OCT 2 8 2019

WAR GIRLS

Also by
TOCHI ONYEBUCHI

Beasts Made of Night

Crown of Thunder

WAR GIRLS

TOCHI ONYEBUCHI

RAZORBILL

RAZORBILL

An imprint of Penguin Random House LLC, New York

RAZORBILL & colophon is a registered trademark of Penguin Random House LLC.

First published in the United States of America by Razorbill,
an imprint of Penguin Random House LLC, 2019

Visit us online at penguinrandomhouse.com

LIBRARY OF CONGRESS CATALOGING-IN-PUBLICATION DATA
Names: Onyebuchi, Tochi, author.
Title: War girls / Tochi Onyebuchi.
Description: New York : Razorbill, 2019. | Summary: In 2172, when much of the
world is unlivable, sisters Onyii and Ify dream of escaping war-torn
Nigeria and finding a better future together but are, instead, torn apart.
Identifiers: LCCN 2019016805 | ISBN 9780451481672 (hardback)
Subjects: | CYAC: Sisters—Fiction. | Cyborgs—Fiction. | War—Fiction. |
Survival—Fiction. | Nigeria—Fiction. | Science fiction.
Classification: LCC PZ7.1.O66 War 2019 | DDC [Fic]—dc23 LC record available at
https://lccn.loc.gov/2019016805

Book manufactured in Canada

1 3 5 7 9 10 8 6 4 2

Design by Tony Sahara.
Text set in Fairfield LT Std.

To my mother

PART

I

CHAPTER
1
Southeastern Nigeria
April 2172

The first thing Onyii does every morning is take off her arm. Other War Girls have gotten used to sleeping without their arms or their legs. But Onyii's phantom limb haunts her in her sleep. In her dreams, she has all her arms and legs and can run. She can run far and fast and away from whatever is chasing her. She can hold her rifle, and she can aim, and she can feel her face with all of her fingers. But then she'd wake up and try to touch her body with a right arm that wasn't there anymore. She never got accustomed to waking up without all of her body there, so now she sleeps with her arm attached, even though sometimes she accidentally crushes and bends some of the machinery. Even though the sweat from her night terrors rusts some of the more delicate circuitry. Even though she wakes every morning with the imprint of metal plates on her cheek. Which is why she gets up earlier than the rest of the camp and spends the quiet morning hours at her bedside station, oiling the gears and tinkering with the chips. In the darkness, the sparks from the metal as she works are the only light in her tent.

Ify sleeps through all of it.

Onyii takes a moment to listen to Ify snore. The birds outside have just started their chirping, but they're still quiet enough that Onyii can hear Ify's patterns. Two smooth snores, then a hiccup. Onyii's dreams are a blur of chaos and blood and screaming. Flashes of gunfire. Rain falling hard but never hard enough to wash the tears from her face. Ify's face is serene in slumber, the tribal scars soft ridges on her cheeks. Her lips turn up at the edges. For almost her entire life, the child has only known peace.

When Onyii finishes, she disconnects her arm from its station and places it against the spot where her shoulder ends. She'd left that battle long ago with a stump. But the doctors had had to cut away the rest of the arm, because it had gotten infected. Now there is only mesh wiring over the opening, so that her socket is more like a power outlet than anything else. Nanobots buzz out of the metal arm socket, trailing wires. The threading then attaches the metal to her flesh. Electricity shocks through her body—a small burst like scraping feet against carpet then touching a doorknob. Then she's able to flex her fingers. She tries out her elbow joints, bends the arm, swings it slowly back and forth, rotating the shoulder, then stretches and lets out a massive yawn. She waits until she's outside the tent to let out her gas.

The world is green and wet with recent rain. The dew hasn't yet dried from the grass. Leaves bend on their tree branches overhead.

Wind whips about her. Engines scream overhead, and Onyii looks up just in time to see aerial mechs, massive humanoid robots, with green and white stripes painted on their shoulders, screech through the sky, as they've been doing for the past year. Shoulder cannons and thrusters attached to their compact bodies. State-of-the-art nav systems. Yet they can't detect the rebel Biafran camp right under their noses. As long as the signal dampener they rigged to hide this outpost from the Nigerian authorities is up and running, they're safe. The government forces can't even see the rebel flag waving right below them. A blue background with half of a yellow sun at its bottom, golden rays radiating outward like lightning bolts.

Onyii stretches her flesh-and-blood arm and shoulder, arches her back and listens to the cracks ripple up her spine, then shakes herself loose. She's still wearing only her bedclothes—a compression bra and athletic shorts that stick to her in the heavy Delta humidity—but it's comfortable enough for a morning run.

She makes her usual circuit of the camp. First, she heads to the camp's periphery, past the school for the little ones and one of the few auto-body shelters—a place where faulty robotics can be tinkered with, where arms and legs can be made. Where the girls can become Augments, given limbs or organs more powerful than what they were born with. Sometimes, it's a place where medical operations happen and people are given new eyes or the bleeding in their brain is stopped and a braincase has to be installed. Onyii knows some of the others sneer at the place, like people only go there to come out less than human, but some of those who look sideways at the people working in there and getting worked on have never seen war. Half-limbs only become half-limbs because they're trying to make someone whole. An Augment is not an ugly thing.

She hangs a left and spots the orchard and the fruit trees that line it. Beyond the orchard, a vegetable garden sits encased in a greenhouse large enough for a few people to enter and roam about in. Rotating spigots programmed to automatically spray water on the plants hang from the ceiling, and artificial light panels line the walls. The camp hasn't needed them for some time, but when the nights get long—too long—they can't let the food suffer.

Onyii spirals outward on her run and passes the mess hall—usually empty this early in the morning. But as Onyii runs by she spots a girl in jungle fatigues with her jacket unbuttoned and draped loose over her shoulders as she leans on her rifle, dozing. Chike. At the sound of Onyii's feet brushing the grass, Chike starts awake and straightens. It's a wonder she doesn't hoist her assault rifle and aim it right at Onyii; she's so jittery. When Chike realizes where she is, she settles back, and her posture relaxes.

It's only me, Onyii thinks, *who will pafuka your head when your commanding officer finds out you've been sleeping on your watch!*

Onyii ambles past. These morning runs double as patrol surveillance. Backup for those on watch. The outpost may be hidden from radars and scanners, but what's to keep a Green-and-White from walking right through their perimeter? At fifteen, Onyii is among the oldest in the camp. The younger ones—some of them new to living on their own and some of them just learning how to be people again after having grown feral in the jungles—have trouble adjusting, staying awake during patrols, concentrating during school, not screaming in their sleep. With some of them, their guns are bigger than they are. But they're slowly turning into steel, turning into the type of girls who can be depended on during an attack, the type of girls Onyii would be happy to have at her side in a fight. Proud, even.

Her route takes her farther out to the practice grounds where weapons training happens. Jungle trees with their broad, heavy leaves hide the girls from above, and there's enough foliage here to absorb most of the noise they make as they shoot toward the shoreline. She gets to the cliff, and below her lies the beach. Melee combat happens here too, when it's scheduled, but during the warm seasons, Onyii will occasionally arrive on her morning runs to see some of the girls already laid out, naked beneath the sun, giggling or roughhousing, and she's reminded that many of them are still just kids. And the sun for them is still a gentle, loving thing. Some of them have never looked up into a clear blue sky, at an out-of-place twinkling, and recognized a drone ready to drop a bomb on their homes. Maybe some of them have seen it and still don't care. Those ones always turn out to be good fighters. Reckless, but good.

In the distance is the water, still more black than blue this early in the morning. Onyii hears the faint sound of metal banging, of water sloshing against steel, and what she sees as specks or small shapes along the horizon, she knows to be the mineral derricks. Old and rusted but still capable of leaching resources from the Delta. Their resources. The blue minerals buried beneath Onyii's feet and, farther out, beneath the ocean floor. This is what the Nigerians are killing Biafrans for. Not a morning passes that Onyii doesn't think about setting charges to those things and blowing them into coral debris. It's been said that the minerals are the divine right of the Igbo, their blessing from Chukwu, the supreme being whose energy powers all of existence. But the minerals are just dust to Onyii. Powerful, important dust, but nothing more.

Other than the Nigerian mechs that streak overhead from

time to time, the derricks provide Onyii's only glimpse of the outside world. *There are more people out there than us and our enemies.* Every time she sees the derricks, she aims an invisible gun at them with her still-human hand.

She doubles back and passes the hangar where the mobile suits are stored. They're smaller than the Nigerian mechs that screech through the sky overhead and closer to the shape of actual humans. Rust spots their armor, and Onyii knows there isn't enough lubricant around for all the gears that need it. But the beat-up suits—stocked with ammo for their guns and equipped with night vision and a neural adapting system—are enough to get by. Then there are the skinsuits. Depending on how old or how big you are, they either fit tightly enough to suffocate or they hang off you like hand-me-downs, even after you press the button on your wrist to compress them. The skinsuits are supposed to collapse to fit like a second layer of flesh for journeys out past the camp, where the radiation gets so thick that skin peels almost instantly.

The ammo crates all have Mandarin characters written on their sides in fluorescent blue ink. But the girls know by looking which containers hold the 7.62 mm bullets and which hold the ammo for the shoulder cannons on the mobile suit mechs. They know which hold the bullets for their assault rifles and which hold the knives for when the bullets run out.

It never seems like enough, the smuggled arms. But orphans never steal enough bread for a feast, only enough to last the day.

Onyii continues towards the Obelisk. But even before she gets to it, she can see sparks arcing out of its base. It looks like a mini mineral derrick, microscopic by comparison, driven into the ground. Beneath Onyii's feet, fiber-optic cables run throughout the camp and beyond, buzzing the earth constantly with charges, zapping the soil over and over to release the water soaked into it. The water is then purified and made available for washing and cooking and cleaning. It also collects the minerals that power nearly every electronic device in the camp.

Today, it's somehow busted.

Onyii crouches at the base and sees a blackened stretch of tech running along one of the cables, ending right before it pierces the grass patch. She didn't build this, so she doesn't know it as intimately as others in the camp do, but she's fixed things before.

She takes a long time squinting at the mechanical carnage before a flash of movement changes the air around her. Suddenly, Chinelo's at her side, all long, gangly limbs. Still, somehow, she manages not to make a sound. The opposite of clumsy. In fact, Onyii remembers the first time she saw Chinelo—tall even as a child—move with a grace she'd never seen before. Covered in ash and soot and blood, Chinelo had moved with the confidence of a general.

Now Chinelo wears a jungle-colored compression bra over her small chest and pants with many deep pockets. A green, patterned bandana holds back her locs. Ancient, obsolete "cell phones"—relics of a different era—hang from her necklace, clacking together to make some weird music Onyii doesn't particularly like.

"You want to break our water, is that it?" Chinelo jokes.

She jokes like that from time to time. Dark jokes about how all the girls here are, for some reason, not made of the type of material to create children. Onyii heard one time that when your water breaks, you are near to birthing a child.

But looking at Chinelo now, the sheen on her skin a glowing mix of night sweat and morning dew, Onyii sees a girl who only knows how to laugh.

"Hurry up now, before we are all stinking, and the Green-and-Whites smell us," Onyii shoots back, smiling.

Chinelo smirks, then her bees buzz out from her hair. Tiny robotic insects that tell Chinelo the temperature and the water density in the air and the amount of radiation in each drop of rain that lands on them from the tree leaves overhead. They tell her how warm Onyii is next to her, and they tell her the state of Onyii's prosthetic arm. As Onyii watches, the bees descend onto the well to tell Chinelo what needs to be repaired. Then they go to work.

Onyii remains crouched on her haunches, a position of battle-readiness. Chinelo sits back in the grass while the robotic bees do their job.

"We need to make a run," Chinelo says like she is telling Onyii to bathe more often. Her Augments are more internal. A braincase for her brain, ways of having data transmitted directly to her, even some metal where bones should be. On the outside, she is as human as anyone. But finely tuned machinery ticks and hums inside her. Still, even with a body that can connect on its own to the camp's network, she is more human than machine. Cyberized, but still, she bleeds red blood.

"And what will we find in the forest that we can't find here?" Onyii stares at the well as light spreads along the once-blackened portion of circuitry.

"That's the thing. You never know. Our tools are rusted, and our guns need ammunition, and just the other day, one of the lights in the greenhouse went out. The nights are getting longer, and our generators won't last."

Onyii wants to tell Chinelo that they've lasted at this outpost for years, that they've made more with less, but it's a conversation they've had a million times before. "And what if there are Green-and-Whites on patrol?"

Chinelo elbows Onyii. "They have not found us yet. Why would they find us now?"

"Because neither of us has bathed in a week." Onyii tries to say it with a straight face, but a smile curls her lips, and she can't hold back anymore, and their laughter echoes into the trees.

Chinelo rolls around in the wet grass, clutching her stomach, as the bees fly back into her hair. Onyii wants to tell her to be quiet, to stop laughing before they alert whatever Nigerian patrols may be nearby. But the sound of Chinelo's laugh warms her too much.

"Let me say goodbye to the little one at least," Onyii says. She pushes herself upright and hauls Chinelo to her feet.

"And maybe we can find some napkins too," Chinelo says, looking at the repaired well to see if it's properly working again. "Some of the girls have begun to bleed."

■ ■ ■ ■ ■

How many years has it been? Even after all this time, it still moves Onyii to see Ify sleep so peacefully. The ratty, coarse blanket rises and falls, rises and falls. Sometimes, Onyii wishes the two of them had ports, rounded outlets at the backs of their necks that some half-limbs have, so that she could plug a wire in and connect it to Ify and see what the little girl dreamed. Maybe dancing and a cool breeze and a pretty dress. No mosquitoes.

Onyii shuffles to Ify's side. The inside of the tent is still awash in blue from a morning that has not yet fully arrived. And she knows Ify will try to resist being woken up so early before her classes, but the girl can stand to learn a little industriousness. So, Onyii sits on a crate by Ify's bed and gently shakes her awake.

The girl's eyes open a little, then grow wide for a second before settling. Even in the darkness, Onyii can see the purple of her irises, flecked with jagged shards of gold, and her breath catches in her throat at the beauty of it.

"Hey, little one," Onyii whispers.

Chinelo waits at the tent's entrance, and Onyii can feel her impatience, but Onyii has made it her mission to spend as much time with Ify as she can. You never know when you might lose a loved one in war or even who that loved one might be. Her days as a child soldier are still fresh in her mind. Too fresh. So Onyii spends several long seconds running her hand along Ify's bald head before Ify turns and pulls the blanket over her entire body.

"Hey." Onyii shakes her, more roughly this time.

"It's too early," Ify whines.

"I have to go on a run."

At this, Ify turns. The girl is learning toughness, Onyii can tell, but there's still a pleading look in the purple and gold of her eyes.

"We have to look for some more supplies. Chinelo is coming with me, so don't worry. I have a buddy. And Enyemaka can keep you company."

"While I do what?"

Onyii frowns. *Is that spice in your voice, Ify?* "While you go over your lessons." Onyii pulls a tablet from a shelf and powers it on. The screen flickers, and Onyii slaps it against her knee, a little too hard, before it casts its light over the inside of their dwelling.

"But, Onyii, I already get high marks. Let me sleep-oh!"

"Fine." Onyii puts the tablet on the bedside table. "Don't study. And in class, when the teacher is teaching, if you like, don't listen. Don't pay attention. Be on your tablet. Play your games. Talk. Chaw-chaw-chaw-chaw-chaw." Her voice rises. "But if you come back to this tent with anything less than first position"—a pause for dramatic effect—"we shall see."

Ify spends one last, brief moment under the covers before she throws off the blanket and swings her legs around.

Onyii gets up and turns before Ify has a chance to see her smile. Chinelo stifles a chuckle.

In the corner, Enyemaka stands, hunched over and powered off. If someone wanted to be charitable, they would say her multicolored armor gives her character. The faded purple metal of one forearm, the pitted orange of one breastplate, the patchwork of green and red and yellow and orange and blue wires that make up her ribs. They'd say it was like a dress sewn out of choice fabric and made into this beautiful gown. A riot of color. But, really, it's just a droid made out of whatever tech Onyii and the others stumbled across on previous runs and during skirmishes with the Green-and-Whites. The metal plates on her legs are rusted at the corners. The sockets for her eyes are dark with grime. Moss runs along her backside, and other parts are fuzzy with fungus.

Onyii stands on her toes, inhales deeply to unlock a series of chambers and valves in her artificial internal organs, and spits a mucus-encased stream of nanobots into Enyemaka's ear. When Ify used to ask how Enyemaka came to life, Chinelo would joke that it was like a wireless connection, with Onyii as the droid's router. Enyemaka's eyes light up. Her gears hum, and she stands upright, squares her shoulders, and scans the room.

"Watch her while I'm gone," Onyii commands.

"Yes, Mama," Enyemaka says back. As she powers all the way up, her voice sounds like two voices at once. Then she walks over to Ify. "So, little one. Mathematics." When she says that part, Enyemaka sounds too much like Onyii for her own comfort.

Onyii grabs her pack from by the tent's entrance and hefts her rifle with her prosthetic arm. "And make sure she shaves," she calls over her shoulder. "Clean. I don't want to see any missed spots on her head! We have a heat wave coming." Then Onyii is out into the chilly morning.

14

CHAPTER 2

Ify waits until Onyii leaves the tent before reaching under her pillow and fumbling around for her Accent. The tiny piece of tech, a ball small enough to fit on the end of an ear swab, has nestled itself in the folds of her bedsheet. When she finds it, a grin splits her face. Enyemaka hovers over her, and Ify instinctively turns her back while she fiddles with the Accent, then fits it inside her ear.

The darkness of the little hut evaporates. Peels away like the skin of rotten fruit to reveal the lines and nodes of net connectivity that bind everything—and everyone—together. Her pillow sprouts a series of pulsing blue dots. The metal beams supporting her roof glow with aquamarine lines. Enyemaka turns into a forest of nodes and vectors. Ify can see inside her and watch the gears turn and the core in her head thrum. She can see how her movements are enabled by the wireless connection from the Terminal that helps power the camp. Enyemaka's rustier parts glow a shade of red that worries Ify, but the rest of her is a healthy blue. With her Accent, Ify can see all of this. All these things happening in the camp's closed network. Bright as ocean water under the sun. Data.

"Remember, Enyemaka. You promised not to tell Onyii," Ify says, frowning at her minder with as much sternness as she can muster. Onyii had forbade her from tinkering with any tech that might interfere with the wireless. And after the second time it had disrupted Onyii's comms while she was on a scouting mission, Onyii had nearly thrashed her senseless. Only at the last moment had Onyii returned to herself. There was a change in her eyes. When she got that angry, a cloud came over them and Ify could tell the storm was coming. But Onyii's eyes had cleared, and she had given Ify only an extended tongue-lashing.

Ify never meant to disobey Onyii, but she would look around at her life to see nothing but questions. And whenever Ify inserted her Accent into her ear, the world exploded with answers. Almost every piece of tech and even unconnected items like her bed and her pillow and the biomass the scouting parties brought back to make their meals with—all of it was explained to her through the Accent in a way that made sense. And right now, she's not messing around trying to hack into Chinelo's comms or into the Obelisk that takes the special minerals from the ground to power the camp. She's just watching. Surfing the connections. Riding the waves. The Accent also lets her talk to Enyemaka without needing to make a sound.

She remembers where she is and that Onyii is still probably near enough to sense her, and she shifts her jaw to put her Accent into sleep mode. Then, shrugging on her shirt, which looks and feels more like a burlap sack than anything a human being is supposed to wear, she takes a seat on the crate before her mirror. Or, rather, shard of mirror.

Okay, Enyemaka, she says cheerfully through her Accent. *I'm ready.*

There's a little bit of hair on her head, just a small shield of silver fuzz, but it's enough to make her itch in the warm seasons. So she sits as still as she can manage while Enyemaka runs the razor smoothly over Ify's scalp. With each stroke, Enyemaka sprays a small puff of alcohol on the nearly shiny space. Ify winces. Sometimes, Enyemaka isn't as smooth as she'd like, and Ify's left with a cut or two that she has to put adhesive over. Then she has to endure the taunts of her age-mates.

"Ow!"

"You should not have been moving," Enyemaka says in her half-robotic voice. "My reflexes are not fast enough to account for your constant shifting."

Always my fault, Ify thinks to herself. "Ugh, I'm finished," she says, without even having Enyemaka inspect her. "You wait outside the classroom this time when we get to school, okay?" There's an extra bite in her voice today, and all that good cheer she felt upon finding her Accent has left her.

By the time she gathers her tablet and her rucksack, daylight shines through the slit in the tent's opening. She's going to be late for school. Again.

■ ■ ■ ■ ■

The cooling unit must be broken, because they've retracted the roof on the warehouse where the teachers hold their classes. Ify sneaks in through the back, but sees that the only free seat, of course, is in the front row. The thought runs through her head to turn back and just skip class for the day, but Enyemaka is blocking her path through the side entrance, so she has no choice but to duck her head and hurry to her seat.

Everyone has their tablets out in front of them with holos displayed, but Ify can't tell what page of the downloaded lesson they're on and so has to stumble through image after image after image of nonsense until her holo matches the others. Some of the girls around her snicker, which makes Ify duck her head even more. She's tempted to turn on her Accent and have the secrets of each of these girls revealed to her. The Augmented ones with their stored search histories not yet deleted, showing the sites they visit to look at barely dressed men and boys. Ify can see all of that and expose them with just a turn of her jaw, but Enyemaka's still in the doorway, and there's no doubt that Onyii would find out. And it's not even the beating that Ify fears so much as the look of disappointment in her big sister's eyes. So Ify focuses on the holo, which is a 3-D projection of a parabolic curve on a graph.

The teacher is explaining basic algebra, not even anything useful. Not like the orbital physics in the ancient textbooks and archived sites Ify studies on her own.

She grits her teeth, and suddenly the world explodes with blue. For a panicked moment, Ify sees the gears and wires inside her teacher and can feel the information from other people's tablets run through her head. She senses Enyemaka's distress, and far into the distance, on the periphery of her vision, a familiar signal: Onyii. So fast she hurts herself, she clicks her jaw and shuts off her Accent. She looks around to see if anyone noticed the shadow signal in their devices, the little blip or moment of static in their tablets or in their teched-up bodies. But no one seems to have noticed. She lets out a sigh and listens to the teacher drone on about how algebra originated in Biafra among the Igbo peoples. How the knowledge was stolen by the Fulani tribe when they invaded from the North centuries ago. Ify wonders what it must have been like to live in a time when Nigeria was newly independent and no longer a British colony, when the Igbo lived alongside the Fulani monsters the teacher is talking about. But before she can follow the thought, everyone's tablets buzz, and the lesson's over for today.

The girls stream out already giggling, some of them playing with their tablets and turning them into music boards to play songs they made and recorded. Ify slips her tablet into her sack and shuffles toward Enyemaka. She reaches up to scratch the top of her head when something slams into her from behind, and she topples forward. Enyemaka's gears groan as she moves to try to catch her, but Ify tastes dirt and turns to find several girls standing over her.

"Eh-heh," says one of the girls, with her hair braided in two dark pigtails coming out the side of her head. The ridges of the tribal scars on her cheeks glisten. "Without her big *sista* around, she is just a skinny *oyinbo*." The others snicker and point at Ify's skin, lighter than theirs, so that mosquito bites show up redder and her bruises take longer to fade. She tries to hide her bare arms in her shirt. Her skin the color of sand, theirs the color of firm ground. She grits her teeth. *Turn on your Accent*, she tells herself. *Hack them. Mess up their systems.* And she could do it. She gives herself a moment to imagine the girls screeching as their tablets explode in their hands or the tech in their braincases short-circuits, making them go blind. Then she pushes herself up to her feet. Whatever she would do to them would get Onyii's attention and, worse, her anger. So she lets it go, just like she does every time.

"She looks like jollof rice gone bad," another of the girls sings.

And that gets the others going. "Maybe she thinks just because she has no *real* family, we are supposed to pity her."

The girl with the pigtails sucks her teeth. "Just some skinny goat Onyii found in the bush all alone."

Ify's cheeks burn. Tears spring to her eyes. The anger is right there, close enough to touch, and she has to fight against it. But if one of them pushes her, if they even touch her, then Ify will give herself permission to lash out. She will tell Onyii afterward that she had no choice, that she had to defend herself, that she had to be strong like her. And that's why the girls will be squirming on the ground wondering why they suddenly can't see or hear or walk.

But the girls relent.

They turn to go, and one of them picks up a stone and flicks it at Ify's head as their group walks away.

Enyemaka stands before Ify, and that's when she realizes she's shaking. Rooted where she stands, hands balled into fists, brow knit into a frown, a soft growl growing in her throat. But the shadow Enyemaka casts over her brings her back to herself, and she takes in a ragged breath.

The android kneels down and raises a hand to Ify's face. The palm opens up and sprays alcohol on the cut above Ify's eye.

"Ack!" Ify slaps Enyemaka's hand away. "Get away from me!" And that's when the tears come. Suddenly, she's running and doesn't care what direction she heads in, as long as it's away from school, away from camp, away from Enyemaka always hovering over her, away from the girls who keep pointing out how different she is.

She stops when the hum of camp activity grows quiet. The small patch of forest she ran into opens out onto an outcropping, and, below it, a beach. Waves of blue-green water whisper against the shoreline. A few heavy breaths later, Ify has calmed down. The noise and fog in her head dissipate. She sits in the grass, hugging her knees to her chest, and stares off into the distance. The mineral derricks are black silhouettes on the horizon. With her Accent on again, their shapes glow bright against a darkened blood-red sky. Even the enemy Nigerian mechs that hover over the derricks shine with pulsing blue light. They swim through the sky in widening oval patterns and leave trails of what looks to Ify like blue stardust in their wake, but Ify knows it is the pathway that's been programmed into them. She can tell the reach of their comms too, and she knows that she and the camp are just outside their grasp. Invisible.

She fishes her tablet out of her sack and programs her Accent to pirate an enemy connection so that she can access the lessons she's been sneaking in outside of school. The headline reads: ORBITAL PHYSICS. And springing out of the text are holographs of parabolic curves and Space Colonies spinning slowly on their axes. She picks up where she left off: Lagrange points and the spaces between planets and moons where the gravity from both bodies can hold a colony in place. Then there are the mechs and the small, nimble jets that fly through asteroid belts, dipping and rising and twirling. But no matter how hard she zooms in, she can't see the pilots. The resolution gets too bad. She knows they're there. She knows there are people in those cockpits, maybe women like the type she'll grow up to be. And her heart thrills at the idea.

Enyemaka appears at her side and stiffly sits down next to Ify.

Ify waits for Enyemaka to chastise her for hopping onto an enemy connection, for going behind Onyii's back and using her

Accent, but Enyemaka peeks over to examine the holograms that emerge from the tablet. Ify holds it out for Enyemaka to get a better look at and smiles at the android.

"You already have a very deep understanding of orbital physics," Enyemaka says in her double-voice. "And yet you do poorly in your mathematics class."

Ify snatches the tablet back. "That's because the algebra we do in class is boring. It's so basic, and they keep wanting me to show my work. So I always get low marks. But in America, they reward you for getting the right answers. That's how you become a pilot."

Enyemaka can't smile. Ify knows this. There's no real face on her head, no lips, and her eyes don't light up to show happiness but to signal that she's been powered up and her battery life is full, but when Ify looks up at Enyemaka, it *feels* like Enyemaka is smiling at her. "Is that what you want? To become a pilot?"

"More than anything," Ify breathes. She has never said it out loud before, and it feels dangerous. But it feels like commitment. She has to do it now that she has said it. And she'll find a way. Maybe when the war ends and there's a free Biafra, they'll get a launch station built, probably somewhere in Enugu or maybe right here where the camp is, and the station will fire shuttles deep into space, where they'll join the rest of the world. Another superpower like America among the Space Colonies.

Enyemaka chirrups. A bell rings inside her. Ify's shoulders sink. Mealtime. But she realizes how hungry she is—she doesn't remember having eaten anything all day. "We must head back if we are to avoid the end of the line," Enyemaka says.

As they head back through the forest, Enyemaka silent and stoic, Ify looks up at the android. "When Onyii goes through your logs at the end of the day to see what I've been doing and where I went, can you erase the part where we went by the beach? If she finds out I skipped afternoon classes . . . I don't want to make her angry. And I don't want her to find out about my Accent. Can you, please?"

For a long time, Enyemaka is silent. It seems like she's sad, almost. She speaks to Ify silently, through her Accent. *You are asking me to erase things that I've touched and heard and seen, the data I have accumulated and added to my core.*

Shame rushes through Ify. Her cheeks burn. Enyemaka sounds so much like Onyii sometimes that it's easy for Ify to forget that, in so many ways, she's just like a child. Figuring out how things work, gathering experiences, organizing the world around her. Learning.

"Consider it done," Enyemaka says, then holds Ify's hand. "That portion of my logs has been erased."

Ify squeezes Enyemaka's mechanized hand and brings it to her cheek.

The android doesn't miss a step.

CHAPTER

3

If Onyii and Chinelo had timed their run for earlier, they could have avoided the mosquitoes. But their skinsuits provide them at least some level of relief. The Geiger counters on their wrists beep, noting the radiation levels around them. Still, the vegetation persists: the fat tree leaves, big, almost like they've mutated; the tall grass that swishes against them, brown and yellow in some places, green in others.

Onyii wasn't alive when the oyinbo went to war with themselves and the Big-Big went off an ocean away and the wind swept red clouds over the entire continent. She wasn't alive when the sky began to bleed. But she's heard stories. Stories of a time before the domed cities and before people started fleeing to colonies in space. A time before the oyinbo— the whites—raced to the stars and built America and Britain and Scandinavia and other places where they were able to— were the *only* ones able to—hide from what human stupidity had done to the planet. A time before Biafra had declared its independence and the war started.

Now detritus litters the forest floor where they walk. Juice packets, torn clothing, bits of broken tech.

Chinelo stoops at a pile of blackened earth, moves some twigs and brush around with her foot, then spots an ancient smartphone buried beneath it all. She picks it up with her gloved hand, her rifle in the other, and blows away some of the irradiated dust. The dust swirls in a cloud before her visor. For a long time, she stares at it, then slips it into her pocket to be added to the string of broken smartphones she wears around her neck.

Mist hovers in the air around them. Visibility is low. But Chinelo, properly cyberized, can see. The level of moisture in the sky. The dips and grooves in the ground, too tiny for Onyii to see, heat signatures of Agba bears or mutated wulfu with their two heads and ridged backs.

Leaves swish to their right. Chinelo puts out an arm, stopping Onyii. They crouch, hidden by bush. The noise is organized. Chinelo squints. Onyii follows her gaze.

Slowly, an animal emerges from the fog. Its skin is pink in the light and glows a soft green in places. Its ribs show, but its four legs are thick with meat. Fur ripples along its spine. Its hooves squish in the mud. A shorthorn.

If they were more than just Onyii and Chinelo, they might have tried to capture it to bring it back, cleanse the meat, and cook it. But they can't spare the ammo, and the thing is just as likely to kill them as it is to feed them.

The beast ambles past them, bending fallen tree trunks beneath its weight, drawing the mosquitoes to it with its radiation-rich blood.

Onyii and Chinelo wait until it is completely out of sight, then a few minutes more, before continuing onward.

In a small clearing, they find more traces of people. Broken

TOCHI ONYEBUCHI

comms devices, more torn cloth, ratty sneakers. The mark of people who left in a hurry.

Chinelo, ever curious, moves to examine the broken and discarded tech. More jewelry to wrap around her neck.

Onyii hisses at her. They're not here for necklaces. They're here for rations.

They continue in silence, pausing briefly as a familiar shriek rips through the air. Mechs streak across the sky. The wind sways the tree branches overhead. Onyii and Chinelo don't stop but crouch even lower as they continue.

"They never think to leave any pads behind," Chinelo sneers.

Onyii doesn't speak for several seconds, then realizes she can't let it go. "Who is 'they'?"

"The refugees, of course. Or whoever leaves all their trash in the forest like this." She doesn't look at the ground, but she manages to step over the upturned roots of a fallen tree. "No, it's just empty Fanta bottles and old mobiles with rusted chips."

"More for your necklace," Onyii says, and allows herself a small chuckle.

"The little ones, if they find us, we can put them to work at least. Give them new lives." Chinelo continues to scan the forest, her head moving left to right, right to left in a steady rhythm. "Teach them how to fix things."

"And the older ones?"

Chinelo shrugs. "If they are women, we send them to Enugu. Maybe Umuhaia. They find some use in the Republic. Maybe they make more children."

"And if they are men?"

Chinelo smirks. "We shoot them."

They both giggle. It feels good to go on a run with a friend.

26

Most runs pass in silence. They're quick things. Run out, find supplies, run back. Or, more often: run out, find nothing, run back. But when Onyii's out with Chinelo, she lets herself move slower. The more time she can spend with her, the better.

"I would like to see Port Harcourt one day," Onyii says, surprising herself. "I hear it's beautiful. And it's right on the water, and you can't see any of the derricks blocking the way, making all that awful jagga-jagga noise." A smile crosses Onyii's face. "And there are proper hospitals and a women's clinic."

"What would we do in Port Harcourt?" Chinelo jokes. "What is there to build there?"

"Biafra." Onyii knows she sounds dreamy when she says it. And normally she would call this stupid. To believe in something as lofty and invisible as the Republic of Biafra. But when she thinks of Biafra, she thinks of buildings of glass and stone and steel that scrape the sky and paved streets and clean fruit that you can eat straight off the trees. She thinks of a place where there is no rust. Anywhere. Where the radiation-poisoned air doesn't scrape against your lungs as you breathe. In this dream, her arm has a proper skin attached to it instead of the black band she always wears, and every time she looks at it, she doesn't have to be reminded that it is metal and gears and circuitry and maybe she can convince herself that it's proper flesh and blood and bone. In this dream of Biafra, she's fully human.

"Wait."

Chinelo sticks her arm out just in time to stop Onyii from stepping on a mine. Onyii can't see the red light blinking under the mud, but Chinelo probably can. If it's not from the Green-and-Whites, it might be from some other rebel group.

Onyii curses herself. This is what happens when you lose concentration. Likely a sign that they should head back.

"Come on," Onyii says, turning. "There's nothing out here. Not today."

But Chinelo doesn't move. She crouches until she's nearly sitting on the ground and peers into the distance. Then she points. "There."

Onyii tries to follow her gaze.

"There."

Onyii squints. Then she sees a small cloud of mosquitoes.

"What is it?"

Onyii riffles through her rucksack and pulls out a small mound of clay. An eto-eto. "Whatever it is, it's still warm. I'll look."

She sits, careful to avoid the mine, and molds the white clay into a something with arms and legs. Then, with a small pin, she pokes two holes in what has become the eto-eto's face. She twists the limbs out a little more until it looks like more of a starfish than anything human.

"This'll do." Then she spits a glob of mucus over the eyeholes on its face. The nanobots in her mucus burrow into the eto-eto's skin. Like Onyii's DNA, biomech colonizing the clay, putting pieces of Onyii into it, animating it so that it becomes a thing she can see through. An extension of herself. Like a mobile device connected to Onyii's neural network by wireless internet.

Its arms and legs wiggle. Then it squirms in her palm like a little baby. It glows blue at its core.

She sets it on the ground, then pats it on its backside, and it waddles forward. What it feels and what it sees and what it hears echo in Onyii's brain like a whisper. A voice underneath her own.

The eto-eto heads toward the mound, then stops and tilts its head, looking it over. At first, it's just leather and torn cloth, but then the eto-eto sees hair. It runs an arm through it, and the hair curls around its white limb. It scurries around and sees that it's a person. A human. And it's breathing.

"She's alive," Onyii says. Before Chinelo can stop her, she's up and racing toward the body. She comes to a stop, drops her pack, and fishes out her aluminum pole stretcher. When she's got it out of the pack on her back, she takes her eto-eto and squeezes it. It makes a soft whirring sound, almost like an exhale, as it powers down. Then she stuffs it back into her rucksack.

Chinelo hesitates for only a moment before helping to lift the woman. Onyii starts, raises her rifle, and peers down her scope into the forest. Something had moved. She spends several moments scanning, though she can barely see through the fog.

"We're safe." Chinelo puts a hand to Onyii's shoulder, and Onyii relaxes. "Help me carry her."

Onyii shoulders her rifle, and the two of them lift the woman and head back to camp.

"You are getting soft, you know. In your old age."

Onyii's in front, but she can feel Chinelo's smirk at her back. "Oh?"

"A year or two ago, you would have left this woman to die."

CHAPTER
4

When Enyemaka and Ify get to the line of stones painted blue in the forest, Ify realizes just how far away from camp she'd run. If she flicks on her Accent, she can easily see the mines buried beneath the ground and covered by brush. She can track the paths and where she's free to walk, but she has already spent so much time online that any more would surely give her away to Onyii. It will take too long to go around the mines. By the time they complete the circuit and get back to camp, there'll be no food left, and the rumbling in Ify's stomach tells her she can't afford to miss this meal.

Mist thickens, and what little Ify could see of the ground vanishes. Her heart sinks. Her stomach twists and turns.

"Come on, little one," Enyemaka says, and holds her hand out. Her eyes are growing faint, and Ify can tell it's because her battery life is running out. But Ify takes the droid's hand, and Enyemaka hoists the child onto her back. Ify drapes her arms around Enyemaka's neck and squeezes.

Step by assured step, Enyemaka makes her way through, walking what feels like a straight line but what Ify knows to be a complicated back-and-forth dance to avoid the traps the War Girls have laid for intruders.

Toward the edge of the forest, where it opens out onto the camp, mosquitoes buzz over something lying still among the leaves. Enyemaka stops, and Ify moves to slip off her back, but Enyemaka grips the child behind her and holds her fast.

"Enyemaka, what is it?"

For several seconds Enyemaka doesn't move, and Ify wonders if the droid has powered off completely, which would be a problem because then Ify would be stuck in her grip, practically glued to her back.

Then the telltale hum and whirr of tech turning back on. Enyemaka straightens but doesn't loosen her grip. "A two-fang. It is not yet dead, but it has been poisoned by the air. It has wandered here."

And that's when Ify sees it. It lies on its side, its flank rising and falling slowly, one head lying on top of the other, both mouths open, gasping for breath. It's as though the mist has cleared to reveal it, and a memory flashes behind Ify's eyes.

She's younger, a baby almost. And the ground is cold under her, and she holds an animal by its neck close to her chest. It's gasping for breath, its chest heaving against Ify's, and she's crying into its fur. Someone has shot it, this animal she cares for, and she has gathered it in her arms while the shooting and the screaming continue outside her room.

Then, she's back.

Enyemaka's shoulder is cold against her cheek, snapping her out of the memory. The droid's fingers press into her bottom, cradling her. The wet air cools her scalp. She shakes her head.

"Let's go, Enyemaka." And she prods her heels into Enyemaka's ribs like she's seen people in her downloaded movies do when they ride horses in the desert. Enyemaka plays like she's galloping in place, and Ify giggles.

Before long, they get to the armory, and from there, it's a short trip to the mess hall for the evening meal.

Between the armory and the mess hall lies the clinic. Ify slips off of Enyemaka's back when they get near. A crowd of girls gathers outside the tent. Onyii sometimes helps with the women or girls rescued from outside the camp or whenever someone catches an infection because of their tech or when some of the girls' night terrors keep them awake. Even though she's scared Onyii will find out about her Accent, she smiles at the thought of seeing her sister again and skips ahead of Enyemaka to the tent's entrance.

She makes her way to the front of the crowd and takes it all in. A nurse named Nneka is leading a bunch of the others around a table that has a woman on it whose face is scrunched up in pain while she clutches her stomach. Ify looks around, then finds Onyii sitting on a crate by the tent entrance.

"Hey, little one," she says with a tired smile. "How was school?"

The woman on the table moans. Ify can't stop staring, as the woman in torn clothes clutches something to her chest. And Ify feels something invisible press against her own chest. The memory of that wounded animal she'd held as a child. And she's caught, trapped where she stands.

A snapping sound brings her back. Onyii's face is directly in front of hers.

"Hey!" Onyii says. "Where's Enyemaka?"

"At her side," the droid says, lumbering past the gathered crowd. "As always."

Onyii looks up and smirks, as if to say, *Are you being smart with me?* "Good." Then Onyii gets up from her crouch. "Well, let's go. It's mealtime."

The three of them head toward the tent's entrance, but Ify turns and sees that Onyii has stopped and is looking at the ground. She's got her fists balled at her sides, and it looks as though she's at war with herself, trying to decide something. The woman on the table whimpers. Then Onyii reaches into her sack and pulls out a piece of clay. An eto-eto!

Swiftly, Onyii forms arms and legs out of the clay and a head with something of a face. She turns and brings it to the woman, and the woman stops her squirming and groaning for a moment to stare into Onyii's eyes.

Ify sees Onyii struggle with being kind from time to time but feels a surge of pride every time she watches Onyii move with love.

The woman grabs Onyii's wrist and tightens.

A bell rings inside Enyemaka, but the mealtime bell already rang.

The machines the woman is hooked up to start beeping.

Faster. Faster.

"Oh no," someone whispers.

"Ify!" Onyii screams. "GET OUT! IT'S A BO—"

CHAPTER 5

The world comes to Onyii as though she's wrapped in gauze. The sounds are muffled, the shapes blurred together, so that it's all colors swimming. The screams and the explosions sound like they're happening on the other side of the forest. But the pain. The pain is immediate. It screams through her limbs. Twice, she tries to get to her knees but can't. On the third try, her head hits something metal. Flecks of something black and gray come off in her hair. She turns around and falls on her back to find the burned-out husk of Enyemaka crouched over her. Enyemaka shielded her from the worst of the blast. There's almost nothing left of the droid. Just its blackened limbs and charred torso. Silhouetted against the light-enflamed medical tent, Enyemaka looks like a silent, solemn tree.

Onyii pulls her way free and staggers to her feet, and that's when she sees Ify. The little girl has her cheek pressed into the dirt, her entire body caked in mud. Skidding to a stop at her side, Onyii pores over her body for wounds, tests her wrists and arms and legs for broken bones, cradles her head in her hands. "Ify, please," Onyii whimpers. "Please, please, please."

And when she opens her eyes again, Ify is looking at her, dazed but very much alive.

Thunder booms overhead, and both their gazes snap skyward to track the arc of a burning mech as it sails through the air. It trails a comet tail of smoke behind it and crash-lands in the forest so close to the camp that the impact tosses Onyii onto her back.

Automatic weapons fire chatters all around them. Katakata. Chaos.

Onyii scoops Ify up in her arms, and the child murmurs in Onyii's ear, "What's happening? Where's Enyemaka?"

"The camp is under attack," Onyii breathes as she runs toward the camp's periphery. On the way, she catches Chinelo leading a small squadron of War Girls from the armory. "Chinelo! The mechs."

Chinelo nods, then shouts a command to Chike, one of the smaller girls in the group, who salutes, then leads the others into battle. Chinelo dashes in another direction. Onyii runs and runs, past the Terminal and past the storage area for the suits and past the greenhouse to a small patch of untended land. Ify hops out of Onyii's arms, and Onyii scrambles around for something but can't find it. She lets out a curse, then starts digging with her hands.

Ify joins her, and they paw and scrape at the ground. Suddenly, it gives way, and dirt and brush fall into what looks like a small underground tunnel.

"Get in," Onyii says, pushing Ify so hard she nearly trips. Before Ify even makes it all the way into the cave, Onyii is moving brush and broken boards and slabs of metal. Sparks fly from her right arm. Some of her circuitry must have been fried in the blast.

"No, wait," Ify says.

"Stop," Onyii shoots back in the kind of voice she hasn't heard herself use in a long time. She grabs a chunk of sheet metal and, gritting her teeth, rips a piece of it off, then twists it into a sharp-ended pike. She tosses it down after Ify. "If anything comes—anything—swing as hard as you can, and don't stop until its blood covers you."

Before Ify can say anything, Onyii covers the rest of the tunnel's opening by dragging the remaining discarded steel over the space, then covering it with brush until she's satisfied that anyone running past won't give it a second look.

Then she's off. More thunder overhead, and the rapid-fire booms of mortar rounds landing in and around the camp. Columns of smoke sway in the air. The attack seems to be coming from everywhere. Onyii runs past the school before getting to the armory, where there are still plenty of weapons. She drapes a bandolier of rifle rounds over her shoulder and grabs a sack and stuffs it with banana clips taped together by twos. All around her, War Girls grab weapons and take up positions. Some nurse wounds. One leans against a wall with her bandaged leg out in front of her. No time to get to her. Not while they're still under attack. Onyii darts into the forest. Before long, she hears footfalls near her, and she drops into a crouch, swinging her rifle in an arc, stopping only when she sees it's Chinelo and a few of the older girls. Onyii doesn't say anything, just nods, and they head in a line deeper into the forest until Chinelo raises a fist, signaling for them to stop in front of a tree.

One of the girls threads a wire out of the socket at the back of her neck, smashes a metal fist into a tree, revealing a control panel, and plugs in.

The ground opens up beneath them, groaning.

Below them are cockpits. Cockpits attached to weapons Onyii hasn't used in far too long. Cockpits attached to a life she thought she'd left behind. When was the last time Onyii sat inside an ibu mech?

Onyii glances down the line. Amaka. Chigozie. Kesandu. Obioma. Chinelo. Then Onyii nods, and they all hop into the cockpits that have opened up beneath them.

Screens glow blue all around Onyii. When the familiar murmur of her console thrumming to life fills the air, it's like she's being held by her dearest friend. Familiar smells and sounds rush back into her brain and muscles. The control board, the gearshifts, the pedals, the triggers. Her cockpit. *Hers.*

She slides her rifle and bandolier over her shoulder, drops them by her feet, and inputs the commands that get the mech to make its first movements.

Thick fiber-optic wires hiss loose, and the mechs disconnect from their underground ports. A platform raises them through the earth so that Onyii's view is first of dirt and then of thickets of elephant grass, then of the tops of the forest's trees. Tree trunks split. The air howls around them. Then there's a loud *thunk* as the platform settles into place.

They are a row of fierce machines, with shoulder cannons and arms outfitted with Gatling guns. Some of them are already holding massive spears or swords or staffs.

Onyii activates her comms and sees the faces of the other girls in a column of holos on the screen to her right.

"Amaka, ready," says Amaka.

"Chigozie, online," says Chigozie.

"Obioma, online."

"Kesandu, online. Let's do this."

"Chinelo, systems go."

Onyii settles into her seat. Tenses her shoulders. "Onyii, online." She grips the gearshift. "Activate thrusters."

She shoots into the air so fast, she's slammed back into her chair. Her skin flattens against her face, against her body. Her bones rattle. Her teeth smash against each other. Branches thwack her windshield. Then there's nothing but the sky above. In the moment, all sound vanishes, and the inky blanket over them shines with diamonds threaded through it.

Her sound systems activate, and all she can hear is *boom boom boom*. Her mech shudders with each explosion.

The others fly behind her, then settle in the sky.

"Amaka." Onyii welcomes the hardness in her voice. "Take Kesandu and Obioma to secure the Obelisk. If we can't access our minerals, we'll lose all power. Chigozie, safeguard the school. Chinelo."

Static, then Chinelo's voice loud and clear. "Let's slice up some Green-and-Whites."

Onyii lets herself smile as their formation breaks apart and they head to their assignments. Just as Chigozie speeds off, an aerial mech, night-black with a green-and-white flag painted on it, speeds past.

"Chigozie!" Chinelo shouts.

But the Nigerian mech has already fired several rounds from its arm cannon into Chigozie's back. Chigozie's mech spirals through the air. Onyii hurls herself at the enemy mech. It gains on Chigozie, darting away from Onyii. It's too fast. Onyii can't catch it. But she speeds straight for where Chigozie will fall and cuts through the air, so fast everything around her blurs.

She twists around so that she's facing up. Right when Chigozie's mech sails over her, Onyii fires her shoulder cannons. Missiles twirl just past Chigozie and crash straight into the enemy mech's core and cockpit. The explosion rattles Onyii. Her comms line buzzes.

"Nice shot." It's Chigozie.

Onyii toggles up her rearview and sees Chigozie's damaged mech arc upward, trailing smoke, but operational.

"I'm fine," Chigozie says. "I can handle the school." Chigozie's mech pauses in the air, then its thrusters fire, speeding her toward the school building.

"Onyii!" Chinelo calls. "I'm getting hungry-oh!"

Onyii detatches a bladed titanium staff from her back and grips it in one hand. Her engines warm around her. Then her mech cuts like an arrow through the sky, and the feeling returns. This is it. This is what she has been waiting for. The katakata. The chaos.

She catches one Green-and-White from behind, slicing clean through its core and racing off before it even has a chance to explode. Still racing forward, she spins and cuts through another enemy mech, then hops higher as missiles pass under her.

Onyii looks down at the camp below her. Crabtanks stomp through it. Their turret guns fire into every building they can find. Onyii charges downward, staff ready, and slices the top off of the first crabtank, then bounces into the air just as Chinelo's missiles hit another. She flips to reorient herself, then charges into a formation of four enemy mechs. They break apart when she gets close.

She drives her spear through the mech closest to her. A second swings a massive hammer at her. She ducks. It hits its comrade, who spins to the earth. Onyii pulls her spear out of the first and guts the mech with the hammer. She pulls it close to use as a shield to take the Gatling gun fire the last of the Green-and-Whites shoots at her. The enemy mech on her spear shudders and writhes with each volley. Onyii charges forward and rams her new shield into the last mech, increasing speed, going faster and faster until she lets go of the spear, cuts off her back thrusters, and gets her front boosters to stop her in midflight. From her shoulder cannons, she lets loose another volley of missiles that turn two enemy mechs into a giant ball of fire.

"Help!" Amaka's voice bursts through Onyii's screen. "I got one on my back. I can't shake it."

Onyii sees them high above. Amaka's mech with its Gatling gun arms hanging at its sides spirals through the sky. A Green-and-White follows Amaka's every move. Onyii flies higher to meet them. They circle, blasting right past Onyii. She gives chase. Rising into the clouds, then diving toward the camp. Spinning and twirling to avoid the missile detonations. Onyii tries to get the enemy mech between her and Amaka in her sights, but it's too fast. Just when the reticle centers on it, the mech shifts or dips or finds cover. Then Onyii sees where Amaka is heading.

"No, Amaka! Don't go into the forest!"

The trees are bunched too close together. Amaka would get caught in the branches. She'd be a fish flopping on dry land.

Onyii pushes her thrusters to go faster and hears something come loose inside her mech. It's starting to fall apart. But she has to get closer. Her cockpit rattles and rattles, but she's able to detach another spear from her back. She brings it forward. And aims.

The enemy mech is getting farther and farther away as both it and Amaka gun it to the trees. Onyii wills her mech to stop shaking. Everything goes quiet. All that exists is what's on her screen. Her target.

She hoists the spear. Ready.

The target reticle goes red.

"Amaka! Dive!"

Onyii hurls her spear as hard as she can.

It moves so fast, it whistles through the air.

They're all heading for the treeline, but at the last moment, Amaka drops out of the sky. The spear flies right into the core processing unit of the enemy mech, sending it crashing straight into the trees.

Chinelo's mech appears next to Onyii's. Finally, a moment to catch their breath. Onyii's body feels like electric currents are running through it. Fire in her veins. Her mind is clearer than it's been in years. The world comes to her in sharper colors. She can practically smell it all through her cockpit.

"How did they find us?" Chinelo asks through her comms.

Onyii hasn't had time to ask herself that question. Too caught up in the thrill of battle. But now that she thinks about it, very little makes sense. The attack didn't begin until the suicide bomber detonated herself. The crabtanks and the mechs appeared almost right after. They must have been close. Onyii remembers the supplies run she and Chinelo had gone on earlier that day. Were they being watched by Green-and-Whites the whole time? But they had been using an isolated wireless connection and had masked it so that it seemed like no one was here. This wasn't a major mineral deposit. There was no reason for enemy forces to have stumbled onto this place. Their home.

Below them, fire takes almost everything.

Girls, suited and armed with their rifles, make ad hoc formations, firing at the crabtanks that stalk toward them. Aerial mechs duel the camp's pilots in the sky above. Others light up the ground surrounding the camp with the bombs they drop. There are too many of them.

Above them, the drone of an aircraft carrier.

Onyii and Chinelo look skyward. The aircraft is so big it blocks the moon. Its back door opens, and out spill row after row after row of enemy mechs. They darken the sky.

"There are too many of them," Chinelo says, breathless.

Onyii trembles in her cockpit. They're going to destroy her home. They're going to take away the only place where she has ever known peace.

They're going to win.

"Onyii, we have to evacuate the camp. They're going to take it."

Onyii grits her teeth and bows her head. Her gearshift and joystick tremble in her hands. When she finally looks up, her cheeks are wet with tears. "They're going to have to kill me first."

As she launches herself at the phalanx of enemy mechs, she lets out an animal cry that fills her cockpit. Her mech's arms unfold to reveal their Gatling guns, and she fires and fires and fires.

Until explosions are all she sees.

CHAPTER
6

The first boom sends dirt and twigs falling onto Ify's head. She coughs and barely has enough time to clear her eyes before another peal of thunder shakes the hole so much it might fall in on her. Through the walls and the ground above her, she hears screaming. People—grown-ups or kids her age—shouting commands. Others crying out in pain or fear or both. It sounds like war. She has her head in her hands and her eyes closed, and as much as she tries to fight it, she's thrust back into that memory. That vision of her as an even younger child in the darkness of her home, holding that dying dog in her lap as screaming and shouting and gunfire surround her.

"No, no, no," she whispers. Her mind jumps to the future waiting for her if she's kidnapped. She has heard stories. Stories about how the Fulani in the North captured girls just like her, how they raided schools and how they burned those buildings to the ground and forced the girls into long-back maglev trucks to be married to the boys they had turned into killers. Stories about what those boys would be made to do to her, what some of them would do on their own. A life in a mud hut where she will be turned into nothing but a machine for making their children. The thought paralyzes her. It drowns out all the noise from above, turns her world into silence.

Ify isn't sure how much time has passed when she hears scratching at the entrance. Something is scraping against the metal and debris covering the entrance to the tunnel. She scrambles backward and paws through the dirt for something, anything, to hit whatever comes through. Once it pokes its hand or foot or head in, she'll get one good shot. Her hand closes around the bladed staff Onyii gave her. Her fingers can barely wrap all the way around it, but she gets into a crouch and hoists it behind her.

The scratching turns to banging.

Boom, boom, boom.

Dents bloom in the metal.

Boom. Boom.

It comes loose. *BOOM.*

The metal door flies inward with a shower of dirt and brush and elephant grass. First the paws. Metal tearing at dirt and stone as the beast scrambles for purchase. Then its head comes through. It looks like a horse's head, but it's attached to the frame of a sleek tiger or leopard. Wires and cables run like veins through it. Its core glows green. Ify can't stop gawking. When it finally lands, it fills the whole space. It stands on four legs and lowers its head. Red light washes over Ify. She can't move. She wants to move. Needs to move. Her fingers shake around the staff. Her arms burn with the effort of holding it up. The beast backs up, arches it back, then gallops toward her. It'll reach her in two strides.

The smell of burning metal fills the air. She screams, drops the staff. It leaps, but sails over her as she crawls for the opening. The gunfire is clearer now. She recognizes the voices screaming. The others are out there.

The gears and pistons in the beast hiss. Ify dropped her weapon. She has nothing.

The beast struggles to stand upright in the tight enclosure, banging its head against the tunnel roof and stumbling sideways as it tries to right itself. It's stuck.

Ify lets herself breathe a half-nervous laugh, then turns to climb out of the tunnel. She stops when she hears the animal make a whining noise. Its legs retract. It frees itself, then springs forward, metal fangs glistening and ready to rip her chest open. She screams, and a blue light flashes over the beast. Time slows. Ify can see its insides, how every wire connects to every gear and every processing unit. How its drives work, how its optic nerves braid each other. Where its command functions are based.

It's only an instant, then the thing crashes into her, knocking the wind out of her. Then, all at once, it's still. Its green core fades. Ify struggles against the thing's bulk. Her legs swing and push at the ground below her. She grits her teeth. It's too heavy. But it's dead. Or off, at least. It won't eat her.

How?

Ify's mind races. One second, the thing was getting ready to rip her heart out, then it was in the air, and now it's turned off, though stuck on top of her. She tries to wriggle free, but it doesn't budge.

The Accent.

Maybe if she can turn the animal back on . . . She doesn't finish the thought. The idea of this thing alive again and glowering at her with those red eyes nearly stops her heart.

What if she can't control it? What if the tech is too different? She's only ridden other connections.

Then she remembers the girls who waited for her outside of class to make fun of her. To torment her and throw dirt and stones at her. She remembers what she wanted to do to them. It all comes back to her like a gust of wind in a storm, and she gets that feeling she always gets before she's about to fight. The rush of blood to the head. The warming in her chest. The way her fists clench. And before she knows what she's doing, she's peering at the beast's metal organs and CPUs.

Her Accent is on. The wireless network is a tangle of noise and activity. She tries to ride waves of connection, but they thin down to tightropes. So many devices wink out of existence around her like dying stars that explode before vanishing. She runs along the network's lines, jumping and sliding from node to node until she finds what she's looking for.

Gears whirr against her chest. The beast wakes up and looks around the small cave for a few moments before pushing off of Ify. Ify coughs and holds her ribs. Luckily, nothing seems broken. Still, it hurts to breathe.

The beast walks backward. Ify lowers herself into a crouch. An explosion outside tosses her to the ground. When she looks up, the beast stands utterly still. She shakes the dirt off of her face before getting back into her crouch. "Okay," she says to herself, quietly. "Okay. Let's try this." She takes one small step toward it, her hand out as though to pet its snout. "Okay, okay, okay. Onyii will surely think me mad for this. But if I can do this . . ." She waits for the thing to lash out and rip her hand off, but it doesn't move an inch.

She scoots forward again. "Okay. Now, sit!"

A moment passes where nothing happens, then it sits. It cocks its head to one side, considering her. But now it no longer looks like it wants to turn her into goat stew.

"Okay. Um. Fetch me that stick." And she points to a tree branch behind it. It retracts its legs to get into the smaller part of the cave, then grabs the branch in its teeth before returning to Ify. It's working. She can barely get a laugh out before another blast collapses the tunnel's ceiling where the branch had been. The ground above her continues to shake.

It's going to cave in.

The beast glows green again, then charges toward Ify. She wraps her arms around its neck and swings herself up onto its back just as the cave crumbles behind them. They crash through what had been the entrance in a splash of dirt and brush and metal, and suddenly, the world is louder than Ify has ever heard it before.

With her Accent on, all the camp structures glow with blue outlines. Ify looks up to see mechs, also threaded through with strands of blue light, streak through the sky like stars. The only things that don't shine are the explosions when missiles hit a mech and blow it right out of the sky, when a crabtank smashes through the mess hall and sets off the generator, knocking one of its own legs out but setting the whole building on fire. When enemy Green-and-Whites accidentally step onto a gravity mine that swirls them into the air in a burst of energy before splitting their mechanized bodies apart.

Ify's beast gallops through the katakata. She looks behind her to find other mechanized half-beasts chasing her. With greater confidence than last time, she twists on her animal's back, then zeros in on the CPUs of the beasts chasing her. A few tweaks to their coding, and they break away to attack their former masters.

Hooves thunder in the distance, getting closer. A shorthorn smashes through a stack of crates, swinging its head back and forth. The crates splinter. Food supplies and rations spray through the air. Stray metal dings Ify right in the head, hurling her from her beast. The world spins around her before she finally comes to a stop. The shorthorn is a mass of meat and metal. Plates and circuitry screwed into it, wires disappearing in its rotting flesh. A corrupted thing poisoned even further by the Green-and-Whites. Kept alive by tech and coded to kill. It looms over Ify, nearly as tall as the Obelisk, then charges forward again.

She narrowly dodges its hooves.

Gunfire from just over Ify's shoulder pings against the shorthorn's armor. Ify turns to find Chike firing with her rifle. Those bullets can't do any damage, even though they draw blood from the shorthorn. It's *ping-ping-ping* until Chike detaches a launcher from her waist and screws it onto the bottom of her rifle. With practiced motion, she slips a grenade out of her chest pouch, then loads the launcher and aims.

"Down!" she shouts, then fires.

The shorthorn's head disappears in a mass of blood and smoke. Ify dashes out of the way just as it falls onto its side.

"Chike!" Ify barely knows the girl, has only seen her from time to time acting as a sentinel for the camp, a guard. She has sometimes seen Chike on the beach in warmer weather, practicing the moves Onyii had taught her and the other girls earlier. But now Ify squeezes Chike in an embrace. "Thank you."

Chike breaks away and nods.

"Onyii," Ify breathes. "Where is she? Is she safe?"

"None of us are safe." Chike whirls around and shoots down another mechanized jungle cat. "They have colonized the animals, even."

A mech swoops down and riddles the ground with machine gun fire. Chike grabs Ify, and they dive for cover. The grass shoots up in chunks with each volley. When Ify looks up, through the crack in a set of fallen crates, she sees one of the girls who had tormented her earlier swinging a metal beam at one of the beasts. It snaps its fangs at her. Each of her swings misses. Emotions duel inside of Ify. That girl has hurt her so much. Has beaten her when Onyii wasn't looking. Has demeaned her. Has made her feel like she could never belong here. But Ify can't watch her die. Not like this.

Ify squints, focusing on the half-beast's circuitry. The green glow at its core changes to blue. It stops. The girl swings and catches it right on the jaw and sends it toppling onto its side. She staggers forward, too tired to raise her weapon for another strike. The beast rises on its haunches, straightens, then gallops in the opposite direction.

Chike puts a hand to Ify's shoulder and leans in close. "What did you do?"

"I can hack them," Ify says back.

"But . . . but how?"

There's no time to explain the Accent, the tech she had dreamed up and put together, the tech she used behind Onyii's back to surf signals and ride wireless connections and see the insides of things, of people. "It's complicated."

"Can you do more than one at a time?"

"What do you mean?"

"The Terminal."

Then it hits Ify just what Chike is suggesting. The Terminal. If she can find a way to amplify her Accent, she can control bigger machines. She can hack them. "The Terminal . . ."

"Let's go!" Chike pulls Ify along. Ify scoops up a fallen pistol and tries to keep pace with Chike as they cut a line through the camp. Chike leads the way, firing at enemy soldiers while Ify sweeps behind them, firing at whatever may try to cut them off from retreat.

Then the platform rises before them. A console station set up on a small dais, a staircase winding around it to the center, where the control panel stands. The Terminal.

"I'll cover you," says Chike, spinning around to fire at beasts and soldiers approaching from behind.

Each boom in the sky nearly throws Ify to the ground. She can barely keep her feet under her, but she makes it to the staircase and, holding the railing, climbs her way up. When she looks at the keys on the touchboard, though, she frowns. The characters. She doesn't recognize them.

"What is taking so long?" Chike shouts from below, her rifle letting off small bursts of fire. She's trying to conserve ammo, Ify realizes. She's running low.

Ify squints at the touchboard, then, tentatively, puts her fingers to it. It hums beneath her, then she feels it. She doesn't have to look at the keys in the board. She can feel them. Her brain knows. Suddenly, she's filled with muscle memory, as though she's done this a million times before. Her fingers blaze over the keys, faster than she's ever typed in her life. And then it's like all the doors in her mind, one after the other, open.

Looking at the touchboard, she can see it all. Can see inside the mechs, the crabtanks, all of it. The connection pathways are as broad as rivers.

She jumps from one node to the next, powering down their cores so that all around her, enemy mechs fall from the sky. The cries of their confused pilots are a whisper in her ears. But she can hear the cheers of her comrades as clear as morning birdsong. The crabtank stomping through the greenhouse stops in mid-attack, its top sizzling and sparking before it lets out a fiery puff. Then the thing collapses onto the remains of their garden. Ify scans in a wide circle around her, touching each node she comes across. Then she closes her eyes, inputs a key sequence into the touchboard, and feels a massive wave of energy pulse out of her. Like an ocean tide with her at its center. The wave expands and expands and expands, and each enemy mech it hits sizzles and sparks before collapsing. A wave of command inputs to alter their coding in mid-operation. They drop like mosquitoes sprayed with antiseptic.

We're winning, Ify says to herself. And all because of her. Because of her tech. Her Accent. She swims through the wireless network she can see in her mind. Dances through it, leaping from comms system to comms system until she stops at one. Onyii. She is inside Onyii's mech. She can hear her. Issuing commands, naming formations. Laughing. *Sister, I am saving us—*

An explosion rips the ground out from under Ify and sends her arcing through the sky, limbs flailing, until she hits the earth. Bones crack. She screams out in pain, clutching her ribs. Her head is a thunderstorm of static and machine-whine. Pain swallows her whole. When she manages to turn around, her eyes widen with shock. The Terminal. Fire gobbles it. The console melts in the flames.

Three soldiers make their way carefully toward her with large rifles Ify has never seen before. Sleek, black, almost plastic-looking. They have masks over their faces, and their eyes glow green beneath them. Night-vision lenses. Ify tries to get away but can't even move. She tries to claw her way back, but they're gaining on her.

Tears leak down Ify's cheeks. They're going to get her. She looks around, wildly, for anything, anyone. But then she realizes why everything seems so different. Her Accent. It's disabled. But how . . .

She has no time to figure it out.

The soldier in the center fires a net out of his gun that wraps Ify and pins her to the ground with magnetic charges. She has no breath in her lungs to scream. Otherwise, she would cry out for Onyii, whose face is still fresh in her mind. And whose laughter still rings between her ears.

They cinch the net with a collar around her throat.

CHAPTER
7

Swallowed by fire, Onyii's mech spins and strikes. Pressing down on pedals and pushing and pulling her gearshift, she feels as though she's become one with the metal encasing her. Her mech rams its fist into the body of an enemy mech and hurls it in a wide arc at several others, ripping out its core. Her mech headbutts another mech. Closes its fist around the rifle barrel of another and crushes her free fist into the enemy's cockpit. Charging forward, she gets her hands on another mech and, in one swift motion, rips it in half. The armor on her own mech shrieks. Pieces of it fall away. A blast hits her from behind. One of her engines cuts out. She turns, and someone's spear sticks her. A volley of gunfire pits her windshield with bullet holes. Then, suddenly, it all goes dark.

Onyii hears nothing. Her console stops glowing. Her comms are dead.

Suddenly, her weight shifts. Something pins her back to her seat. Her controls slip out of her hands. Everything's sliding.

She's falling.

No no no no no.

She can't remember how far up she was or what position she's falling in. But she must be facing down. She fumbles behind her for a cord, praying it'll be where she needs it to be. Her seat straps dig into her chest. The velocity keeps pinning her arms back. She doesn't have much time left.

She fumbles with her human hand. Can feel the bones close to snapping, the joints already popping. New tears spring to her eyes. Pain needles every inch of her body. Her mech catches on something, throwing her whole body forward, then back. Her thumb jams against a button and snaps. But a panel bursts loose behind her head, and a wire uncoils. She grabs one end through the pain and jams it into a socket on her Augmented forearm, turning herself into her mech's battery. It might kill her. But then, so might the fall.

Her mind explodes with sensation. All the noise and smell and texture of the world hitting her at once. Blood spills from her nose. But then everything powers up. Her console comes to life, and she pulls at her joystick and gearshift. Pulls and pulls until she's about to dislocate her shoulders. Her windshield display powers on to show her the fast-moving ground. She pulls and pulls and pulls, tries to get her mech to move against the wind.

One last jerk and she's upright. Her fingers blaze over her touchboard, and thrusters open on her legs to slow her until she comes to a shuddering stop. A hundred feet above the remains of the school building.

Through all the noise in her head—the amplified buzzing of cicadas, the whimper of wounded girls, the hiss of emptying gas tanks—Onyii searches for the sound of gunfire. Nothing. She turns her mech to the sky. The enemy mechs fly in an arc toward the massive aircraft carriers floating at the camp's edge.

"Where are they going?" Without warning, she pitches forward in her seat and vomits. Her belt still holds her back, so it all ends up in her lap. Dizziness slams into her like a missile. "The forest," she murmurs.

Her mech first leans, then floats slowly into the trees. The sound of elephant grass whispering against the mobile suit's flanks settles the beating of her heart. A few minutes later, she finds a charred clearing, shattered tree trunks forming a blackened circle around the space. She tries to land but can't get her thrusters to do what they're supposed to, and the mech collapses into a heap, its legs bent beneath it.

Onyii lets herself hang sideways in her seat for several seconds. Blood drips from her cheek. She tries to reach and wipe away the vomit on her pants, but her arms refuse to move. Strength leaks out of her. But she fumbles for her belt. A click.

She falls onto her human arm and yelps. For a few moments, she lets herself lie there, curled in a ball, shivering. Her teeth chatter. The forest is quiet around her. And for that small bit of time that she has to herself—that she doesn't have to share with anyone—she can hide and feel her pain. Where no one can see.

She does not know how much time has passed, but the cold slowly lifts from her. She struggles to sit upright, but when she twists, she sees her legs: a mangled mess behind her. Useless. Strangely, there's no pain.

Ify. She has to get to Ify.

Gritting her teeth, she pulls herself to her disabled console, fishes under the board for the latch, then nearly collapses with relief when the hatch hisses open.

Outside, the mist makes a wall of gray she can barely see

through. She blinks. Something's wrong. She crawls through the open space and falls onto the grass, and that's when she finally puts her hand to her face. Her right eye is gone.

Panic tightens its grip on her lungs. She knows things have happened to her body that should bring pain, but she feels none. Only numbness. She remembers Ify, and all thoughts about herself vanish, like mist evaporating. She has to find Ify.

Leaves whisper around her. Movement. She stills.

Shapes form in the fog. Black silhouettes. Shorthorns? No, people. Soldiers. It does not matter to Onyii that she has no gun, that she has only one arm, that her legs are broken beneath her. That her right eye is gone. She will fight with whatever she has to get Ify back.

The shapes break apart. Three of them. And something behind them. Being dragged.

Onyii grits her teeth. With her good arm, Onyii tries to push herself up but fails and falls into the mud. They're heading straight for her. The world blurs. She's dying. Onyii knows it the way she knows the direction of gravity. But she must save Ify.

They stop. Their shadows darken her ruined body.

She tries to push herself up, fails, and tries again, each time splashing into the mud until it has gotten into her nose. The Nigerian soldiers standing over her talk in hushed whispers to each other. One of them chuckles.

Then one of them kicks Onyii onto her back, flips her over like she's just a piece of brush. But now she can see their faces. They hide behind masks that cover everything but eyes that glow green from their night-vision lenses.

But one of them, when it sees Onyii's face, squints. Its whole body tenses, then it leans in while another has its gun trained on her. The first one's face draws close to Onyii's. So close the puffs of air that filter through its mask with each clean breath brush radiation-thick frost onto her bloodstained cheeks.

Onyii strains to see the bundle they had been carrying behind them. Enough of the mist has thinned for her to see that it's a body wrapped in a net. Metal binds the body's ankles together, another collar closed around its neck. It must be a trick of the light, or Onyii's missing eye playing with her mind. But she sees the bundle stir. Sees it come to life in its restraints. That brown cloth isn't a bag. It's a mud-splotched shirt. A shirt so big it nearly reaches the bundle's ankles. The only size of shirt Onyii could ever find for Ify.

With her good hand, Onyii reaches out.

A boot presses onto her chest. The one that had been examining her before steps hard on her and points its gun at her forehead. This is how it's going to end.

"I know this one," it says in a voice Onyii recognizes as human. "We've met before."

"How do you know?" asks one of the others, annoyed.

"I've killed many *udene*, but only one have I maimed." With its rifle, it gestures to Onyii's crushed metal arm. "I took its arm." It cocks its gun, ready to fire.

The other one puts its hand to the first one's rifle barrel and pushes away. "Let me. You, take her to the ship." The figure nods back at the bundle, attended to by another Nigerian. The bundle twists and writhes. Ify. "I will be with you shortly."

Their eyes catch. And that's when Onyii knows in her heart that Ify sees her. That Ify knows she tried. She tried so hard to save her. Onyii won't let herself cry. She can't give the Nigerians the satisfaction of seeing her weak. So, even as the one who'd called her *udene* goes back to Ify and drags her away, even as Onyii is left alone with her executioner, even as her vision blurs and the world fades away, she doesn't let herself cry. She allows herself one last thought. A word. A name.

Ify.

Her dear sister's face is the last thought in Onyii's head before she hears the gunshot ring out.

Onyii opens her eyes.

The soldier is still standing over her. But its gun is aimed into the tree branches. Smoke twists from its barrel. The soldier lowers its rifle, never taking its eyes off of Onyii. It taps the side of its head, then Onyii hears words buzz into her brain.

"Do not thank me for sparing your life." A woman's voice. More Nigerian mimicry. It only sounds like a woman. "You will not live much longer anyway. But know that I am not like him," she says, gesturing in the direction of the Nigerian soldier who left. "Daren and I share blood and a mission, and that is it." Then, for a long time, silence. "I will not apologize for what he did to you the last time you two met. You must have been children, but this is war. And we will win it."

Then, like a crow taking flight, she vanishes into the forest.

CHAPTER

8

Ify wakes as they are dragging her through forestland. Pebbles and twigs catch under her. Scratches bloom on her cheeks. All is darkness around her. Her eyes eventually adjust to make out the shapes of trees and the silhouettes of some of the soldiers, who are careful to stay out of the moonlight. She can't hear war sounds anymore and wonders how far from the camp they've dragged her.

A dream. It must have been a dream. Onyii on her back with soldiers standing over her. Onyii slowly getting smaller and smaller as Ify was dragged away. Smaller and smaller until the fog swallowed her up. Then the gunshot. No. It must have been a dream. Onyii is still alive. Ify has to get back to her.

That's when she remembers she's trapped.

Her hands are pressed against her chest, her ankles clasped together. She can only wiggle and barely that. Whenever she tries to move her head, to shift her gaze so that she sees something other than ground, pain pinches the back of her neck.

The world is so black without her Accent. She tries to shift her jaw and get it working again, but the forest remains dark. There's none of the telltale hum of life.

The soldiers dragging her stop. The one holding up her legs lets go of the net's end. Ify's ankles smack the ground, and she yelps. The collar around her throat burns her. She grits her teeth and tries not to make another noise, tries not to anger the thing they've clipped around her neck. She just lies there, trying to slow-breathe her way through the pain.

For some time, no one moves. Ify tries to raise herself. Wherever the soldiers are, they must be standing as still as the trees—stiller, even. A slight wind knocks leaves from tree branches overhead. Ify wants to call out, to curse them, to shout for help, to proclaim the greatness of Biafra, anything, just to make a defiant noise, to show them she won't go quietly. But without her Accent, she feels defenseless. Powerless. She's just a little girl.

She smells morning before she sees it. A sweetness in the dewy grass beneath her head. Then warmth. Through the trees, along the horizon, blue begins.

They arrive at a clearing, and the air seems to shimmer. She gasps as the distortion morphs into an aircraft.

Its silver wings stretch out from its top and then bend to dig into the ground like anchors. It has a sleek oblong body, large enough to fit at least a half dozen land mechs. The back door unfurls itself like an elephant's trunk, revealing a yawning emptiness.

The Green-and-White that had been dragging Ify reaches down, then stops. The soldiers freeze. Then they all look to each other, and one of them darts off into the forest. Ify tries to focus her hearing, tries to remember if she'd heard anything or imagined it. But it's not long before the soldier returns, holding a War Girl by her hair, so high that her feet dangle and swing above the ground.

Ify's eyes widen. The girl she saved. What is she doing here?

Metal bands hold the girl's wrists together behind her back. The soldier who caught her looks to the one who had been dragging Ify, then at the others. Ify realizes there are now five of them. They all trade looks, and Ify realizes they're all talking, only not out loud. Like she does with Enyemaka. *Did* with Enyemaka.

The girl catches Ify's eye, and they stare at each other. The girl's lips are pursed shut. She can scream, Ify realizes, but she won't. She won't give the enemy the satisfaction of hearing her scream. Blood streams from a wound on her head, runs over one eye, but she manages a defiant look, every so often squirming in her captor's grip.

The soldiers look at each other, one shakes their head, another nods insistently, and their silent argument continues. All the while, Ify and the girl hold each other's gazes, and Ify tries to squint her forgiveness at her. Tries to tell her without moving her mouth that she's sorry for the anger she felt and that she's glad the girl is still alive and that maybe now she will make an effort to learn her name and maybe they can grow close and even in the northern bush they can—

The girl is dropped to the floor, and the soldier holding her pulls a pistol from their waist and shoots her once. In the head.

"No!" Ify screams through the pain lancing her neck. "No!" Tears blur her vision and slide down her cheeks. This feeling of fire burns up to her face and through her head, so that it feels like she will burst any moment. When she opens her eyes again, even though the world is hazy with pain and tears, she can see that the girl is gone. Likely dragged into the forest and not even given a burial.

They're going to kill her too, Ify realizes. When one of the soldiers stands over her, she glares at them and lets herself be filled with rage and hate. Her chest heaves with each breath she takes.

The soldier takes off their mask to reveal a face like Ify has never seen before. Hair in silver locs comes down to the soldier's shoulders. Their eyes are many-colored, irises cut through with gold and brown and green. Like hers. And their skin. The soldier's skin is brown. Sand-colored. Light. Like hers.

"It's all right, Kadan. Little one." The soldier squints, then reaches through the netting to wipe tears from Ify's cheeks with rough, gloved fingers. "Soon, you will be home." The soldier speaks with a type of voice Ify has never heard before. Deeper. Lower. And the soldier's face is shaped weirdly. No oval, but a flat chin and a sharp jawline. She'd seen boys in holos from her tablet. In movies always getting into trouble and being saved. They looked like this. But those were humans. These are Fulani or Hausa.

The soldier squats all the way down to Ify's level, rifle slung across its back, then reaches for her collar. "You have to promise me," it says in its weird voice. "You have to promise me that when I take this collar off, you will not scream."

Ify wants to ask if the soldier will kill her. She can't believe it speaks like her. But she manages a nod.

The soldier touches the collar, then taps a sequence into a keypad on its wrist. The collar lets out a puff of air, then falls into the soldier's hand.

Her throat still feels raw, and she can't move any of her limbs, but she asks, "What are you?"

The soldier looks up at the others, then lets out a chuckle.

Ify's eyes go wide with bewilderment. This isn't a beast, not some type of hairy animal. Not like what she was taught Nigerians looked and sounded and smelled like. But it's clearly an enemy. "What kind of animal are you?" Maybe if she can get its name, she can study it, learn it, find its weakness.

The soldier smiles at Ify. It looks like a version of what Onyii might have looked like had Onyii been born the enemy. But then again, these things aren't born. They're made out of evil and metal.

Lights come on in the aircraft, and gusts of wind begin to blow as its engines power on. The soldier swings Ify onto its shoulder and walks lightly to the opening. She wants to fight, to bite and kick and scratch, but the energy has left her. She can't stop thinking of the girl they murdered, the girl whose name she'll never know. The girl who has left her to this future she must bear all alone.

A soldier emerges from the forest. The one who they had left behind with Onyii. The one who had killed Onyii. No. Onyii's still alive. *I have to get back to her. She needs me.*

The soldier sets Ify down on a metal bench and presses a button that loosens the net so that it falls away. The other soldiers sit on benches that line both sides of the craft. The back door curls itself shut.

"What kind of animal am I?" It chuckles as shadows swallow its face. "I'm a boy."

CHAPTER

9

In the memory, the ribbons on the bedposts in the girls' dormitory are pink. And Onyii sleeps with her textbooks beneath her pillow. She hears about how children who do that sometimes get teased, but none of the girls in her school tease her. Today, however, when she wakes up, she sneaks a small tin out from under her pillow. Inside are pieces of wrapped-up toffee.

She spent the whole night dreaming of Adaeze, who was a few grades above her and thus slept in a different dormitory. And all last week, as Ada didn't show up for class, the girls whispered about what might have happened to her. Then Onyii had found out what Adaeze had done. Onyii listened, enraptured, as the rumor made its way through the dorm and found her, the rumor that Adaeze had watched her brother enlist in the New Biafran army. The rumor that Adaeze had wanted to join him but that families were limited to sending only one child. And, besides, who would wash the laundry and clean the home? But Ada had snuck her way to their encampment. And when they found her, a soldier took her outside to the front gate and called her parents. Her parents had sent an older sister to come get her, but Adaeze had said no and sent her back home. Then a brother-in-law, her sister's husband, had come to collect her and had reportedly grabbed her arm to drag her away, but she had found a sharp stone and cut him. Finally, Adaeze's mother had come to the army camp's front gate and had wept, begging Ada to come home. But she had refused. To give Adaeze's mother some relief, the commander had told Ada's mother that Ada could be sent to a camp run by and for women. Ada would be surrounded by people just like her, and her mother would not have to worry about the things that happen to girls in war.

It's this thought—a camp of women warriors—that fills Onyii's head as she leaps out of bed and readies herself and dresses in her clean school uniform. She's dreaming of the front lines even as she bursts into her principal's office and drops a piece of toffee on his desk. The principal looks up from his paperwork and smiles and says, "Happy birthday."

Onyii giggles. "It's not my birthday," then she's out the door.

She hands a piece of toffee to all of her classmates in science class, and those girls follow her to her mathematics class, and by the end, they are all howling and hugging her and weeping into their palms and begging her not to leave. They all know what she wants to do and where she wants to go.

But she is going to fight.

"Why should I sit and waste my time?" Adaeze had told her one afternoon in a courtyard well before she had made the decision to leave. "I don't want them to build this new country without me. And I'm tired of having to maintain all this hair."

Onyii had beamed at the older girl. Looking at her, she had never seen a more beautiful sight.

A different memory takes her. Onyii is flying. Her mech shudders around her as she tries to escape the bullets firing at her from every direction. On her screen, Adaeze's mech darts and arcs and spins, trying to shake the enemy mech chasing her. Onyii tries to get the Green-and-White in her sights, but every time her reticle settles on it, it dodges.

"I can't shake it!" Adaeze shouts over their comms system.

Onyii's mech rattles her bones. She grits her teeth and powers forward, trying to get closer to Ada and the mech chasing her. She almost doesn't notice the beeping until it's too late. She spins just in time to catch the enemy mech that had charged at her. But the force of the blow sends her careening through the air.

Her mech goes dark. But she can hear the wind outside, howling around the tons of metal she's trapped in as her mobile suit hurtles toward the ground. Just as she's about to hit the treeline, her mech comes back to life and the thrusters stop her fall. Above her, a single mech hovers. It's a machine with no face, no eyes, no mouth, but she thinks she can see it grinning.

She tries to find Ada, but the mech that rammed into her charges for her. She darts out of the way. "Ada!" she calls out.

Static.

"Ada!"

The enemy mech is on her tail. She weaves and dodges, but it's too fast. Missiles screech past her. For the first time, she feels fear. It seeps into her bones. Makes her hands shake on her gearshift. It makes her heart trip-hammer in her chest. *Don't let it conquer you.* That's what Ada had told her during their training. *As soon as you feel fear, you've lost.* But Onyii can't stop it.

Her mech is slowing down. Bullets stitch along its side.

Explosions boom through the sky. Each noise makes her want to cry.

"Little udene," she thinks she hears someone say just as the enemy mech closes in on her.

Suddenly, it appears in front of her. A transmission beams into her visual display, intruding on her comms. It's the enemy pilot.

She sees his face. His silver eyes. The silver braids running down past his shoulders. He's so young. As young as her.

"Little udene," he says again. There's a giant hammer-like object in his hands. He raises it.

All of Onyii's training leaves her. She raises her hands, foolishly. As though her mech will follow her movements and block the blow.

But the enemy swings, and all Onyii sees is darkness.

■ ■ ■ ■ ■

Onyii wakes up with a start.

Softness, fabric against her skin. A chill. But she can feel threading all around her. She opens her good eye. Through the canopy of leaves, starlit sky overhead, slowly breaking with dawn. She blinks. Static, then voices. Familiar voices.

She's in a blanket.

They're carrying her in a blanket. Her sisters. Then it all comes rushing back to her. The attack on the camp. Her mech landing in the forest, the Green-and-White who had spared her life as she lay bleeding and broken on the ground. Them dragging Ify away.

Ify.

She starts, then moves to get out of the blanket.

A screech pierces the night. They drop her.

Pain rips through her back and neck. But after a moment, she grins. She wants to laugh. Pain. Pain means she's alive. Pain means she isn't paralyzed. She lifts her right arm and slowly turns on the ground to see that it's connected by a wire to the back of Chinelo's neck. Onyii's grin widens. *Chinelo's okay.*

"Onyii!" Kesandu calls out from Onyii's left. "Onyii, can you hear us?"

Chatter drowns out the rest of what Kesandu might have said.

Onyii tries to stand upright. Her legs have been straightened by splints. She looks up to Chinelo, whose bees swarm around her head.

Chinelo stoops down. "Onyii," Chinelo whispers, grateful, then wraps her in an embrace. "We thought we lost you."

Kesandu stands next to Obioma.

"*Chineke*," Kesandu curses. "We thought you were dead-oh."

Obioma looks at Onyii as though she's watching a ghost grow skin and bones right in front of her. Like she's afraid of Onyii. Onyii glares at her with her eye.

Chinelo smacks Obioma on the back of the head. "Are you mad? Are they cooking fried rice inside your brain? This is your sister. Look like you are happy to see her." Obioma rubs the back of her head and offers a sheepish grin.

"I am happy-oh," Obioma says beneath her breath. "No need to fire the back of my head like that." She looks to Onyii. "Sister, we are happy to have you back." She grows shy again. "I did not know we could fly mechs the way you fly yours. If I can learn to fly like that, I will be very happy."

Onyii smiles at the little girl. Only a few years older than . . .

"Ify." Onyii leaps to her feet. Her legs buckle beneath her. Before she can stagger to her feet again, Chinelo is by her side, putting an arm over her shoulder.

"Rest, Onyii," Chinelo tells her quietly.

Onyii breaks away. "No. Ify. They took Ify." But she has no energy left.

Chinelo leans in close and pulls a gel packet from a pouch at her waist. A steroid boost. "Here, have another one of these," she says, sliding the packet into Onyii's mouth.

Energy fills Onyii. She feels herself become more solid. She feels like she's gained control over her body. She can stand unassisted now. But she's still woozy.

"I gave you one after I repaired your arm and connected to you. It was enough to bring you back, but you are still very weak."

Onyii brings her face close to Chinelo's. "I need to find Ify. Give me something stronger."

Pain shines in Chinelo's eyes. But she pulls a vial out of her breast pocket and hands it to Onyii. "It's Chukwu," Chinelo says, hesitating for a moment before handing Onyii the vial of crushed crystals. Chukwu. What they call the precious minerals they mine from the ground to power their machines. What they call the powder they grind it into and ingest. The energy of the supreme being that gives strength to all things. Onyii has heard of others who did it, who said it felt like inhaling the universe, who then died soon after. "Just a little. It will give you more strength. But we need to get you to a healing bath. We might still be able to salvage one. Rest, then we'll get Ify."

Onyii looks at the vial, then turns her back to the others. She bites off the top, then tips its contents onto the back of her hand. Glittering powder. When she sniffs it into her nostrils, fire bursts to life between her ears. All of a sudden, everything is in high definition. It is almost too much. But then the burn subsides. Her shoulders relax. She can see. As though she still has both eyes.

For a moment, she thinks about making a run for it. But then she looks back at the others. The Nigerians didn't kill Ify. They took her. That means she's still alive. They will get her back. Onyii inclines her head toward the edge of the forest. "*Oya,*" she says, suddenly the leader again. "Let's go." The Chukwu surges through her, and it's almost a struggle to keep from breaking out into a run or attacking the nearest object. So much strength and power sits inside her.

Chinelo disconnects from Onyii's arm, and the cord snakes its way back into Chinelo's neck. Together, they walk.

Then, there it is in front of them.

Smoke billowing in columns throughout the camp. Blood and shell casings all over the ground. The gutted husk of an enemy mech lies on its side, crushing the infirmary. A pilot lies slumped out of the broken cockpit window.

Footsteps, then Chinelo's voice. "The Obelisk is out. They bombed it. Took out the Terminal too. We have no more power."

"Amaka?" Onyii asks. "Chigozie?"

Kesandu and Obioma look at the ground. Chinelo softly shakes her head at Onyii, then gestures at the ruins of the camp.

In the distance, faint but growing louder, a rumbling.

Something's coming.

CHAPTER
10

Ify can't stop staring at the boy sitting across from her.

He has his rifle upright between his knees, and as the aircraft hums around them, he leans on it like he's tired, and suddenly, Ify recognizes him as human. A boy, like he said. He doesn't seem like an irradiated monster come out of the bush like most Northerners are supposed to be. Like what Ify learned about in the holos from history class. Like what she'd seen in the vampire movies she and the other girls pirated on their tablets. It's startling to see one up close. To see it having skin just like hers and eyes and hair and two hands and two feet.

Her head throbs, and she squeezes it between her hands, as though she just needs to push hard enough to get the pain to leak out. She hadn't noticed it during the battle, but now that there are no more explosions and peals of thunder around her, the thudding of her brain against her skull is all she can hear. It's gotten worse since they dragged her onto the aircraft.

The boy slings his rifle over his back and grabs onto a strap hanging from the craft's ceiling. Almost like a monkey, he swings from one to the next until he arrives at Ify's bench.

Too exhausted to push him away or even to growl at him, Ify

just lets her head hang between her knees. If she vomits, let it not be on herself.

"What is the problem, Kadan?" His voice is smooth, even as it seems to dip, like it's gliding just above the earth.

"Don't call me that," Ify hisses. "I don't even know what it means."

A pause from the boy. "Then tell me your name. So I can call you something else."

Ify wants to lie, but the hurt keeps her from thinking, so she just blurts out, "Ifeoma."

"That is a beautiful name, even if it is the name they gave you. In our language, *kadan* means *little one*, but you do not speak it yet, so I will call you Ifeoma until we can come up with a better name for you."

"A better name?"

"A name fit for a Nigerian."

Ify swipes weakly at him.

He doesn't even bother to swat away her hand. "Now, let us see what is the problem." He grabs Ify by her face. A gentle grip, but Ify knows this type of hold. She knows that with but a thought, the boy could snap her neck. She knows that he could gouge out her eyes or worse before she'd even be able to scream or blink. So she remains still.

As he looks at her, Ify realizes that his left eye is not flesh and blood. It's mechanized. It twitches one way, then another, scanning her head. It reminds Ify of the beasts that attacked the camp alongside the Nigerian soldiers. The beast that burst into her hiding space. The beast she was able to hack and control. And that's when the thought hits her. All she needs to do is bide her time. They have not killed her yet, which means she is useful to them alive. Which means that they will continue to keep her alive, long enough for Ify to come up with a plan of escape. And maybe she can make sure this one is no longer around to chase her.

The eye ends its scan. Then he shifts his grip, holding Ify by the back of her neck, tightening, and tilting her head up. He puts his free hand by Ify's ear, and she hears—too loud—the whirr of machinery under the boy's skin. Just like with Onyii's arm.

"This will take only a moment."

Before he finishes the sentence, his elongated fingers dive inside her ear, sending shock waves through her entire body. She seizes, but he holds her neck so tightly that she can't even move her head. Her teeth chatter. Her fingers spasm. Inside her ear, she can feel nanobots swirling and hear metal spinning. And when her eyes close shut, she can imagine the boy's tech digging into her brain and lobotomizing her, making her useless. She wants to fight back, tries to, but the boy has paralyzed her. Then, after what feels like forever, it ends.

She slumps in his grip.

He brings his re-formed hand back before his eyes, palm up, and squints at a tiny metal sphere resting in a groove on his glove. With a flick of his wrist, he bounces it so that sits between his thumb and index finger. Then he brings it to his Augmented eye.

Ify gasps. Her Accent.

She tries to reach for it. But the boy squeezes her neck, and she goes limp again.

She struggles against him but can only turn her eyes to look at him. She's completely powerless as he turns her Accent over in his fingers, scrutinizing its every millimeter.

"So this is it," he breathes. "This is the device that has been swimming on our connection." He doesn't bother to mask the awe in his voice. "An external ghost box. With a VPN enabled to mask its IP address, and SEIM capabilities to keep from being hacked itself. Nearly impregnable. Child, how did you do this?"

He loosens his grip, but Ify refuses to answer.

"We have this in Nigeria, but it takes a machine as tall as me and with enough server space to be noticeable by anyone with a second set of eyes. But here, you've turned it into a device that can be activated even by a red-blood." He looks to her, then, without warning, lets her go. "That's what you are, isn't it? A red-blood."

Ify rubs the back of her neck. "Is that another Northern slur? Something you call Biafrans before you violate and kill them?"

A look of disappointment whisks across his face before it's gone. "It means only that you are zero percent machine. You are not an Augment. You are as Allah designed you." He looks at her Accent. "Which makes this all the more remarkable. There's no node or outlet on you. I discovered this when I scanned you. Nowhere on your body is there a place for a cord. But with this"—he holds up the Accent—"you have turned yourself into an invisible router."

"Not so invisible," says a Nigerian soldier farther down on the bench. "That was the signal we followed to find this camp." This one, Ify recognizes as the one who murdered Onyii. "You are sloppy, Kadan." When the woman looks at Ify, rage erupts in Ify's bones, and Ify knows that there is no bond between them and can never be. This woman would murder her as easily as the boy murdered Ify's schoolmate. "Or maybe you wanted to be found."

"You're lying!" Ify shoots back. Then she looks into the boy's face. "Tell her she's lying. You said yourself. This was invisible. I could not be detected. By anyone."

That familiar look of disappointment comes across his face, but this time doesn't leave. "I'm sorry, Kada—Ifeoma. But there is no other way we could have found your camp. It was Masked. Daurama is correct. You were not the invisible one. You were the one calling for our help."

"I was *not* calling for your help! You are the enemy. You attacked us. You murdered my sisters."

The boy's face scrunches in anger. "They are *not* your sisters. They are your kidnappers. For years, they have forced you to live in the dirt, to scavenge for supplies in the forest. To learn from outdated lesson downloads. They are backward, and they have forced you into their violent ways. And it is clear that they have brainwashed you."

"Don't talk about Onyii like that! You are the murderers. You killed my friend right in front of me."

"Was she your friend?" The boy's voice is soft, but the question rings between Ify's ears. "Is that what she was?"

Ify turns away. Tears burn her eyes, but she can't tell who they are for. Are they for the girl? Are they for Onyii? Are they for something bigger? For the home she has just lost? The home where so few people had accepted her? The home where her truest friend was an android? She feels her heart begin to harden but stops it. No. They were her family. This boy is trying to trick her.

"In Abuja, you will thrive, Ifeoma." He holds up her Accent. "Before, this would have been considered magic. I'm sure the Biafrans would not have approved. They would have called this witchcraft. I'm sure you had to hide it from them."

How does he know? Is he reading my memories? But how? I'm not connected.

"But in Abuja, this would have gotten you the highest marks on your final exams."

"What?"

"I cannot even begin to imagine the algorithms you had to figure out in order to get multiple security-management platforms layered on top of each other in this tiny thing. And to have it not generate its own network but map itself to others to gain immediate access? Astounding. You will have us on the moon before the year is out." He's smiling. With his teeth. And to Ify, they shine bright enough to light up the darkened aircraft interior.

Daurama scoffs behind him, but the boy's smile doesn't fade.

He touches her shoulder. "Ifeoma, you are special. You are brilliant. Where you are going, you will be praised for it. And challenged. Nigerians are competitive. And our children learn from an early age how important is our technological advancement." He raises the shield over one window, and light spills into the aircraft in a beam. "Look."

Ify peers out the window. They have left the forest and now, below them, is blighted wasteland. Animals skinny with radiation poisoning or thick with blight from polluted water roam hardened ground so red and brown it looks like a giant scab. A few humans walk the wasteland in baggy, patched-together radiation suits, breathing through old masks. But the only homes Ify can see are huts and occasional shacks sheltered beneath shimmering blue domes. Air-cleansing half-spheres, likely powered by the minerals beneath the soil. But this place looks ravaged. It looks like nearly every living thing has been snatched from it, so there are only the dead and the dying.

"This is southern Nigeria. Our Middle Belt is where prosperity begins, but the seasons have grown more and more extreme with each year. And the tax on our land is already too great." He leans into Ify. "We are working on technology to . . . reverse the tide, as they say." He smirks at his joke. "The climate is changing, and we must change with it." He pauses for a moment. "Is this a project that interests you?"

Ify's gaze roves over the landscape, trying to take it all in. It's almost too much to process.

"Ah, yes. You have likely never been beyond your camp. Well. There is so much more of Nigeria for me to show you."

And that's when the hunger hits her. The same hunger that had her downloading pirated lesson plans on orbital physics. The same hunger that had her studying outside of class, in her bed with her tablet splayed before her and her stylus running back and forth over her screen as she scribbled equation after equation. That hunger to know.

How are the Northerners like this?

The boy puts his hand out. Ify's Accent sits on his palm.

Ify takes it. Suddenly, it seems like something different, bigger. It's no longer some tiny sin she has to hide from everyone. It's a technological achievement. It's not a mistake. It's a marvel. It's something to be proud of.

"What do I call you?"

The boy smiles. "Daren. It means 'born at night.'" He takes off a glove and shows Ify his light skin. Light like hers. "The sun was not shining when I was born, so I came out of my mother like this." He laughs, and Ify is so shocked that she can't help but join him.

Ify catches herself. Guilt burns in her cheeks. How can she let this happen? She has betrayed Onyii. Even sitting next to this soldier and not trying to kill him, she has committed a sinful act. But she can't bring herself to hate him. She can't bring herself to scramble along the aircraft floor for a piece of shrapnel to jab into his neck. She can't see herself strangling him, snapping his voicebox with her thumbs like Onyii taught her to.

"You are not alone," Daren says, as he puts his hand on Ify's fist. *Is he being kind, or is he restraining me?* She can't decide. "So many others whom we have rescued have the same battle rage inside them. So many others whom we have rescued, they believe their kidnappers loved them, cared for them. But that was not their tribe. That was not their family. I bet they told you all sorts of things about us. That we live in mud huts." He leans toward Daurama. "Do we live in mud huts?"

Daurama gives a thumbs-up sign and a rare smile. "My mud hut has wireless internet and wallpaper televisions. What does your mud hut have?"

Daren laughs. "In Nigeria, we paper the walls of our mud huts with advanced engineering degrees."

Ify doesn't have time to respond. An explosion thunders through the aircraft. The floor beneath her rocks and shudders, and she falls forward, barely able to brace herself in time. Daren grips the wall, then the straps hanging overhead. Daurama is up and moving about the hull. They shout to each other in a language Ify can't understand. With her Accent disabled, she can't translate the words. So she has to hold on to the ledge of the bench while smoke fills the cabin. Everyone presses a button on their suit, and their masks appear. She's the only one without a mask, and she coughs so hard it feels like her lungs are coming through her throat. Through the smoke, Ify sees Daurama glare at her.

Daren notices and says something to Daurama, and Daurama vanishes into another part of the aircraft. All the machinery beeps its distress. Wind rushes by them outside. They're spinning. Daurama is yelling now. The smoke stings Ify's eyes, and she squeezes them shut. Someone yanks her from the bench into the air. It's Daurama, her fingers growing tighter and tighter around Ify's neck.

CHAPTER
11

It's not long before the maglev Range Rovers, sparkling in the morning light, bulldoze their way out of the forest and into the camp. The headlights shine into the faces of the surviving girls. Onyii has one arm wrapped around her stomach. She aches all over and can barely stand. The Chukwu she took is wearing off. If not for Chinelo holding her upright, she'd be on the ground right now.

The Rovers, for having gone through the forest, look pristine, covered in dewdrops that bead their black frames. Some of the girls have their hands up in front of their eyes to shield against the glare. Some of them stand with their fists at their sides or their fingers close to the trigger of their machine guns. The vehicles form a semicircle and sit for several near-silent seconds before shutting down and lowering to the ground. The camp has stopped burning. It lies dead, smoldering behind the girls, and Onyii wonders how much of it the people in the jeeps can see.

As the lights continue to beam the girls blind, a door opens and out steps a man in an olive-green military uniform with red stripes on sleeves rolled all the way up to his biceps. He steps in front of one set of headlights so that he's silhouetted, and Onyii can tell this is purely for dramatic effect. To make him seem greater than he is. But Onyii knows the uniform, knows the type of man who wears it, knows that this thing in front of her is just that. A man.

She straightens and stares straight ahead into the lights. Mercifully, they turn off.

By now, a number of soldiers have come out of their jeeps. Some of them have their assault rifles ready. Some of them sway anxiously from foot to foot. They are new. They've seen less combat than Onyii has. They've probably spent most of their careers in base camps, fetching this man's water and making him coffee. Onyii wonders if they've ever even fired a gun before. Onyii knows their type.

The one in the middle, with the rolled-up sleeves and the beret tilted to the side, the one with the single scars running like tear streaks down his cheeks, has his thumbs tucked into belt loops. His boots make little splashes in the ground now covered in blood and ash. And his gaze roves over them, scrutinizing. Trying to pick them apart.

With the sight of this man comes a flood of memories. Onyii with a high-powered rifle of her own, making her way through the bush on a raid. Onyii taking cover behind crates in enemy facilities before charging in and having the enemy soldiers fall before her onslaught. The flash of light that took her arm from her. Surgery. More combat. And all of it done in a deadened, unfeeling haze. That was another lifetime. That was someone else. Someone she can't afford to become again.

"So," says the man. "This is the camp, then." His accent is thick. It makes his consonants more vivid. Turns his short *i*'s into long *e*'s. He takes a few steps forward. "And you are the War Girls, eh?" He sneers.

Some of the other soldiers behind him snicker.

The commander walks over to Kesandu. Kesandu's back straightens. She readies her fists, raises her chin. "And you," the commander says. "What poor husband did you run away from?"

Kesandu's hands shake at her sides, and her bottom lip trembles. The man must remind her of someone. Someone who hurt her deeply.

The commander smirks, then turns away from Kesandu, and Onyii worries that Kesandu will hit him in the back of the head, one good punch at the base of his neck, paralyzing him, then get them all killed.

"They are disgusting," one of the soldiers says loudly enough for Onyii and the others to hear. Some of the younger ones flinch as though they were hit in the chest. Onyii can't keep herself from moving for the soldier, but instantly, the guns go up, the entire row of them aimed at the girls' hearts.

The commander chuckles. "They are dirtier than you, yes," he says. "But that is only because they have killed more enemy soldiers than you." He walks to the soldier, who begins to quake when the commander gets near enough. "Maybe I should throw you in the mud, so you can roll around a little, get yourself dirty like them." He turns to face the girls. "Now. Who is your leader?"

Chinelo glances at Onyii. Before Onyii knows what's happening, Chinelo steps forward. Onyii realizes she hears buzzing. Her good eye darts back and forth. Chinelo's bees. She's armed them with flares to blind the soldiers if they get ready to fire. It may not save the girls completely, but it would give Onyii and the others time to gun down a few of the soldiers and find cover.

"We were just minding our business," Chinelo says, spreading her arms. "Making our jollof rice, not being a bother to anyone." She waves behind her to indicate the camp. Even though it lies destroyed and sparks spray from the Obelisk and the Terminal is a pile of rubble and twisted metal, it is still impressive. They had built a beautiful thing.

Onyii wonders if any of the men arrayed against them can imagine what the camp must have looked like before the Green-and-Whites arrived.

"We're just a camp on the outskirts of the Republic. Collecting refugees fleeing the war and teaching them to be good citizens for the Republic of New Biafra. See, we are even teaching them the proper war songs." Chinelo turns around and raises her arms like a conductor. Onyii glares at her as if to say, *Do not make this a game!* Chinelo smirks, lowers her arms, and turns back to the commander. "I would have them sing for you, but we have not had much time to prepare. If we'd known you were coming, we could have gotten ourselves ready to make a proper welcome." Onyii hears the rebuke beneath it, and she's sure the commander hears it too. *If we'd known you were coming, we could have saved our camp. And the girls in it.*

"Refugees, eh?" the commander says. "It seems like you are keeping just the girls. What do you do with the boys? Kill them?"

Chinelo doesn't answer the question. Instead, she nods to the soldier who had that earlier outburst. "They seem to have found something to do with themselves."

The commander sucks his teeth and looks past Chinelo and

the others. He juts his chin out, puts his hands on his hips, and starts walking like a slow chicken. "So. A school. A greenhouse. Even an armory." He makes like he's walking to Chinelo, then he turns his head to Onyii. "But you are using Biafran resources to power all of this." He stomps his foot. "This is Biafran soil. Everything under it belongs to Biafra." Still looking at Onyii. "And you have not even asked my permission."

"We do not know your name," Chinelo calls from behind him, still joking. "Tell us your name, and maybe we can properly ask your permission, sah."

The commander leans in toward Onyii. "My name." Then he walks away, toward his soldiers, and turns. Everything is a grand gesture with him. On the battlefield, he would have been shot at least thirteen times by now. "My name. Is Godswill Ugochukwu Emmanuel Chukwudi. Brigadier General of the Free Biafran Army. Middle Striker for the Biafran Super Eagles Football Team and Current Record-Holder in Goals Scored during the League Season. But that is too long a title, and if I send you into battle and you say yes, you will be killed before you can finish saying the whole thing. So. You may call me General." He whirls around to face Chinelo, his pistol aimed at her temple. "But you. You talk so much. Tell so many jokes. Just chaw-chaw-chaw-chaw. Tell me." He presses the barrel of the gun into her hair. "Does this get you out of trouble or into it?"

Onyii moves without thinking. A single, fluid motion in which she ducks, scoops a bit of shrapnel from the ground, and has its tip pressed against the man's neck. She can feel every gun pointed at her.

Chinelo is completely still, but she glances a command at Onyii: stand down.

Onyii already knows. If any hurt comes to Chinelo, then it will be over for this Brigadier Eagle or whatever he calls himself.

Chinelo's bees buzz, but none of the soldiers seem to notice them.

"It is too bad my army has no need for court jestahs," the brigadier general sneers. "You can and you will serve the war effort, however." He holsters his gun, and after a moment, Onyii drops the shrapnel and steps back. The brigadier general smirks, then raises his voice so everyone can hear. "This camp and its contents are being seized by the Republic of New Biafra. This is now our property." He nods to his soldiers, several of whom break away and begin rummaging through the camp for anything that can be salvaged. The remaining soldiers still have their guns pointed at the girls, so it feels like yet another violation they can do nothing about. "This camp is being requisitioned so that it and those who have maintained it can serve the war effort. An inventory will be made of what is recovered. In the meantime . . ." He sweeps his arm in the direction of the forest.

Maglev trucks with long backs rumble into view. Tarpaulin covers their back shelves. Onyii's heart plummets.

The backs of those trucks are like black holes that would suck Onyii and the others in and never spit them out again. The last time Onyii found herself staring at such an entrance, she was a child. A child swept from the bush and given a gun. A child no older than Ify . . .

At the thought of her little sister, Onyii turns back to the camp and starts walking, but a hand grips her wrist hard. Obioma. Her eyes, which used to be young and watery and unsure, have turned hard. She no longer looks at Onyii as though she were a ghost.

"Our sister is gone," Obioma whispers. "If she is even still alive."

Onyii tries to shake herself free, but Obioma's fingers dig into Onyii's wrist. "She is not *your* sister."

It is meant to hurt Obioma, but Obioma frowns as though she has no time for this. "If you leave now, they will find you, and they will shoot you. And they may shoot some of us while they wait. We must stick together."

And Onyii searches for the moment that finally hardened Obioma, the moment she went from quivering child to quiet strategist.

"Together, we can plan our actions. Together, we can bring back our girls."

And that's when Onyii realizes there is more to this than Ify. If girls were kidnapped instead of killed, then there are more than just Ify out there. Waiting for their sisters to come get them. Onyii can't get them all on her own.

"Chop-chop-oh!" the brigadier general shouts, clapping his hands together. "Come with me, and we will keep you safe."

Kesandu speaks through gritted teeth. "We were safe here."

The brigadier general raises his head to acknowledge the voice he has just heard, sniffs the air, then looks to the demolished camp and the husks of detonated mechs that litter it. "Does not look so safe now."

Every nerve in Onyii's body aches to go search for Ify, but Obioma is right. She can barely stand, and even if she were able to make it to her mech, she'd have to power it with her own body. She'd barely be able to leave the forest.

"Let us bury our friends-oh!" a girl cries from the crowd. Onyii doesn't recognize her. She might have been one of Ify's schoolmates. Other girls kneel down by the child and console her while she wails into her hands.

Onyii is the first to step forward, toward the trucks.

"New Biafra thanks you for your service," the brigadier general whispers as she walks past.

Onyii hops onto one of the flatbeds and crouches by the edge while the other girls follow. Some of them go with Kesandu into a separate truck. Obioma calls for the others to come with her in a third.

When all the girls are loaded and the scavenging troops have returned, bags laden with the tech the girls had put together, the brigadier general slaps the backs of the flatbeds like horses, and they start off into the forest.

A few fires still smolder. A few pieces of machinery still crackle and pop. And somewhere amid the dead bodies are Amaka and Chigozie. Onyii hasn't even been given the chance to bury them.

CHAPTER 12

When Ify opens her eyes, she sees Daurama's face. Daurama holds Ify so high off the ground that her feet dangle. The visor attached to Daurama's mask drops, so that Ify can see the full hatred in the young woman's eyes.

"She did this," Daurama says to Daren.

"No." He struggles to stay upright, gripping the straps. "It must have been the other one."

Ify remembers the girl they killed in the forest. She must have attached an explosive to the craft before they caught her. That's what she was doing, not running away. Guilt spikes through Ify's heart that she'd ever doubted the girl. But then the aircraft dips into a sharp somersault. Ify slips from Daurama's grip, and Daren leaps and holds her against his chest as they hit the ceiling.

Everything is too loud. Daren pulls something from the ceiling, and Ify realizes it's a mask.

"I don't have enough time to put the whole suit on you," he says almost quietly. Too calmly. "But slip the mask on, and it will help with your breathing."

Ify finds the opening and slips it on, and all of a sudden,

the world fills with numbers and percentages and color bars. Data.

"Do not worry, little one. Those are just your vital signs. You're okay." He hugs her tighter and reaches behind him and slips something out of a fold in a container that flew to the ceiling. A blanket. Beneath Ify's fingers, it feels sleek like the skin of their suits. Oily.

The spinning aircraft flings them against a wall. Daren grunts but manages to keep wrapping the blanket around Ify. "Stay still, little one."

More shouting from the cockpit.

Daren continues to wrap her up, and as the blanket comes over her shoulders and arms, it hardens. She can move inside it, but she can't get her arms out. Can't break free.

"It's okay, little one."

"What about you?"

He says nothing as he wraps the last bit of blanket over Ify's head and it hardens into a cocoon. Then he manages to reach for a strap and holds fast as he brings Ify closer. Her body tenses. Too many feelings war inside her. She hears pieces of the aircraft's armor fall away, engines blow out, consoles fry themselves into oblivion. The shouting grows fevered, then ordered.

Then there's nothing but silence. As though everyone inside, even the Nigerian soldiers she can't see, has come to peace with what's going to happen.

When she looks up, Daren's eyes are closed.

The window he had opened still reveals the world outside, now a blur of red ground and blue morning sky. Swirling and swirling and swirling.

Daren's breathing slows. "Trust me," he whispers.

Ify hold his gaze, shivers.

A wall bursts open. Wind sucks Ify straight into the open air, where she spins so fast the world turns into a mass of colors around her. Blue, brown, red.

Then, nothing but darkness.

CHAPTER

13

The road has smoothed out.

Onyii can tell they've left the forest and the farthest reaches of their camp because the roads are actual roads. No potholes, no swerving to avoid mine traps. No low branches slapping windshields, and no elephant grass choking the underside engines and the magnetic charges of the maglev trucks.

It makes things better for the girls in the back of the flatbed truck. Even in the darkness cast by the tarpaulin stretched overhead, Onyii sees some of them squirming, holding broken limbs and trying not to cry. Some of them have let the rocking of the truck lull them into sleep. A few of them even sleep peacefully, and Onyii is grateful they've found a few moments of quiet. Others hold themselves tight in their sleep and murmur and thrash their way through nightmares.

With a piece of metal she breaks off of one of the metal beams supporting the tarpaulin, she digs into her prosthetic arm. Her sleeve has peeled away in places, revealing the clockwork underneath. Gears and energy packs connected by tendons; pistons lined up with joints. Her hand is still intact, but her forearm is exposed to the elements. She tries to flex her hand into a fist, but stiffness in her fingers stops her. With the piece of metal, she digs around in her forearm. Sparks jet out. The sound of sizzling reaches some of the others. Onyii's skin where it lies in flaps on her forearm starts to char. But then she hears the clink. A piece of shrapnel lodged between two cylinders, pressing against a bed of nerves. Onyii taps at it. She grits her teeth as pain shoots up her arm and shoulder. Reflexive tears pool in her closed eyes. But she forces them back open and digs around, tapping, each tap sending needles of fire through half of her body, until she hears the shrapnel come loose. A massive sigh escapes her. Halfway there.

She hooks it with her piece of metal and drags it back until she can find an opening big enough for it. Then she pins it down, raises her arm, then lets it go. The piece of shrapnel falls into her lap. Onyii's metal arm follows. That took too much energy out of her. Sweat beads her forehead and makes her back and shoulders shine. Her shirt is dark with it.

She glances at the other girls and wonders how many of them are thinking of escape like she is. Some of them squint at the ceiling as the truck moves, working out plans in their minds. But relief simmers in the eyes of others. For them, all that matters is that the battle and the dying are over. For now.

They had tried to hide. Onyii had tried to make a peaceful place for them, a sanctuary where they could stay and avoid the fate that she had had to endure. And just like that, the swirl of memories returns. In some of them, both her arms are flesh and blood. In others, she is already mangled. Scarred. But in all of them, she has a machine rifle in her hands and a machete strapped across her back over her bandolier of bullets. The gun is nearly as big as her. She is eight years old.

Onyii remembers cutting her way through the bush, knowing how to look for the depressions in the earth that mark improvised explosive devices buried beneath the soil. Moving under cover of night to the villages on the outskirts of Nigerian towns and leaving behind a trail of bodies. Her leader had called it liberation, but there was no freedom for the enemy farmers who had lain in pools of their own blood. The weeping families, the people who filled the graves. After a while, her leader had forbidden the digging of graves. Takes too much time, he had said. But they had moved. In an ever-widening semicircle.

The Green-and-Whites had tried to bomb them out of hiding, but the forests were too thick, and they were too good at hiding in them. When the troops would try to fish them out, Onyii and the other militia teams could ambush them easily and steal their gear. Then the Green-and-Whites had been foolish enough to send mechs after them. Mechs that Onyii and the others captured with far too much ease.

Those were the early days of the war, when victory came with the snap of a finger. When everyone had underestimated the strength and the determination of the Biafrans. The War for Independence.

She remembers the joy with which everyone had cheered when they'd secured the airfield with its spaceport and had gained shuttle access. Some had cried in celebration. Others had remained stoic, but by then, Onyii could read the interior emotions of everyone around her. She could tell who was happy with the progress they had made. She could tell who was still thinking of all that they had lost to get there.

She remembers the bombing campaign that took the airfield

from them, and she remembers the battles in which they barely managed to hold on to the port.

Her memories come back to her as strategic maneuvers, as troop movements her leader had commanded her and her group to follow. She remembers why they had to do the raids they did. But sometimes she remembers the raids themselves, the people begging to be spared. But her leader had told her, "They attacked us first." And that was enough for Onyii.

Another memory sneaks up on her.

This time, she's back in school. Still a child. And all the girls in her class are lined up in a row at the front of the room, in front of Teacher's desk. Teacher walks up and down the line of girls with a switch in his hands, absentmindedly tapping it against his skinny calf muscle. In the haze of the dreamy memory, Onyii does not remember Teacher's voice, nor does she remember Teacher's face, but she remembers his gnarled hands, where the knuckles seemed more like swollen bug bites than what should exist on normal human hands. And she remembers Teacher asking them why they were at church when they should have been sleeping, preparing for afternoon class. And Onyii knows this is not a question they are meant to answer. She knows that either way, answer or not, they will be beaten. So the girls say nothing, and Teacher goes down the line and commands each girl to stick her hand out, and Teacher swats their hands in a single swift motion that makes each girl yelp and hold her hand. One girl bounces from foot to foot, biting her lip against the pain. They are all around Onyii's age, except for Kachi, who was so gifted in school that she skipped several grades. Kachi, who is so small that a single blow would break her.

So when Teacher gets to Kachi, Onyii sticks her own hand out.

"I will take Kachi's strike," she says, head bowed. "If you shall do it, do it to me."

And she remembers her Hausa teacher standing over her, looking at her in shock, before a wide smile stretches across his face. "Okay," he says in the memory, before winding up and giving Onyii two of his strongest strikes, blows so powerful that they bring Onyii to her knees.

Her hand had gone numb for the rest of the day, and it was a full week before she was able to properly move her fingers again. A week of bathing her hand in ice water every night. A week of not being able to dress herself quickly. A week of having to learn how to write with her other hand.

In the back of the flatbed truck, Onyii flexes her metal hand into a fist. So much of that memory remains vivid in her mind. She can still hear the whistling of the switch as it cut through the air.

The flatbed truck makes a sharp turn, and some of the sleeping girls are jostled awake.

Where Onyii sits, she can see all of them.

I would stick my hand out for all of you, she wants to tell them.

But, as the sound of a gate clanging open rings loud enough for everyone to hear and the truck slows to a stop, Onyii remembers that Kachi had died in the first year of the war.

"Oya, come out!" barks a soldier from outside. "Hurry up-oh!"

Onyii leaps out into a campground that offers no shelter from the blistering sun. Everything is too bright.

There is only one soldier at their truck, and he grabs Onyii's arm, but she breaks away and swings the piece of metal she's still holding up to the man's neck. "I will watch them all come out first," she hisses. "You will not separate me from my sisters."

After a moment of shock, the soldier snorts. "Fine, you stupid goat." Then he backs away.

The first of the girls comes to the edge of the flatbed and raises her hand to her eyes to shield them from the sun.

"I am here," Onyii says, reaching her arms out to catch the first girl as she jumps from the edge of the truck. Onyii catches her and helps her gingerly to the ground.

She does this for all of them until the truck is empty and the girls surround her, some of them clinging to her torn pant legs.

"It's okay," Onyii says, and she knows she's lying, but she has learned that sometimes it is her job as big sister to lie to them, if only to bring them a moment of peace. Of relief.

If you shall do it, do it to me, she says to the world. To the war that is waiting for them.

■ ■ ■ ■ ■

With Onyii and her charges gathered, the soldier leads them deeper into the camp, where the other truckloads of girls await in a cluster. Familiar faces put Onyii at ease. Chinelo is there, along with Kesandu and several of the others.

The sun sucks the moisture out of everything. The buzzing doesn't come from mosquitoes. It comes from metal sizzling. Tent flaps billow in a breeze that brings no relief. A few mechs stand stationary at the edges of the encampment.

One of the tents is bigger than the others, and out of it strides the brigadier general. His face shines with sweat. He takes off his beret to wipe his forehead, then slips it back on. The soldiers guarding the girls stand at attention when the brigadier general nears. He waves them at ease with a smile that chills Onyii.

On their way in, peering from the back of the flatbed truck, Onyii had counted two Diggers, machines to plumb the earth for the minerals that powered so many of the devices in her own encampment, their energy supply for their wireless network. Here, she sees no Obelisk and no Terminal, no way for them to communicate with the outside or with each other. Two aerial mechs rust in the distance, their giant frames towering over the men who lounge in the shadows they cast. A part of her can't believe this is actually the Biafran military and not some gang of rebels or random terrorists come to collect child brides. She had seen them in action over the years, prowling roads and dipping into the wilderness to snatch up unsuspecting girls and make them slaves.

At the thought, Onyii hugs a few of the girls closer to her side.

"You must be hungry after your journey," the brigadier general says to Onyii. He ignores Chinelo, as though to say, *No matter your tricks. I know that you are the one who leads them.* "We have food waiting for you in the barracks. You have arrived just in time for lunch. Impeccable timing-oh!" He snaps his fingers, and the soldiers all move at once to surround the girls with their guns at the ready.

Onyii moves to walk with them, but the brigadier general holds a finger out.

"No, not you. You come with me."

Onyii tenses, can feel herself readying to attack. It takes every nerve in her system to keep from lashing out, but Chinelo catches her gaze and, with a single look, reassures her. A cloud of insects surrounds the girls, as Chinelo brings them tightly around her. Not mosquitoes, Onyii realizes. Chinelo's bees.

Her muscles loosen a bit, and Onyii turns back to the brigadier general and follows him to his tent.

It is almost the largest structure in the entire camp, and a heavy metal desk sits right in the center of it with glass paperweights and a tablet and stylus on it. A half-eaten apple spoils at one corner.

Around them are ammo crates and shrines to gods Onyii can only guess at. A whole bunch of useless things.

The brigadier general takes a seat behind his desk.

There's nowhere for Onyii to sit. She wouldn't have taken the seat had he even offered it.

"I can see from the look on your face that you are not impressed." He pulls a narrow tube from his breast pocket. It looks like a small cylinder wrapped in fanta leaf. He examines it, then runs it beneath his nose before putting it between his teeth and lighting it up. Instantly, acrid smoke fills the tent. Even though the walls are right now open to the elements, the smoke hangs in the air, and Onyii sneers at it.

"I did not see any equipment to mask your activity."

He smirks around what Onyii remembers is called a cigar. "That is because we are analog. You were digital. And so are the enemy. And they could see you because of it. The price of connectivity." He detaches an old black device from his hip. "This? They call this a walkie-talkie. It uses radio frequencies. It is old, not like myself." He places it on the table, almost too hard. But it doesn't break. "I am a young man. I will live forever."

"What do you want with me?" Enough of this man's babble. If there is no connectivity, then they must be piloting their mechs dark. If they have so few Diggers, how do they fuel their aerial units? Maybe they already have minerals gathered and prepared. Onyii's mind races through possibilities, taking apart escape plans as quickly as she can put them together.

The brigadier general leans back in his chair. "I wanted to see with my own eyes."

"See what?"

"God's Right-Hand Man." He chuckles but chokes on his cigar smoke. When his coughing settles, he still wears a smile on his face. "It turns out, God's Right-Hand Man is a woman. The Child with Demon Eyes. I'd heard of you in the early days of the War for Independence. How you would go where no one else would before anyone else would. How, often, you didn't even have to be told. You simply followed the smell of the Nigerians. And you killed all who crossed your path. Then, when you were old enough to pilot, you brought death to them from the skies. No one fought like you, the story goes."

Onyii's hands turn to fists. "That was a long time ago."

The brigadier waves his hand, makes a dismissive noise. "A few years. Maybe a few more than that. Is not so long. But you are still a child. Time has not decided to choke you in her fingers yet."

"What do you want?" *Besides hearing yourself talk and talk and talk.*

"I want you to live comfortably." He kicks his booted feet up on his desk. They thunk. Too heavy to be just muscle and bone. Metal. He's an Augment. "I want you to have riches beyond your wildest imaginations. I want you to never again have to reach up to snatch a mango from its tree. I want mangoes to be delivered to you. I want you to have servants making ogi for you and frying akara to complement the ogi. You will never have to work again, and you will be able to purchase anything it is in your heart to even want. You just have to return to service." He puffs and lets out a thick cloud of smoke. "Become a soldier again."

"I never stopped being a soldier."

After a moment, the smile fades from his face and he rises from his desk. Now that Onyii knows to look, the man's steps are heavier. He leaves prints in the dirt wherever he walks. "That's right. That is why as soon as you arrived, you started measuring my camp's defenses. Maybe you were doing so to tell me how you can be of help." He stands so close she can smell the mix of acrid cigar smoke and sweat wafting through his clothes. "Or maybe you are trying to escape." He leans so close their noses nearly touch. "Is not as easy as you think."

Faster than Onyii can see, the man grabs her arm and pries the piece of metal out of it. She'd completely forgotten she had been holding it. The brigadier general smiles at it, holds Onyii at arm's length, then draws the metal slowly along the side of his neck where Onyii had aimed earlier, before the journey here.

Blood the color of oil spills from the wound, but the brigadier general manages to pry it open with two fingers, revealing metal plates and pistons working beneath them. "You would not have even scratched me where it matters." He lets go of his neck, then calmly strides to his desk and pulls out a tube of MeTro surgical sealant. It is like toothpaste, and he draws a line of it along the wound. The skin seals, and soon there is only the faintest scar. The bloodstains remain, but the bleeding has stopped. Then he tosses the tube to Onyii, who catches it in one hand, before sitting back down at his desk. "So, riches will not do it. Shall I appeal to your patriotism? Your love of the Republic of New Biafra?"

Onyii is silent.

"Do I have to threaten your age-mates? Is that what you want?"

Her fists tremble. She glares her fury at him, measures the distance between them. She wonders how quickly she could cross it and get at his neck, snatch a paperweight, leap over the table and jab out an eye, disabling it, before inevitably finding the outlet that must be somewhere at the base of his neck and ripping it open.

"Killing me won't help you."

"But it will feel good."

His smirk widens. He spreads his hands, as though to give up. "What do you want?"

"I want to find my sister."

"Your sister?" He gestures to the station's entrance. "Surely, she is out there somewhere. Are they not all your sisters? You are your sisters' keeper."

"No." She knows she sounds too firm when she says it, like she's denying the others. And that's not what she means, but she can't figure out how to say what she needs to say to this disgusting man who has them all trapped. "There is one girl. When the Green-and-Whites left, I went to her hiding place, and she was no longer there."

"And she wasn't among your dead?"

They hadn't had enough time to really look, but Onyii says, "No. She wasn't."

"And you think they have taken her?"

"Yes. I will find her. I will bring her back."

"Back to where?" The brigadier general raises his voice in anger for the first time since he's spoken to Onyii. "What home are you bringing her back to?"

Through gritted teeth, Onyii says, "We'll make a new one."

The brigadier general throws up his hands in defeat. "Chineke mbere," he curses, then slumps in his chair like a deflated skinsuit.

Onyii hears footsteps coming from behind. The soldier salutes when he gets to the edge of the station.

The brigadier general beckons him. "What is it, lieutenant?"

"The crash site you had us examine." He has a scratched and weathered tablet in his hands and wipes a coat of dirt off of it before handing it over. The brigadier general glances at Onyii, then swipes across the screen a few times before spreading his fingers then closing them again over the tablet. He tosses it with too much strength to the edge of his desk, where it teeters.

"Your sister," he says, almost like a scowl.

"What?" It comes out of Onyii as a gasp. She snatches up the tablet and tries to see through the dust smudging the screen. With the palm of her hand, she swipes and swipes. Then, when she can see the touchscreen, her fingers dance over the controls. The image rises before her as a hologram. A three-dimensional projection of someone's line of sight.

They're in a forest. There are a few of them. Biafran soldiers. Then the image glitches before they find themselves in a stretch of desert. They crest a ridge, then what they see fills Onyii's vision.

"Only animals would do such a thing," says the brigadier

general. But there is no outrage in his voice. Only disdain. "But that is, I hear, how they are made up in the North. Living off of the land like that, we are maybe the first true human beings they see. And they never learn that they are not supposed to eat us. That they are not supposed to do these sorts of things. That it is only beings who are less than human who do these things. But, enh. You can command a dog, but you cannot reason with it." He shakes his head. "The only thing a dog can teach a human is how stupid it is. And that—"

The tablet snaps clean in half.

"What did you do?" shouts the lieutenant, running to Onyii's side. He raises a hand to smack her, but stops. His hand is raised mid-motion, but Onyii, hunched over the shattered tablet device, can only feel him staring his fear into her back. He is scared of her, and Onyii does not care, because what she saw still lives behind her eyes. Burned into her brain. Flaring so hot and so bright that tears come.

Tremors take hold of her. First her hands, then her arms. Her legs tremble.

Then she feels it growing inside her. A warmth that blossoms into heat that radiates throughout her chest, fills her face. It's the same feeling she got while piloting her mech, fighting to protect her camp. Letting all her soft parts fall away until all that's left is steel.

The soldier standing next to her backs away.

Onyii doesn't move when the brigadier general arrives at her side.

He shakes his head and sucks his teeth. "I told you. This is what they do." He bows his head. When he looks back at her, there's a new look in his eyes. Concern.

She can taste copper. She looks straight into his face. "I will fight."

His expression softens. "For the glory of Biafra."

She closes her eyes and feels the last of her kindness, her too-soft self, wash away. What she saw forces itself to the front of her mind so that it will always be just behind her eyelids whenever she closes her eyes to sleep. It will always haunt her. Drive her. Complete her.

"No. Not for Biafra," she says. "For revenge."

INTERLUDE

Waves shimmering in sunlight. Static. Voices. An argument. Children. Girls. Fighting over a bulubu ball. Static. A flower. Petals lifting slowly underneath fingers made of cast iron and powered by nanomachines. Static. Embers rising from fire like fireflies. Smoke billowing into the air. Screaming. Static. An eto-eto waving its doughy arms while a young woman carries it in her arms across a room. Static. Two girls, sisters, smiling at each other. Static. A woman on a table, cradling the eto-eto. Static. Screams. Static. Static. Static.

Enyemaka hums to life. She still smells smoke.

She's crouched, arms bent as though hugging something, someone. Memories flit through her central processing unit. Was she protecting something? Someone? Her sensors tell her that her back is scarred, that whatever explosion leveled the building she's in must have come from behind her.

Slowly, she uncurls herself and rises.

Bursts of static still fill her vision from time to time, but her backup systems thrum inside her. She can feel, in the wires that serve as her veins and arteries, the nanomachines repairing her.

Sensory input overwhelms her. Sights, sounds. The stillness

in the air. She walks out of the decimated building she woke up in, and before her is nothing but carnage. Small buildings collapsed on each other, flexiglas littering the charred ground. Fallen mechs tower over her, sideways beasts in slumber. Everywhere, bodies. Whole or in pieces, they lie strewn about, utterly still. All the dying is done.

She does not know what happened here, but she can guess. From how the mechs lie, she can tell where in the sky they fell from. She knows the make and model of each of the shell casings from every bullet fired. Information about blood type rolls down her feed with each puddle she walks past. These bodies are broken. Some of them are clothed in what she recognizes as the Nigerian flag. Others wear patches on their jackets showing the flag that belongs to the Republic of Biafra. She doesn't remember who this land belongs to, whether it is Biafran or whether it lies within Nigerian territory. All she knows is that there were once people here. Learning and playing and fighting and healing. She remembers two girls in particular. One older, so dark she glowed blue in the moonlight, the other small and sand-colored with irises shot through with purple and gold. When she stops taking in signals of the outside and returns to the fragments of memory, she can see them. Saved on chips in her brain.

The bodies dressed in all black must be the enemy. But Enyemaka does not see any enemy here. The bodies dressed in black belong to people who showered and learned and played and fought and healed just like the girls Enyemaka remembers. Their skin, where it shows in the places where their uniforms are torn, glows blue as night gives way to dawn.

Nanobots, swimming through her veins, send commands to Enyemaka's brain.

With deliberate steps, she finds a portion of empty land at the camp's center and begins digging. When she has made a hole large enough for one body, she carries one of the fallen girls and lays her in it gently, then finishes the burial. She finds a nearby plank of metal and bends it into a cross, then sticks it at the head of the grave. She does this with each of the bodies until all the graves form neat rows, their crosses glinting in the growing sunlight. Then, instructed by the nanobots in her brain, she starts walking away from the camp.

She does not stop walking until she reaches irradiated desert.

An aircraft lies sideways and broken in the dirt. Red sand already covers a portion of it. Everywhere else, there is nothing but redland.

At first, Enyemaka believes the sizzling in the air to be simply radiation. The type of energy that eats away at metal just like hers. She shouldn't stand here too long. But, for some reason, she can't leave. There's a mystery in the air. Something, someone was here.

More memories. The small girl with the big eyes pressed against her back, arms around her neck. Then, the two of them sitting together in a forest, studying the constellations. Then, Enyemaka gently shaving the girl's head. Enyemaka knows this child. She must find her. The child will have answers.

The energy powering her softens. The nanobots slow down. The heat of the Redlands has been eating away at her battery life. She has not yet learned self-preservation. She does not know hurt. So Enyemaka does not know that the radiation in the air has already started corroding the important parts inside of her. All she knows, as the nanobots slow into hibernation and eventually die, is that there was once a young girl whose head she shaved.

A word bubbles up into Enyemaka's consciousness, recovered from the charred and torn wreckage of her memories. A word that binds together the disparate images and sounds in her consciousness—fingers on rose petals, a hand rising in a classroom, someone staring through the scope of a rifle. A word that fills in the gaps. A word that stays with her as the light in her eyes grows dimmer and dimmer.

Sister.

PART

II

CHAPTER 14

Four Years Later
Abuja, 2176

The elephant grass reaches to Ify's shoulders.

Her gown shimmers in the sunlight. And this should make her a target for the beasts that roam before her, but the light bends around her to make her invisible. She can tell because the world—the blue sky and the green grass and the acacia trees that dot the landscape—all shines golden. Data beams back into her, through the *kimoyo* beads on her wrists and around her neck. Also outlined in gold is the herd of animals munching on grass while the morning mist hangs around them.

Some of them are armored, mechanized so that their biomass melds with wiring and machinery, but others are simple flesh and blood and muscle. These are what interest Ify. The animals all seem to recognize their shared nature. The metal doesn't scare them. They aren't mutated shorthorns or wulfu, made crazy and irrational by radiation poisoning. They are more beautiful than that.

Her Accent, amplified by her beads, allows her deeper access to the biomech horse. She can see the energy canisters that power the animal's circuitry. They take what it eats and convert it into fuel. She can see past the pistons and the gears and zero in on the heart that changes red blood to inky black oil. She's seen tech like this built in labs as a means of Augmenting animals and the food they produce, controlling the populations, monitoring their intake and their health from afar. So much metal. Somewhere, there is an opening. This animal is a self-contained entity, seemingly unconnected from the communications network that blankets the Nigerian Republic, connecting every open device and properly teched person to each other, but there still has to be some way in. There has to be a way to hack it. She's done it before with less sophisticated equipment. She can do it again.

Data of the biomech horse's vital signs appears on the holographic screen that she holds in her hands. Another trick of the light. She taps a few keys, and data from the other animals, including the lynxes that surround the horses, floods her screen. Someday, she'll be able to hack pure red-bloods. But first, she has to figure out how to get into the core processing unit of this horse. She imagines triumphantly riding it back into the capital, a scarf whipping in the breeze behind her, the horse galloping so fast that other Nigerians in the street jump out of the way. She imagines her horse vaulting over the cars of a speeding rail hyperloop train and coming to a dramatic stop right in front of the presidential palace, rearing once for dramatic effect and neighing loudly before coming to a rest.

But so far, nothing. Her Accent can't detect any opening. The animal's system is entirely self-contained. It seems unhackable. But *seems* is the operative word here. If Ify has learned anything in the four years since her rescue from the Biafran rebels, it's that nothing is as it seems.

For several minutes, she stands and stares at the puzzle of the animals grazing. There has to be some way. Even though her legs start to stiffen, she doesn't want to sit down and lose sight of them. Like so many proofs, the key, the algorithm, the piece that will allow her to control them, is right in front of her. She just needs to find it.

She likes coming out to the fields and being away from the noise of the capital, where so much is happening all the time. Data. So much data coming into her system. The speed of maglev cars, the records of citizen encounters with the police, the mineral count of the jewelry the wealthy wear, the last time cyberized citizens went to their mechanic for their regular checkup. So much data swimming around her. Whereas, out here in the fields, the data is instead the wind that kisses her cheeks and the grunts of animals having their meals in peace, blissfully unaware of her presence. Some of her minders chastise her for being such an outdoor girl. She knows, behind her back, some of the boys call her a Bush Girl, because she spent so much of her early life in the woods with the Biafrans. But she doesn't tell those children that she has records of each of their remarks, stored and ready for playback whenever she wishes. Not just that, but conversations they don't believe anyone else can overhear, conversations that contain their hopes and fears and who they have crushes on and who cheated on which exam and who hopes to earn a scholarship to get to America and who everyone thinks is too stupid to even get an apprenticeship in one of the hundreds of labs throughout Nigeria's Middle Belt. The perks of being part of Abuja's surveillance team. At the ripe age of fourteen, it still sounds odd to her ears to be called a Sentinel, but she now wears the title with pride. Before, some of her age-mates made fun of her for having been raised by

Biafrans and for the tribal scars Onyii had given her. Now the majority of them only think those thoughts, but even those aren't safe from a Sentinel sitting in the watchtowers scattered throughout the capital.

She lies on her back in the grass, her hands behind her head, and stares up at the clouds. Nano bees emerge from the thick braids that hang to the small of her back and dance before her face. Her own guardians. The ambient noise of their buzzing is enough to put her to sleep.

When she wakes, the sky is much darker. Then she blinks and realizes it's a shadow.

Oh no.

She scrambles upright. The animals behind her freeze. Without looking, she knows their ears have perked up, their systems have seen through her cloak. Light no longer bends around her to hide her. Now she stands awkward and nervous, and they can tell she doesn't belong here, so they gallop away. There goes Ify's vision of riding like a true warrior into the heart of the Nigerian Republic, commanding the respect of every loyal citizen.

Daren doesn't look angry. Instead, her adoptive brother has that ever-present smirk on his face. Like he's more bemused than anything. His silver dreadlocks glow in the midday sun. Biafrans would scold her for skipping class as a child. But Nigerians are kinder. They're genuinely more curious about the world, more eager to nurture that curiosity in others. And whenever Ify walks through the capital or any of Nigeria's major cities and sees how intricately the transportation systems have been interwoven or how the public universities are often the tallest buildings in those cities, topped only by the mosques, she is told that it is all the mark of a Nigerian's curiosity. Brilliant ancestors laid the foundation, "and our curiosity built the towers that stand upon it," Daren always says, like a mantra.

"So this is where you go when you skip class." He has a bundle under each arm.

"Sometimes," Ify says, with her head bowed, waiting for her tongue-lashing.

Daren looks around and inhales deeply. "It is much quieter out here. You don't mind the smell?"

"Smell?" And that's when Ify remembers she'd calibrated her Accent to override her olfactory senses. Another thing she'd learned how to do after she'd had her Accent fused to her inner ear. She can't smell anything. At least, not when she doesn't want to.

Daren laughs. "Most children spend all day looking at screens and not seeing the world around them. Or they are always listening to their jagga-jagga music and not hearing the world around them. You, Ifeoma Diallo." He laughs and places his metal hand on her shoulder. "You choose not to smell the world around you." He shakes his head, that smirk growing even broader. "I must say, that is quite impressive."

"I get data overload in the city," Ify says by way of explanation, kicking at the dirt.

"Certainly." Daren cups the back of her head, then brings her close. There is so much metal just beneath his skin, but he feels warm to the touch. His silken robe is one of the softest things her cheek has ever felt. "Would you like to watch a shuttle launch?"

Ify's eyes go wide. Her heart races. "A shuttle launch?" She squirms in his embrace and looks into his eyes. "Really?" She wants to ask him what she did to deserve this treat and tries to think back on whether or not she recently scored high marks in her class or received praise from her supervisor in her laboratory sessions. But nothing comes to mind. This is like surprise cake. And, well, not everything is a problem to be solved.

"Yes, Kadan. But we must hurry. They do not time these things at our convenience."

A sound reaches them from the city, muffled by the distance. But the singing tune, almost like a wailing, is clear. Daren hands Ify one of the bundles. Prayer rugs.

"Before we go," he says, smiling.

Together, they unroll the prayer rugs in the grass and as the muezzin launches the call to prayer, they make salat, the prayer proper Muslims must perform five times a day. When they finish, they roll up their rugs, and Ify hands hers back to Daren.

His maglev car, sleek and shaped like a teardrop, waits for them at the bottom of a hill, and Ify skips in leaps and bounds toward it, her gown flowing wildly, joyfully around her.

CHAPTER
15

Giant metal wings and cockpits and arms and legs and bits of dashboard sail through the air, trailing wires that spark and grow flames. The debris rains down on the enemy encampment below. The pilots inside those mechs are dead. Either that or their dying screams have been caught in their throats and all they can let out are blood-rich coughs. But by the time all the pieces hit the ground, the men and women who pulled those gearshifts and who pressed those console buttons and who tried to fight against Onyii, the Demon of Biafra, are no longer alive.

Onyii's engines flare, and she accelerates over a line of trees bordering the Nigerian camp to land with a skid among another group of enemy mechs. The pilots are too paralyzed by fear to begin firing. And with her bladed staff, she swings, cutting the first in half before twirling and slicing a diagonal blow across the second, moving faster than any mobile suit has ever moved before. The other pilots regain their senses and begin firing, but Onyii leaps into the air, a short burst of her thrusters, and those enemy Green-and-Whites accidentally fire at each other. Onyii lands just as they explode before charging into another cluster of mechs. Several of them launch themselves backward into the air and fire their heavy ordnance. Onyii jumps from left to right and left again, raising her shield to block the heavy cannon fire, then charges into the air toward the one with the heavy gun.

She sees their formation take shape. They make a diamond in the sky. The mechs fire. She raises her shield just in time, then her arm flips back at the elbow to reveal her own guns. Several blasts from her guns hurl her back. The formation breaks apart. One of the mechs charges her, ramming into her shield. She spins herself and hurls the mech attached to her shield to the ground. Her engines flare one at a time to stop her spin. Then she flies straight for the downed mech. The blade of her staff pierces its cockpit.

A new quiet fills the sky. They're retreating.

But something disturbs the air behind Onyii. She whirls around, staff in hand, to slice through the mech that had charged at her. One last victim who had fancied themselves a warrior. Now nothing more than scrap metal to be salvaged by Biafran soldiers. The separated halves of the mech detonate. Onyii's shield rises to cover her cockpit. The force of the blast pushes her back but leaves only singed armor.

Now the quiet feels real. Earned.

She's not even breathing heavily. The battles are getting easier and easier. She suspects it's because they've heard of her by now. The warrior on the front lines. The inhuman pilot who destroys Nigerian mechs as though they were flies to be swatted out of the sky. And who has no fear of death. With her mechanized eye, the outlet at the base of her neck, and the tech that covers half her face before running down her shoulder and back to her Augmented right arm, she barely looks human. She looks like something much more evil. The Demon of Biafra.

Her mech stands upright. The moving gears and plates make music for her ears. She can see the destroyed camp before her. Can see the fires rising from their Terminal, can see the bodies of dead soldiers littering the ground outside the mess hall and the ammunition depot. Many smaller mechs lie in pieces, some of them self-detonated to keep the Biafrans from getting their technology. But other soldiers either died before they could activate the self-detonation sequence, or they ran. Maybe they watch the takeover of their camp from what they mistakenly believe to be the safety of the forest. Maybe some of them have run farther out into the desert outside the forest, splashing through river on the way.

A hissing sound fills her cockpit as the latch above opens. Onyii's cord unplugs from the outlet at the base of her neck. Slowed by stiffened limbs, she climbs the ladder behind her and stands on a shelf made by her mech's chestpiece. Even after four years and with all the changes that have been made to her body, the aftermath of battle is still the same. She can see it all now without the data, without the heat signatures that turn bodies into red silhouettes against a green background, without her mech's Geiger counter tracking the amounts of radiation in the air. Without her coordinates and those of enemy mechs constantly flashing before her eyes. There's birdsong, strangely enough. Short trills, like the birds are testing the sky, waiting for the next cascade of mech limbs to fall from the clouds or waiting for gunfire to rip apart their trees or for fire to burst from the ground beneath them.

Onyii wants to tell them it's okay for them to sing, but in her heart, she knows she would be lying to them. The peace secured here in the capture of this enemy camp is only temporary. There can be no peace, no real peace, until Biafra is a fully recognized nation. Until Nigeria ceases attacking completely. There are days when Onyii feels it is only a matter of time. And there are nights when she knows the fighting will be ceaseless. When she knows, in the deepest recesses of her mind, that the fighting will last as long as there is an enemy.

So she looks down on the ruins of the camp as Biafran jeeps emerge from the forest like ants beneath her, scurrying over the spoils. The Biafran soldiers, in uniforms the same color as the Nigerians Onyii just beat, spill over the pieces of downed mechs. Technicians plug their devices into the consoles to download what can be salvaged from the mechs' processing units. Some of it is meaningless: memories or communications between soldiers and their families elsewhere, a father telling his son to continue doing well in school and win a scholarship to America, a young woman telling her younger brother that he is the man of the house now and that, while she is gone, he must protect their ailing mother. But some of the data could be enemy coordinates. At other camps, whole maps have been recovered that have allowed Onyii and the others to ambush convoys or sneak up and perform pincer maneuvers on unsuspecting encampments.

When the younger troops gather up enough courage to sometimes ask why Onyii moves so fast, she tells them it's for that reason. To kill the pilots before they have a chance to destroy valuable intel. But this, like the peace she would have told the birds about, is a lie. She moves as fast as she does for the thrill. The faster she moves, the more reckless her movements, the more all-engulfing the high. The truth is that it's a drug. She got a taste for combat as a child. And like a child given their first sip of palm wine, she had hated the taste. Now, hate or love has nothing to do with it. She needs it.

■ ■ ■ ■ ■

The Biafrans have erected a structure with translucent polyurethane walls and metal supports, with a plastic tent flap for an entrance.

In the beginning, Onyii would stand before the brigadier general's desk. But now she sits without even asking permission. "My body is tired," she might say by way of explanation. And no one can challenge her, because they have seen what she has done to the enemy forces. They've seen the Demon of Biafra up close and lived to tell about it. But only because she is on their side.

The brigadier general has a holo map of the territory pulled up, connected by a cord to a charred piece of machinery that looks to have been pulled from one of the defeated mechs. A generator has already been plugged into an outlet. Diggers work outside to plumb the depths of the soil for the minerals that will sustain their camp's operations. "Good work, soldier," he says to her, smiling, as though the work she does is part of some funny performance. "Without help from the Commonwealth Colonies in space, the Nigerians are no match for us. Or, rather, no match for you." When he raises his eyebrow and smirks, Onyii feels as though he has coated her in oil. "We are nearing the Middle Belt. Just beyond that is the Nigerian stronghold. But with this latest victory, we have secured enough of a buffer zone between Biafra and the Green-and-Whites that we can at least pretend to function as a proper nation."

Onyii raises an eyebrow at him. Someone looking at her would say she is being cocky and disrespectful, her legs spread, one draped over an armrest, her arms slung every which way. But it is comfortable. And she's earned that, at least. "Proper nation?"

"You know, with school exams and reliable electricity outages." He grins. "All the annoying things that exist in proper nations. Maybe we will even one day have trains that run late. And potholes in our streets. Just like they do in the North."

Onyii sneers. "Why would we be like them?"

The brigadier general slaps his hand on the table. "Is a joke, soldier." Then he pulls a cigar from his breast pocket and lights up. "What will you do to celebrate your victory?"

All Onyii can think about is Chukwu, that mineral mixture that will numb her aching joints and slow her racing mind. "Plan for the next maneuvers."

"No rest for the Demon of Biafra."

She has hated that moniker ever since people first began whispering it just within earshot. She hates when she hears it from her comrades. She hates when she hears it from the enemy. She hates when she hears it from her commander. But, to her, it's like the pain in her bones. The ache in her limbs. The fire-like needles that spike up and down her spine. Just a part of life. As much as the blueness of the sky and the blackness of recently charred earth. As much a part of life as sweat and mosquitoes and birdsong.

"Well then, soldier." He puffs on his cigar. The acrid smoke fills the room. "You are dismissed."

Onyii forces her body to fold itself together, then stand. Her joints scream at her as she salutes.

She leaves behind the soft hum of the generator for the earsplitting sound of Diggers at work and soldiers shouting over the noise and laser saws cutting away pieces of metal from the Green-and-White mechs. It's all so very loud.

No one notices Onyii finding a space in a tiny alleyway between two tents. No one notices her pull a small vial from a pocket at her waist and pour a line of powder—crushed minerals—onto the back of her hand, just under her knuckle. And no one notices her hungrily snort it.

Every time she takes Chukwu, she remembers that first night in the forest when a single hit of the powder Chinelo had given her had fully restored her broken body.

Her eyes roll into the back of her head. The noise around her fades and fades and fades. The sky turns from blue to pink, and the birdsong returns. And this time, it's no longer short bursts of gunfire but a full song, with rises and dips, with a melody she can discern, a melody that reminds her of a song from long, long ago.

CHAPTER
16

Ify stares out the window of the car she shares with Daren. Whenever she returns to Abuja from elsewhere, she remembers what the city was first like to her. Even four years ago, it was all reflective surfaces. An entire city made out of glass. Glass skyscrapers so tall their tops vanished in the clouds. Glass domes threaded with gold atop every mosque. Flexiglas lining the high-speed railways. You could see through everything. There was light everywhere. Blinding, overpowering light. But that had just been Ify's eyes, sensitive from so much time spent in the bush among natural light, accustomed to dull colors and a sun that shone on her from far, far away.

In the beginning, people gawked. At least, they did when they weren't cheering or crying with joy or pointing at her and proclaiming the greatness of the Nigerian military. She'd been afforded very little rest before she'd been paraded out for everyone to see, still clothed in her rags, still smelling of Biafra, still wearing the tribal scars she'd been given by the War Girls, but a girl returned. Rescued. The only survivor of her family's massacre. Her homecoming turned into a spectacle, televised for all the world to see. She had escaped. It's only now, four years later, that journalists and politicians and other children have mostly stopped asking her about what it was like among the savages. Now she is just like any other high-achieving student with good enough marks to one day earn a place at a piloting school in America.

But the memory of her arrival here is never far from her.

When they had repaired her Accent and fused it to her, the entire world was a mess of data. Numbers and letters and gauges spinning around her, shouting at her. It was Daren who taught her filters, how to turn some of the data-gathering off while leaving other parts on.

In their car, the leather feels soft as melted butter beneath Ify. Childishly, she squirms on it, moves back and forth and giggles. Daren shoots her a glance, as though to chastise her, but he just winds up smirking. Ify turns to the window and watches as men and women—some of them cyberized, some of them Augments—pause briefly in front of stores and offices, waiting for their identities to be scanned. The Augments sport prosthetic hands or legs, some of them with completely metal arms in their sleeveless djellabas. The cyberized Nigerians look just like anyone else on the outside, but fiber-optic wires and microchips make up their insides. Their brain sits comfortably inside its titanium casing. Couples sit silently in restaurants, having full conversations over their comms systems. Parents silently discuss the weather while their children run around, giggling out loud in the streets. Silver spheres float high above the streets—surveillance orbs. Ify looks up and sees all of the watchtowers they are remotely connected to. Everything in this city is monitored.

The two of them ride in silence for several minutes, turning onto the expressway and gliding high over the pedestrians below. They hew to the air-traffic corridors while trains arc upward against the side of glistening towers.

The gravity was set before they got into the car, so that when it goes sideways and when it twirls upside down for a bit in a slow barrel roll, Daren and Ify remain in their seats. However, Daren has his hand out, and as they spin, the folded paper crane in the center of his palm remains still.

The car finishes its circuit just as Ify reaches forward and, for a brief moment, detaches from her seat and floats in the air. Then they're right side up again, and Ify holds the crane gingerly to make sure she doesn't crush it. It looks exactly like all the others.

The image comes back to Ify in a flash: a hospital floor littered with paper cranes. Pieces of paper torn from somewhere Ify couldn't see from her hospital bed and folded with one hand— one new, mechanical hand—into little bits of origami, then dropped onto the floor as if that's all the new hand had energy for.

She remembers waking up in that hospital. Feeling no pain and seeing nothing but the bright lights above her. She was encased in something that refused to let her move. A cocoon. Then, when the fog of panic had cleared from her mind, she remembered the aircraft crash. The explosion that shook their frame, the way the craft had spun in the air. The shouting. Then the feeling of being buffeted from all directions by the wind. The pain of so many bones breaking. Then silence. Somehow, the blanket Daren had wrapped her in had saved her. Had trapped her and hardened its shell around her, protecting her body.

Daren would tell her afterward that he had equipped the blanket with a homing beacon, a distress signal in case anything happened to them. He would say this after the doctors spent weeks and weeks stabilizing him after the crash. After they had replaced several organs and fabricated an entirely new skeleton for him. After they had rewired much of his nervous system to accommodate cyberization. After they had built him a braincase and successfully transferred his consciousness to it.

One of the first things they had done was replace his arm. And Ify had lain on her bed, silent except for the occasional whimper, as doctors took her cocooned shape and submerged her in a pool of liquid several times a day. Until one day, she managed to turn her head, the cocoon loose enough to just barely give way, and see beneath the curtain that separated them, the man's fingers working. Absently. Mechanically. She couldn't tell where he'd gotten the paper from, but the hand moved without hesitation.

And that's how she watched him get better.

The first cranes were misshapen, one wing much larger than the other or with folds in all the wrong places. But then they became cleaner, more symmetrical, until they were wonders of geometry. Over and over and over, he would fold them, then drop them on the floor.

Daren didn't mention the paper cranes after they'd both left the hospital. But occasionally, she would find him in his office and one or two new ones would sit at his desk's edge. Sometimes, Ify tells herself that he makes them for her. That when he was near death, he had reached for her. And making cranes was how he had kept himself stimulated, active, alive.

Ify feels at home in the car with Daren. The entire city moves beneath them, abuzz with activity, but here, above it all, she has him to herself. And every time he looks at her, thinking that she doesn't notice, he smiles, and Ify's heart thrills. Someday, she will earn a scholarship to America, where she can work to build magnificent things among the Colonies, see space and so much of what it contains. Study the planets up close, meet the stars where they sit, and bring that knowledge back to Nigeria. She dreams of building extraordinary structures that will beat back the waters that gobble up more and more shoreline with each passing month. And she will figure out ways to harness that energy and power entire cities with it. She will figure out how to terraform those parts of pasture in the North that the desert has conquered. She will study and learn how to resettle those tribes. She will make Nigeria a beacon of light on the continent. She will make Daren proud.

When she was younger, it all felt like a dream. Like a thing for her to think about so that she wouldn't give too much thought to the girls who bullied her or to the ways they all had to scrounge through the forest for supplies or how the lights in the greenhouse would occasionally give out, spoiling their crops. Here, everything is proper and working, and she will study and learn how to make it even better. It feels like prophecy. Like the course has already been set.

The launch station shimmers in the distance.

Their car descends along an air tunnel until it glides just above paved road with giant magnets strewn underneath the asphalt.

The launchpad and the buildings surrounding it glow like a temple. Like somewhere people go to in order to pray. The car makes it to the first barrier, and the guards nod to Daren. When the car passes through, she feels as though she has entered hallowed ground.

A shuttle launching into space. When Daren talks about it, he sounds casual. He has probably watched this sort of thing many times. But for Ify, each time it's like watching a miracle happen.

In the road, a platform rises above the ground, and the car heads into a tunnel with fluorescent lights all along its ceiling. Eventually, they stop in a garage. Daren steps out of the car, and Ify follows. Before Daren can make it to the elevator, Ify hugs him and buries her face in his hip.

"You're welcome, Kadan," he says. Then, "One day, it will be just me watching the shuttle launches. You will be on the other side, waving goodbye to my tiny little frame as the rocket takes you into space."

As they make their way to the observation deck, Ify takes hold of Daren's hand with one of hers. In the other, she carefully cradles the paper crane.

■ ■ ■ ■ ■

Ify has her olfactory sensors turned on when they reach the observation deck and Daren greets the men in suits. Men whose skin looks like paste. White men. Some of them sweat. Ify can hear the cooling systems in the others, the cyberized ones, working fast and hard to keep them comfortable. More than any human beings, they resemble the near-colorless clay out of which children made dolls. *Oyinbo*. Man with peeled skin.

"Must we stand so close to them?" Ify whispers to Daren.

He squeezes her hand, too hard, and Ify knows this is

punishment. She's to be on her best behavior in front of what her Accent tells her are mining executives from the American and British Space Colonies. For the occasion, he has draped his silver locs regally over both shoulders.

Guards man every entrance and exit, and they stand stiffer at attention when they see Daren. The white men see it, and Ify thinks she detects a note of fear in their expressions. But Daren is all ease, practically gliding over the ground as he shakes their hands. Ify suppresses a shiver as she watches his smooth skin touch their slimy palms. But she hides her grimace as much as she can.

As far away as they are and even with the thick glass between them, Ify can hear the rumble of the shuttle preparing for launch. The commands from the guard station come through muffled, but Ify can trace the words they form. The rapid-fire instructions. Then someone stating coordinates, announcing launch calculations. Finally, the countdown begins.

Smoke billows out of the rocket's bottom and turns into a sort of dress for the shuttle. With a whooshing sound, the supports fall away. Then Ify hears the thunder of engines powering on. There's that first push, like the shuttle is leaving a womb, then it goes farther and deeper into the sky, and Ify cranes her neck to watch it soar higher and higher. Light twinkles around it, and she can tell that it has detached its secondary engines. Even where those large hunks of machinery will land has been calculated, and Ify knows sand pits buttressed by netting wait to catch the falling engines. All of it has been planned and accounted for. She can't tell what's on the shuttle, and most of her doesn't care. It's enough just to watch the miracle of space flight happen.

Daren stops his conversation short for the moment and turns to watch with Ify. She glimpses the same wonder glowing in his eyes. "Allahu akbar," he whispers just beneath his breath. A moment later, he has returned to the mining executives.

Ify hears Daren quietly say her name. One of the oyinbo tries to sound it out. Ify knows she shouldn't spy on them, but she can't help herself. The brief glimpse she already stole through her Accent revealed a world of possibility to her. Their suits are black, their shirts white, and their bellies protrude, as though to suggest how much prosperity they enjoy. "Look how well we are eating," their bellies say to Ify. But she doesn't have to look at them to have her Accent beam their information to her, which makes the prospect of spying on them even more enticing.

She easily learns their names. The letters after them seem to signify where they went to university. They contain the names of places Ify recognizes from her studies. Maybe this is where they have gained their professional expertise. Then she scrolls through their biometrics and frowns at their blood pressure numbers and their body mass index, and a neurological scan reveals a slowness that shocks her. How can anyone who thinks so poorly become so successful in America?

It is said that in the Colonies, the color of your skin bestows certain advantages. In Nigeria, everyone is the same color. Here, your success is based on your ability. Ify is smart, so she is surrounded by the smartest. Just like the most gifted athletes are surrounded by the most gifted athletes.

These mining executives are a mystery to her. But she can tell from quickly cross-referencing their titles and company names with the library database she has constant access to that they represent companies eager to get the minerals beneath Nigeria's soil. The minerals that power the whole country. Ify suppresses a snort. They cannot even generate their own self-sustaining energy sources.

Their conversation turns to Biafra, and Ify's mind quiets. They are talking about mechs now, and just as they mention them, diagrams of the giant humanoid robots appear before Ify's eyes. She taps her wrist beads to create a screen on which she can play a simple jewel-snatching game and look like she's not eavesdropping. Anyone with half a brain can see through her ploy, but she persists. They talk about mechs and a land that seems so far away, but that Ify knows in her head is very geographically close. Again, they mention mineral deposits, and Ify realizes that's why Biafra has come up so often.

Daren lets out a soft chuckle. "The Biafrans," he tells the oyinbo, "they think those minerals are some gift from their supreme god. And this supreme god has lesser angels flying around, planting yams in their fields. Such primitive peoples do not deserve these resources."

It still quiets Ify's heart to hear talk of Biafrans like this.

The war mechs are supposedly a gift to Daren and the Nigerians. Daren calls them Igwe. Despite whatever deficiencies they may possess, the Americans cannot be beat for the quality of their war machines.

She knows what they will be made to do, where they will be made to go. She can see the dirty Biafran camps they will drop bombs on, the rusty Biafran mechs they will slice through and gun down as though they were made of paper. And her heart aches, because it means Daren will be gone fighting.

When she chances a glimpse at him, her heart swells. Nigeria's Super Eagle.

They celebrate him at all of the football games. Before every match, they salute him. The cheers become particularly feverish whenever Nigeria hosts a foreign team. And when one of Nigeria's strikers scores a goal, the entire pitch erupts. The scorer backflips or does something similarly acrobatic and point with both hands at Daren, wherever he sits in the crowd, silently saying, "We do this for you, Great Protector of Nigeria." And Daren always says that he is no king, no prince, no member of any royal family. This is a democracy, after all. He is just a lowly mech pilot. And everyone laughs, knowing that he has single-handedly turned the tide of several decisive battles since the beginning of the civil war. If Nigeria now stands on the cusp of crushing the fledgling Republic of New Biafra, it is because of him.

The men all let out a chuckle, Daren's softer than the others, and they shake hands again. Ify tries not to cringe. Daren comes next to Ify.

"Did you get to see it?" he asks her.

There's still a light trail of smoke arcing into the sky, left over from the shuttle's flight. "It was awesome."

Daren pats the back of her head, lightly squeezing her braids. "That is exactly the word I would have chosen." For a long time, they stare at the fading chemtrail. Then Daren says, "I know you worry about the war and how long it will continue. We are almost done." He talks about it like war is only adults' business, like it is a very long discussion that she couldn't possibly hope to understand, and it's one of the few times she grows impatient with him. "Soon, there will be peace." He leans in close. "And maybe then the smelly oyinbo will leave us alone."

Ify chuckles at his joke, but her heart's not in it.

On their way back to the garage, she thrusts her hands into her pants pockets. The fingers of her right hand smush something, and she pulls out the paper crane, crumpled beyond repair.

CHAPTER 17

Onyii wakes up hanging by the straps in her cockpit. She hears the sawing sound of a lightknife cutting through the hull of her mech. Sparks rain down on her as the laser blade screeches into the metal above her. She is a child. This is a dream. But she cannot escape it.

She scrambles for her buckle and falls to the ground just as the first piece of metal above her head peels back. Somewhere in here there must be a rifle, a pistol. Anything to defend herself against the Nigerians who shot her down. Or to make sure she's not taken alive. Above her, metal tears free, and there's a rush of air as they pry her mech open, and suddenly hands grab her and yank her twisting body out of the downed machine.

Sweat has made her entire body slick. She feels the type of warmth under her skin that means a fever is on the way. Ada. Where's Ada?

She tries to fight the soldiers, but they are bigger than her. Practically giants. One of them rams the butt of a rifle into the back of her head, and her legs buckle, sending her to the ground.

They drag her to a spot where several more soldiers wait, among them the pilot who had cut her down. His mask is off, so his full face shows. Onyii knows what this means. She will not leave this place alive.

Already, some of her comrades writhe on the ground in pain. Some of them twist and squirm wordlessly. Someone howls. Onyii looks to her right to see a splash of red and a sizzle before Nigerian soldiers toss another Biafran to the ground. Her heart races. They're going to torture her. Her gaze flits back and forth at the waists of the Nigerian soldiers, trying to see if any of them has a weapon she can steal.

They drag her to a tree stump with a sheen of red already coating it.

One of the bigger soldiers pulls her arm forward while the other holds her still. The first soldier slams her arm, outstretched, onto the stump. As much as Onyii struggles, she can't break free.

The pilot who slammed her out of the sky steps forward. He flicks his lightknife to life. The blade is as long as his forearm. His steps are slow, deliberate. The grin on his face belongs to an animal.

Onyii strains her neck to look up at him. She bares her teeth in a snarl. She still struggles in the grip of the bigger soldiers, but she knows resistance is futile. Still, she can't let them see that she's given up.

"You better kill me, Nigerian dog," Onyii hisses. "If you leave me alive, I will hunt you down."

"Udene," the pilot says in a pitying voice, shaking his head. "With what arms?"

He raises his blade.

■ ■ ■ ■ ■

Something jostles Onyii's leg. If it's a rat or some other tiny animal, she won't swat at it. She can't be bothered with punishing it for obeying its nature. And if it's some sort of snake, let it bite her. Fog floats in her brain. The world is a mess of blurred colors. The nudging doesn't stop. Instead, it grows more insistent. It's a boot. Someone's boot.

The world's edges sharpen. Everything becomes clear. The fog dissipates. She's being attacked. She rolls on her back and spins to her feet and has a knife out in one hand. But she moves too quickly. Vertigo hits, and the world spins again. Just as she's about to fall, a hand latches on to her wrist and pulls her upright. Onyii blinks. Even though the sun is shining brightly enough to turn the other person into nothing more than a silhouette, Onyii can tell who it is.

"When is the last time you showered?" Chinelo asks her. "They call you the Demon of Biafra because anyone who gets close to you can find out what hell smells like."

Onyii tries to blink the dizziness away. Chinelo slings Onyii's arm over her shoulder. She smells like the perfume made out of crushed flowers. And her uniform is crisp, the lines straight and ironed, her patches without a speck of dirt on them. When they leave the shadows cast over the alleyway and come out into the sun, Chinelo's skin glows. No sweat on her body. No stains at her armpits, no sheen on her brow. Onyii lets her head rest on Chinelo's shoulder as Chinelo nearly carries her forward, and Onyii hears the machinery whirr just beneath Chinelo's skin. A cooling system? Onyii wants to ask her. *That sounds like cheating*, she wants to say. If only to see once again the wry smirk Chinelo would give her in return.

"We'll have your Buru Ibu transported back to Enugu."

Chinelo talks like this is a regular conversation, even though the opiate haze has returned to Onyii, blurring the edges of her world. "I've been speaking with the brigadier general. He took some convincing, but I managed to communicate to him that you could use a break. You have almost single-handedly cleared our way to the Middle Belt. So, we will give you a sabbatical."

Onyii's feet drag. She can barely feel her legs. She glances behind her and sees a child keeping step with a gun over their shoulder. A hat obscures the child's face. The child doesn't walk, the child marches. Like a machine. Onyii can barely keep her head lifted. Her mouth feels as though it's stuffed with cotton. She can't even muster up the saliva to spit on the ground. But she wants to call out to the child. Ify . . . Ify . . . It can't be. It must be the Chukwu in her head, short-circuiting her machinery and tugging at memories. No. Ify is dead. Buried in a mass grave.

Chinelo shifts her grip. A door opens, and suddenly Onyii finds herself inside a maglev Range Rover. She's the dirtiest thing in it.

A hazy voice calls out and, if Onyii understands correctly, asks her if she wants any water. Onyii, silent, leans back against the cushions. They mold to her body. She could sink into them.

She's sober enough now that if she closes her eyes, she knows, nightmares will greet her. She'll find herself hunched over the tablet the brigadier general gave her all those years ago, staring down into the thing that had cast the very light out of her world that day.

Bodies, mangled and maimed. Limbs piled haphazardly on top of each other. Some of the bodies are riddled with bullet holes. Others show disconnected wiring where arms have been severed, while others show bone that hasn't yet bleached in the sun. There's a moment when the bile rises in Onyii's throat, but cold follows right after it. Her body shutting down. Something deep and necessary inside of her freezing over.

On top of the pile, maybe the freshest kill, lies what remains of Ify, disfigured beyond recognition.

Onyii knows the proper thing is to weep. But she cannot mourn, even now. Mourning won't bring Ify back. Neither will killing. But Onyii knows how to do the latter. So she clings to it like a piece of driftwood in oil-coated ocean. It is all she has left.

When Onyii drifts out of the memory, she looks out the window and sees the one- and two-story shops of Enugu's central business district. Enugu. The capital of Biafra. Igboland. Occasionally towering over the shops are the microflats: one-room living spaces where the residents share a communal kitchen. The flats face each other and form a square into which the compound's entrance leads visitors and residents. "Face-me-I-face-you," she had once heard them called.

Flags wave in the breeze that descends from the surrounding hills.

People fill the streets but part when they see the military convoy coming. Then come the cheers. Onyii can see their mouths moving as they shout what she assumes to be praise at them. Children run alongside the jeeps with their flags held high. *Ojukwu, nye anyi egbe ka anyi nuo agha!* Ojukwu, give us guns to fight a war!

Chief Chibuikem Moses Tunde Ojukwu. Prime minister of Biafra.

Onyii can't tell if Chinelo's been speaking at all. And she can no longer detect the presence of that ghostly child she'd seen earlier, that spirit of Ify. The drug has worn off. Chukwu has left her.

The jeep eventually rumbles to a stop in the courtyard of an apartment complex. The towers surrounding the courtyard rise stiffly into the air. At some of the large windows, people stand and watch her. Onyii's door opens, and Chinelo reaches in to get her out, but Onyii waves her away, takes a moment, then hops onto solid ground. It takes her a moment to gain her bearings, but soon she is upright.

Chinelo leads Onyii through the courtyard, where children tend to a garden, watched over by a white-bearded man. He must be a teacher of some sort. Then they get to an elevator that whisks them up several floors.

The only light in the hallway shines through a window at the end. When they arrive at the last unit in the hall, Chinelo presses a keycard against the pad. The door slides open.

Inside is a bed and nothing else.

"I told them luxuries like a wallpaper TV and a fruit basket would be wasted on you," Chinelo says, smiling. "The people here, they don't see too many warriors from the front." She pats Onyii on the back. Softly. "I am telling you to rest. Not just as your friend, but as your commanding officer." She then slides the keycard into Onyii's palm and closes her friend's fingers over it. "So you don't get locked out." Chinelo steps back past the threshold. "One of the girls will come find you in the morning." Her face softens. Some of the humor leaks out of it, so that sadness shimmers in her eyes. "It's good to have you home, my sister. The shower is down the hall." Just as Chinelo's lips curl into a smile, the door slides shut.

Onyii's limbs ache again. When she finally lies down on the

bed and her head falls onto the single pillow, she feels relief.

There's soft pounding up and down the hallway outside her door. She's too tired to move. Then she hears the voices of children.

"Doot-doot-doot-doot-doot!" one child shouts.

"Brrrah-pa-pa!" from another.

Then comes: "Yahk-yahk-yahk-yahk!"

And all throughout, giggling while they bound up and down the corridor. Onyii tries to force herself to smile, to enjoy the sound of children playing so close by. But she knows what sounds they're making.

They're mimicking gunfire.

CHAPTER
18

Ify slips beneath her bedsheet wearing a skinsuit whose warming and cooling systems can be adjusted with the press of a few buttons along her collarbone. She sets it to auto-detect mode, and it connects to her nervous system. This way, it can adjust her body temperature without her having to wake up and input a new set of commands each time she grows uncomfortable. Her hair is newly washed and collected in a wrap. Her body is clean from ablutions, and her heart is cleaned by the night's prayers. But she doesn't deactivate her Accent just yet.

In bed, she twirls a bead on her bracelet, and a hologram appears before her face. At first, the image shimmers with blue, then a layer of gold flashes over the strands of light that form the outlines of people in a room. Then the colors fill out, and Ify finds herself looking at the men in the observation deck.

With a thought, she's able to dim the light of her bedroom, a single in a dormitory full of doubles and the occasional triple. But it's not like Ify has a whole lot to decorate it with. No family 'grams or old artifacts like books made out of paper passed down through family lines. No jewelry, no clothes or decorations from older siblings. So the light from her hologram casts its colors over a nearly bare desk with a few tablets on it, some kimoyo-bead bracelets and anklets she's been experimenting on, and several paper cranes, long since browned and crinkled by time.

However, no one else can hear the dialogue she can.

The air around them steams with their forced ease. They're trying so hard to feel comfortable around Daren, but they're too stiff or they're too floppy and loose, and when they do laugh, they laugh a little too loudly.

But one of them speaks with confidence, just above a whisper, as though he were actually worried Ify might overhear, about mineral deposits and corporations. He mentions something about making Daren very wealthy, and that's when Daren stares down the man, and Ify wonders what has happened between them that turned Daren's mood so quickly. Then she sees it in his stance, the way his chin is held high. *I am not like you*, he is saying with his body, with his aura. She doesn't have to hack his brain to know it. *Not everything I do is for myself.*

There is nothing new to be gained from watching them like this. It's only an opportunity for Ify to see how well she was able to hack the nearby surveillance camera to get this downward-facing angle of the group. It also pleases her that the audio quality is as good as it is.

One of the oyinbo says: "You have a word for them, don't you? Udene? Vultures?"

That silences the group. It is the man who spoke with confidence before. Ify remembers his vital signs being healthier than the others. He seemed fit, even though it was clear that much of his body is mechanized. His eyes are the color of ice, and his hair looks like the sun has leached all color out of it.

Daren frowns at the man and is quiet for a very long time

before he says, "That is what we call them." In the 'gram, he is utterly still, like he is tensed to leap at the man and grab him by the throat. And Ify can tell from the way everyone else waits that they are nervous he'll do exactly that. "And I can tell you," Daren says, taking a single step toward the man, "that you do not want to know what they call you."

The recording freezes in that moment. Daren is inches from the man's face. The oyinbo's features twist just a little bit, eyes on the verge of growing wide with fear. It makes Ify proud to see that Daren has this effect on strangers.

Then her thoughts turn to images of Biafran mechs flying through the air, engaging Nigerian forces in battle. Vultures.

All of Ify's earlier joy has evaporated. She looks at the shimmering scene before her, then, without another thought, deletes the recording. She doesn't want to be tempted to watch it again. Her bodysuit cools her skin and regulates her heartbeat, preparing her for sleep right on schedule. But her mind won't stop working.

It still troubles Ify to hear someone say *udene* and mean someone like Onyii.

CHAPTER
19

It takes Onyii a few moments to remember where she is. She tries to get up, but stiffness has her glued to her bed. She realizes this is the most rest she has gotten in at least a month, maybe in the past four years. So much fighting and moving from camp to camp. Onyii is used to sleeping standing up with her rifle leaned against her shoulder. Or she'd close her eyes in her mech and catch a minute or two of slumber before orders arrived to head out to the next battle.

Onyii looks around the room and can't find her rifle anywhere. There's no change of clothes, only the jungle-camo combat pants and the torn dark-green shirt she slept in. Sunlight pours through the window. She can tell from the angle that it's morning. But her mind still feels fogged. Her body aches, like it's eaten too much sleep too quickly, and now she must sit with the indigestion.

But Onyii pushes herself upright, through the pain and the creaking joints, and flexes the fingers of her metal hand. With her human hand, she touches her cheek and feels the bumps and impressions left by the metal. She can't help but chuckle at herself. Some habits never die.

When she's able to get to her feet, she stretches her back. Then she stretches her human arm and bends down to touch her toes. Popping sounds run all down her back. She takes her time with each stretch, even when she sits down to continue them. It gives her time to reorient herself, to remember her last battle and clearing the Nigerian camp, then Chinelo coming to find her in an alley snorting God, then the ride in the jeep. Enugu comes to her in flashes, like a glitchy holo recording. And all the while, that specter of a child that felt like it was hovering behind Onyii just out of sight. Ify's ghost.

After her stretches, she sits on the ground and presses the heels of her palms against her eyes. Her head is clearer now than she remembers it ever being.

Then she leaves the room.

She wanders down another hall and finds herself at the edge of a larger common room. The furniture here is in disarray, moved and angled every which way with boys draped in all sorts of configurations over it. One boy lies upside down on one couch, his legs wagging in the air while he tosses a ball up and catches it. Others are sprawled out with one leg over a chair's armrest and the other angled toward the floor. Onyii counts fifteen of them, almost all teenagers. But still just children. The brigadier general would have found work for them.

A little boy arrives at an entrance just next to Onyii and is about to enter when one of the boys on the couch, without looking, says in a deep voice, "Toluope, switch on the light."

The little boy, a plate of food in his hands, obediently goes to the light switch and makes it halfway before another boy, on an opposite couch, says in a deeper voice, "Toluope, if you touch that light, I will kill you."

A bunch of the teenagers laugh, and one of them, the one sitting upside down, says, "Don't bully my brodah. Otherwise, you will receive a courtesy slap from me."

"Oya, go, go!" says one of the bullies, and the little boy joins the upside-down one by the couch.

A loud *clack clack clack* gets everyone standing at attention. In a doorway not far from Onyii stands a young woman with a stick in her hands. She bangs it two more times against the doorframe. Everyone, even the little boy with the food, is upright and at attention.

"Hand combat training in five minutes, which means you need to be dressed and outside in two!" says a familiar voice.

The boys scramble, some of them still smirking over a shared joke, and scatter down various hallways. All around Onyii is the whisk of doors opening and closing and the thump of bare feet against the floor.

With the room emptied, the leader walks in and shakes her head at the mess. She turns. That's when Onyii sees her face.

Kesandu.

Kesandu's eyes become wide. Whatever hardness was in them before vanishes, and she runs to Onyii and wraps her tight against her chest.

She holds Onyii out at arms' length and looks her up and down. Even now, in the midst of joy, her grip is firm. "Oh my goodness, Onyii. I heard you were here, but I couldn't believe it. We've heard so many stories of you on the front, but Chinelo is always telling us that half of them are made up. Oh my goodness, oh my goodness. It's really you." The words tumble over each other. It's like Kesandu is a child again.

And that's when Onyii notices the boy, maybe eleven or

twelve years old, who stands just taller than Kesandu's hips. His skin where it's exposed is patchy. Discolored in places. Like he has vitiligo.

"Oh!" Kesandu says, following Onyii's gaze. "This is Kalu. My abd." She puts her hand on the boy's head. "Kalu, this is your Auntie Onyii."

The boy is stone-faced. Not afraid, not curious. His eyes betray no emotion. He wears a shoulder holster and has a knife in a scabbard at his waist.

"Say hi to your Auntie Onyii."

The boy sticks out his hand. Fast, like he's drawing a gun.

Onyii takes the boy's hand, and his fingers squeeze. Too hard. The gears in Onyii's hand whirr and hum with activity until the boy lets her hand go.

"Let me bring you to the others," Kesandu says while Onyii rubs her hand. "They are at the firing range. They will be happy to see you."

As they leave the common room, Onyii can't take her eyes off the boy. "Your abd?" she asks Kesandu quietly.

"Yes. He is very skilled. I will show you when we are outside."

Onyii tries to find the word in Igbo, but it does not exist. She has only heard it spoken by the Fulani and other Nigerians in the North.

In Arabic, *abd* means *slave*.

■ ■ ■ ■ ■

Wind takes the staccato sound of gunfire up into the hills, then through the mountain ridges that surround the firing range. Kesandu drives the jeep up the barely covered magnetic rails leading to the field. When they get there, Onyii sees the young women scattered about, some of them clustered together, while little boys just like Kesandu's abd stand at their stations with their boxes of ammunition beside them and fire at targets Onyii can't yet see.

Before they crest the rise, Onyii can hear their voices. They sound older, which makes sense, given it's been four years. But how much can a person change in four years?

When the jeep comes to a rest, Kesandu and her abd, Kalu, hop out. Onyii's a bit slower, but as soon as she gets out, her legs falter. She leans against the hood of the jeep to stabilize herself, then looks up to see Kesandu and Kalu up ahead, Kesandu saying something Onyii can't hear and gesturing back toward Onyii.

Some of the girls drop what they're holding. Some of them run toward Onyii. Some of them simply stand where they are and smirk. Satisfied. Like they won a secret wager. Obioma is the one who comes running. She stops halfway and shouts back over her shoulder, "Who said you could stop shooting?" The pistol shots that had ceased start up again.

When Onyii and Obioma meet, Onyii takes a few seconds to look her over. Obioma slaps Onyii's shoulder with the back of her hand and says, "Eh-HEH! The prodigal daughter has returned! We heard stories-oh! We heard stories about you!" She drapes her arm over Onyii's shoulder, and Onyii's left wondering who this new woman is. She seems worlds away from the shy, trembling leaf of a girl who barely survived the raid on the camp four years ago. It is as though something has been unlocked in her. She walks Onyii to the center of the range. There stand a few women Onyii's age, but she doesn't recognize them. They could have come from the camp, but the years in between then and now, Onyii realizes, can make a person unrecognizable. She knows she should feel joy at the reunion, at having found a friend alive and well. But when she reaches inside of herself, she finds nothing. Only numbness.

Obioma brings Onyii to their circle, and they introduce themselves.

"Ngozi," says the one with box braids coming down to the small of her back.

"Ginika," says the one in a sleeveless combat vest with half of a sun tattooed on her left shoulder.

They each shake Onyii's hand, then step back, as though they're waiting for her to say something. Waiting for her to be like all the stories they've heard of the Demon of Biafra.

There is no Demon of Biafra, Onyii wants to tell them. *There's just a War Girl.*

Onyii nods over Ngozi's shoulder at the little boy with the assault rifle pressed against his shoulder.

"Ah," Ngozi says, smirking, "Nnamdi." She walks toward the boy, and the rest of the girls follow.

Nnamdi has his rifle ready and aimed, while the abd to his right arranges the semiautomatic pistol rounds on his table. His hands and neck have the same patchwork discoloration as Kalu's.

"All right, begin," says Ngozi.

Nnamdi lets loose a series of three-round bursts aimed at targets five hundred meters away. The targets rattle each time he fires, shaking as if possessed. Then, after each burst, they right themselves. He calmly sets the Beretta AR70/90 on the table and waves to someone far in the distance. A spotter. On the table lie a box of ammunition and two spare clips.

"Nnamdi!" calls the the spotter in a clear voice that rings over the field. "One, clean shots to chest and head. Two, clean shots to chest and head. Three, clean shots to chest."

Onyii expects the boy to smile, but he has the same expressionlessness as Kesandu's abd. Mechanically, Nnamdi detatches the butt of his rifle, hefts it once again, and holds it at his hip. Ngozi puts a hand to his shoulder.

"That's enough for now," she says.

The boy's hands fall to his sides, and he stands still, like an android waiting to be told what to do.

"What is he?" Onyii asks.

"He's a survivor," Ngozi says, smiling.

Ginika calls back over her shoulder. "Golibe! Oya, come here!"

From not far away, a young boy walks, a Benelli shotgun resting against his shoulder. "Yes, Mama," Golibe says, his near-bald head scratchy with newly grown hair.

"Oya, go and clean up some of the ammo. And help your spotter bring in the targets."

With that, the boy dashes off toward the field into which Nnamdi had been firing earlier. He moves fast, with regular strides. Onyii can't help following his movements.

"The abd are special," Ginika says, taking her gaze from Golibe. "It helps to not see them as boys."

"What?"

"They are weapons. It's a new program Chinelo put together. Each of us is paired with an abd. We train them for special missions. Clandestine operations. The things too delicate for a mech pilot to bash her way through." She doesn't raise her eyebrow at Onyii, but Kesandu can see the tension in Onyii's balled fist and moves to stand between them, all the while pretending all is well.

"After the Nigerians bomb a town or a village, we sneak in to see who can be rescued. Some of those we rescue are alive enough to survive cyberization. We give them new bodies, repair their minds, and hand them an opportunity to serve their country and fight for Biafra. We condition them, and we train them. As you can see here."

Onyii watches it all, and maybe it's the extra rest she's had, but she sees the images too clearly. She can picture the rubble left behind after an aerial bombing campaign launched by the Green-and-Whites. She can picture the families buried underneath, the Biafrans whose cries for help are choked by dust. She can picture the rescue teams racing from location to location, trying to pull bodies from their makeshift graveyards. And among those rescue teams are the girls here, looking for boys whose bodies can be salvaged. Whose bodies can adjust to someone else's arms or someone else's legs. With skin grafted on from over a dozen people. A collection of body parts fused onto an artificial skeleton. A collection of other people's memories thrown into a single braincase. The skin discoloration makes sense now.

"They're synths," she says bitterly. It was a synth that bombed their camp all those years ago, a body implanted with just enough neural data to fake being a person, then sent on its mission. No soul. No thought to call their own. She had only seen adult synths. Androids fashioned to resemble fully grown humans. These are something new.

Kesandu draws closer to Onyii. "We're giving them a chance

to strike back." More quietly, she says, "This is what they would want."

"How can a synth want?" Onyii looks at her metal hand, then flexes. So this is what Chinelo meant by *sabbatical*. She's just preparing Onyii for a new type of mission.

"Where's Chinelo's office?"

Obioma puts her hands to her hips and laughs. "Oh, you will see her just like that?"

"She thinks she can just throw me in a boys' dormitory and forget about me, eh?" Onyii smirks, then reaches in an ammunition crate for a pistol she tucks into her belt. "Never mind. I will find her myself. You continue playing with your children."

She tries to sound like she's joking, but she still feels ill at ease. All the while, one of the abd has been firing his pistol. Even now, the sound of gunshots firing at regular intervals follows Onyii all the way off the range.

CHAPTER
20

When Daren had told Ify about Biafra's child soldiers, disgust had been her first reaction, rumbling in her stomach and her heart. But in the days that had followed, the disgust gave way to something else, a realization: she was almost one of those children. A child trapped in war-filled southern Nigeria. This is what they would have turned her into if they'd had enough time. This is the thought she carries with her as Daren takes her on a tour through a camp filled with detention centers for recently captured Biafran soldiers. To everyone else, she is an aide to a senior officer in the Nigerian Armed Forces, Kato Mobile Defense Unit, dutifully documenting the war effort and assisting the officer in administrative matters. An honor no other student at the Nigerian Consortium for Social and Technical Sciences has been given. But she knows this is just Daren's way of making sure they spend time together. It's always nicer when Daurama's not around, despite how much Daren seems to delight in his blood sister's company.

The concrete startles her. All of the buildings are made out of it, not of the glass and steel she is used to seeing in Abuja. Everything here is blocked off from view, where, in Abuja, everything is available for everyone to see. Here, even the guards wear masks.

"Why don't they show their faces?" Ify asks Daren. Their robes flow around them, shimmering. In Ify's helmet, radiation readings roll down her screen. A Terminal has not yet been installed here. As this had been previously unconquered territory, the poisonous air has not yet been totally cleared. But Ify doesn't worry. The helmet is just an extra layer of protection. Her Accent reassures her that levels here are low enough that a quick bath in the regeneration pools back home should be more than enough to clean away any dust or chemicals carrying residual radiation.

The pathways between the concrete buildings are still unpaved, and little clouds of dust puff up around Ify's ankles with each step she takes. The hem of Daren's robe is red-brown with irradiated grime, but he seems unbothered.

"Can you show me?"

"Show you what, Kadan?" He looks ahead like he's staring far into the distance past anything she can see.

"One of the rehabilitation centers. For the children." She wants to tell him so many of the things roiling inside her, so many of the thoughts running around in her head. Her memories of her time in the camp with the Biafrans, how she almost shared the fate of these children, the possibility that they might someday share hers. It heartens her to think of the children as fellow Nigerians. To clean them up, give them proper showers, provide them with proper hygiene, proper education, to give them homes and to teach them how to behave in them. "I want to see them."

"Are you sure you don't want to see the school we are building farther down the way? It is a basic structure, but that is only because this camp is meant to be temporary."

"I want to see what they look like."

Daren hesitates, then smiles and looks around for the nearest detention center. Inclining his head, he makes a turn and leads Ify down another dirt pathway.

It's only after he nods to the two masked guards outside and they enter a dark anteroom that Ify realizes that Daren never answered her question about the masks. One of the guards inside the anteroom approaches Daren and looks down at Ify for a moment before looking back at Daren.

Daren smiles at the guard. "We are just conducting a tour of the facilities. This young one is one of our brightest students from Abuja, and she is interested in studying the rebels. She thinks when she grows up that she will become an anthropologist, but I personally believe she'll grow into a desire for space exploration."

Ify frowns at Daren. *Why is he telling these lies?* She doesn't want to "study" the Biafrans. But then she turns the thought over in her head. Isn't that just what she intends on doing? Talking to them, observing them, tracking their habits. How is that different from the physics she studies in the classroom or the half-mech animals she watches in the fields and tries to hack? To understand?

She doesn't have the time to reach a solution before the guard barks a few orders to others who man the station, then looks down again at Ify.

"I'm sorry, but I will have to take your jewelry, miss."

"What?" Instinctively, Ify clutches her kimoyo beads. The thought of entering a new space without them chills her.

Her Accent is so much lesser without their amplifying power. There's so much data she'd be missing out on. And she'd have no way of reading the children, of getting their health levels and gauging their mental agility, of seeing what effect, if any, that sustained contact with the radiation has meant for their bodies. She backs into Daren, who puts his hands on her shoulders, almost like an embrace.

"It's okay, Kadan." He rubs warmth and reassurance into her. "We will retrieve them when we leave."

"But why do they have to keep them here?"

The faceless guard steps forward. "Even though the rebels are caged, they may try to use our technology as a weapon. They are very clever, despite their lack of intelligence. And we must not give them any means to bring about an escape or to cause any harm to Nigerians in this facility." Behind his mask, his face seems to soften. "It is for your protection. And ours."

At that, Ify looks at her bracelet, then reluctantly twists one of the beads to power it down. Then she slips it over her hand, twists a bead on her necklace, and detaches the magnet fasteners at the back of her neck. She hands them to the guard, who puts them somewhere Ify can't see, and Ify almost reaches for her Accent, then stops. Removing that would be too painful. It is clasped to her skin, like an earring but inside her ear. She would be utterly lost without it. She stops herself just in time. The guard doesn't notice.

When the guard is satisfied, he leads them through a skinny passageway that opens out onto a wider corridor. The whole place is made of stone, and when Ify tries to turn on her Accent, she realizes why. To block signals. To keep people from connecting to larger networks. She tries to imagine what it must be like to be shut off not only from the net but also from the possibility of it.

They turn a corner and head down another corridor, this one lined with one-room cells, some of them empty. The thresholds to the rooms look clear, transparent, as though there is nothing there, but Ify sees the shimmer in the air and the beeping light above the doorways that tells her a force field keeps these children in their cages.

"The rebels wear collars around their necks," the guard tells Ify and Daren, "so that any unpermitted movements will result in an electric current being run through their body. Some of them, however, have adapted to pain and can withstand more. So we have a fail-safe device installed. If a rebel strays too far from their designated location, the collar detonates."

Ify recoils in horror. When she looks into the cells, she sees individual boys, many of them dressed in unclean rags. Brown with mud they must have crawled through at some point. Unwashed. Most of them keep their heads bowed, their bodies utterly still. She can't tell if they do this out of shame or out of something else, a more violent impulse. Others look their captors straight in the face, expressionless and defiant at the same time. These have a hollowness in their eyes.

"Are they all like this? Held separately?"

The guard does a scan of each cell, turning his head back and forth regularly, like he is on patrol. "The older ones who have undergone Augmentation, we keep apart. They may try to form closed neural networks and plot an operation."

"Are they all boys?" Ify sounds more like a scientist than a concerned human being, and it bothers her.

The guard sneers. "The Biafrans do not value their women." And he leaves it at that.

Ify frowns. She knows that's a lie, but what will she say? That she used to live among them? That the soldiers who raised her were among the fiercest she ever saw? That, in the camp, women were leaders and teachers and gardeners and soldiers? To speak of the Biafrans that way would probably mark her for treason.

"Their families send them to war, because they believe it to be a patriotic duty," Daren says, his voice calm and level. Like he's talking about how a caterpillar walks. "Some of them go feral in the jungle. These are only partially cyberized." Daren steps to one of the cells and looks down on a boy who curls in on himself. "And the work is sloppy." It's as though Daren has to keep himself from spitting on the boy. Ify has never seen him like this.

She draws herself up and turns to the guard. "Are they all enemy combatants?"

For a moment, both Daren and the guard are unable to hold back their surprise.

"Under Article Three of the Centauri Convention on the Rights of the Child, members of a tribe under fifteen years of age cannot be categorized as enemy combatants. They are civilians. Even if they are given a weapon." When the guard and Daren look at each other, Ify continues. "That means they cannot be held captive for longer than seventy-two hours before being granted access to civilian shelter within the borders of the enemy state."

The guard rounds on Ify. "Child, you—"

Daren raises a hand that stops the guard in his tracks, then calmly turns to Ify. "And that is why they are in the process of building a school for these children. Even though many of them pretend to be refugees fleeing war and even though we can see through their deception, we give them shelter." He looks to the guard, as though for confirmation. "Here, they are fed. Housed. Kept safe from whatever militia may be trying to kill them for fleeing or being captured."

And look at how they are treated. She crouches down onto her haunches and tries to look into the boy's face, but he won't lift his head. Ify tilts hers to the side, tries to get a better angle. But the child stays absolutely still. And she knows that to activate her Accent would alert the guard, who is most certainly Augmented himself. Before her, on the other side of that invisible cell door, is a problem she can't solve. Yet.

She stands, smooths her gown. "And the red-bloods?"

This time, it's Daren who is taken by surprise.

"Is everyone who passes through here cyberized?" She makes sure to emphasize *passes through* to let the guard know she has no intention of pressing the detention issue. If he needs to say this is just temporary so they can continue to commit war crimes, let him. He will stay out of her way if she lets him. "Are the red-bloods kept in a separate facility?"

Daren nods at the guard as though to say, *I have control of this situation, trust me.* So the guard nods his assent, turns, and says, "Follow me."

They round another corner, and the guard hurries them down the next corridor, probably to keep Ify from seeing what's in each of the cells. They pass through a sun-drenched courtyard, then into another wing. Here, however, the hallways are wider, and the group slows down enough for Ify to notice, in one wall, a window opening out onto a large room.

Adults walk around the room, but they don't wear any armor. Just robes with green and white stripes at the ends of each sleeve. Here, the kids cluster in groups, some young enough to barely be walking. A few of them rest against the wall; these ones seem older. But, through the flexiglas, Ify can see movement. She can see children talking to each other. Some of them are animated, others withdrawn. But they all seem . . . alive.

"I'd like access to that room, sir," she says to the guard. She has grown into this role and knows that she has special status. She is among the favored of Abuja. The brilliant ones who are charged, from an early age, with guiding the country well into the future. She will go to the most prestigious universities. She will command a seat at the same table as those who run the Space Colonies. So who is this lowly guard to deny her access to a room in a children's prison?

The guard taps his earpiece and speaks a few words, then a door farther down the hall opens up. Ify leads the way, and when she is inside, she sees the drawings that line the wall. She walks to one of the pictures and sees a compound sketched out, seen at an angle from above with soldiers toward the center of the page around what she realizes is an explosion. The captured moment finds the limbs frozen in mid-flight. A shaheed. A suicide bomber. Someone in a military vest stands at the bottom right corner of the page, looking both at the scene and at Ify. Another sketch shows a Nigerian aircraft, the green-and-white flag displayed prominently on the side, while what look like Biafrans with guns fall away beneath the gunfire. When she turns around to a circle of children, one of them can't stop laughing. He scratches his scalp and giggles while looking very shy. Toys litter the ground, untouched.

A woman, one of the guardians, steps to Ify and Daren and smiles.

"Some of them have been making progress today. It is easier to reach them than to reach those who have been cyberized. The Biafrans altered their limbic systems when they cyberized them, changing their emotional centers so that they no longer feel things like grief. But these children?" She indicates the circle behind her with a sweep of her arm. "There is hope."

Ify inclines her head toward one of the older boys leaning sullenly against the wall. "And him?"

The guardian lowers her head. "Some of them feel guilty. For getting captured." She is not afraid to speak at full volume, and Ify realizes it's because she believes none of the children can understand the Arabic-infused Hausa she speaks. "Some of them were elite soldiers sent to training camps in the forest. They were given better food and shelter than they'd had in their villages. They were the hope of their families. And now they are prisoners."

"Do they get outside?" Ify asks. "Do they see the sun?"

"They are permitted an hour of natural sunlight. But because they are fully red-blood, they cannot spend too much time in an environment with too much radiation." She sighs. "Some of them even refuse treatment and have to be . . . forced . . . into their healing baths."

Ify frowns, then walks to the circle with the giggling child.

Some of them raise their heads when they see her.

She sits down on the rug with them and smiles.

"I drew the picture there," says one of the boys, pointing to the one with the aircraft. "And when I get better, I want to be a pilot. I want to help my country."

Ify smiles.

"I want to be a civil engineer!" shouts another.

The giggling boy grows quiet.

"And you?" Ify asks, smiling.

He hides his face behind his hands, then peeks through his fingers. "I don't like violence," he says, his words muffled by his palms. "War and blood. I don't like it. I have hope for peace." He pauses. "Sometimes, if my mommy give me money to eat biscuit, I dey buy twenty leaves of paper to draw. I see myself among de great artists of de world. Sometimes, there is too much dust here. It makes the water hard to drink, and it's hard to see things."

"Like what?"

"Like the roses."

Ify blinks.

"The ones that grow on the wall."

Ify frowns, looks around, and sees nothing but the pictures on the wall. As she's looking, the papers start to shake. The ground begins to vibrate. Daren runs to Ify's side just as an explosion erupts outside.

Everyone falls to the ground. The guardians sweep blankets from a closet and gather the children together. The older boy who had been relaxing against the wall scurries toward the rest of them, frightened out of his nonchalance.

Daren is on top of Ify. Dust falls on them both. The lights flicker, then turn back on. Outside, soldiers shout orders to each other. Ify closes her eyes, and suddenly she's back in the camp among the other War Girls. She sees the mechs flying overhead and raining fire on their home. She remembers Onyii in her own mech speeding into the air and battling their attackers, who are in crabtanks with legs that crash through the school and shatter the greenhouse. It all takes hold of her. She can smell the char, hear the katakata of gunfire, see the dirt and stone and metal shoot into the air in columns with each explosion.

Then, everything grows silent.

For several long seconds, nobody in the room moves. Their guard is gone. Now more soldiers line the walls, peering out the windows but making sure to stay out of any line of fire.

One of the boys, the giggling one, is smiling.

"What was that?" one of the nurses asks.

Daren must have forgotten Ify is there. That is the only reason Ify can think of for why he says, without hesitation, "One of the udene detonated himself just outside the compound."

The giggling boy stares directly at Ify. He's not laughing anymore, but his smile chills Ify. "Roses," he says. "When the dust is gone, there will be new roses on the wall."

Ify's heart sinks.

Roses.

The boy thinks the bloodstains on the walls of the compound are roses.

CHAPTER
21

It takes some wandering and curtly asking a few officers and soldiers for directions, but eventually, Onyii finds the main compound, what she guesses is the military headquarters for this unit operating out of Enugu. It looks a lot like a school campus extension. There are still signs that say UNIVERSITY OF ENUGU throughout the courtyard and along the hallways, but none of the people here look like students. Only young women and boys manning their stations, some of them behind turret guns on tall towers, others lounging on overturned crates with their rifles cradled in their arms.

Inside one of the compound's buildings, Onyii roams the hallways. The map she downloaded is outdated and doesn't indicate whose office is whose. But everyone lets her pass, and she suspects it's because her reputation precedes her. Maybe Chinelo has personally told them who she is, that she is to be given free rein of the campus. Maybe they've heard of what she has done to the Green-and-Whites. Maybe a photo of her has already been circulated to everyone's tablets. Onyii scans their faces for any reaction. She is used to seeing fear in the eyes of others. But some, even the occasional officer, glow with respect for her. Some even salute her, even though she bears no rank. She's felt for so long like some wandering soldier, like some ghost, not a part of any formal military or any structure, just a whirling demon who flies wherever pointed and swings her bladed staff and fires her shoulder cannons and cuts through enemy forces. Going wherever the brigadier general tells her the enemy is. *Ojukwu, nye anyi egbe ka anyi nuo agha!* Ojukwu, give us guns to fight a war!

She stops at what looks like the doorway the others described. Wood paneling around double doors. Two guards out front. They look to her and nod, as though to say Chinelo isn't busy at the moment. Even though she's not accepting visitors, the Demon of Biafra is permitted entry.

One of them presses her thumb against the keypad by the door, which opens inward toward the room.

Onyii sees Chinelo standing behind a desk, leaning over it and looking down at a holo, then walks through.

As soon as the doors close behind her, a blow strikes her right in the cheek.

She topples, but just before she falls, she regains her balance. Just in time to block another blow. And another. The hands come fast. A boy's hands. Too fast. But she catches one fist, and just as she winds up to hit the boy attacking her, he breaks out of her grip, ducks, and rips two fierce punches to her rib cage, then an uppercut that sends her staggering back. He rushes and tackles Onyii by the waist. She uses her momentum to flip him and kick him off.

He flies into a bookshelf, and several thick books fall on his back.

Onyii goes to kick him, but he grabs her leg. She leaps into the air and, with her other leg, catches him across the face. He puts his hand to his face as Onyii spins herself upright. She has just a moment to catch her breath.

The boy launches another blow. She blocks it, then another, then another. Lightning-fast. She catches each with her palm, then her forearm. The next rolls off her shoulder. He gets closer, starts to smother her. How is he able to move this fast for this long? And how does his small body contain such power?

Onyii remembers the gun in her pants.

The boy swings for her head. She ducks, skids behind him, so that she can aim her gun at the back of his head. He spins and knocks her hand away. The bullet hits the window. Onyii swings again, aims lower. That bullet hits the floor. Again and again, she pirouettes and just as she's about to get a shot off, the boy knocks her hand away. She tries again, the boy hits her wrist so hard it sends the gun flying to the window.

The boy leaps into the air to deliver another blow. Onyii blocks it with her metal wrist and takes less than a second to note the boy's surprise before sweeping his legs out from under him. She goes to stomp on his head, but he rolls away, just out of reach. Then he catches her downward kick and flips her backward.

She lands on her feet and blocks a blow aimed for her chest. A blow so strong it pushes her backward. She counters with her elbow and nearly catches the boy in the throat, but he grabs her hand and twists. Joints pop. Onyii flips herself over and out of the boy's grip, and their hands shoot for the other's throat, so that they're caught in a stalemate.

Only then does Onyii hear Chinelo behind her desk shouting for them to stop.

"Chineke mbere!" she curses. "God help me!" Under the distress, there's a note of laughter in her voice. They both look to Chinelo, locked in each other's death grips, bleeding from the mouth, hair a dusty mess. Chinelo shakes her head. "Chiamere, stand down."

Reluctantly, with a beseeching look in his eyes, Chiamere releases Onyii from his vise grip.

After a moment, Onyii does the same, then massages her throat, coughing. "Let me guess," Onyii says when she gets her breath back. "Your abd."

"Are you done test-driving him?"

"He attacked first." Onyii straightens her clothes, puts a finger to her lip, and looks at the blood it comes back with. "Didn't even see it coming," she says, more to herself than to anyone else. She's never seen someone move so fast in hand-to-hand combat. And to take such advantage of so cramped a space. She realizes that each time she tried to fire, Chiamere had angled so that there was no chance of Chinelo getting hit. All the while, he had been holding back.

"He's programmed with a prime directive: to protect me at all costs. Even if that means sacrificing himself. He's a soldier just like you, Onyii." There's a note of defensiveness in her voice. "He can fight as well as the rest of us." She smirks at Onyii's bloody lip. "Maybe even better." Then she pushes off her desk and folds her arms. "I've something to show you. Follow me."

She leads Onyii through a back door and into what looks like a sparse bedroom with little more decoration than Onyii's.

There's a bed and a bedstand with a tablet on it. A lamp by the far wall. And a boy standing just in front of the bed, dressed in suspenders and a bowtie. He can't be older than ten or eleven years old.

Chinelo stands to the side, glancing with satisfaction at one then the other. "Onyii, meet your abd, Agu."

For a long time, everyone stands in silence. Then Onyii, nervous, asks, "Do I shake his hand?"

"Whatever you want."

"What did you do?"

"I baffed him and cooked him suya like a good woman," Chinelo croons. "What does it matter what I did?"

Onyii frowns at Chinelo's unhelpful sarcasm, then returns to her abd. She has no idea what to do.

Chinelo leaves, then comes back with Onyii's gun. She hands it to Onyii and says, "Let him show you what he can do." She presses her hands over Onyii's and lowers her voice. "Tell him to take it apart."

Onyii hands the gun, butt first, to Agu.

Agu holds it in front of him like he's never seen a pistol before.

"Take it apart," Onyii says.

In seconds, the thing lies in neatly arrayed pieces on the bed. Even the spring has been taken out. When Agu is finished, he holds his hands behind his back and stares into Onyii's eyes, unnervingly.

Onyii can't believe what she's just seen. But the events of the day make all of this seem less strange. She has seen what boys who look like Agu can do. She has seen how easily they can break things. "Now put it back together," she says.

Agu reaches for the gun, but Onyii grabs his wrist.

"Close your eyes." Then she lets go.

Agu takes a moment to close his eyes. Then his hands dance

over the parts until the gun is back as it had been. The boy exhales, then opens his eyes and hands the repaired gun, butt first, to Onyii.

This time, Onyii's shock passes even more quickly. Now she's smirking. The boy's impassive face breaks open in a smile. Like he has brought home the highest marks in his class for his big sister to see.

"Welcome to the Abd Program," Chinelo says, grinning.

CHAPTER
22

For a long time, Ify sits alone in the maglev limousine. With her Accent back on, she's able to connect to the vehicle's surveillance and can see through its windows, can rotate the cameras to see how the dust has settled. She can get the cameras to curl on themselves and show her just how thick and tinted the windows are, how the entire limousine is built to withstand blasts from buried mines and rocket-propelled grenades. It is through the cameras that she can hear. But Daren stands far enough away, chatting with the guards and camp administrators, that she can't hear him. What if he's also telling Daurama what happened through his comms? Ify tries to imagine the woman expressing concern for Daren's well-being but not once asking about Ify. Daurama has never cared much for her.

The entire compound has shut down. Almost nothing moves outside. At least, nothing that isn't supposed to. There had been a man selling balloons earlier. He had had them tied to the handle of his cart. He is nowhere to be found. Now the ground mechs are much closer. And soldiers stand by their military-issue hoverbikes. Where, before, one had to squint to see them, now they stand practically on top of the newly built town. All construction noises have stopped.

Ify gets the cameras of the car, small beads the size of raindrops, to stop moving. It feels too much like she's playing a game. But as soon as she stills, terror grips her body. Her arms shake with the memory of the rumbling floor. Her legs go numb. She hears a loud whine, then it's like earplugs muffle every other noise in the world. She can't scream, can't cry, can't whimper. Tears leak down her face. Her heart kicks and bucks inside her chest. She can't breathe. It feels as though she's trapped. Wrapped tight in an invisible blanket choking the air out of her lungs, squeezing the sense out of her brain.

A door lifts open, then closes shut.

She snaps out of her trance to find Daren sitting opposite her, eyes closed, head leaned back against his headrest. He heaves out a sigh so big it seems to deflate his body.

"Are you all right, Kadan?" he asks at last.

Ify nods, then looks away, out the window. She doesn't know what she's looking for, but knows that she can't bear to look him in the face. "It won't always be like this." It comes out as a sentence, but she means it as a question.

Daren's expression softens. He moves to sit beside her. "You care for them. This is important. But you can't love someone into common sense. You can't love them into peace."

"They're caged like animals in there. At least we let actual beasts roam the pastures. But them?" The sobbing takes her by surprise. For a while, she can't speak. She feels Daren's arm around her and wants to shake him off, but can't find the strength.

"I should not have taken you here," he whispers into her hair.

She pushes away. "No. Don't say that. I wanted to come." She fights for more words. "I want there to be peace. It shouldn't be how it is right now. We are all Nigerians."

Daren shakes his head. "No, it shouldn't. And you are right. We are one nation. But I see the way you are with them, and I worry for you. You cannot meet the unreasonable with kindness. It is like you keep digging hoping to find water. If you are dying of thirst, one drop of that dirty water will feel like the best water you have ever tasted. When you are dying of thirst, you will drink it all without question. And after so much thirst, you will not even listen to those who are trying to tell you that there is another well twenty feet away."

"You called them *udene*!"

At this, Daren stops. His brows knit into a frown. "They are willing to send children to kill themselves for their foolish cause." He speaks through gritted teeth. "They would have done that with you had we not rescued you. Had we not returned you to your home."

"What home! That was my home! That was my family!"

"They were *not* your family!"

"Onyii was my sister!" Ify sniffles and fights back her tears. "She was not udene! She loved me. She cared for me. She was just trying to protect me." She is about to say it, but stops herself.

"Say it." His fists are balled at his sides. He seems like he is made out of metal. "Go ahead. And. Say it." His fists tremble. "Protect you from what?"

Ify can't stop shaking.

"Protect you from *what*?"

It comes out as a bark, like a bullet spat out of his mouth and aimed straight for her chest. It paralyzes Ify. "From you," she whimpers, as she finally sees him in all his fierce and controlled power. He seethes with energy. It sounds as though the air crackles with it.

But he relents. Neither of them speaks for the rest of the ride home.

CHAPTER
23

Onyii watches Agu aim the Mauser C96 semiautomatic pistol at the target two hundred fifty meters away. The wind picks up as the sun slowly descends behind the mountains, casting the firing range in rays of pink and gold. Kesandu and Kalu are packing up their things, and Onyii glances at the two of them as Kesandu palms the back of Kalu's head. Ngozi stands silently a couple stations down, looming over Nnamdi as he picks up the shell casings from the afternoon's training. Kesandu stops at the top of the ridge and looks over her shoulder, waiting. Onyii wonders what she's waiting for until Ngozi looks back at her and their eyes catch. Something silent passes between them. Whatever it is, it makes Kesandu smile. Then she and Kalu are gone. Ngozi sees Onyii watching, and her frown pulls down the tribal scars on her cheeks. Those scars, three small, vertical lines on each cheek, mean she must have come from some kind of wealthy family. The type of family to look at someone like Onyii, half-covered in Augments, and suck their teeth.

Onyii spits on the ground and looks to Agu.

"Oya!" she shouts. "Are you waiting for the moon to give you permission? Go!"

The gun has only enough available room on the grip for one hand, so Agu has to stabilize his gun arm with his free hand. The first shot goes wildly to the right of the target. He stands there, silent, then resumes his stance, firing again. The next shot wings one of Nnamdi's targets nearly a dozen meters to the left. Again, closer to his own target but still laughably off-mark. Ngozi snickers. Tears spring to Agu's eyes.

"Try holding it sideways," Nnamdi whispers. "Hold it sideways, and you can use the muzzle jump to create a horizontal sweep. Instead of trying to force it under control." He backs away with his armful of shotgun shells.

Agu tries it and aims a little to the right of his target. When he pulls the trigger, the stand-up target swings backward. In the next instant, the one beside it does the same until he has successfully hit all five in a row. A smirk ghosts across his face before his expression turns stony again.

Onyii draws closer to Agu. "It took you all day to hit your targets, according to the spotter." Then she leans in closer to Agu's ear. "Do you know why I had you use the Mauser?"

Agu has no answer.

Onyii shakes her head. "That is too bad." The first drops of rain start to hit the tables. "Go load up and resume shooting. Also, move the targets to three hundred meters. Keep training until you can hit them all and figure out why I made you use that gun in the first place."

Ngozi and Nnamdi are already up the ridge. Onyii stuffs her hands in her pockets and follows after them. Dinner will be ready soon.

In the warm mess hall, a few of the abd sit together around a mountain of gari. They each have a rinsing bowl and a bowl of pepper soup next to them. They scoop out handfuls of gari, roll them into balls, and dunk them in their soup as they chatter softly to each other.

Onyii looks up from her plate of rice and stew every so often, toys with the fried plantains on top, then looks back down again. The chatter from the abd and the patter of rain against the roof and the low hum of the generators powering the lights fade away. She feels herself drifting.

In the memory, Onyii's hands move of their own accord.

Muscles tensing and loosening as she grips the slide of the machine pistol, slides it back, flips the catch, and pulls it off. The barrel falls out, landing with a muffled thud on the tablecloth, followed by the spring, and before long, the entire handgun lies in a neatly ordered display, piece by piece. She stares at it for a long time, memorizing each component, how they all fit together, and in forty-five seconds, she has the whole thing back together again. She repeats the exercise, her mind going blank, becoming empty space. The movements are instinctual until pain pricks her finger, and blood drips onto the cloth.

Stunned, she watches the small pool grow larger with each drop. Coming back to herself, she sucks on the wound.

A tray clattering on the table snaps her out of her reverie. She half expects to see Chinelo, who is always playing practical jokes on her, but it's Kesandu. Onyii forces a smile, then returns to her meal.

"You've grown an appetite since we were just War Girls in the camp," Onyii says.

Kesandu's mouth is already full with puff-puff. She chews fast and swallows even faster. "Someone has to eat all this food. And I am willing to make that sacrifice." She lets out a sigh.

"I saw you and Agu earlier. The Mauser is such an old gun. Nobody uses it anymore. Why are you having Agu train with it?"

"Muscle control, owning your nerves. That's what it's about. If he can't learn to control the muzzle jump on an outdated Mauser, he'll never learn the intricacies of a SIG." Thunder booms outside. "Speaking of which, have you seen him?" She nods toward the group of abd, who have finished their meal and are now busing their plates. "He's not with them, and when I went by his room, he wasn't there either."

Kesandu's eyebrows rise. "Have you checked the range?"

"What? There's a thunderstorm outside. It's been hours. No one in their right mind would just stay out there and . . ."

She rushes out of the mess hall as fast as she can, Kesandu close behind her. Dread makes her limbs feel as though she's made entirely of lead, but eventually they get to the range, and when Onyii gets close enough, she can see a lone figure standing by one of the metal tables, arms stretched forward.

Agu's teeth chatter. His arms tremble, and he struggles to hold the gun in his hand as he pulls the trigger. The recoil nearly throws him onto the ground. The intervals between shots grow longer and longer.

Out of ammo, he shuffles to another table where, blood running along his fingers and melding with the rainwater, he thumbs more bullets into his empty clip. He staggers back to his station, stands still for a moment, then collapses.

Onyii gets to him before he hits the ground, and she scoops him up in her arms. "It's okay," she whispers, not quite knowing why. "It's okay, it's okay." Together, the three of them rush back to shelter.

■ ■ ■ ■ ■

When she tries to go to sleep in her own bed, she can't. So she lies awake, staring out the window, waiting for the rain to stop.

The campus is rich with greenery the morning after the storm. By the time the sun is halfway to its peak, the wood benches have dried. Onyii makes her way outside and sits, absently tapping a pebble against the wood of the armrest. Kesandu emerges from the compound, wearing a long olive-green coat, and smiles, then starts drawing a pattern in the mud with the toe of her boot.

"He was just following orders," Kesandu says, like she's trying to reassure Onyii.

Onyii looks into the middle distance and, for a long time, says nothing. Then she turns to Kesandu. "Are they all like that?"

Kesandu stops drawing in the mud. "What do you mean?"

"Broken." She frowns, trying to figure out what she wants to say. "Kalu seems well-adjusted, but maybe that's because you've had him for a while. Chiamere seems to work just fine for Chinelo. And Nnamdi and Ngozi seem like they are working well together. Maybe Agu's broken."

Kesandu shrugs. "They're all broken at first. And they never really get fixed again, but that's life."

Onyii looks to her friend. "How do you keep Kalu from doing stupid things like what Agu did tonight?"

Kesandu looks to the compound. "It's a brain thing, I think. They're all relearning how to move. How to behave." She meets Onyii's gaze. "Have Agu learn penmanship. Or an instrument. I taught Kalu the xalam. But now he's got blisters on his fingers from all that playing." She chuckles. "I don't know. Maybe Agu can learn the piano."

"But I don't know how to play the piano. How would I teach him?"

"Hah, who says he has to learn from you?"

■ ■ ■ ■ ■

The studio is a mess of instruments with dust everywhere and the soundproof sheeting peeling in places from the walls. But a little ways from the center of the room, Agu sits on a stool with a touchboard balanced on a flexible stand in front of him. He stands and turns around at the sound of Onyii's entrance.

"I was told to meet you at fourteen thirty, sister." He always says it as *seestah*, which makes Onyii keep forgetting he's not a child. He's a synth.

She snaps her fingers, and orbs light up the room. Then she takes a seat next to him on the stool. "You can sit now."

For a long time, Onyii sits in silence. *What am I doing?* She tentatively puts a finger to the board, and a single note rings out. A little dulled, as it's been a while since the board was cleaned. But still fresh. She puts her hand back in her lap and is staring at the board again when Agu puts his own finger to it. There's a look of curiosity on his face, and in that moment, Onyii can swear she's looking at a child.

She touches a different part of the board, and a lower note hums. Agu reaches out with his left hand to do the same. His eyes light up.

Onyii touches a third key, more confident this time, and Agu does the same, then Onyii touches another, faster, and

Agu mirrors her movements. They go back and forth, touching random keys, and Onyii knows they're just making noise, but she can't stop the smile from spreading across her face. When she looks at Agu, a smile has split his lips as well.

After a moment, she stops smiling, then gets up. "That's enough for today."

For the briefest instant, a look of pleading fills Agu's eyes, then it's gone. "Yes, sister," he says before rising and leaving.

She tries to look and sound like a commanding officer, like she's concerned with just his training and that she needs him to be ready for more combat sessions. But she knows why she made him stop. His fingers haven't healed yet. He had smeared blood all over the board, and he hadn't even noticed.

In bed later that night, rising melody wakes her. Like an aircraft slowly angling its way upward. Sleek and silvery. Then the dip. All low notes mingling together before the tune unscrambles itself. It turns confident.

Onyii is slow to get up. But she follows the music all the way down to the studio. The door opens before her. But when she steps inside, Agu doesn't move. Doesn't turn around. Doesn't even hear her. A cord extends from the back of his neck to a console Onyii hadn't seen earlier against the side wall. She realizes with a start what he's doing. He's downloading music.

His shoulders are swaying back and forth as his bandaged fingers glide over the board. He had come back to this place without Onyii telling him. She hadn't issued any commands, hadn't adjusted any of his programming, hadn't altered his prime directive. He . . . he *wanted* this.

Onyii has never heard a synth express want, but this is the most beautiful thing she's heard in her life.

CHAPTER
24

Outside the Nigerian Consortium for Social and Technical Sciences, Daurama waits.

Ify stops short, standing at the top of the broad marble steps while Daurama stands with arms folded beside the sleek, bulletproof van that will take her from school to her quarters. Normally, Daren waits for her after school and they walk through the streets or spend time afterward in the parks. Sometimes, he even takes her to the top of the Millennium Tower in the center of Abuja. But the sight of Daurama means that Daren must still be angry with her.

Sullen, she makes her way down the steps. Before she reaches the van, Daurama has the door opened, then climbs in after Ify and slams it shut.

"You're late," Daurama says. It is probably the most that Daren's sister has spoken to her in years. Ify realizes with a start that they are rarely in the same room. If Daren and his sister are together, Ify always catches Daurama just as she's leaving. She could never bring herself to ask Daren why she hated her.

"I'm sorry," Ify murmurs. She looks out the window as the city passes them by.

Suddenly, the van stops. Without a word, Daurama reaches under her seat and pulls out what Ify realizes is a rolled-up prayer rug. When the door opens, Ify hears the chanting, then the door shuts, and Daurama vanishes. Ify climbs on her seat to peer through the window at Daurama facing eastward, knees on the rug, encased in a translucent tent hastily erected by her guards. With a start, Ify realizes what time it is.

She fumbles underneath her own seat but comes up empty. Her heart sinks. That chanting, broadcast from the loudspeakers all around Abuja: the call to prayer. How could she have missed it?

Her heart races as she scrambles to find a substitute rug. She's still searching by the time the door opens and Daurama climbs back in. Daren's sister has the look of someone who has just woken from a peaceful nap. She even looks Ify in the eye and smiles.

Daurama places the folded rug back underneath her seat and keeps that smile on her face as the ride resumes. In one hand, she holds a string of beads that she thumbs through absently. Somehow, the expression Daurama wears unsettles Ify. It reminds her of something—someone—from long ago. She barely remembers, but she knows she's seen that look before.

"What were you whispering just now?" Ify asks, then silently chastises herself for interrupting whatever peace Daurama has found.

"Allahu akbar."

An instinct to fear that phrase arises in Ify. Long ago, when she was a War Girl, she was taught that this was what savage Nigerians said before they killed you. It's what they screamed before bloodshed. And, for so long, Ify could only see it coming out of mouths contorted by rage, twisted by hate. The mouths of monsters. But since arriving in Abuja, she's heard it constantly. Whenever the elderly dorm prefect stretches in the evening and makes her way down the hallways of the building to make sure all the girls are asleep as they should be. Whenever the Super Eagles score a goal. One time when Daren went animal-watching with Ify and they happened upon an unAugmented deer and her young.

Daurama still has that dreamy gaze in her eyes when she continues. "I first consciously heard those words when I was a child. Maybe five years old. My mother prayed in front of me. When she kissed the ground, she did it with her whole body. So filled with love. She would come up, whisper it, then gently kneel again. Her nose would touch the prayer rug, and I remember thinking it tickled her." Her smile widens. "It was so graceful."

"That's beautiful," Ify says, wondering if, instead, she should say, *Allahu akbar*.

"But that is the first time I *remember* hearing it, not the first time I heard it."

"When was the first time you heard it?"

"When I first came into the world. Those were the first words my father whispered into my ear." Her gaze focuses on Ify, and it's filled with love. "As I'm sure your father whispered it into yours."

When the van comes to a stop, Ify is still staring slack-jawed at Daurama. So many questions dart through her brain. *Who is this woman, and what has she done with Daurama?*

The older woman climbs out, and Ify sees that they've arrived at the library. That's right. The Colony Placement Exams are in a few months. She has to study. But the shock from Daurama's words still hasn't left her.

"Don't worry," Daurama says by the open door. "My brother is not angry with you. He is just busy. He sends his love."

Just as Daurama's about to leave, Ify calls out, "Daurama!"

She stops and raises an eyebrow.

"I want to go on hajj. With you and Daren." Is this what Daurama had been waiting for? To see that Ify really believed? That she no longer prayed to the gods of the Biafrans? Is that it? She realizes that it is not a small thing to want, to wait for. To see conversion happen in a person. To know for certain that they share your faith, this quiet, understated part of your being. *Yes, I am a proud Muslim*, she wants to tell Daurama. She wants to shout it. But, instead, she waits.

"Sure, sister," Daurama says. "I must leave for some time. But as soon as I return from my next mission, we will prepare. And you can finally make your first hajj."

Sure, sister. Those two words stay with Ify the entire rest of the afternoon. She isn't able to study a single lesson.

"Allahu akbar," she whispers into her tablet, grinning. Glowing.

CHAPTER

25

Onyii lies prone by a window in the stone tower of a bombed-out building. She has been lying there for a long time. In the memory, she's a child. Barely ten years old.

She rises to stretch her legs and glance out the window at the abandoned street below. Night has fallen, casting everything in a dark blue hue. When she hears footsteps from down the hall, she scrambles to the window and puts her eye to the scope of her sniper rifle. She is not supposed to have left her post, even for a second. And when Adaeze enters, Onyii tenses to see if her handler will have noticed she spent a few moments away from her post.

Onyii lies on the floor of the tower with her sniper rifle before her and with Adaeze behind her. *I will get it right.* This is her chance.

Their target, a prominent Nigerian official, leaves the building, having snuck out and avoided his own security detail, probably for a breath of fresh air. This is her chance.

Onyii adjusts the zoom and thinks of Adaeze and hopes that when she finishes, she will see that look on Ada's face that she saw when she first joined her as a soldier. A soft, warm, proud smile.

Onyii pulls the trigger.

The sound of the dream-gunshot raises Onyii from her slumber.

It takes her nearly a minute to calm her breathing. Sweat chills her skin. She searches for her satchel and fiddles around the pockets for that little vial of Chukwu, but when she finds it, she tips it and sees nothing but emptiness. Angry, she tosses the vial across the room.

Already, Onyii feels antsy, like she's spent too much time standing still. She realizes, rising to her feet, that she misses the inside of her mech. The glowing screens, the feel of the gearshifts in her hands, the hum and whirr and groan of the metal moving around her. She closes her eyes and wraps herself in her arms and can feel the warmth running through her body. She feels like she herself has begun to glow. The moment passes, and she stands alone in the too-quiet room. With a sigh, she slips into a pair of combat pants and leaves.

She has finally mastered the compound's hallways and corridors, and, pretty soon, she arrives at Chinelo's office. Light spills out from under the closed doors. A different set of guards stands outside the office.

"Is she in?" Onyii asks, and one of them nods. "She taking visitors?"

The two look at each other, trying to figure out what to do next.

Onyii wants to push past them, assert herself, but she's tired of fighting for now.

One of the guards puts a finger to his earpiece. Onyii expects him to say something, but his eyes glaze over, and she realizes he's transmitting information. Then the guard's eyes return to normal. "You can go," he says, softly. He presses the keypad, and the door whisks open.

Onyii is on her guard as she walks through, ready to defend herself, but Chiamere stands by the far wall, arms folded. He stares at Onyii when she enters.

Chinelo has a holo out in front of her, a rotating three-dimensional display of a launch site, it looks like. "Can't sleep?"

"Never could," Onyii says back.

The 3-D map vanishes, and Chinelo looks up. "How do you like him?"

"Agu?"

"Yeah."

Onyii smirks and scratches the back of her head. "He's learning how to play the piano."

Chinelo squints at Onyii for a second before saying, "Is he, now?" She folds up the projector tablet on her desk, then walks to the front and leans against the edge. She folds her arms just like her abd. "Do you want to see him in action?" When Onyii raises an eyebrow, Chinelo continues. "It's only been a few weeks since you got here. Normally, I'd wait for the bonding period to finish between a sister and her abd before bringing them into combat, but we just received intel on something big. And we can't afford to wait."

Anticipation thrills through Onyii. She tries to steady her voice and not let it show. "What is it?"

"We just got word that the Nigerians are expecting a shipment of mechs from the British Space Colonies. They'll be dropping off somewhere along the coast and heading inland from there.

The Commonwealth Colonies are supposed to be neutral in this conflict. But they've been meeting with the Nigerian military. One of their best pilots has apparently been leading the deal. Sucking at the white man's teat. If we can do this raid right, we can expose them and maybe get other nations on our side. And we can steal their hardware while we're at it. What we don't take, we destroy." She frowns at Onyii in silence for several seconds. "You ready?"

And Onyii knows that Chinelo is asking if she'll stop snorting those minerals. If she'll get herself clean and put herself back together. If she can keep the bad thoughts and bloody memories at bay long enough to work with others and get this mission done. Chinelo doesn't need the Demon of Biafra for this one. She needs Onyii.

This is her chance.

I will get it right.

"Yes."

■ ■ ■ ■ ■

It doesn't take long to summon the others, and an hour later, they are all seated at a massive table in the center of the briefing room connected to Chinelo's office. On it glows a digital map of the world. Chinelo stands at the head of the table and swipes across the touchboard in the head console. The vision zooms into a map of Nigeria, green where the Nigerians rule, red for the poisoned irradiated zone of the Redlands that winds like a jagged wound across Nigeria's middle, and yellow for the portion of southeast Nigeria under Biafran control.

Though Chinelo's voice is low, it carries through the room.

"The mission is to gather and broadcast intelligence about the mechs sent from the Commonwealth Colonies, show proof that the neutrality they speak of is a farce and they've been helping the Nigerian government commit genocide against the Biafrans, steal what mechs we can, then get out of there as fast as we can."

The young women lean against the consoles lining the walls while their abd stand beside them, eyes glazed as they download information. It's unnerving to look at, the abd downloading scenarios and calculating probabilities while Chinelo speaks. It reminds Onyii that, at the end of the day, these boys are machines.

"Makoko needs to be awake for this plan to even get off the ground," Chinelo says before swiping again at the tablet. The image zooms in further on a slum just outside of Lagos. Makoko is a small water city with shanties jutting out from the mainland. The buildings rest on rusty metal stilts sunk into Lagos Lagoon's muddy bed. In the hologram that rises out of the table screen, people crowd along the wooden walls, waxy with wear, of those buildings. Others travel from their schools to their homes and their shops in canoes. Hawkers stand in their own boats, shouting up at people walking across the rickety bridges with their wares in their outstretched hands.

"It won't be as noisy as Lagos," Chinelo continues, "but it should be enough motion and busyness to mask us. They still use generators there. We'll fly low and settle along the coast in a little enclave here, not too far from the city. There's enough brush to hide us. Then we'll disable the mechs. We won't be going back to them. We'll get to Makoko, and from there, we'll head inland to the Okpai oil fields."

Ginika unfolds her arms. The half-sun tattoo on her shoulder glows blue in the light from the hologram. "Why not just go through the forest?" When she points at the table map, the image of Makoko falls away, and they're staring at a two-dimensional image of southeastern Nigeria again. "That way, we avoid detection."

From a nearby corner, Obioma says, "Too close to Lagos, which is still a Nigerian stronghold. They still hold too much of the coastline."

Her abd breaks out of his trance to say, "And there are many shorthorns in that forest. And two-fangs and Agba bears."

"If they are a problem for the Nigerians," Obioma finishes, "they will be a problem for us."

Chinelo looks from Ginika to Obioma, then returns her gaze to the map, shifting to the Okpai oil fields. She pulls up a map of what looks like an abandoned structure with drilling towers rusty from disuse. Trailers fill the field at random. Then a larger multistory building connects outward to two large octagonal structures held up out of the water by struts at each corner.

Kesandu brushes away the shock of hair covering her eye. "Where are they hiding the special mechs?"

"Somewhere underground," Onyii says, realizing belatedly that she said the words out loud. "The map's incomplete, isn't it?" Onyii meets Chinelo's gaze, and it feels almost like a challenge. This is the first time someone has pointed out a hole in her plans.

"We have no idea what the lower level looks like," Chinelo confirms. "We'll be going in blind."

The air grows tense between them. Suddenly, Onyii barks out a laugh. Everyone looks at her in confusion, even Agu. But she palms her stomach and quiets down. "That is just how I like it," she says at last. "This plan of yours was starting to sound too safe. You should know by now that I don't do *safe*."

The others smirk. Their expressions seem to say, *Neither do we.*

"All right," Chinelo says, turning off the display. "We head out before dawn. Everybody, get some rest."

As they stream out, Chinelo goes ahead of Onyii. When she reaches the entrance, she looks back at Onyii with a question in her eyes: *Was that challenge to my authority real?* Onyii stares back, then winks. *You were starting to sound too full of yourself, sister,* she thinks. *You are still the girl who jokes about how badly I used to smell. Don't forget that.*

CHAPTER 26

Ify sits in the balcony while, below, the men—scientists and lawmakers and government advisers, all with their specific colored stripe at their right shoulder—surround the large table at the center of the room. Another one of Daren's security conferences. There are very few people with Ify in these top rows and only a few more in benches toward the entrance to this particular hall. Today's session is a boring one: climate control and forest fires. And, indeed, some of the government advisers sit against the wall with their heads bowed and their knees crossed, their dangling feet bouncing and twisting idly to some music they're probably listening to in their half-sleep.

Daren is one of the only government officials standing. He takes position, arms folded on one side of the table, his back to Ify, while the scientists face him. Nervously, their gazes flit from Daren to the advisers lining the wall, as though they're unsure of whom they need to try harder to convince.

"But you see, that very rule mandating fire suppression is the problem," says a scientist with a light fuzz of gray on his otherwise bald head. "The landscape south of us is too complex, too diverse. Rising temperatures dry out the higher elevations.

Insects that harsh winters would normally kill survive and kill more trees, eating them from the inside out. And dead trees burn more easily than live ones."

"I still don't see any problem with the Sunrise Rule," says one of the ministers with a fez on his head. His robe is all white, almost blinding. He lounges in a chair by the wall, and his red-slippered foot bounces in and out of a beam of sunlight coming from a window above. "Any forest fire that breaks out, extinguish it by sunrise."

"And leave more dead trees on our mountains and near our towns like so much kindling!" The scientist, spectacles sliding down the bridge of his sweat-slick nose, turns to the table, pulls a tablet out of his coat, and inputs a sequence. A hologram rises from the table: a fire spreading like a knife scar at the bottom of the border with the Redlands. Flames silently lick the air. The hologram changes angles, and it looks as though the camera is flying through the blaze.

A drone must have taken this footage.

From this view, the fire looks suddenly real. The closeness of it. It reaches roadway, and Ify realizes that the fire has spread to more populated areas. Still sparse but not quite wilderness. And that's when they all see the maglev cars lining the road, made black and gray and calcified from having roasted. Shapes lie scattered on the road. Misshapen black lumps. They could have been anything. Or anyone.

The drone camera angles upward, and it appears as though fire has consumed everything, but then the drone shoots into the sky, and they watch everything from above.

With a single swipe of his tablet, the scientist wipes away the vision. "Before the Sunrise Rule, fire would regularly clear out the deadwood. Now all those trees are left to stand dead and skeletal, waiting for fire to smolder and reach them."

What do you think?

Ify starts. That voice. *Daren?*

You have a nasty habit when you get tired of drifting into other people's heads.

It's true. With her Accent on, every Augmented person within her network becomes a glowing node, and if she doesn't pay attention, she will float toward them, like a moth drawn to flame. If she's not careful, she can drift straight past the barriers put up to protect a person's brain, accessing all of their information, everything that makes them them. Ify smirks. *They shouldn't leave their doors open.*

Daren's shoulders rise with a single chuckle, but he doesn't look her way. Instead, he faces the table where, just a moment earlier, fire had roared. *What do you think?*

People choose to live there. And they know the land.

Daren nods, then raises his head to face the scientist. "Many of these people did not heed the evacuation order until it was too late. They decided long ago that they would not be scared every time a plume of smoke rises in the air."

The scientist has a pleading look in his eyes. "But, sir, not everywhere is meant for human habitation."

Ify frowns at the scientist from her seat in the balcony. *How does he know where those people are meant or aren't meant to live?*

"Maybe they are fire-adapted," Daren says. He walks over to the table and touches some of the buttons on the console closest to him. It's the aftermath of the firestorm. There are still people there, crawling out of holes they had dug or bunkers they had prepared, some of them emerging from desert perilously close to the Redlands but far enough from the fire to guarantee safety. And slowly they pick up and put their lives back together. "Maybe they are working not to exclude fire but rather to learn to live with it."

A transmission buzzes over his private channel. Ify's still inside his head. She can still see everything. She's about to disconnect, but Daren, forgetting that she remains inside his head, opens the message.

"Sir, there's been an attack," says the voice on the other end. "An oil outpost off the coast. In the Delta region. They have hostages."

Ify gasps. This is not what she expected. But she can't turn away. Not now.

Do we have surveillance images?

A holoscreen appears before Daren's face and fills with a series of images that are almost entirely black. The images enhance their resolution, then zoom in, then change their brightness. They show figures clad in all black manning positions along walkways circling the massive octagonal buildings propped up by beams. A wide view of the structure reveals nearby oil derricks. Mechs face out from the shore toward the water. Another set of holos reveals more figures inside the facility, frozen in mid-run on metal walkways, standing guard with their high-powered rifles outside generator rooms; then, in one small space, several of them form a circle around men bound and gagged, smushed together so that their backs face each other. Some of them are unconscious, others bleeding.

In another room, darker with fuzzier resolution, the silhouette of two giant mechs, so tall their heads vanish in the shadows.

Igwe. The word swims across Ify's consciousness. Igwe. Those are the mechs Daren had been talking about with the oyinbo.

Along a walkway by the cockpit of the first Igwe are two figures frozen in a crouched run. He zooms in on one of them, enhances the photo, then zooms in further.

Ify's blood goes cold. She leans forward in her seat, squinting closer at the hologram.

That face.

"No. You're supposed to be dead," Ify whispers.

Even with the new machinery covering half her face, even with one eye replaced by cybernetics, even with the metal having grown from her shoulder all the way to her head like it is colonizing her, Ify recognizes that face.

Onyii.

Her sister.

The transmission ends so suddenly that it leaves Ify in a daze. Her Accent shuts off. The absence of Daren's mind stings, then numbs. A shiver runs through her.

She comes to just in time to see Daren rush out of the hall.

CHAPTER
27

They enter forest past the Makoko slum in the early morning. Agu shifts the pack on his shoulders, grunting beneath its weight before marching forward through the knee-high elephant grass. Trees with fat leaves weighed down by morning dew tower over them. Shadows move across their field of vision. Onyii has her mechanical eye turned to heat detection so she can better see the bodies of living things they come across. And better eliminate all that stands in her way. Agu cranes his neck to see Onyii detaching herself from the shadows almost a dozen paces ahead.

They reach the precipice of the forest. From there, they can see the east wing of the oil processing plant. It has the look of an abandoned city. Something left behind. But there's precious material in there. Material precious enough for the Nigerians to hide behind this smokescreen. They know it. They've gone over the intel, verified the sourcing, cross-checked it where they were able. And they know that the Nigerians are not above just this sort of trickery. They are arrogant enough to leave something so valuable so unguarded because they think the Biafrans will fall for it. But underestimating Biafra will be the death of them.

Agu swings his pack to his front and takes out and unfolds the tripod for his rifle. Then he pulls out the weapon, clicks on a scope, and adds an extension to the barrel. He lies on his stomach in the wet moss and props the extended barrel on the tripod's catch. In another moment, he is all set up. And Onyii knows from his training that he is capable of lying like that, unmoving but completely alert, for at least half a day. For now, they just need to provide cover until the coast is clear. Half a minute in, his fingers dance on the rifle grip and on the barrel. Absently playing a piano that isn't there.

Even though Onyii is supposed to continue facing the forest to protect them, she takes cover with him in the bush. Tallgrass hides them. And she knows that, with normal, unenhanced sight, no one could see that two bodies lie hidden against the ground, ready to strike.

The war is nearly done. What are your plans for after? Onyii asks Agu.

For nearly a minute, Agu is silent. Then he says, *I don't know.* He adjusts the zoom on his scope, then switches it back, and Onyii knows he's just giving his hands something to do, either to keep his fingers limber or because he is nervous. Do synths get nervous? But when Agu speaks again, his voice is different, if only slightly. *I am having memories. Of playing the piano. There are people around me, listening. Sometimes, there is only one person. But this person too is smiling. They are liking it when I played the piano. I think I am liking it too.*

After a moment's shock, Onyii smiles at the thought. She had just been following Kesandu's suggestion for making Agu a better killing machine. It had not occurred to her that before Agu was made into a synth, he had had a whole other life. A feeling of pride, followed closely by gratitude, swims through her. If she has connected him to his past somehow, and maybe made him happy, then she has done a good thing. For once, she does not care whether or not this will make Agu better at covert operations.

But those memories are false.

Onyii starts.

They are implants inserted into my core processing unit to help me have more range of emotion and make me better in espionage operation. As abd, I am having training not only for combat missions but also for subterfuge, and my creators are believing I need to pretend to be a full red-blooded human to the greatest extent possible. He pauses. It is the most he has spoken at once in all the time Onyii has known him. *After the war, I will serve in whatever capacity you see fit.* Then, from him, silence. A wire emerges from the outlet at the back of his neck, and he pulls it out with his free hand, then plugs it into the outlet by the chamber of his rifle. Now what his rifle sees, he sees. The rifle is no longer an extension of him, but he an extension of it. Just another weapon.

Onyii's comms buzz. She blinks away tears she had not realized were forming. She hears Kalu say, "My position is blocked by foliage." Then she digs into her pack and pulls out a mound of putty.

Muscle memory takes over, and her fingers rip off a piece, then mold it into a small doll. With her nail, she digs small crescents into its face for eyes. Then she pulls a cord out of the outlet at the back of her neck and plugs in. Blood and fluid rich with nanobots flow into the putty, filling it out. Like DNA inserted right into its form. After a moment, its extremities wiggle. Then the lumps become small arms and legs. It squirms in her hand, and she sets it on the ground. In short order, four eto-eto join the one wiggling its stubby arms in the air. Once they are all lined up, they nod at her mental command and fan out, beaming all the information they encounter into Onyii's tech. Radiation levels, heat signatures. Footprints that glow in her sights to reveal patrol patterns.

She grabs the loose end of her cord, then connects it with a second outlet just behind Agu's ear. That way, she is able to beam the information she receives to him, and he can then relay it to the other abd. As soon as the network is established with Onyii as the router, Onyii notes the change in the air. She doesn't detect any movement from where they are all stationed, but she can tell that enemy patrols are dropping, taken out by the other abd.

"Finished," Agu says.

They pack up and hurry, moving in silence over deflated soccer balls and broken wooden boards that look like they'd once been fashioned into something you played a game with. Maybe, once upon a time, children came here to play. Or they came to siphon off oil from the nearby pipelines. Onyii can tell from simply sniffing the air that no child has run through this dirt in some time.

By now, the Makoko slum outside Lagos must be humming to life. Pretty soon, it will be fully awake.

Onyii and Agu find shelter near a small trailer, and Agu pulls out a small hard drive that unfolds into a tablet. Onyii rises slowly to peek inside the trailer's windows, scan for activity with her rifle slung behind her back and her pistol in her hands. Nothing. Through the smudged window, she sees a few scattered pieces of tech, some retail electronics, what looks like a music player. But no one has lived here recently.

Small shapes wiggle in the distance. Onyii's eto-eto. They scramble through the scrub brush and into her arms, where she deflates them, then puts the clay back in her duffel bag.

A hologram map rises out of Agu's tablet. It shows the floor plan, then breaks open to reveal multiple floors, but then, close to the tablet's surface, static.

I can't plug into any of the surveillance cameras in the facility, says Golibe over their connection. *Closed circuit.* Which means no piggybacking.

Agu folds his tablet and puts it away. Onyii is about to dash ahead of him when he grabs her wrist.

"It is too quiet," he whispers.

Onyii frowns. "That is because they want us to ignore this place."

He shakes his head. "Too quiet even for that."

"What do your sensors detect?"

He frowns at the earth. "Is not my sensors. Is something else. Deeper." Instinct. His human parts.

She kneels down to meet his eye level. "Hey. We will survive this. We will complete the mission. We will expose the Commonwealth Colonies, and we will force a ceasefire. Then there will be peace and no more of this."

"This does not matter to me." His voice is no longer even. Something is fighting inside him. "If you tell me to fight, I fight. If you tell me to kill, I kill." He's struggling to find the words he wants. Then he settles. "I will protect you." And that seems to calm him. "I will protect you," he says again, almost like a mantra he needs to repeat to himself.

"You will protect me." It's not a question when it comes from Onyii's lips. She feels her heart lift. That's when she realizes what just happened. Her whole life, she has fought for others, protected others. Agu is a child, but he is willing to die to protect her. He wants nothing more than for her to stay alive. She wants to pat his head or scratch his scalp, but she realizes the gesture will likely confuse him. However, she does let herself smile. A fleeting twist of the lips before she turns and leads him to the shelter of another trailer, then to a large shipping crate stranded in the middle of the field, and finally past the rusty smokestacks that tower over them to a side entrance hidden in the shadows of a metal staircase.

They stand on both sides of the hidden door, rifles at the ready. Agu's fingers detach and plug into the keypad by the door. The lights blink rapidly over the keypad, the door whispers open, and she charges in.

CHAPTER
28

Ify races out of the conference hall and winds her way down the halls until she's out in the bustling streets. She doesn't see Daren anywhere. People walk around like normal. It's early in the morning. They need to shop and eat and flirt and go to school just like they always do. That's when Ify remembers that what she saw is secret. It was stolen from inside Daren's comms. Hacked. That, in and of itself, could be a punishable offense. But Daren would understand. He would always understand. Ify has always just wanted to be close to him, to understand him. She shouldn't have heard it. She should have disconnected. But he had let her in. *That is what love is*, she tries to tell herself as she races to the building where the officer corps holds its meetings.

She punches in the code to the front gate and enters, then remembers she can't look watchful. Without an escort, however, she draws suspicious glances from the guards at the front gate.

"I need to find Daren," she says to the impassive soldiers.

They answer her with silence.

"I am—"

"We know who you are," one of the soldiers cuts her off.

They don't even sweat, which is how Ify knows they are Augments with cooling systems built into their cybernetically altered bodies. "This building is forbidden to anyone who does not have the required security clearance." There's a hint of a sneer on his lips, like he can't believe Ify's audacity in even coming here.

But how many times has she walked into this very building? Seen its halls and wandered its corridors and studied her lessons while Daren took his meetings in secured rooms nearby?

"Officer Diallo is away at the moment," says the other soldier, this one kinder.

He must be on his way out of Abuja already. But maybe he's still somewhere in the city.

"Thank you," she says absently, before hurrying back the way she came. A Terminal. She needs a Terminal.

She turns on her Accent, and the world glows with gold thread lining every edge, connecting every node in the city of Abuja. Everyone connected to the network is revealed to her. And among the nodes are the surveillance orbs moving slowly along every boulevard, every alleyway, scanning every rooftop. Guiding them are the Watchers in the towers dotted throughout the city. If she can access the same tech as one of those Watchers, she'll be able to find Daren.

In a few minutes, Ify finds the nearest tower, an obelisk-like structure made of gleaming metal and transparent flexiglas, like an old-fashioned watch whose glass surface reveals all the gears and motors within, the intricate latticework that makes the whole thing tick. At the tower's back is a lift, a transparent cylinder that comes down around her. She puts her thumb to the keypad, praying that her status as a Sentinel will grant her access. Sweat slicks her thumb so it slips, and she wipes it on her shirt and tries again. "Come on, come on." She's not officially a Watcher, only sometimes involved in the surveillance operations of Abuja, but she is close to Daren. And being close to Daren has gotten her into more places than anything else she's done. The keypad blinks green, and the chamber swivels open. She boards a platform that provides her a view of the entire quarter as it raises her higher and higher.

Her heart races, completely at odds with the placid scene before her, the people milling around the Sahad Stores and hanging out by the Millennium Tower in the city center. If only they knew what she knows . . .

When she gets to the top, the opposite side of the cylinder opens, and she passes through a gateway to the station where a Watcher sits before a Terminal with a helmet on, connecting him by way of wires to the fiber-optic cables that wind their way through the tower and patch him into every surveillance orb. Ify needs that helmet.

She doesn't want to disturb the Watcher, but she's running out of time. So she walks to the Watcher's side with purpose and puts a hand on the young boy's shoulder. He doesn't seem to register any surprise. Maybe he's that locked in, but Ify senses beneath her fingers a tension in the boy's back.

"Shift change," she says with a small catch in her voice. "They are running tests in Katampe Exterior Zone and need another Watcher to provide backup."

Ify expects resistance, expects the Watcher to push back, to ask her when the order was given out. She expects him to check on the Watcher in the Katampe Exterior Zone and see that nothing is amiss. It's a stupid, simple lie, but Ify can think of nothing else.

A moment of silence passes. Up here, everything is quiet. She cannot even hear the wind whipping the Nigerian flags scattered throughout the central zone. Then comes the sound of wires unhooking. The boy slides the helmet off his head, and his afro puffs out. He wears flowing green-and-white-striped robes over a black bodysuit, and when he stands to his full height, he's even smaller than Ify.

"Okay," he says, smiling. As soon as he unplugs, he's a kid again. He hands Ify the helmet, then scampers away.

Stunned at her luck, Ify blinks after he vanishes.

She settles into the seat, then fits the helmet over her braids. She doesn't need to connect, so the wires in the floor stay where they are. But she activates her Accent, and suddenly, the entire world goes white. It's too much. The helmet amplifies the reach of her Accent, so that where, before, she could only see what was in front of her, she can now see in all directions.

Her body seizes. There are no safeguards against all the information crashing into her. Every smell, every flash of color, every murmured phrase or piece of chatter. It's too much. She grips the edges of her armrests, her nails digging in. Blood leaks from her nose.

She hadn't erected any filters before plugging in, and now the entirety of the city's sensory outputs beams directly into her skull. If she doesn't stop this quick, she'll lose consciousness. It'll eat away her brain, fry her neurons, and she'll be a vegetable.

IP addresses flash before her, glow, then wink out of existence. Hundreds at a time, thousands per second. She needs to find Daren. A single pulse widens her range. The orbs allow her to go even farther, taking her Accent's abilities with her. Where the orbs see and smell and hear, she too can see and smell and hear. Suddenly, nodes pop up in a line through the city. Places where Daren logged in or connected. Like footsteps. Closer. She leaps from one location to the next, fast as lightning, until she finds empty space to the south. He's heading south. In a mech.

She focuses and makes one final leap, bounding over acres and acres and acres of sparsely networked land to find Daren leading a formation of mechs flying low over forest. They're heading for the oil derricks. They're heading for Onyii.

His signature appears in front of her face, and she latches on to it.

Ify's chest heaves. When she raises a hand to wipe the blood from her nose, her fingers tremble. Then her eyelids grow heavy. Oh no. What's happening? Her hand falls to her side. She can feel her body going limp. *What's happening to me? No. No no no no no.*

As she goes under, she sees before her a blinking red light, tracking over the electronic map of Nigeria accessed by her Accent. She tries to send Daren a message through his comms, the most important message she has ever written, one that could save lives. But she can't remember what it is.

"Daren," she whispers aloud, not realizing it. "Daren."

She goes limp.

CHAPTER 29

They open the door and enter a storage room filled with unmarked crates and discarded bodysuits. Air filtration masks hang from hooks in the wall. The dust is so thick that each step leaves a footprint. Onyii adjusts her mechanical eye to account for the new darkness and sees no heat signatures. They have to find a way underground. She tests the floor with her heel. Everything sounds solid.

A door in the far wall opens out onto a corridor.

They proceed as a pair, then Onyii points one way, taps Agu twice on the shoulder, then proceeds the other way, and they break away at the corner to regroup at the opposite corner. As Onyii moves, she switches to her pistol and holds her knife at the ready. In close quarters, her rifle will only get in her way. She hears a pained grunt and a thud, but calmly continues her circuit. When she finds Agu again, he's stooped over the unconscious Nigerian security officer dressed in all black with a Nigerian flag patch on his left shoulder. A cord leads from the back of Agu's neck into the back of the guard's. Agu's eyes glaze over as he downloads the man's contents, then disconnects. The cord slithers back into the outlet in Agu's neck, and the seal closes over the opening like a scab healing. Together, he and Onyii carry the body back into the storage room, where it will collect dust out of sight.

Once back in the hallways, Agu leads Onyii to the door he found and uses the code from the earlier keypad to open it.

They step out onto metal grating that rings the giant circular expanse before them, at the center of which stands a gigantic pillar. Agu crouches, aims his rifle, and fires. Just as Onyii comes down to one knee, she sees two guards, one ahead and one to their right, collapse. She aims her rifle up at the ceiling and scans for another walkway, then they both look down to see absolutely nothing. Along the wall, there are four lights glowing in metal consoles. There are no ladders, no obvious way of getting up or down to the other walkways. The consoles must control the platform. That has to be their way down.

They go to the first, and Agu puts his hand to it. He focuses as his fingers extend and break into segments that type a lightning-fast sequence into the keys of the console. The blue-and-red wheels above it spin until their red parts all angle in different directions. Something unseen unlocks. He must've stolen the code from the guard when he hacked the body. A loud hiss sounds, followed by steam. But they can't see anything changing. They look at each other before proceeding to the next one. Agu does the same. The wheels form a different pattern. Immediately the floor opens out beneath Onyii. She falls, but, a moment later, something jerks her up. Agu has his hand wrapped tightly around her wrist. She watches her pistol and knife fall into the cavernous depths. They seem to fall forever, until Onyii hears a tiny splash.

Agu pulls Onyii back up, and she comes to one knee to catch

her breath. Slowly, they shimmy to the next console. Agu hacks it, then more hissing rises from below. They proceed the same way to the last console.

This time, when Agu finishes, a giant rumbling fills the space.

They raise their rifles at the ready. Out of the water far below rises a giant pillar with an enclosed platform on top of it like a helmet. Glass rings its middle, rusted metal running along its top and its bottom. Water slides off of it in mini rivers. It comes to a stop when it meets their level. Then its front opens and a walkway haltingly unfolds to reach them. Rust and wear line the metal walkway, but Onyii and Agu hurry across it in case it decides to betray them like the other walkway.

Inside, Agu looks for another console or something to control their descent, but, before he can find anything, the front opening closes, breaking off the walkway, and the chamber starts to descend into the water.

The walls rattle all around them, so hard that Onyii's teeth chatter. The two of them hold on to the guardrails sticking out of the wall. The air pressure changes once they go underwater.

The container grinds along rails. She can hear it struggling, then it jams into place and begins to lift.

It rises only a short way before it stops. Agu takes a moment to get to his feet, and Onyii rushes to his side to prop him upright. For a second, he rests his body against hers, then he becomes alert and battle-ready again. Onyii wipes the blood from her nose, then nods, and, guns at the ready, they wait for the container door to open.

The door groans open, shedding water. A stream of it rushes in to fill the container up to their ankles. *Oh no.* They're not all the way above water. Then the door jams. More water rushes in, then Onyii realizes what's happening. The rails moving their container have stopped working. If they don't get out soon, the whole container will fill with water and very well might break from its rails and submerge them completely.

She slings her rifle behind her and splashes through the water to the door. Already, it's up to her thighs. She's able to slip her fingers through the opening and pull, but the door doesn't give at all. Agu joins her and they pull. Nothing. The water level rises and rises. Now her waist is completely underwater. Agu struggles to keep his feet planted on the ground. They pull.

Onyii's arms strain with the effort. She can feel her joints stretching to their snapping point. In her mind's eye, an image flashes: Agu's body floating facedown, lifeless, in the water. She grits her teeth, closes her eyes, but she slips in the water and falls. It's high enough now that she falls completely. When she gets upright again, it's up to Agu's neck. His face is firm and expressionless, but veins pulse at his temple with the effort. His whole body is being pushed to its limit.

A painful ripping sound, then a spray of gears and wires. Agu falls back into the water as blood and oil spill from his torn arm. Onyii pulls him close to her, his face against her chest as, using her metal arm, she pulls with all her strength. *I have to save him, I have to save him, I have to save him.*

The door groans, then slides all the way open.

One arm wrapped around her abd, Onyii swims out and finds the nearest ledge. When her fingers find purchase on the edge of the platform, she almost cries with joy. She pushes a stunned Agu onto it, then climbs up, soaked through.

Agu has his broken arm cradled across his chest and tries to sit up, but falls back down. Onyii pulls him to her and rests his head in her lap and, before she realizes what she's doing, softly shushes him. She rocks back and forth. When he tries to rise, she presses down on him. *Stay still. Rest. It'll be okay.* The thoughts whisper through her. Agu must hear them, because he calms.

"My arm," Agu whispers.

The skin is torn in places, and the gears that had served for joints just below his shoulder have come loose. Wiring bunches at the tears, some of it severed.

Onyii reaches for her bag, then realizes it's gone. It must have slipped off her in the container. And now it's unreachable. She pats her pockets, then opens one on her vest to pull out a small, wet tube of MeTro.

Agu's arm hangs from his shoulder, the skin ragged, the inner machinery exposed. She holds it together with one hand, puts the MeTro tube in her mouth, and fishes in her vest pockets for more tools. She manages to hold the small implements in her fingers as they unfold. Her fingers shake. She closes her eyes and wills them to be still. Never before has she been nervous in the field, especially when it has come to caring for a wounded comrade. But now her heart races, and she struggles to keep the images and the worry from filling her head.

The machines in her hand whirr to life. She goes to work, drilling and fusing, snipping wires where they need to be snipped, wrapping others together with a small band, connecting them to circuits, hardening over singed outlets, all work she has done on her own arm a thousand times. When it looks like Agu's arm is sufficiently repaired, she pulls the skin together and squeezes out MeTro sealant along the tear, melding the break into scar tissue. Without knowing why, she leans forward and blows softly on his forehead. A memory comes to her: she did the same to Ify when monsoon season had given her a fever.

It takes a moment for Agu's breath to slow, but eventually, it returns to normal. He looks up at her. A smile ghosts across his face, then is gone. He sits up from her lap and tries to flex his hand into a fist. Some of the fingers refuse to move, others bend halfway but can't finish.

"Sister," he says, then with a finger of his good hand, he points.

Onyii follows his gaze and sees them.

Behind her, towering so high that their heads disappear in shadows, gigantic bipedal, humanoid machines, each painted a different color. Terrifying mobile suits, one of them with a mega rifle attached to a forearm, another with a massive staff clipped to its back, another still with bladed chains coiled on a wrist-catch. Onyii stares in awe.

The Igwe. This is what they are after.

With her mechanical eye, she zooms in and snaps photos of their features. The cockpit located in the torso, the advanced precision-targeting screens in their faces, their jet propulsion systems, the specs for each of their individual weapons, as well as the ammo caches attached to them, containing their bullets, their missiles, and the generators for their lasers. These are the things that could level entire villages, that could make Onyii's tiny mech look like a mosquito.

When she finishes, the connecting cord snakes out of its outlet at the back of her neck, and she plugs its loose end into the outlet at the back of Agu's neck.

She hears static, then a sharp whine, and disconnects. The damage to his arm must have short-circuited parts of his nervous system. Dread fills her stomach. He can't download her intel.

Onyii tries to connect remotely with the others but gets only static. They must be too far away. Or maybe the walls are too thick, blocking out any signal.

With no way back, they're trapped. Onyii looks around, then sees up above, on a landing, a console just like the one Agu had hacked in the other room. They race to it, and Agu puts his good hand to it. His fingers detach, and after a few seconds of fast typing, lights flare on in the underground hangar.

They hear the grinding of metal moving against metal, and water starts to rush in. Lights burst to life in the eyes of the Igwe. Now Onyii can see that thick cables connect them to the walls. A quick scan reveals the path to Onyii. A long, thin metal grating staircase that will bring them chest-level with the giant mechs. She and Agu race up the stairs and along the metal walkways until they each get to the cockpit of a different Igwe. When they get near enough, a slot on the torso unfurls, and inside lies the cushioned chair and the consoles and touchboards of a mech, a seat Onyii has not occupied in far too long.

She jumps into hers, and Agu follows suit.

Onyii feels as though she has leapt into the embrace of an old friend. Even though the text is in a language she does not understand and the controls are all in different places—the foot pedals, the gearshifts, the weapons board, the jet activators— her muscle memory takes over, and it's as though she's been piloting this mobile suit all her life.

The water rises over the platform on which the Igwe stand.

A new set of controls glows at Onyii, and she calls up an informational description on her screen. "They can transform," she breathes. She inputs a sequence on the touchboard, and the Igwe folds in upon itself until it turns into a massive robot horseshoe crab. It's as though electricity runs through Onyii's veins. She can't remember the last time she was this excited.

Agu's face appears on her comms screen, and she taps a sequence of keys that transmits the instructions to him. On her screen, she watches his mech do the same.

Together, they plunge into the water.

They follow what appears to be a tunnel. Doors open as they approach, before they finally find the open sea. When they break the surface of the water, the fog lifts from inside Onyii's head. She can see and feel the rest of the world now. The bottom door of the Igwe storage room closing is a distant sound.

Onyii establishes a connection with Chinelo, but as soon as Chinelo's comms recognize her, Onyii hears the muffled sound of automatic gunfire. It's coming from inside the facility.

Chinelo allows Onyii into her comms, and through the bees Chinelo has deployed for surveillance, Onyii sees the aftermath of the shooting: one of the abd, Golibe, nursing a bleeding arm; a worker in a jumpsuit on the ground with a pool of blood spreading beneath her; then a group of other workers of different shades and skin tones huddled together with their wrists and ankles bound and with gags in their mouths.

"The dead one is a Nigerian," Chinelo explains. "Named Daurama. She was an officer and soldier for the Nigerians, guarding these workers and running patrols of the facility. When they discovered we were here, they beamed out a distress signal. She tried to attack Ginika, but Golibe put her down."

"And the hostages?" Onyii asks.

"Internationals. Some of them are from the European Colonial

Bloc. From space. It turns out more countries than the British have been providing secret aid to the Nigerians."

"Let us go!" shouts one of the hostages after he shrugs his gag loose. "We have nothing to do with—"

One of the abd silences him with the butt of a rifle.

Chiamere approaches Chinelo and says something to her that Onyii can't hear.

Then Chinelo says to Onyii, "We have a problem. The Nigerians are coming."

Onyii turns to face their way back. Already, on the distant shoreline, a dozen Green-and-White ground mechs glow blindingly in the light of the midday sun.

CHAPTER
30

It feels like so long ago, but Ify remembers every detail. She is sitting in a chair with blinding lights pointed right at her face. Someone has come and put a brush to her cheeks and her forehead, then a small pad to smear on some chemicals. When she sees the question in Ify's eyes, she says it's to help with the lighting. Someone else brushes the back of her neck, while a third person tries to straighten her dirty brown shirt, the shirt she has not changed out of since she was captured. Rescued. That is what she is supposed to call it now. Her rescue.

She looks for Daren and for Daurama, but they are nowhere to be seen. Maybe they are in another room.

The lights are too bright, but a woman in a Colony-style suit sits down on a hovering chair across from Ify and crosses her legs. People busy themselves around this woman too, brushing her cheeks and blotting her forehead, and she acts like they're not even there.

"Can you spray her?" the woman asks, and Ify knows she means her. "They can see and hear her, but they can't smell her, and I shouldn't have to either."

Ify wants to tell the woman that if she'd had the chance to

bathe since she was held in that tiny recovery room—little more than a cell—and before she was given her small meal and before she was shuttled all around this strange new city with no one to guide her, then she would have. And she wants to call the woman a rude name, but she can't think of any. Words fail her.

She hopes Daren is all right. She hasn't seen him since she left the hospital. Since the doctors said she'd recovered from her injuries. That plane crash comes back to her in a rush of memories: the explosion, the spinning, Daurama grabbing her by the neck and threatening her, Daren calming her down, Daren wrapping Ify in a blanket then opening a door and pushing her through, spinning, spinning, and more spinning, then a pain greater than any she had ever known.

Then she woke up in a hospital. With Daren in the bed next to hers.

In her hands is one of the paper cranes she'd scooped up from the floor and held close to her ever since. She can't let it go. If she loses it, maybe she'll lose Daren too. And she can't let that happen. She has to be strong for him. She has to be ready for when he recovers and comes back to her.

One of the helpers sprays a chemical all around Ify. She sneezes, but this seems to put the woman across from her at ease. The woman's face softens.

She leans forward. "My name is Safiya," she says softly, in a deep voice. "I'm going to be talking to you today about what you went through."

"Are you a doctor?" Ify asks.

Safiya chuckles. "No, I am a news reporter. We want your story to be broadcast to all of Nigeria, so they can know that one of theirs has been returned to them." She puts a hand out and touches Ify's knee. "You've been through so much. If, at any point, you want to stop, just let me know, and we can take a break."

Ify has to be strong, so she nods. *Okay.*

The woman leans back, satisfied. "Are we ready?" she asks the air. Then she looks at Ify, stares at her, and says, "We have with us today a young child rescued less than a month ago from Biafran terrorists in a daring mission launched by the Nigerian military. This child had been captured many years prior, after her family's gruesome murder at the hands of the terrorists, and now she has been returned home, thanks to the courage and intelligence of Nigerian Armed Forces mobile-suit pilots. This girl has been through unimaginable trauma but has decided to speak out about the horrors she endured in the wilderness. Here to tell her story is Ify."

CHAPTER
31

"We have to get back to them," Onyii says over her comms to Agu. On her screen, she sees Agu nod. The oil facility and the coastline are farther away than Onyii expected but still close enough that she can get a clear signal from the others. She uploads a direct feed from what Chinelo sees, and smaller screens pop up revealing what her bees detect via their surveillance capabilities. Onyii sees the hallways, the metal staircases, the walkways, the cavernous warehouse rooms, all of it.

"There is a space beneath the struts," Agu tells her. "We can hide our mechs there. My schematics of the oil facility reveal easy access to where the other sisters and the abd are located."

She accesses the floor plan stored in his CPU. And she sees it. From a position underneath one of the struts, they can climb a steep ladder that will bring them to the underside of one of the struts, then onto a walkway circling the octagon. Vents then will lead them to the exact room where the others hunker down with their hostages.

Onyii establishes a link with Chinelo. "Have they tried to communicate at all? Even to demand release of the hostages?"

Through Chinelo's eyes, Onyii sees the others shake their

heads. "Nothing but silence. They've sealed off every entrance and exit." There's no despair in her voice, nor futility. Instead, she speaks with grit and determination, and Onyii already knows that Chinelo means to go the distance. This girl who used to concern herself only with fixing things and with learning how to make their tech more efficient, how to keep the lights in the camp greenhouse from going out or how to make sure the water filtration systems worked perfectly—this girl is ready to die for her nation.

Onyii's heart sings with pride, but there is a note of despair in it. She does not wish that she could avoid death, only that someone as curious about the world as Chinelo might live to see peace. The wonders Chinelo could accomplish if the Nigerians were not on the cusp of annihilating them, Onyii can't even imagine.

Onyii and Agu arrive at the space beneath the strut where they are hidden from the aircraft and the aerial mechs above. Their Igwe bob in the water, the tops of their shells just peeking above the surface.

Onyii's door opens, and she climbs out to stand atop the giant robot. Even though most of it is underwater, she feels its massive expanse. Were it fully above water, she could take more than one hundred paces and not reach the end of its shell.

Agu goes straight to the ladder. Onyii follows, taking some of the personal ammo from the cockpit of her Igwe. Her abd takes a moment to try flexing his fingers again and getting his arm to work like new, but he ends up just pushing the fingers of his broken hand into something that can grip a ladder rung. Then he begins his climb. Onyii follows after him, ready to catch him should he fall.

When they reach the platform, wind buffets them. They crouch low. They are ready. They make their way, quickly and quietly, along the grating that rings the strut until they get to the vent. Onyii slings her rifle behind her back and, with a single jerk, tears the vent off. When it stops clattering, she freezes. Bootsteps. The enemy is near. The footfalls start up again. This time, faster.

Holding her rifle close to her side, Onyii shimmies into the enclosure, while Agu, on one knee, aims his rifle in a sweep, ready for whatever's coming around the corner.

"Agu!" she hisses, once she's in. "Oya, come!"

He does one last sweep before edging himself in feet-first. Onyii is almost at the end of the vent, where it opens up onto a generator room, when she hears gunfire. Agu.

She shimmies her way forward, but Agu shouts, "Onyii, get back!" Then the place fills with silver-flecked purple gas. A chaff grenade. More gunfire, then an explosion.

The vent buckles, then collapses, and Onyii slides down, unable to catch anything in her grip, legs flailing, until she crashes through the vent's gate at the other end and lands on her back. She has her rifle out in front of her, aimed at whatever's waiting for her here, and finds herself staring at the other end of Kesandu's rifle.

Kesandu barks out a laugh like she can't believe what just happened. A moment later, Agu comes hurtling through the vent. He lands in a roll and comes up with his rifle at the ready.

"The chaff grenade," Onyii says.

Agu gets to his feet when he sees he's among comrades. "I fired it back out at them. And sent a small projectile after it that pushed out the smoke and let the wind outside take it. When the vent collapsed"—he points above—"that is closing off the airflow."

Chinelo and Ginika and Obioma look at Agu with surprise, then at Onyii with playful admiration.

"Well, it seems they have bonded just fine," Obioma says with a smirk.

Onyii steps forward, and that's when she sees, around a corner, the huddle of hostages sitting on the floor. Ngozi and Nnamdi stand watch over them. "Show me the dead one," Onyii says.

Chinelo leads her down a passageway and around another corner, and there, slumped against a wall, is a young woman in a torn jumpsuit. Beneath her jumpsuit, she wears skintight body armor. Onyii kneels down, puts her fingers to the Nigerian's neck to feel for a pulse before tearing away at the partially ripped suit. She raps her knuckles twice against the young woman's chest and feels the toughness of her armor. Not strong enough to stop one of their bullets.

Onyii freezes. Those eyes. Her hair is different, which is why she almost didn't recognize her. But when she sees the dead woman's face, she knows it instantly. The memory rolls over her like a tsunami. Onyii, caked in mud, lying in the forest grass, her legs a tangled and ruined mess in front of her. Smoke hisses from the disabled ibu mech behind her. She's on her back as she watches a Nigerian clad in all black drag Ify away. And then this one stands over her, rifle aimed. She waits for the others to leave, then fires into the air. She spares Onyii's life.

Onyii looks at her now, the pool of blood still wet beneath her. Her name was Daurama. Then Onyii wipes any and all emotion from her face.

"Let's go," Onyii says, leaving Chinelo to guess at what's going through her war-sister's mind.

The two of them rejoin the others.

"Has a decision been made?" Onyii asks, then jerks her head in the direction of the internationals.

Chinelo takes her aside. "This place was supposed to be guarded only by enemy soldiers, if at all. We thought we'd just be dealing with mechs and synths. But they can be our way out."

"And you don't think the Nigerians will kill them anyway and blame it on us?"

Chinelo's brow furrows.

The oyinbo begins to shiver.

"Look," crows Obioma. "He is shaking like a leaf."

The other hostages have their heads bowed in defeat. They will find no kindness in Onyii. Ginika joins Onyii and says in a quiet voice, "If we let them go, they report back to their handlers and we are exposed."

Chinelo's frown deepens. "And if we kill them, we cause an international incident, and all the goodwill the prime minister has fought to get us with the Colonies evaporates." She is their leader, and Onyii feels all their heads turn to her, waiting.

To the others, it may seem as though Chinelo is the very picture of calm, but Onyii can see her struggling with the decision. She may be able to fool them into thinking she is their calculating, strategic leader, always ready with the answers to their questions or the solutions to their problems. But Onyii sees a girl who wanted nothing of this, who had no desire for bloodshed or gunfire, who picked up a rifle only reluctantly.

This is what war does to us, Onyii tells herself.

Chinelo straightens.

"What is it?" Onyii asks her.

"They're getting closer."

And Onyii knows that Chinelo's bees have detected the movement, that they are tracking the course of the enemy soldiers storming the facility. They're running out of time.

While Ngozi and Nnamdi stand watch over the hostages, the others get into a tight formation.

"Were you able to transmit the intel?" Chinelo asks.

"No." Onyii shakes her head. "Down below, our signal was blocked."

Chinelo waves her finger at the ceiling. "And they've jammed our signals here too. We can't reach the outside world."

"So the intelligence we have fought so hard to get dies with us, then?" This from Kesandu. She tries to sound courageous and sarcastic, but her voice wavers. Ngozi shoots her a look Onyii can't read.

"Chiamere," Onyii calls. After a brief glance at his sister, the abd walks to Onyii. Onyii snakes her cord out from the back of her neck and plugs into Chiamere's outlet.

"What's wrong with Agu?" Chinelo asks.

Without looking up, Onyii responds, "He was hurt when we were down below. He sustained damage to his arm that affected his nervous system. I can't plug into him anymore."

"Then how will he share the intel?"

Onyii looks up from the top of Chiamere's head. "Remotely. Once one abd has it, they can all download from their shared consciousnesses on their closed network." When she finishes, she disconnects from Chiamere and holds the loose end of her cord out to Chinelo. *You're not a synth, but you're almost more machine than human*. Onyii doesn't want to say it out loud, to even suggest that Chinelo is anything like the abd, that she is anything other than a red-blood, even with all her tech. So she just holds the cord out silently, waiting for Chinelo to take it.

Chinelo does, then plugs it into her own outlet at the back of her neck. Onyii feels the information flow from her to her friend like water in a river. When it's finished, Onyii's cord pops out of Chinelo's neck, then recoils back into Onyii's.

"All right," Kesandu says, when it looks like everything is finished. "Now what? We're still trapped."

"We can fight our way out," Onyii says, "or—"

They all freeze.

Chinelo and Onyii look at each other, then out into the middle distance. Their comms are receiving a message—the same one. On a holoscreen projected in front of them is a face. The face of a young man whose silver dreadlocks fall down past his shoulders. He wears a black bodysuit just like the one worn by the dead Nigerian soldier. This one glows with life. On the screen, the young man's face and shoulders are bathed in multicolored light. He's broadcasting from inside a mech.

At the sight of him, Onyii sucks in a ragged breath. Her body seizes. The line in her shoulder where her flesh ends and her metal begins chills and burns at the same time. Those eyes . . .

Her mech crashing. Her arm laid out on a tree stump. A lightknife flaring to life. A single downward slice. It was him.

"My name is Shehu Daren Suleiman Sékou Diallo, commanding officer of the Nigerian Armed Forces, Kato Mobile Defense Unit, A Class. I am offering you the chance to surrender. Free the hostages and leave with your lives. Or else we will be forced to destroy you."

CHAPTER
32

The quiet of the courtroom is what Ify remembers the most. After all the lights and the cameras and the loud noises of this new city called Abuja, it was the quiet of the courtroom Daren had brought her to that struck her.

The courtroom is cavernous. Arabic script lines the walls and arcs over the domed ceiling. The floor is covered in geometric patterns that remind Ify of lessons she vaguely remembers reading through on a broken tablet in the camp. Benches fan out on both sides of the central walkway, and toward the front, there is a table and a set of chairs on each side facing what looks to her like a throne. Next to the throne, on both sides, are two large chairs with cushions so plush they look like you would sink into them if you sat down. In each chair sits a bearded man clad in glistening robes. All of the men sitting in the chairs have a cap on their heads to match their gowns. Purple and deep blue and orange, each dressed in a different color.

Daren, holding Ify's hand, stops at the end of the path. Around the room stand guards with guns at their waists and green-and-white sashes across their chests. Daren bows his head briefly, then says, "Honorable qadi. Asalaam wa aleikum."

The man in the center, adorned in a silver djellaba with a single green stripe down the center, nods to acknowledge him, "Wa aleikum es salaam." Then he raises his chin to address the few people scattered throughout the courtroom. "We are gathered here today in the High Shari'a Civil Council of Abuja to determine a matter of *kafala*. Petitioner, state your claim."

Daren lets go of Ify's hand and takes a single step forward. "I, Officer Shehu Daren Suleiman Sékou Diallo, soldier and mobile-suit pilot of the Nigerian Armed Forces, wish to adopt this young girl into my family."

The man at the center looks to Ify. "Child, what is your name?"

Ify snaps out of her daze and says, first with a soft voice, then louder, "Ify."

"And what is your family name?"

"I . . ." The question hurts her heart, and she loses her words.

"Honorable qadi, this child was rescued from enemy forces. Her family was murdered by terrorists. She . . . she has no family name."

The man frowns. "Is she a Muslim?"

The moment catches Daren off-guard. He puts a hand to his heart. "She is prepared to submit to the will of Allah."

"Do not be so swift to speak for her, young man. If she is to join your family, she is to join the wider family of Muslims all over the world." He leans forward in his seat. "Child. Are you a Muslim?"

Ify cannot come to an answer. She does not know. She knows that Onyii had taught her to hate all Nigerians who were not Igbo. She knows that Onyii had once told her all Hausa were dogs, beasts that could never be called human, that the Fulani were made of metal and evil, that Igbo gods had cursed them for praying to Allah instead of to them. But she also knows that Daren was kind to her. That he saved her from that airplane crash. That he is with her now.

Tears pool in her eyes.

Daren raises his head to the judge. "Honorable qadi, are we not taught that the poor and the orphaned are to be the first to receive help if we can offer it? This child has no one but us to care for her." He quiets. "She may not be my blood, but I will love her just the same. *Call them by the names of their fathers; that is juster in the sight of Allah. But if you know not their father's names, call them your brothers in faith, or your trustees. But there is no blame on you if you make a mistake therein. What counts is the intention of your hearts. And Allah is Oft-Returning, Most Merciful.*" He steps back and is once again at Ify's side. "I will give her my family name."

She can't stop staring at him. Love. That is what he said. He will love her.

The judge leans back in his chair. *"Did He not find you an orphan and give you shelter? And He found you wandering, and He gave you guidance. And He found you in need and made you independent. Therefore, treat not the orphan with harshness."* He does not take his eyes off of Daren. "You are prepared to accept this child as your kin?"

Daren nods.

"Raise your hand and repeat after me."

Daren raises his hand.

"I swear by Allah," the judge begins.

Daren's mouth moves to follow.

"I swear by Allah that I will protect and care for this orphan

child as is my duty under Islam, as proclaimed by the Prophet Muhammad, peace be upon him. I will keep her safe. I will feed her the food of my house. I will give her the clothes from my back. She will be to the world as if she were my blood. I swear to keep her as close to me as two adjacent fingers on one hand. I will love this child as the children of the Prophet, peace be upon him, were loved by him. This, I swear before Allah."

When Daren finishes, he looks down to Ify, and now tears pool in his eyes. "Ifeoma Diallo," he says, almost like he's trying the name out on his tongue, seeing how it fits.

"Diallo," she says back. Already, she feels at peace.

CHAPTER
33

Onyii makes sure to memorize the young man's features, the shape of his face, the length of his hair, the color in his eyes, the light shade of his skin. She imagines the look on the brigadier general's face when she brings back this commanding officer's head. The thought of finally killing the dog who maimed her, who has haunted her dreams ever since she was a child with a rifle . . . it takes all of Onyii's effort not to let the smirk form on her lips.

"Fulani dog," Kesandu sneers. Onyii glances behind her to find Kesandu glaring at the projection. A rage she's never seen in the girl before. Her shoulders heave. Her hands tighten on her rifle. Veins rise on her neck. "You know nothing but how to kill. Women, children. It's all the same to you." She takes two steps forward, coiled, lumbering movement. "And you do it so often that you do not even remember them. But with each village you raze, each town you bomb, each camp you raid, you create a thousand new enemies. This is what happens when children have to watch their age-mates die. We will overrun you. And we will win."

The Nigerian officer's face remains impassive. He looks as

though he has heard this sort of thing many, many times already. "I did not expect you to negotiate," he says. "But I wanted the record to show that I did give you the chance to surrender." Then the screen vanishes. The transmission ends. The others begin to confer, but Onyii continues to stare at where the screen had been. It pleases her to have an individual face to focus on now. She is no longer fighting a teeming mass, an entire nation. She can direct her rage, her violence, at this one. If she kills this one, maybe she will be satisfied. She repeats the vow she made all those years ago, this time with the name of her tormentor: *Shehu Daren Suleiman Sékou Diallo, I will kill you.*

She turns to find Kesandu fighting to get herself back under control. This man must have hurt her personally too. Maybe he led the bombing campaign of her village. Maybe he was the soldier who orphaned her. Maybe Kesandu is like Onyii and only needs a single face on which to focus her hatred. One target to bear it all. One person on whom to revisit revenge for all she has suffered.

"Do you think we have time?" Onyii asks Chinelo.

"Not much," Chinelo says back.

Agu steps forward, the scar still bright on his shoulder. "They will not bomb the facility while their soldiers are in it. The soldiers are for the surgical strike and to secure as many hostages as they can before killing some of us. Then they will bomb the facility to ensure we all die."

"We are innocent!" shouts one of the oil workers again. "This is not how you bring about peace!" Ngozi hits him with the butt of her rifle, and blood spills from the new wound at his temple.

"Peace is not given," Ngozi says in a voice as hard as the

metal of an Igwe. "It is taken. For so long, they have visited violence upon us. It never starts with machetes. It starts with shutting the Igbo out of government. Then it becomes giving all the good jobs to the Hausa and the Fulani and the Yoruba. Then we are accused of crimes we do not commit. Called animals. They say we *infest* this country. Then we become the reason the Sahara grows larger and more and more of Nigeria turns to desert. We are blamed for the drought. We are blamed for the radiation. Then we are thrown in jail. Then we are murdered."

Onyii watches Ngozi's face tighten her tribal scars. They make her look regal. Like the tribal royalty to which she probably once belonged.

"We have tried peaceful protest," Ngozi continues. "We have tried marching. We have tried registering even those Igbo in the hinterlands to vote in the elections." She speaks not like she's reciting from an article or from some downloaded history but from life experience. She speaks like someone whose parents argued politics over the table at family dinners, like someone who was carried in her father's arms during those peaceful marches. She speaks like someone who knew a period before war. Before it all turned to violence. "You do not meet hate with love. Some will say that when a hateful person makes you hate, they win. But those people will never say what exactly it is that that hateful person wins. They will say that if you resist hate and meet it with love, that you win. But they never tell us what we win. We see with our eyes. We see that the only thing we win is death by machete. Isolation. Massacre." Her frown deepens. "They did this."

A moment of quiet settles over the group.

Chiamere, Chinelo's abd, grabs her attention and whispers to her. When Chinelo looks up again, her eyes are wide and determined. She has a plan.

"Gather, gather," she says, bringing everyone close together. "Chiamere believes there is a high probability that officer will try to contact us again. During that first transmission, he did not try to gather any information. He did not ask about how many hostages there were, but they definitely know there are hostages here; otherwise, they would have already attacked. His comms channel was encrypted. Which may be why he was able to get through to us. Or maybe they have some other way of piercing the static. Either way, it is our opening. Our abd will hack the signal, then use this Daren's comms system as a VPN to transmit it to headquarters."

Kesandu leans in. "But to headquarters, it will appear as an enemy transmission."

Chinelo replies, "We have to trust that they will know better and open it."

Obioma snorts. "Or guess right."

Chinelo nods. Grimly.

From Kesandu: "So we wait until he contacts us again."

"We have no choice."

"There is someone else with him." This from Kalu. Everyone turns to face Kesandu's abd. "The pilot is cyberized. Someone has already hacked his channel."

"What?" Onyii asks, eyes wide. Who could this be? An enemy? An ally they don't know about?

"And they are connected to Abuja, the Nigerian capital."

This time, everyone gasps.

Chinelo is the first to recover her composure. She grins.

"That's it. We don't send the transmission to headquarters. We send it to the enemy."

Kesandu lets out a shocked, hopeful breath. "We broadcast it all over Nigeria. Show them what their government has been hiding."

Chinelo nods. "And *they* will automatically beam it to the Colonies. This is how we will use their own technology to best them."

They can't believe their luck. Obioma whispers a silent prayer of thanks.

Onyii thinks of the dead Nigerian and that night in the forest when that young woman had fired her rifle into the air then left. Too many memories. Too many emotions. Onyii obliterates them with a thought. *I have a mission to complete.*

The already familiar buzz of a transmission from a Nigerian node fills Onyii's head. She looks to Chinelo, and Chinelo nods. She feels it too. Together, they project the broadcast, and Daren's face reappears on the screen before them.

"Come to reconsider your position, goat's son?"

The Fulani pilot's brows knit together in a deep frown. "We already have soldiers converging on your position. Show us the hostages, and we will order them to stand down."

"That easy?"

Onyii glances at Chinelo and sees that she's biding time. The abd and the other girls stay out of view so that it looks like Chinelo and Onyii are the only ones in the room.

"I would not have thought you Nigerians would cave so easily."

"You forget," Daren almost growls, "that you too are Nigerian. We are all Nigerian."

Chinelo puts her hands to her chest. "I am Nigerian because

a white man said so. I was Igbo because my tribespeople long ago said so. And I am Biafran because I say so." Her hands fall to her sides. "Even now, you seek to guarantee the safety of your colonizers. These oyinbo. They don't care about you. They care about your minerals. They care about your machines. They care about what is under the feet of Biafrans. That is why they are aiding you. You share no culture with them, and they share no culture with you. And yet you are letting them help you destroy your Igbo brothers and sisters."

Daren flinches, and that's when Onyii knows the signal went through. He detects the activity on his comms network. But he is too slow to prevent it. It's out there.

Pretty soon, it will be splashed over every news outlet in Nigeria and in space. How the Commonwealth Colonies have been shipping weapons of mass destruction to the Nigerians in violation of their stated neutrality as well as galactic human rights law. The Colonies will condemn Nigeria's use of such weapons. The consequences will ripple outward. Military changes, political changes. Stones in the pond that, once the water stills, will mean a ceasefire. Peace.

They did it.

"Are you done with your little speech?" Daren asks, condescension thick in his voice.

Chinelo squares her shoulders and puts her hands on her hips, satisfied. "As a matter of fact, I am, Your Highness Master Goat."

Daren grits his teeth at the insult in a rare show of anger, then calms himself. "Now, show me the hostages. Once they have been confirmed as alive, I will give the order to call off the soldiers in the facility."

The foreigners shuffle forward in their dirty, rumpled

jumpsuits, hands and wrists bound in solid metal restraints. One by one they walk past the screen before they are once more out of view.

Daren's eyes move back and forth, searching. "There was supposed to be another. Where is she?"

Onyii's heart races. The dead one. Daurama. How does Daren know the last hostage is a woman? She sees Chinelo racing through that question and more. Onyii says, "She was deemed a danger and had to be separated. She will be among the others when the hostages are freed."

The nervousness shows in new wrinkles on the young man's forehead. "I need to know that she is safe. I need to see her." He's starting to panic.

The dead woman was not an ordinary Nigerian soldier, Onyii realizes. She was someone close to this man. Onyii hardens inside. That changes nothing. Everyone has lost someone precious. She feels a note of satisfaction. Already, they have hurt this man.

Daren lashes out. "Show me Daurama or I will bomb you until the water glows."

"And risk punishment from your commanders and condemnation from the Space Colonies?" Chinelo's smirk widens. "Perhaps you should calm down. Maybe get some fresh air. You get the hostages we send you or you get nothing. That is the deal."

Daren grows quiet. Even though he doesn't take his gaze off of Chinelo and Onyii, they can tell that he is receiving orders from his commander. "Fine," he hisses through gritted teeth.

"We will send you confirmation when they are ready for pickup." Then Onyii ends the transmission. When Chinelo looks her way, Onyii says, "If we'd remained on the line any longer, he would have suspected that we were stalling for time. At least this way, we can still hope that he is in the dark about what we have planned. They still think our mission here is to take hostages."

Chinelo grins. "Look at you, the master strategist."

A shy smile makes its way onto Onyii's face.

"Auntie," Agu says to Chinelo, "we have taken two of their Igwe. They are below us right now. My sensors do not detect any activity around them."

Kesandu's eyebrows rise. "Is there room for all of us?"

Chinelo turns to her. "No need. There's an Igwe for each sister, and a smaller mech for each abd."

Kesandu, Ngozi, and Obioma all gasp at once. Some of the abd look to each other and grin.

"I know the way," Agu says, and the expressions of the others brighten until Agu says, "but the entranceways are blocked. After the first transmission, they were sealed off."

"But then what about the hostages?" asks Ngozi. "They will have to let the doors back open if they want the hostages out alive."

Chinelo scratches her chin. "And it's clear that it's not simply that pilot's decision. They want the hostages."

"So what do we do?" asks Obioma.

Onyii looks up from her rifle. "We give them the hostages."

Agu has Chiamere's duffel bag in his hand and drops it before the group. The flap hangs open. Onyii takes out a brick of plastic explosives.

"And insurance."

The sisters grin.

CHAPTER 34

Gold threads through Ify's memory. Her legs dangle over the small ledge overlooking the beach. Behind her, Onyii stands with her arms folded, squinting at the sunrise. But Ify only has eyes for the stars. They wink into nothingness, the blue-black of night giving way to the gold and purple of early morning. And when they vanish, they take the constellations with them. A crown. A belt. A shorthorn.

Ify knows some of those stars are Colonies. A giant pinion—a smaller gear—meshed with a larger annular gear. Outside, in noiseless space, the earsplitting grinding of titanic amounts of metal against each other. But on the inside, due to technological wonders she can't even imagine, no such sound. People walking and eating and studying and learning and being brilliant, going about their lives in breathable air and habitats supporting stable bodies of water. She has glimpsed pictures of the Colonies in her pirated lessons and images she wasn't supposed to have downloaded. She knows what they look like, but they are still a puzzle to be figured out. The biggest puzzle of all. If people could build those, what else could they build?

Chukwu, the supreme being that powers all life, is everywhere.

Ify can feel him in the ground underneath her. And she can feel him in the warmth of the rising sun. Anyanwu. The word comes to her from her religion lessons. The sun as revelation, the source of all knowledge, and Chukwu its author. Ify brims with so many questions. How things work, how they happen, how the world is put together. With each new day comes the promise of answers.

"Onyii?"

Her big sister has her hands wrapped behind her head, elbows outstretched, back arched mid-yawn. "Yeah?"

"What's outer space like?"

And Onyii looks to the sky, and Ify can tell she's trying to follow Ify's gaze and see what she sees, but now the Colony star has winked out. All that's left is the memory of the sight. There's no way Onyii can see it, but they both stare anyway.

"I think it's quiet," Onyii says at last.

"You ever been?"

Onyii shrugs. "Not yet." She turns to Ify. "Wanna go?"

"Yes," Ify says, breathless, her gaze still inclined toward the stars. "More than anything."

"Well, do well in school, and I'll take you." She snaps her fingers. "Oya, time to get ready."

After a moment, Ify gets up, brushes the grass off her butt, and follows Onyii back into the camp, skipping and dreaming of space.

CHAPTER
35

It takes no time at all for Onyii to form eto-eto out of the C-4.

The hostages stand in a loose circle while the young women strap the C-4 to the skin under their shirts. When Onyii sees that they were not given body armor, she shakes her head. *The Nigerians see you as completely disposable. They did not even bother to pretend to protect you, stupid oyinbo.* Before long, they are finished.

"You are being strapped with C-4," Onyii says in the voice of a doctor describing a condition. "You will notice there is no timer attached, so you may ask yourself how these are capable of detonating. Look closely, and you will see these eto-eto moving their arms and legs. That means they are sentient. And they are connected to me. That means that I control them. And with a thought, I can detonate them." She looks into the eyes of the golden-haired oyinbo. "Do you understand what I am saying? I am the timer."

He gulps.

Onyii backs away to address the five remaining hostages as a whole. "There is nothing you can do to alter the eto-eto made out of this C-4. There is no time limit on them. As long as I am in geographic range, they are under my control. Additionally, that means that if I am attacked and my attention diverted, I will detonate them, and you will all lose your lives. Painfully. Once I am out of range, the C-4 will disarm itself. And you will be safe."

Kesandu and her abd, Kalu, step forward.

"These two will escort you to the roof of this strut and remain with you until we believe we are safe. Then they too will leave. The C-4 will not disarm itself until we are *all* out of harm's way. Try to interfere, and you die. Try to warn the Nigerian Army about any of what we have done or plan to do, and you die. Make me angry, and you die. Do you understand?"

The golden-haired oyinbo takes a moment to blink through his sweat, then nervously nods. The others hang their heads in sorrow and manage only gentle, docile nods. They will all comply.

"So now we wait," Chinelo breathes to Onyii.

"Now we wait," Onyii says in return.

The girls gather. Kesandu and Kalu are the last to join them. First, Kesandu faces Ngozi and sticks her hand out to grasp the other girl's forearm. Ngozi looks at it for a moment, rifle in her hands, before grabbing Kesandu's forearm and pulling her into a tight embrace. They embrace for so long and with such fierceness that Onyii can only wonder at what things were like for them before she arrived. What relationships formed before she walked into their lives. Onyii remembers the stolen glances at their training camp, those wordless moments that happened when they thought no one else was looking. When the two break apart, they look each other in the eye for a long time before kissing like it is the last time they will have the chance to.

Kesandu then makes her way around, embracing each of the sisters in turn, whispering into their ears and looking them in the eye lovingly before moving to the next, until she gets to Onyii. "I was very happy to see you returned to us," Kesandu says.

"I was happy that God returned me to you."

Kesandu glances quickly at Ngozi, then back. "Take care of her for me. Please."

Onyii nods. The one sister she can't seem to get along with. She almost laughs at the irony.

Kesandu heads to the group of hostages. "Kalu, oya. Let's go."

Kalu breaks away from the abd, who had all been huddled together, whispering among themselves and grabbing forearms and embracing in imitation of their sisters.

They are learning to display affection, Onyii thinks with a smile. *If they practice this enough times, it will become muscle memory, and real affection will follow.* She lets out a soft chuckle. *So, this is how a synth learns to love.*

Kalu leads the hostages to the entrance of the room, with Kesandu bringing up the rear. The door is closed tight before them, and they all wait until they hear a massive thunk, the warning siren barking a few times, then the hiss of the door opening. Then the seven of them vanish in a cloud of steam.

The massive door hangs open, and the others charge through, then scatter down the stairways that flank the main passageway. Once they hit the floor, everyone turns to follow Agu. Agu winds them down corridor after corridor, through narrow spaces between boilers and up and over fallen pipes, all with a broken arm.

"Here," he says, panting. They stand over a solid, nondescript patch of concrete. He points at the ground, and Onyii realizes what he means.

Onyii tears a chunk of C-4 from her breast pocket and fashions it into a charge right in the space's center. The others back away as far as the enclosure will allow. The explosion is louder than Onyii intends, and the ground shakes underneath them, but right in front of them is a hole big enough for all of them to go through at once. Chinelo puts her head through, as does Onyii, and they see it all just as the first chunks of concrete hit the water.

Chinelo whistles. "Hey! Jackpot-oh!" She taps Onyii's shoulder. "Hey, if we are trading with the Nigerians, they can gladly keep my little horsefly if I get to take this dragon."

Ngozi slaps her hand on the stone. "Chinelo! Now is not the time!"

And Onyii catches a glimpse of what they might have been like before things became so serious, before so much blood was spilled. Joking. Fun.

The abd pull ropes and magnetic fasteners from their bags and secure the fasteners and rope to the ground. Then they shift so that the fasteners face them, and they grip the fasteners and brace themselves against the floor. Each of their sisters grabs a rope and launches herself over the side, rappelling down until she lands on the torso shelf of a different Igwe. The abd follow after them, then yank the magnet fasteners from the floor and let them fall into the water. Agu and Onyii rappel down to the platform they stood on just hours earlier.

Behind each Igwe stands a hunched aquamech, built for land and water like the Igwe but smaller, more compact. A variation of the ground mechs Onyii used to pilot so often.

Obioma gestures toward an untouched pair. "We leave these for Kesandu and Kalu?"

Onyii shakes her head and shouts up at them. "We cannot risk it! When we leave, we will sink them into the water. No one will have them."

Obioma winks. "Kesandu will be jealous."

The cockpits open all at once, and the sisters climb into their Igwe. Their abd hop from shelf to shelf until they get to the cockpits of the aquamechs. In an instant, the lights of every machine glow to life.

Onyii looks to Agu. "Go with the abd. I will ride with Chinelo."

A steel rope ladder falls from the torso of Chinelo's Igwe and sweeps Onyii upward so smoothly that she topples onto Chinelo in her seat. For a second, they are a tangle of limbs, and as they try to extricate arms and legs and move elbows and push at shoulders, Onyii catches herself giggling. It surprises her, but on Chinelo's face is only satisfaction. She doesn't look surprised at all to find Onyii happy. They are touching, and Onyii can tell that this is the only thing either of them wants.

Onyii's smile softens, and she settles into a space to the left of Chinelo's seat, where she'll be out of the way. "There is a door at the bottom of this room that I believe is pressure-activated and—"

The Igwe rocks and shudders, then Onyii sees through Chinelo's screen that the Igwe has a giant laser rifle in its hands. Without warning, it pulls the trigger. Steam rises, hissing from the water. The metal of the trapdoor groans as heat and radiation melt it apart. Then a massive crash as it falls away and water rushes into the chamber.

They dive under and swim in tight formation.

When they break the surface, the sky is purple with dusk. The dying sunlight makes the water around them shimmer.

"And where have you parked your car?" Chinelo asks.

Onyii points back toward the facility. Their Igwe turns and cuts a path straight toward it. Panic creeps into Onyii as they get closer. Agu and Golibe cruise just behind them in Golibe's mech. Relief floods into Onyii when she sees the familiar sight of their mechs' hulls breaching the surface of the water, bobbing up and down like beacons.

Chinelo comes to a stop beside one of the mechs, and when Onyii opens the cockpit and steps out, she sees Agu on the other side doing the same. They share a look before hopping into their Igwe.

When she's back inside her own cockpit, lights come to life around her.

With her comms, she dials into Kesandu's frequency. "We're all set. Agu is sending Kalu the coordinates to the hangar n—"

"Where is she?" The voice bursts through her system. Static, then Daren's face appears before her. Furious. He has lost all composure. "Where is Daurama?"

Onyii maintains her calm. It fills her with satisfaction to control him like this. "The hostages are carrying C-4 fused to their bodies. I have the detonator. You will let my comrades and I go free or I will detonate each and every one of those hostages."

"Where is Daurama?" he screams. "Where is—"

She ends the transmission. "Let's go," she says to the others. They break out from under the shadows of the facility, and just as they are about to rejoin the others, the water bubbles beneath them. "What?" Onyii whispers to herself. "Chineke!" she shouts. "Scatter!"

But the last of her words is drowned out by the cannon blast that shoots out from underwater and tears through Nnamdi's mech. Ngozi gets out of the way just in time, but the left half of her Igwe is melted. They all transform into their humanoid molds and jet into the air.

"What was that?" Chinelo shouts over their comms.

As they ascend, the water swirls beneath them, then up bursts an Igwe like they've never seen before. It has legs, arms, a cockpit, and a head, but the rest of it is a cascade of scales and armor with jets shaped like angel wings sprouting from its back. Attached to one arm is a laser cannon, while the other hand holds the shaft of a massive hammer. The enemy Igwe speeds toward her. Its body is torqued. *He's going to swing that at me*, Onyii realizes just in time to slip out of the way.

Her Igwe's reflexes still surprise her. She is not used to being this agile, to having the controls obey her immediately, to having a machine submit so readily and so fully to her will. In one motion, she twists in the air, flicks a rifle into her hands, and fires at the enemy Igwe's head.

But it's gone.

"What is that?" Chinelo asks, backing away with Chiamere to give them more space for combat.

"I am your god," the enemy pilot says before speeding down toward Ngozi's damaged mech, which isn't able to transform and stays stuck in the water. That voice. It's him. Daren. "This Alusi model is the avenging angel that will bring about peace." It torques its body, readying its hammer once again, poised to strike a defenseless Ngozi when Obioma rams her Igwe into it.

Obioma and Daren splash along the surface of the water, jets firing then cutting off then firing again so they can stabilize themselves. When Obioma is upright, she extends her mech's arms and fires missiles from her wrists. The missiles twirl toward him. But he swings his hammer up, sending the missiles high into the air before they detonate so loudly everyone's mechs shake and rattle.

"How is he that fast?" Onyii murmurs in shock and awe.

Chinelo charges forward, a sword in her mech's hands, and swings. The Alusi catches her blow and flings her away, firing from the Gatling gun that appears on its shoulder. Bullets riddle Chinelo's Igwe. Chiamere dashes down from the sky, where cloud cover had hidden him, using the shield on his mech to deflect the bullets and keep Chinelo safe. He detaches a hatchet from its catch on his leg and swings. The Alusi smacks away the blow, but Chiamere flips his mech, lands on the water, and charges forward. Each blow sends sparks into the air. The two dance over the lagoon, their jets keeping them afloat. Agu aims himself at the Alusi's back and readies his own hatchet.

The Alusi wraps its arms around Chiamere and flies into the air. Agu misses and pitches forward. Onyii flies into the air after the Alusi and Chiamere. As she gets closer, she sees it squeezing Chiamere's mech at the waist. No . . . his cockpit.

She pushes her engines to send her even faster. Chiamere's mech struggles in the Alusi's grip, pushing and striking, denting the metal, but the Alusi won't let go until something loud snaps, and metal grinds together. Chiamere's mech stops struggling. After a moment, the Alusi lets go. Chiamere's mech plummets into the water. It lands with a massive splash. A column of water erupts into the air.

There's barely a moment of silence before Chinelo screams over their comms and charges forward, a bladed staff in one hand, her blade-studded chain uncoiled on her opposite wrist. She flings the chain forward at the Alusi, but it dodges it, then charges forward with its hammer. Agu sends a volley of missiles at it. It tries to get out of the way, blocks the missiles with its hammer, but the blow knocks it sideways.

Onyii can't stop staring at where Chiamere has fallen. Chinelo's abd. Gone. Then it takes her. That rage. She welcomes it.

Agu rushes through the smoke from his missiles. He and the Alusi clash in the air. Each time their weapons meet, a boom sounds over the water.

This Alusi is trying to defeat all of us. Then: *I will kill him.*

Conscious thought leaves Onyii, and she blasts herself forward. She flicks her rifle into her hands and fires. Agu and the Alusi break apart. Onyii charges through the space between them, shifts in the air, clips her rifle back to her thigh, and detaches a pair of scimitars from her other thigh.

They take a moment to consider each other, Onyii and the Alusi. Then they charge. Finally, her chance.

Their first clash sends a shock wave through the air that ripples in the water. A boom follows. Onyii breaks away, charges again. Just as she expects, the Alusi raises the hammer to block. Onyii catches the shaft with one of her scimitars and flips it away, then, with her other scimitar, slices cleanly across the Alusi's chest.

A gash opens up on the Alusi as it flies backward.

Onyii continues her onslaught. The Alusi, with one arm, tries to time its hammer swing. But Onyii is too fast, spinning in the air to dodge it, then jabbing her scimitar through the Alusi's elbow. She pulls away. A shower of machinery falls into the water. She jabs again and again, but it won't drop its hammer. Its Gatling gun spins on its shoulder. Onyii cuts her engines and drops into the water just in time to avoid the volley. From underneath the Alusi, she dashes upward, scimitars ready. Too late, she sees the laser cannon aimed directly at her. Daren must have flipped it around.

She tries to adjust her engines, but she can't get away in time. The barrel warms with light. This is it. She was so close.

Something crashes into her.

She hurtles through the air and rotates to see a mech caught in the blast, paralyzed in the column of purple and pink and red energy. Almost immediately, parts of it disintegrate. Obioma lets out a cry. Her abd. Her abd is the one who knocked Onyii out of the way. Obioma, in the distance, flies straight for the Alusi.

"No!" Onyii shouts. "Obioma, don't!" But she's too late.

The Alusi swings its laser cannon in an upward arc, the blast slicing straight through Obioma's Igwe.

The sight of Obioma's Igwe falling toward the water in two jaggedly cut halves snaps Onyii out of her haze. *How is he this powerful?*

Out of nowhere, Golibe's mech crashes into the back of Daren's Alusi. Its arms wrap around it, pitching it forward just as Ginika rams her Igwe into its chest. Together, they hold Daren still.

"Go!" Ginika screams. "We can't hold him forever! Go now!" Then, in a quieter voice, so low Onyii thinks she's not meant to hear it, Ginika says, "Golibe, let go." Ginika's mech tightens its arms around Daren's Alusi. "Let go, Golibe. Escape. That's an order." The Alusi flexes. Ginika's losing her grip. "That's an order!" she screams.

The Alusi flexes again, and an electric pulse explodes from it. Ginika's Igwe goes dark just as Golibe's mech darts out of range.

He disabled her!

The Alusi's lights shut off for a second, and it dips before it powers back on again, swinging its hammer in one swift spin, crushing Ginika's cockpit and slamming her into the water.

Golibe stops and turns, and his entire mech seems to tremble.

"Do it." Chinelo's voice snaps Onyii back into the present.

Then, a moment later, an explosion so loud they hear it from this far away.

The oil facility. All heads turn in its direction. The struts are a mess of fire and collapsed metal. The C-4 explosives have been detonated.

The Alusi spares the rest of them a brief glare before it jets away, straight for the burning facility.

Chinelo's voice cuts through Onyii's daze. "Come on!" she orders. "This is our chance."

"Kesandu," Onyii murmurs. "Kalu." They must have died on the roof of the strut. Onyii remembers how Kesandu said goodbye to everyone in that generator chamber. Like this would be the last time.

"They died protecting us." Then a pause. "Ngozi? Ngozi, can you hear us?"

Static. Then, through the static, a faint "Yes." Then, "But my Igwe is too weak to move. The propulsion system is damaged beyond repair."

Chinelo's Igwe flies down to Ngozi and hovers above the water. "Here, join me." Chinelo's cockpit opens. Ngozi climbs out the top of her mech, then takes Chinelo's outstretched hand and joins her.

Onyii looks around. The waters have nearly stilled. Beneath the surface lie so many of their comrades. Dead. All those lives, all those histories. The love they dared feel for each other in the midst of all of this. Gone.

The remaining Igwe fly away into the night that has fallen over the lagoon. As much as Onyii tries to convince herself, this does not feel like mission accomplished. Her hands shake on her gearshifts.

They don't stop shaking until the Biafran coastline comes into view.

When they land on empty coast and climb out of their mechs, Onyii descends the steel ladder as fast as she can, scrambling for the bushes, where she vomits. It pours out of her. All of it. Even when there's nothing left, she retches. Her whole body shakes.

What is this? she keeps asking herself. *Is this grief? Is this fatigue? Is this fear?*

No. She can't afford to let it be those things. The Demon of Biafra never felt those things. Only rage. That's what this is. Rage.

Her body stops shaking.

CHAPTER
36

Ify's eyes flutter open. When she wakes, the sky is purple-red
with dusk. Fog fills her head so much that the first time she
tries to get out of her chair, she nearly collapses onto the floor.
What happened? She shakes her head and immediately regrets
it. Where there had been quiet before, there is only ringing
now.

She looks around. The watchtower. How long has she been
here?

She's still wearing the helmet. Gingerly, she takes it off her
head, then slips out of the chair and crawls forward to the front
end of the flexiglas encasement. She has to blink a few times
for her vision to clear, but when it does, she sees the streets
filled with people. Every single person in Abuja is outside now.
But none of them are moving. They are all staring upward at
one of the dozens of billboard screens littered throughout the
capital. Each of them plays the same thing. But Ify can't hear
a word.

She shifts her jaw to activate her Accent out of habit, then
stops. The memory of what happened to her is still too real.
The pain, the overwhelming flood of sensory input, the way it

had almost overpowered her. She puts a finger to her ear, and it comes back with blood.

Images come to her that must have been from some sort of dream. The inside of a mech cockpit, controls glowing back at her. The ease and calm of piloting on instinct . . . Onyii. Ify's eyes shoot open. She was in Daren's head. She saw Onyii. And Chinelo. Then she remembers what must have been a battle. Laser beams firing and tons of metal clashing against tons of metal and screaming. So much screaming. By Allah, it wasn't a dream.

She looks to the billboards. Images of giant mechs in flight over a lagoon. Explosions everywhere. Then a Biafran woman appears on-screen, wearing a mask that only shows her eyes. Saying something. But all Ify can focus on are those eyes. . . . Onyii. The woman's mouth moves soundlessly.

So many questions.

The camera switches to a broadcaster who stands on what looks like the edge of the forest. A chyron strip moves at the bottom of the screen: "Biafran terrorists attack abandoned oil facility. Take hostages."

Behind the broadcaster, the news camera reveals a row of armored mechs with their cannons trained toward the facility. In the distance, the horizon shimmers and shifts. Water. They must be right on the edge of the shore.

Ify hears footsteps behind her.

Armed police rush in. One of them tackles her to the ground and presses his knee into her back, while two more aim their rifles at her face. What is happening?

She screams out in pain as someone twists her arm behind her back. Tears spring from her eyes.

"What are you doing?" she cries. "Ow! What is happening? What are you doing to me? You're hurting me!" She says it over and over, "You're hurting me!" until one of the soldiers shouts, "Shut your mouth, udene!" Which stuns her into silence.

One last officer steps in. She first sees only his boots, then is able to turn her head slightly to see him standing over her with a tablet in one hand. "Ifeoma Diallo, you are under arrest."

"Under arrest? For what? What did I do?"

"You have been charged with providing material assistance to terrorists and hacking Nigerian surveillance to disseminate enemy propaganda in violation of security code one six two, subsection four b. The crime is treason, the penalty for which is either solitary confinement for a period of fifty years or death."

Ify's eyes go wide. She thrashes against the soldier on her back, even though fiery pain shoots through her shoulder. No. No, this is all wrong. There must be some mistake.

"Daren!" she shouts. "Daren! Where is Daren? Daren, please help!" It turns into an anguished scream. "Daren! Daren, please!"

"Shut up your mouth!"

Anger seizes her, chills the blood in her veins. "You are making a terrible mistake," she hisses. "I am a member of the A Class and personal aide and secretary to a commissioned officer of the Nigerian Armed Forces. I am the highest scorer at the academy and the youngest contributing member of the Nigerian Consortium for Social and Technical Sciences! If you know what is good for you, you will get off of me *now*!"

The officer on top of her relieves the pressure just long enough to haul her to her feet and slap her across the face.

Tears run down her face.

"That is enough," says the officer with the tablet in a quiet voice. The one who announced that she had been charged with treason. "To me, you are none of those things. Your school marks, they do not matter. Your closeness with our government, it does not matter. You are an Igbo who we rescued and to whom we have shown kindness, and you have betrayed that kindness in the worst way possible."

"No, I am n—" She realizes that if she finishes that sentence, she will be denying her life among the War Girls. She will be denying Onyii, denying the family that she had had before she was brought here. And she realizes she can't do that.

The charging officer frowns at her, waiting. When she says no more, it seems to confirm something for him. Something dire. And all the protest leaches out of Ify's body. "Restrain her," he says.

One of the officers pulls a device from his belt and, with a flick of his wrist, gets it to unfold into a pair of braces that he fastens over her forearms so that they are held close together in front of her.

The officers lead her out of the chamber and back to the lift. Questions mob her. But beneath them all, a single thought: *I was so close*. To Daren. To Onyii. All she'd wanted was to reach them.

All she'd wanted was peace.

CHAPTER
37

"Push harder."

Chinelo's voice arrives metallic and monotone over the intercom in the far corner of the large training room. Three months since the mission at the oil derricks, and this is the only way Onyii has heard Chinelo speak. Hard and without feeling. She and Onyii stand on the other side of the glass in an observation room, looking down on Golibe. The boy, shirtless, spares them a glance before bracing his hands against a large metal sphere as big as him. Sweat drips into his eyes, slides down his chin, and runs paths over the wires connected to his patchwork chest and back and shoulders. He flexes, fingers splayed.

A railway-like groove holds the sphere and swirls its way to the other end of the chamber. As Golibe pushes, he has to keep changing the ball's path. It groans against the metal grooves.

Red digital numbers on monitors in the observation room record his level of force, as well as his vital signs. A few technicians and doctors, sent in to monitor the group after the mission at the oil derricks, hunch over their consoles. Others stand with their arms behind their backs. The data is beamed directly into their tablets.

One of the doctors shakes his head. There's a number panel in Golibe's room, and he glances at it before lowering his head and bringing his shoulder into the effort to increase his leverage. He grits his teeth. The sphere moves faster. His brows knit together, and Onyii doesn't have to look at his vital signs to know he's in physical pain. The look on his face is enough.

What is he thinking? Onyii crosses her arms. She wonders if he is busy reliving his last moments with his sister. Before that Nigerian pilot disabled her mech, then caved in her cockpit with his hammer, smashing Ginika into the watery depths of the lagoon. Is he replaying her last words? Does he hear it all, or is the memory soundless?

Or has he blocked it out entirely?

He pushes until an electronic beeping sound signals for him to stop.

"Proceed to Station Two," Chinelo orders, her voice level.

Chinelo seems just as opaque. Shut off.

The mission broke all of us, Onyii lets herself think before returning to Golibe's training.

Several of his wires detach from him, but others stick despite the layers of sweat and grime that coat his skin. Golibe moves to the other end of the room, arms stiff at his sides, toes resting against the edge of the red line that shows the fifty meters he has to run.

Chinelo gives him a moment to pause before saying, "Go."

Legs pumping, Golibe darts to the opposite red line, exactly fifty meters away, taps it with the tips of his fingers, then cuts through the air to arrive at his starting point, going back and forth for exactly ten minutes. For a human, it would be punishment of the most extreme order. But Golibe is a synth.

Just like Agu. Just like Chiamere. Just like Nnamdi was. And Obioma's abd. And Kalu.

"Stop," Chinelo says in that mechanical voice of hers. "Station Three."

Golibe heads to a two-handed bar attached by its middle to a cable. The cable lies coiled in a neat circle on a space shorter than the distance between his shoulders. He sets his feet apart, bracing himself.

"Pull," says Chinelo.

With all his strength, he pulls, the length of cable tightening against his effort.

"Harder," says Chinelo.

Maybe Chinelo *is* punishing him. Is there any other reason to strain him this much? What could she be looking for by putting him through this?

Golibe's hands tighten on the bar, knuckles cracking. His eyes glaze over as his body seems to move without him.

"Enough," Chinelo says.

But Golibe doesn't move. His body continues to shiver with effort.

"Enough," Chinelo says, louder.

He's still pulling.

"Golibe, that's enough!"

He doesn't hear her. Can't. Suddenly, a loud pop sounds, and he staggers backward, a stunned look in his eyes. His left arm hangs limp at his side.

Behind Onyii, the doctors recite numbers and record their results. Another one enters Golibe's training room through a side door and fits him with a sling before leading him out to the personal physician waiting for him.

Chinelo heads off to another room without a word. Onyii follows. It disturbs her to see her war-sister like this. It is as though Chinelo has been turned into her complete opposite. Where before there were laughter and jokes, now there is only angry, determined silence. Onyii recognizes the anger, the need to hit things while being surrounded by things you're not supposed to hit. But it seems so strange to see it in Chinelo.

In the smaller surveillance room, Chinelo takes a seat beside one of the technicians and focuses on one of the screens. It reveals a doctor's examining room.

"How's your arm, Golibe?" the doctor asks, with what sounds like actual concern in his voice.

"It is fine, sah."

The man gestures to an empty swivel chair, and Golibe takes the seat. A small window of silence opens between them before the doctor pulls a tablet out of his drawer. Chinelo zooms in to see the tablet opened up onto a photo album. The doctor enlarges the first photo, then rotates the tablet for Golibe to see. Each face has a number beneath it, and immediately following each face is a picture of hands or eyes or the closed lips of a smile. Patiently, the doctor scrolls through them.

"Which ones do you know?" the doctor asks.

"Number one is Chinelo. Numbers three, seven, and fifteen are Kesandu, Ngozi, and Obioma. Numbers four, eight, and sixteen are their abd. Number twenty is Onyii. Number twenty-three is Agu." He pauses. "The rest, I do not know."

Onyii can't tell if Ginika's face is among those on the tablet. Did Golibe see it and not recognize her? Has he already forgotten her? Has he chosen to?

"How did I do?" Golibe asks.

"You did fine," the doctor replies, as though Golibe were an actual boy.

But Golibe's shoulders slump. "I'm getting worse." He lowers his eyes.

"Just try not to exert yourself too strenuously over the next few days. Watch your arm. And remember to record your dreams tonight."

Well after Golibe leaves the examination room and heads back to his dorm on campus, Chinelo stares at the screen.

Onyii wants to ask Chinelo if they are all like this, if this is how they mourn, how they deal with loss.

Is this what Agu would do if he lost me?

■ ■ ■ ■ ■

In the mess hall, Onyii watches Chiamere and Agu eat in silence. Chinelo sits down across from her. Onyii wonders if Chinelo notices the silence that hangs over the abd too.

She catches Onyii staring and glares. For a moment, their eyes meet. After a beat, Chinelo's face softens. "With the program suspended indefinitely, we may not be able to rebuild our teams."

"The Biafran government or whoever gives the orders here, they must still need us for something."

"You see what condition we are in, Onyii. What mission could we possibly accomplish?"

That silences Onyii until she looks up at the abd again. "Is Golibe in his room?"

"Why are you so fascinated with him?" Chinelo barks without looking up from her rice and stew.

Onyii gives Chinelo one last look before wordlessly busing her tray.

She doesn't know why Golibe's behavior bothers her so much. They were never close; he was Ginika's. In fact, she should be lucky Agu is alive and well after everything that has happened. Maybe she needs to know what happens after a sister dies. Maybe she needs to know what Agu would do.

"Maybe I'm just drawn to orphans," she mutters wryly to herself as she approaches the hall where the abd sleep.

Golibe's bedroom looks like it could have belonged to any of the abd. No decorations on the wall, no toys or tools scattered across the made bed. No holographic photos rising from devices on the windowsill. The table is empty of ammunition and weapons.

Onyii goes to the window and opens it to allow some fresh air. That's when she notices something peeking out from beneath Golibe's pillow. It looks like some sort of disc. She lifts the pillow to find four shiny metal discs laid out in a row on the bed and some sort of outdated player with a small screen. She picks up the first and turns it over in her fingers. The discs are tiny and old-fashioned. These days, data would be beamed or collected directly in a recording device. No need for external hardware. Onyii slides the disc in the player, and Ginika appears on the screen.

Her tribal scar lines her cheekbone. Her chin rests in her palm, her gaze focused on something outside the photo's frame. The picture seems more interested in her hand and her fingers than her face. Her face seems blurrier, more out of focus than her chewed fingernails and her smooth knuckles. Onyii never saw Ginika smile like that.

She slips each disc into her pouch.

Agu's room is just down the hall. She doesn't know why she's been avoiding him. Part of her wants to make sure he's okay, but another part of her is afraid of what she'll find. And yet another part of her is furious that she's allowed herself to grow this close to him.

A distress signal blares over her comms.

No words, just the continuous roar of a red alert and the thunder of bootsteps in the direction of the chapel.

Onyii runs as fast as she can out of Golibe's room and down the halls of the dorm.

By the time Onyii arrives at the chapel, a crowd has already gathered.

No one has their weapons drawn, but a murmur hangs over the crowd. At the center of the circle is Golibe's body, laid out on his back with his arms slightly spread, like a boy lying in the grass and staring at the sky. A single gunshot has taken away half his face. The gun is in his hand.

But what chills Onyii is the smile.

The only time Onyii has ever seen that look on his face.

CHAPTER
38

Ify doesn't know how long she's been in this cell alone. But it's long enough for the visions to have become a regular occurrence. It always begins with a buzzing. Then a sharp pain in her jaw. Then she is plunged into a distorted hallucination plagued by static and blurring images. Smells that move from one extreme to another, day that turns to night then day again before her very eyes. Katakata.

She squeezes her eyes shut and grips her head in her hands and screams. She does not know how long the howl erupts from her throat, but when she stops, she hears soft singing, her mother's voice, lilting and swaying in Yoruba, like elephant grass in a gentle breeze:

> *Ekun meran, mee!*
> *O tori bo igbo, mee!*
> *O torun bo dan, mee!*
> *O fe mu un, mee!*
> *Ko ma le mu o, mee!*
> *Oju ekun pon, mee!*
> *Iru ekun nle, mee!*

The leopard stalks the goat, baa!
It searches the forest, baa!
It searches the bush, baa!
It wants to capture it, baa!
No, you can't capture it, baa!
The leopard's eyes are red, baa!
The leopard's tail stands on end, baa!

And Ify's mama holds Ify by her wrists, bouncing her on her lap, and every time she imitates the goat, she puts her nose to baby Ify's nose and scrunches her face, and baby Ify giggles without control.

Ify watches the scene play out with tears brimming in her eyes. She lies on the floor and tries to push herself up to her knees. Her mama and her younger self rest against the far wall, and she reaches toward them. They feel so real.

"Mama," Ify whimpers from the floor, knowing the vision isn't real but unable to stop herself. "Mama." Her mother's hair comes down past her shoulders in thick, silver locs, and her face is lined with only a few wrinkles, not marks of age so much as marks of wisdom and strength. Beneath her gown are muscles, but her skin is so soft it glows in the natural light that shines in the memory. "Mama."

Ify crawls closer and closer until she can hear the song clearly. Her mother twists her in the air with each bounce, and now baby Ify can't stop giggling, and halfway through her mother's fourth time singing the lullaby, she clutches baby Ify tight to her chest and whispers in her hair, then she pats her back, and baby Ify lets out an unselfconscious burp. Ify can't stop crying. She gets closer to the vision, close enough to touch the hem of her mother's garments, but as soon as she puts her hand down, the vision is gone. There is nothing but her empty, too-white cell.

"Make it stop," she whimpers.

Her bottom lip trembles, then pain explodes in her head. She collapses to the floor. Her Accent. It feels as though her Accent has lit the inside of her skull on fire. "Take it out! Take it out!" she cries. "Take it out!" She climbs to her feet and stalks toward her door and bangs, each blow gathering strength. "Take it out! Take it out! Take it out! Take it out, take it out, take it out! Take it OUT!"

The door slides open, and guards dressed in black with green-and-white patches on their arms snatch her off her feet. She struggles in their grip, but secretly, she's glad. Their grip feels real. And during the interrogation that awaits her, she knows she will be speaking to a real person. She knows she will hear a real voice. Maybe a real hand will slap her or figure out some other form of torture. But it will all be real. In that interrogation room, the smells, the sounds, the sights, all of it will be terrifyingly, gratifyingly real.

CHAPTER
39

In Chinelo's office, the recording of the surveillance footage plays
without sound. It reveals a view from high up: the bell tower.
Much of what it watches is cast in shadows, but Onyii, sitting
with Chinelo behind her desk, doesn't need to change any of
the settings on the tablet out of which the hologram footage
emerges to know what she is watching. She has watched this,
alongside Chinelo, at least a dozen times already.

Golibe stands half in the moonlight, half in the darkness.
For a long time, he is still, as though he's nothing but a tree or
a small boulder. Then, in one motion, he brings the gun to his
eye, arms just barely long enough to aim it correctly. A silent
explosion of light from the muzzle flashes. Then the boy topples
onto his back, his arms splayed out just like how they'd found
him.

"Ritualized," Chinelo says to herself. "A double tap through
the left eye."

"Who pulled the trigger the second time?" Onyii asks.

"He did," Chinelo replies, powering off the tablet and turning
in her seat to look at Onyii. "Muscle reflex before his brain
shut down. He'd calculated the muscle reflex to kick in and get

his finger to pull the trigger one more time." She pinches the bridge of her nose and lets out a sigh that seems to deflate her. "We thought we could do it ourselves."

"Do what?"

Chinelo sobs. Onyii can see in the way her body tightens that she's struggling to keep from crying. "We'd imagined this as an elite unit, and the Abd Program was to be an extension of our own family. Those are the strongest bonds, so, it follows, we would fight hardest for those we considered family. We would operate in secret, do those jobs the government or the army couldn't take credit for. Those jobs that the people behind the peace effort could still disavow. We would get dirty so they didn't have to. Anything to free Biafra. It was . . . it was a way to keep the War Girls together. To let us run our own way. And now . . ."

"It's dangerous," Onyii says, "what you've been doing." Her mind works through the pieces she's figured out so far: the intense relationship between the sister and her abd, the conditioning, how much the synths look and sound and move like humans. Like little brothers.

Chinelo barks a hurtful laugh and gets to her feet. "And who are you to tell me what is dangerous?" Her words have turned sharp, bladed. "What do you know of what is dangerous and what is not? You've wanted to die ever since you lost Ify. Every single day, I've watched you try to kill yourself. You fly into battle and leave your team behind, even when you do have backup. But most of the time, you don't even bother with a team at all." She draws close to Onyii, so that they stand nearly nose to nose. "Don't think I didn't read your field reports. I know all about how you've been fighting these past four years." She snarls. "If I'd waited a month to find you, you would've been dead." Then she steps back, her teeth bared in a sneer. "You. You're mostly metal anyway."

Onyii's fist cracks Chinelo's jaw so hard that Chinelo staggers to the floor. Onyii can only stare stunned at where her prosthetic fist has swung. Her arm is still extended, frozen in the motion. She'd moved without thinking. All body. Her mind had evaporated. She had struck her best friend. She could have killed her.

Chinelo gets to her feet, rubbing her already swollen jaw. It takes her a few seconds to catch her breath. Then she wipes the stream of blood running down the side of her mouth and turns to go.

Onyii is too stunned—by Chinelo's words, by the punch—to follow her out.

■ ■ ■ ■ ■

Onyii finds Ngozi sitting on a bench in the central courtyard of the campus. Weeds fill the cracks between the cobblestones. Fallen leaves from the trees that line the paths litter the ground. This is just another sign of the absence of the abd. No one around to clean.

Ngozi stares at a spot on the ground. She has that look in her eyes that Onyii has already seen in so many. Staring at nothing, but seeing everything. She has the look of someone reliving the worst thing that has ever happened to them. Nnamdi's death. Her cheeks are slack, the tribal markings on them sharp against the dulled color in her face.

With a start, Ngozi notices Onyii, then settles. In another

time, Ngozi, startled, might have reached first for the pistol at her side and fired at whatever had surprised her. But now there is no battle-readiness. As though her training has left her completely.

She returns to that spot on the ground. "Maybe this is why Obioma never named her abd."

Onyii stands a little behind the bench Ngozi sits on and thinks back to that kiss she had shared with Kesandu before Kesandu and Kalu had gone off to their deaths. Ngozi had seemed so alive with Kesandu's body pressed against hers. Filled with fire. As though when their lips touched, Kesandu had breathed her own spirit into her lover's body.

"It was her second," Ngozi says. "Obioma had lost an abd early on. A mission gone wrong. Afterward, she'd tried to act as though everything was the same, but we knew she had changed." Ngozi shakes her head. "She'd grown too close." She turns in her seat and looks at Onyii. "That's what happens when you name them. You get close."

We're falling apart, Onyii says to herself. Golibe's suicide, Ngozi's sorrow. Chinelo's rage. *The mission broke us.*

"Now they're all gone." Ngozi says it without emotion. She grits her teeth. Her body tenses. "Why don't those Green-and-Whites just blow up another village already? Maybe we can find some more bodies. Make some more abd, eh?" When she looks back at Onyii, tears stream from her eyes.

Take care of her, Kesandu had commanded Onyii.

Onyii sits on the bench next to Ngozi and holds her shuddering frame in her arms while Ngozi weeps into her shoulder.

She remembers the discs in her pouch. The photos Golibe

stealthily took of Ginika. The photos he hid for himself, maybe to look at before bed or in quiet moments between training sessions. His sister. Whom he loved.

■ ■ ■ ■ ■

Onyii and Ngozi stand at attention in Chinelo's office, their hands clasped behind their backs. Anything to maintain a sense of order after so much has changed.

Chinelo stands behind her desk and looks out the window that opens out over the courtyard.

She must have seen Onyii comforting Ngozi. Onyii wants to be angry at someone else witnessing a moment so private. She wants to stay angry at Chinelo for saying what she said earlier. But the anger slides through her fingers like so much red desert sand.

Chinelo turns to face them. "I called you into my office today, as the two remaining sisters in the Abd Program, to tell you that I've been ordered to shut the program down. As of this moment, the unit is dissolved. Permanently."

Ngozi receives the news with a stone-faced expression.

"That's all. You are dismissed."

Onyii and Ngozi are headed to the door when Chinelo says, "Onyii, stay."

Onyii and Ngozi share a look, and there's a kindness in Ngozi's eyes that Onyii has never seen before. "Thank you," Ngozi mouths before leaving and closing the door behind her.

Onyii balls her fists as she faces Chinelo. "Yes, captain?" She spits out the title like venom.

"The remaining abd have grown unstable, and we cannot

let their aberrant behavior continue. We have been ordered to terminate them."

"By whom? Agu is fine!"

Chinelo's voice is as cold and hard as the metal in Onyii's fist when she speaks. "Have you spoken to him since the mission? Even once?"

It's true. There was so much to do in the three months after the attack, after the doctors and technicians and other personnel had been sent in to watch over the unit. Being put on hiatus should have meant more downtime, but Chinelo had always been away on meetings with Biafran leadership, and Onyii had spent almost all of her time learning her Igwe. Was Agu going to end up like the others?

"Who knows what damage an unbalanced abd might do? To you? To anyone else? This is an order." She turns her back to Onyii and stares out the window. Looking at nothing. Seeing everything. Maybe she's imagining Chiamere's final moments. Maybe she's already planning how she'll do it. "They're just synths anyway," she says to herself, as though she's forgotten that Onyii is standing mere feet away. "They're just synths." She looks over her shoulder. "You're dismissed."

CHAPTER
40

Daren is not coming for her.

The moment Ify realizes this crystallizes in her mind. Her lip is split, and she shivers from the ice water her interrogator has been dumping onto her in buckets. The room is filled with cold, unforgiving chill. The freezing floor numbs the bare soles of her feet.

Her interrogator walks around her with orbs of light circling his head so that only his eyes show. Sometimes, he wears a mask; other times, he doesn't bother to. When she can muster the energy, Ify locks eyes with him.

But now the realization hits Ify like a fist through her chest. Daren isn't coming to save her. She is alone. She doesn't feel bottomless sadness. Instead, she feels freedom. Liberation. *I am the only one who will care about me*, she realizes. *I am the only one who can save me. I am all I have.* She clenches her fists at her sides, rattling the chains that bind her to the chair. *I will survive this.*

She sits on the chair now and lets herself shiver while freezing water soaks her through. It is only by letting go of her body that she can protect her mind. She has walked through so much of her life believing the flesh and meat inside bodies so easily hackable and broken, so easily understood and manipulated, but now she sees that she was wrong. Her skin is hard. It endures. It grows scar tissue to make itself stronger. It molds itself. It adapts. It persists.

"When you visited the detention center in Nasarawa State, how did you communicate with the Biafran rebels?" the interrogator asks.

Ify stares straight ahead. "I was never in contact with Biafran rebels."

"How did you coordinate the attack on the Okpai oil refinery?"

"I knew nothing of the attack on the Okpai oil refinery."

"But you knew who was leading the attack on the Okpai oil refinery."

"I knew nothing of the attack on the Okpai oil refinery."

"You recognized the face of the one known as the Demon of Biafra? Who is this woman?"

"I knew nothing of the attack on the Okpai oil refinery."

"How were you in contact with the Demon of Biafra?"

"I knew nothing of the attack on the Okpai oil refinery."

"Why would you betray your people for the terrorists who attacked the Okpai oil refinery?"

I knew nothing of the attack on the Okpai oil refinery. It is a lie. She had peered into Daren's comms. Then she had climbed a surveillance tower and hacked into his mind while he flew toward Onyii. But she remembers nothing after that. She never reached Onyii.

"We traced the signal to you. When the broadcast went live on our screens, we traced the transmission back to its source. A single watchtower. With you in it."

The interrogator stops and stares at her in silence for several long minutes. Ify doesn't raise her gaze to meet his. The orbs cease their revolution around his head and hang steady in the air, lighting only portions of his face. A chair appears out of the shadows, guided by magnetized strips beneath the floor, Ify has surmised. The man brings the chair to him by holding his hand out, and that is how Ify figures out that he must be an Augment. He can probably read all her vital signs on his visual display: her blood pressure, her heart rhythms. It is probably how he knows when she is telling the truth, when she is lying, and when she has given up on thinking her way into an answer.

But when he sits down in the chair, his body unstiffens. He has the chairback in front of him and rests his arms over the top, then places his chin on his crossed arms. And he stays like that for several more silent moments, staring straight into Ify. "Your screams," he says. "You scream because you are seeing things?"

The question startles Ify. Is this part of the interrogation or something else? "Y-yes."

"You are seeing the things that are in your mind?"

"Yes." She thinks of the visions. Of her mother.

He taps his temple. "It is because of what is in here. Your device."

"My Accent?" But it can't work in there. She has lost her second sight. She can see nothing inside her cell but what anyone else with working eyes can see.

"So that is what you call it." He rests his arm on the chairback. "The walls in your cell are thick. But we can detect your device from the outside. And we can change its signal."

Ify lets out a gasp that surprises even her.

"You may think the torture happens here. But really"—he points out past the room—"it happens there."

Ify doesn't know what to do with this new knowledge. She knows she can use it somehow, twist it to her advantage, but she can't figure out how just yet. So she straightens in her seat and raises her chin.

"Eventually, we will go through enough of your memories to find what we are looking for." He shrugs. "Or you could tell us what we need to know now, and it will stop."

For a moment, Ify feels a fluttering in her chest. A promise to end her torture, to stop the visions from consuming her. All she would have to do is tell them what they want to hear. It doesn't have to be the truth, the whole truth, and it may just buy her time instead of freedom. But she salivates at the promise. Then her will kicks in again, and she stills herself. She becomes as cold and unfeeling as the chair on which she sits.

Her interrogator notes the change in her posture and sighs, like he is disappointed. Then he gets up from his chair and, with a flick of his wrist, sends Ify's chair out from under her, pitching her onto her side. She can't move with her wrists bound to the chair's back, so she is forced to lie there with her cheek to the cold, wet floor while the interrogator walks over to her and undoes her restraints.

Her arms fall limp around her. She knows better than to resist when the guards come in to bring her back to her cell. It is like she is going to be thrown back into water and left to drown. But she is grateful for this chance to speak to someone human. It is like coming up for air. And even if her mind knows that she will once more go underwater, she is grateful for the breaths she was able to take.

■ ■ ■ ■ ■

When Ify, her back stiff from all the time she has spent on this bare bed, opens her eyes and sees Daren, she thinks this is yet another dream. She waits for the scene to play itself out. Will this be Daren consoling her after the girls at school have finished bullying her? Will this be Daren bringing Ify to the laboratory where Nigeria's premier scientists work to build the weapons that will secure Nigerian victory? Will this be Daren in a field watching Ify try to hack animals, then, growing bored, turning her gaze to the stars?

But this Daren doesn't move. He just stands in the opened doorway to her cell. And he looks haggard. His cheeks have hollowed out. His skin has paled. One of his hands trembles and, with the other, he holds it still until the tremors cease. This is Daren as she has never seen him before. He looks like he has been reduced, like he has been made into just a fraction of the Daren she has known her whole time in Nigeria. He's real. This is not a vision.

"Where were you?" she hisses through her teeth, surprised she still cares about his answer.

He takes a few steps into her cell. The door closes behind him. There's nowhere for him to sit, so he takes a seat at the end of Ify's bed.

Ify recoils.

"I heard about what happened," he says in a voice that sounds, like the rest of him, reduced. Weakened. While she has been busy making herself strong here, he has been out there growing soft. "After the hostage incident at the oil facility, I was demoted. I let the architects of that tragedy get away. I'd killed so many of them, but the one truly responsible, the Demon of Biafra, I had let her escape. And, for that, I can never be forgiven."

She holds back a sneer at his self-pitying tone.

"Then I heard that you had been jailed. And since my removal from the combat field, I have been working furiously to clear your name."

Ify's face remains impassive at this news. When she was first captured, she longed to hear these very words from Daren. But she's moved past that. Right now, on this bed, staring at the back of the young man who had once been her protector—her brother—she sees only the weakling who abandoned her in her time of need. "How long have I been here?" she asks in a voice that wants information and nothing more.

"It has been three months since the hostage incident."

It sounds like no time at all. It feels like forever. "And what are you doing here?"

He turns so that, when he looks over his shoulder, he can see her, and she can see a portion of his face. "I am here to tell you that you got your wish."

She frowns at him.

"A ceasefire will be declared. There will be peace between Nigeria and Biafra." He looks to the floor. "All it took was for me to lose Daurama." That self-pitying tone again.

For some reason, it hurts to hear Daren say it that way. *He never accepted me as a true Nigerian.* She stuffs the feelings of regret and hurt down where they cannot be reached. Then she sits up on her bed. "And the crimes I've been accused of?"

"Political crimes. You are a political prisoner. But now that the war is over, the charge no longer applies." When he says, "We must move forward," Ify hears no conviction in it. He cannot let go.

Ify contemplates his words, then looks up straight into his face. "Before I leave, I want one last thing."

A new sadness shines in his eyes as he realizes that she has made her decision. "Yes?"

"I want you to take it out." At the question in his eyes, she continues: "I want you to remove my Accent."

"But why?"

Because it has made me vulnerable, she wants to tell him. *Because it led to all of this. Because I can't control it. Because others have learned to use it against me.* But instead, all she says is, "It is what I want."

Daren lets sorrow remain on his face as he nods. "I will grant your wish." He rises from the bed and heads to the door. "Our doctors will be with you shortly," he says in the doorway. "Before I go, there is one thing I must show you."

Ify wants to refuse him, wants to snarl and spit at his feet. But he looks so broken. So small. She doesn't nod or say anything, but she softens her expression enough to welcome him.

He puts his hand next to her face. Then a digit plunges into her ear. Her Accent hums. The world bursts into golden light.

CHAPTER
41

Onyii wanders the campus. It feels as though everyone is hiding. Nothing moves. Not even the wind stirs.

Maybe if she looks everywhere and cannot find Agu, she can go back to Chinelo and tell her that her abd ran away or that he simply could not be located. That maybe it would be too much trouble to track him down, that maybe he sensed what was coming and took care of their problem for them. But when she gets back into the dorm and walks down the halls of the boys' quarters, the only sound she hears is a touchboard playing piano music. Softly.

Normally, there would be joking and talking and bare feet stomping down the corridors. And it would have been enough to drown out the sound. But now that there is nothing else to mask it, it is all Onyii hears. Her heart sinks.

She walks to his room and stands at the door for a long time, simply listening. She presses her forehead to it and closes her eyes, trying to think her way into what she needs to do.

Instead, she sees that last battle playing out in her head. So much death. She sees flashes of every raid she led, every battle with Nigerian mechs. Every mobile suit she sliced through or shot down or decapitated. Every pilot or soldier she gunned down. She sees the sisters and the abd in that room in the oil facility in their last minutes together. Their faces appear, one by one.

Is all this death punishment for all the killing Onyii has done? Everyone close to her seems to lose their precious thing. She lets herself remember the camp of War Girls and her last moments with Ify. Then she lets herself remember the first time she saw Ify. How small she was in that dark, empty home. Maybe this is the true power of the Demon of Biafra. Everything she touches turns to dust. Everything she strikes. Everything she caresses.

That's it. She'll leave. She will do this one last thing, and then she will run.

She will begin the process of erasing Agu, the campus, the War Girls camp, and the missions that led her there from her memories. She will journey to the Redlands, live there so that the poisoned air and the blood-red sun will peel away at her mind, corrode her braincase. She wants to remember nothing.

She just needs to do this one last thing.

She presses her thumb to the pad next to Agu's door, and the door slides open.

Agu is on the floor by his bed with a small touchboard in his lap. His fingers stop. When he looks up into Onyii's face, he smiles.

"Is it time for training?" he asks.

Several seconds pass before Onyii comes out of her daze. "No, Agu. We're just going for a walk."

He's up on his feet in the next moment and pulls a satchel from the bed. In it, he stuffs his touchboard. He opens his drawer and begins to pull out a pistol and a box of ammunition.

"Don't," Onyii says. Too harshly. "You won't need that today."

He does not hesitate to put it back. Together, they walk out into the late afternoon sunlight.

■ ■ ■ ■ ■

Onyii has only ever seen these mountains from afar. The closest she has come is looking at their cloud-shrouded peaks from the valley in which the teams conducted their firearms training. There was always a band of rocky terrain just below the summits, but green was the primary color. Layer upon layer of forest.

Now, with Agu a little bit ahead, she walks through to find it all just as lush as she has imagined. But quieter. No beasts like those that roam the jungle outside the War Girls camp. No two-fangs or wulfus or whatever radiation-poisoned monsters roam and terrorize the Redlands. Not even mosquitoes.

Some of the fat leaves have fallen from the trees. But most of them provide a canopy to protect people and insects from the rains of the oncoming monsoon season. It's cooler here. The sun, where it casts bars of light through the trees and their foliage, is kinder.

Maybe he'll want to see the sun one last time, Onyii tells herself. For some reason, it feels wrong to end his life in darkness. This needs to be kind. Not like the others. This killing is different.

A sunlit pathway leads out of the forest and curves around the edge of the mountain, out of sight. Agu, perhaps sensing Onyii's thoughts, looks back, and Onyii nods. He bounds ahead, holding his satchel at his side. Onyii follows at her deliberate pace.

She finds him on a small shelf, open to the sun, that looks

down on the whole campus below. How small it all becomes from this far away.

He's sitting down, his satchel at his feet. Onyii stands behind him. Close enough to know she won't miss. Far enough away that Agu won't be able to reach her in time if he decides to resist.

She knows he won't resist.

She slips her pistol out of the holster at her waist in one motion. Flicks the safety off. And she waits. For what, she does not know. Maybe for a crow to caw loud enough to hide the sound of the gunshot. Maybe for another animal to stir and startle Agu out of this moment of marveling over the view. Maybe she's waiting for an Agba bear to charge out of the forest, and the two will battle it, and Onyii will return to Chinelo to tell her that Agu is still fine, that he hasn't been broken, that his prime directive is still in working order.

But there is only silence.

She raises the pistol, sighting the back of his head. It should be instant. Painless.

She feels Adaeze near, as though her trainer stands a mere few feet to her side, just out of her field of vision. It's a ghost, she knows. Maybe a malfunction in her Augmentation, tickling that side where belief in the gods comes from. Maybe the mission broke her too, and this is how.

But she decides not to fight it. Without turning to the vision of her handler, she asks, *What do I do?*

The ghost of Adaeze is silent.

What did you do? You left me, but before that, what did you do? How did you stop? And Onyii knows that the ghost understands that she means *stop killing.*

In the silence that follows, Onyii's gun hand wavers. Her

mechanical arm has never shaken like this. She frowns. It's stupid to wait for a ghost to respond to you. She is just delaying.

Just as she tenses to pull the trigger, the ghost says, *I stopped killing*.

And that's enough to still Onyii's hand. It falls to her side. She bows her head. Sobs threaten to erupt from her, but she grits her teeth, steels herself against them.

"Leave," she says at last. "Run away, and don't ever come back."

Agu grows unnaturally still. Like how he is when he is in a sniper's nest waiting for a target to appear.

"I don't care where you go or what you do. I just never want to see you again." She does not holster her gun. "You have twelve hours to get as far away from here as possible."

He doesn't move.

Don't make me shoot you.

Then, slowly, he stands up and faces her. There is no expression on his face. "May I take this with me?" He brings the touchboard to his chest and hugs it.

The question startles Onyii. And just like that, tears pool in her eyes. She nods.

Something like a smile curls Agu's lips, then vanishes. He walks past her back down the trail and into the forest.

She turns to where she felt Adaeze standing moments ago and shakes her head. No, just a ghost.

■ ■ ■ ■ ■

Onyii is nearly finished packing when she sees Chinelo in her doorway. After a moment, Onyii resumes packing, refusing to look her in the face. Quiet hangs in the air holding the motes of dust that float in the beams of sunlight cast through the windows.

"Where will you go?" Chinelo asks in a voice so low Onyii almost doesn't hear her.

"I don't know. Anywhere."

Then nothing.

Onyii finishes, then zips her bag shut. She rises to her full height, and Chinelo's head tilts, and there's a beseeching look in her eyes that Onyii can't remember ever having seen. *Ask me to stay*, Onyii wants to tell her.

"It's official," Chinelo says. Her hands shake at her sides. Her fingers are covered in blood. Chiamere's. Did he fight back when she did it? "The ceasefire. They are going to make the announcement in a week. A broadcast." The words come out of her haltingly. "We won." Tears burst out of her. "Onyii, we won."

Just ask me to stay, Onyii hopes her eyes say. *Please.*

"We did it." She takes a step closer to Onyii and slams a hand on her human shoulder, trying to smile through her sobs. "You and me. We get to build a . . ." She struggles. "We get to build . . ." Then she falls to her knees and wails. She buries her face in her bloodstained fingers and wails and wails and wails, and her body convulses, wracked by a pain Onyii cannot imagine. "What have I done?" Chinelo says, when she's finally able to look up at Onyii. "Tell me it was worth it. Tell me all of this was worth it. Please. Tell me. Please."

How many times has she asked herself those very same questions? Just as much blood stains her fingers. The special sorrow of survivors. That is what Onyii hears in Chinelo's sobs.

And that is what finally convinces Onyii to get down on her knees, take Chinelo in her arms, and open the gate. So that Chinelo can hear her anguish too.

Crying, they hold each other until well after the sun sets. By the time the stars appear and they've fallen asleep, they are a blissful tangle of limbs, at rest at last.

CHAPTER
42

Ify lies on her back in a field of light and slowly sits up. All around
her is white.

Suddenly, the world turns into static, like what would happen
to her screens if someone's signal interfered with hers. Then it's
night. Everything is evening-blue. And quiet.

She looks around to see that she's in some sort of dwelling.
A home. It came out of nowhere: the mud-and-stone walls,
the windows, the roof. Then, slowly, furniture forms, first as
pixels, then as things that she can reach out and touch. Like it's
building itself. First an overturned couch, then the remains of
a shattered table. Glass litters the floor of the room she sits in.

Then she hears the whimper.

She turns and sees a shape curled against the far wall. She
squints, then lets out a gasp. It's her. She's in . . . a dream?

Sound comes in short bursts. But all she can hear is gunfire.
Short, staccato fits. Bullet casings clinking against each other
as they fall into the grass outside. This . . . this is her home.
She doesn't quite know how she knows. She recognizes none
of it. But she knows. In the deepest parts of her, she knows.
Her gaze darts back and forth over what used to be the living

room, taking in the damage. Then she looks back at that other vision of herself. This Ify is younger. A child. And she's holding something in her lap. A dog. Its fur is uncombed but slick with wet darkness.

Someone screams. The voice, so strange but so familiar, brings Ify to one of the windows, and she peers out into the dirt courtyard. Someone small, as tall as her maybe, drags someone else along the ground. A woman. The woman kicks and screams and claws at what Ify realizes is a metal arm. The hand, whose steel glints in the moonlight, holds firm onto the woman's braids as clouds of blue dust rise to trail them.

Ify's heart pounds in her chest. More faraway gunfire.

The attacker brings the woman over to an open area where more people are huddled, their backs to each other, their hands and feet bound in metal restraints. They weep around the cloth used to gag them.

Dread curls in Ify's stomach. Her heart beats even faster. That face. She's seen it before. The small attacker joins others clustered nearby. They're soldiers. But they wear no uniforms. Just baggy clothes, their rifles, and masks. The young soldier stands over the hostages. She's just a child. The rest are adults. Ify can't stop looking.

Then, without warning, one of the prisoners pushes forward and rams one of the soldiers in the knee. The child soldier steps to the side, aims its rifle, then fires a single shot.

"Mama!" Ify hears herself scream. The word comes out of her before she knows what's happening. "Mama," she whispers. The realization comes rushing in after the word. She's not in a dream. She's in a memory. She's trapped in a memory.

The prisoner stops moving. The others wail.

Someone clad in all black, almost rags, holds a small recorder up to the face of a man who stands behind a row of children, all of whom have their rifles aimed at the backs of the heads of the hostages bound before them. The man speaks in words Ify cannot hear. But then he stops speaking. Ify cannot bear to keep watching. But she cannot keep from listening. Gunfire lights up the night. Then comes the clinking of the last bullet casings. Then silence.

Moonlight falls through the window, illuminating the feet of the little girl still in the room. Ify knows it is herself. Can tell in the utter stillness of the child, the vise grip she has on the dog bleeding against her chest. Bootsteps draw closer, and Ify watches the child soldier burst into the room and sweep it with its rifle. The soldier stops when it sees the younger Ify. And for a long minute, the soldier just stares, then lowers its mask to reveal a face Ify can't believe she's seeing.

The girl is younger. The scars are fresher. But the face is the same.

Onyii.

After what seems like forever, Onyii walks over to the younger Ify and grabs her arm. The girl doesn't budge, but Onyii is too strong and pries her arms apart. Then Onyii lifts the dog into her own arms. The younger Ify's robe is covered in blood. For a moment, Onyii looks at the now-dead dog, then she walks back out of the room and into the field surrounding the compound. Ify turns away from her younger self and follows Onyii out of the room but stops and can only watch as Onyii carries the dog to the shallow grave dug just on the edge of the forest. She doesn't drop the dog in but rather kneels, then slowly rolls the dead animal on top of the bodies already gathered there.

One of the soldiers sidles up next to her, but she doesn't face him. She merely stares into the grave. "Anyone else in there?" he asks her, in Igbo, his mask muffling his voice.

"No," says Onyii.

The other soldier chuckles with his belly, then heads Ify's way. Onyii's hand shoots out. Her fingers wrap around the man's wrist. "Hey! What now? What is wrong with you? Hey! Let go! You are squeezing! Ow! Jeezos!" He falls to his knees with Onyii bending his arm awkwardly behind him. "What is the matter with you?"

"I checked," she says in a voice drained of all emotion. "There is no one left in that house."

After a few more seconds, Onyii releases her grip, then walks toward the other soldiers. She doesn't even bother looking to see if the man believes her. She knows that he will simply trail behind her, nursing his broken wrist.

When Ify looks at her younger self, she sees a girl unmoving with her arms at her sides, as though she were already dead.

But Ify knows what happens next. Onyii will return, alone, and find her in that same spot. And Onyii will carry her just as she'd carried that dog, and Onyii will bring her to camp and raise her and tell her that she is Biafran, that she had been captured by the enemy and that she has been rescued. That she has finally been brought home.

■ ■ ■ ■ ■

When Daren disengages from Ify's Accent and she finds herself back in her cell, she can't move. Tears stream down her face.

"It is a lie," she says. Then her voice hardens. "It is a lie." Anger courses through her. "It is a lie! That is not what happened! You implanted that memory."

Daren's extended fingers retreat and reform. He takes his time slipping a glove over his hand. "Even if we did possess the technology to fabricate memories, I would not have done that to you. I can only pull what data already exists."

"But how? If it was my memory, how could I watch myself? It's not real!" She seizes on that hole in Daren's explanation, tries to force it open even wider. "I could not have remembered all of those things."

"The rest of the data was pulled from the surroundings." He looks at his hand when he speaks, smoothing out the glove's wrinkles. "She was the one who took your family from you."

He rises to his full height, still more like a shell of his former self, and leaves before Ify can shout at him. Even if she had called out to him, told him that he was evil for telling her these lies, that he was doing this only to hurt her, she would not have fully believed it. She had known.

A piece of her had known all along.

■ ■ ■ ■ ■

The doctors arrive to remove her Accent.

They will put Ify underwater to prepare her body, bathing her in the healing fluids that will strengthen her system before they operate. Then they will use their tools and technology to remove the cursed device from Ify's ear. It feels odd to think that this is how they will blind her. They will remove her second sight by pulling something out of her ear. But she will, from then on, see the world differently. She wonders what it will look like.

Whether it will still have the same colors, whether she will see light differently, whether shadows will be deeper or paler. She wonders if the world will be blurrier or if she will be able to tell a smile from a frown with the same quickness she used to have.

Afterward, they will place her unconscious body back in the water and fit a breathing mask to her face while her body heals, then they will free her.

Questions race through Ify's mind about what awaits her. But she finds a way to still them. She conjures up a face. A single face. The one she will search for. The one she is sure to recognize. The face of the person who began this cycle of hurt. The face of the person she will kill in order to end it.

As the water from the healing chamber passes over her face, she thinks of Onyii.

■ ■ ■ ■ ■

Daren doesn't ride with her to the border.

Except for the guards, she's the only one in the van. None of the soldiers they pass on the winding road to the edge of Nigerian-held territory pay them any mind. The closer to the front lines they get, the quieter things become, as though all that Nigeria cared for was war. Without that engine, the war machine sits still. How much of the energy that powered Nigeria, that made its citizens active, that drove its scientific advances was drawn from war?

The border station is small. There is a large gateway for vehicles and a smaller one next to it for individuals. Both are connected to a metal trailer that sits comfortably in the shade of a hovering roof.

The guards stop the vehicle and escort her out of the van. She's passed off to another set of guards who walk her to the gate. The air between the two metal poles of the gate shimmers. A scanner. When she leaves, they want her to have truly left everything behind, to take no piece of Nigeria with her into whatever wilderness she walks.

The border station feels like the last living thing before the desert spread out ahead of her.

She does not know where she is, only that there are patches of green somewhere along the horizon. The world's colors are sharper, the humidity of the oncoming monsoon season heavier. But her body feels harder. Her insides, tougher.

She will need to be those things to do what she knows she has to do: Find Onyii. Avenge her mother's death.

She clenches her fists at her sides and takes her first step forward.

INTERLUDE

Enyemaka's eyes open onto darkness. But the inside of its face fills with rising heat. The ground in front of it, sheathed in night, grows bright. Spotlight. Enyemaka's eyes are like spotlights. The rest of the metal body hums to life, and the droid straightens out of a crouch. Bits of rust flake off of it. The world comes to it in a rush as its systems power back on. Sight, smells, sounds. Images that are not from the present intrude on its vision. Fingers fondling flower petals. Mechs half-submerged in the grounds of a camp, sideways after having fallen from the sky. A girl's shaved head. Warmth blossoms in Enyemaka at the memory of her face. It does not know why. It has no more memories attached to the girl. When the droid tries to reach for them, it finds only emptiness. And that is when it remembers it is in the desert. The Redlands. The radiation has corrupted its memory files.

"WOO-HOO!"

Enyemaka turns at the sound.

A figure leaps up and down and flails its limbs. Arms. Legs. The words come back to Enyemaka piece by piece. Then comes the word *human*. When the human stops pumping its fist into the air, it starts babbling. A moment passes before Enyemaka realizes that the sounds coming from the human are familiar. The human is speaking Mandarin.

"I thought you were done for!" the human exclaims. The expression on its face reminds Enyemaka of the little girl whose head it once shaved. A smile. "Hello, my name is Dr. Liu Xifeng. I am a scientist."

Enyemaka looks down and sees a cable extending from a slot in its side and ending in a device the human holds. The human glances at the device's screen, swiping and tapping at it. After a moment, Enyemaka realizes that the cable glows in the night because it contains its data. It contains Enyemaka. As power flows into Enyemaka, it feels the nanobots coming back to life. They are not as they were. They don't carry the same whisper. The commands they feed Enyemaka are automated. They latch on to the bits of memory that remain. Then, suddenly, visions return to Enyemaka of the camp where it buried the soldiers. That is the last task Enyemaka accomplished.

The android straightens with purpose. That is what Enyemaka must do. Enyemaka takes a step forward, then another.

"No, wait! Wait!" The human scrambles to collect its gear: the device it holds as well as what Enyemaka knows to be a battery pack, a Geiger counter for the radiation, and a sled-like contraption it straps onto its back.

The cable snaps loose from Enyemaka, and the human—Xifeng—grows even more frenzied.

"Wait, wait, wait! You're not fully charged yet! And the radiation is still infecting you! We have to get you to safe ground!"

But Enyemaka keeps walking. Signals, distant and fleeting like fireflies seen from far away, ping in its head.

"Where are you going?"

Enyemaka turns and activates its own projector to display a visual recording of its last memories: the camp as dawn spreads through the sky, the blood long since dried and no longer shining in the light, Enyemaka carrying each corpse—some of them in pieces—to carefully and uniformly dug pits, depositing them softly, then burying them before affixing a marker.

Xifeng stares in wonder. "You . . . you're burying them," the human whispers.

"And I record their passing."

Enyemaka turns its back and starts walking.

"I want to come with you." Xifeng stumbles to Enyemaka's side, burdened by her equipment. "Let me help."

And that is how it begins for them.

Enyemaka follows the signals pinging in its head, soft whistling from comms that survived battle, until they arrive at another site of carnage. Enyemaka documents the scene by scanning it and feeding the data into Xifeng's storage device. Then, together, they dig the graves and bury the dead, Nigerian and Biafran alike. When they are finished, Enyemaka follows the next signal to its end point.

On one battlefield, Enyemaka senses familiar traces of nanotechnology. In this spot and on the ground now are things both machine and human, that exist somewhere in the space between Enyemaka and Xifeng. "Augments," Xifeng calls them. Nanobots swirl in the air like flies above some of the corpses, and, sighting Enyemaka, they fill the android with their data. And that is how Enyemaka discovers there is a young woman who pilots a mech and whose name is Onyii. Who made her.

A piece in the mystery of Enyemaka's self slips into place. Her. Not *it*, her.

One day, they stop at the crest of a ridge to find a near-endless army of androids who look like slimmer versions of Enyemaka lined up in rows, mechanically digging at the ground, then moving forward together to dig more. The ones at the back make movements like they are reaching into a bag and putting something into the recently turned earth. A single groove in the land. Hard soil cracked open by unthinking metal hands. Their bags, little sacks pockmarked by holes, have been empty for a very long time. And yet they continue to plant.

"Someone left them here," Xifeng says with sorrow in her voice. Any traces of a human or a factory or a corporation are gone. Maybe dead and buried beneath their feet, maybe somewhere up in the sky.

Enyemaka does not quite know why, but she already feels linked to these things. A word rises to the forefront of her mind: *sister*. They are her sisters.

She walks down the ridge and puts her hand to the shoulder of the nearest robot and mimics a thing she keeps seeing in her memories. Enyemaka puts her face to the side of the robot's head and ejects nanobots. They may have begun as someone else's, but they passed through her, became her, and now they will pass through this android too.

The android stops immediately, then turns to consider Enyemaka. Then Enyemaka does what she has seen in many of her memories, not just those she was born with but those she collects at each grave site. With the light in her eyes, she smiles.

Then, as day turns to dusk turns to night, Enyemaka marches among the androids, breathing life into them, populating them with her data until they have all stopped. Together, they head up the ridge to where Xifeng has set up camp.

Xifeng's mouth, when she finally sees them, hangs open.

Enyemaka gestures behind her to her family. "They will help us record what has happened here. And they will help us bury the dead. This is now our programming."

Something strange happens to Xifeng, something Enyemaka has not seen the human do yet. She has seen the human grin at her. And she has seen the human quietly weep when she does not think Enyemaka is watching. But she has never seen the human weep and smile at the same time.

Enyemaka smiles back. And, together, they walk into the night in search of the next field of corpses.

PART

III

CHAPTER 43

Nine Months Later
Benue State, Southern Border
Nigeria, 2177

Onyii always has the option of piloting a drone from an air-conditioned room, lit by the walls of monitors circling her. But she prefers to fly an aircraft. It's what Ngozi and Chinelo have taken to calling a pencil plane. A light propeller-driven passenger plane with stabilizers in case she needs to hover. It's an old model, nothing like the military aircraft left over from the war. And Chinelo has warned her against using a mech to do these recon runs. She might be mistaken for a combatant.

Still, there's no one out here on the border of the Redlands to shoot her down, even if she were in a mech.

Below her, the earth is red clay. Brown rivers run through it. Were Onyii to stand at those riverbanks, her Geiger counter would beep so fast it would break. Radiation hangs thick in the air and glows beneath the soil. Beasts occasionally roam, bigger than they have any business being, and often with more limbs than they have any business having. Shorthorns, two-fangs, wulfu. Even larger scaled lizards that crawl on six legs like small dragons and fly in the air in bursts that look more like large jumps.

There's the occasional hut or dwelling. Most of them are covered by a translucent blue dome that Onyii knows keeps the irradiated air out. A way of protecting the inhabitants and filtering the air that comes through. Scavengers leave their dwellings dressed in close-fitting hazmat suits with spiderlike antennae sprouting over their shoulders, spinning to tell them what is in the air, what is in the ground beneath their feet, and what is in the water into which they dip their buckets.

It's land neither the Nigerians nor the Biafrans want to touch just yet. But maybe someday Biafrans will have the technology to terraform this place. To reverse the tide of ecological destruction and gather these scavengers, these left-behind, and bring them into the Biafran fold.

After a few circuits with no refugee sightings, Onyii banks to the left, circles around, and heads back in the direction of the unpoisoned land. Green sits on the horizon in the distance. Already at the edge of the Redlands, eco projects have sprouted up. Testing facilities where scientists will begin figuring out how to make the Redlands livable.

To her right, she spots a hill cleaved almost in two by an invisible line separating verdant greenland from blighted redland. And on that hill, in the distance, a house.

Without giving herself a moment to hesitate, she banks her plane farther to the left. The thing rattles gently around her. Where that might frighten others, it invigorates Onyii. She wants to hear the looseness in the metal, the way each slat, each gear, each plate moves through air. She passes back into redland but right where it abuts a small hill at the top of which lies the cabin with its tall, too-green grass.

As her aircraft lowers itself, a cloud of red dust rises. She lands, then punches in a sequence of buttons on her console and shifts the gear forward. When everything powers down, she flicks the switch against the wall to her right, and the flexiglas pops open on one side.

Onyii gets out, hops to the ground, and shakes the stiffness out of her legs. After some more stretches, she cranes her neck to look up the hill to the underside of the cliff. At her feet, a beetle and a scorpion keep pace with each other, the beetle trudging through grass, the scorpion skittering along on red earth. But they never cross.

At a point along the hill's base lies a small flowerbed. Onyii heads toward it. A path reveals itself, winding up the hill. How many times over the past nine months has she made this trip? And yet it still feels new. Like she's going to get to the top and find that the person she's looking for is no longer there.

But, every time, she makes the walk. She doesn't count her steps, just takes one, then another, falling into the rhythm as she gets higher and higher. Her thoughts evaporate during the trip. She wonders if this is what it's like to pray. Or to meditate. She had always assumed when people had their heads bowed or stared into space that the machinery in their heads was at work. It was calculating trajectories or formulating sentences. It was preparing them to interact with the world. Or they were in contact with another similarly connected person. Two ends of one phone line. But for Onyii, it is the only time her world is quiet. Not even the buzzing of mosquitoes can reach her.

Which is good and well, because when she gets to the top, she knows she needs to be steadied emotionally to walk up to that front door, past the small yard where goats munch on grass and past where the dirt turns into a stone pathway, and raise her fist to knock.

She stands at the threshold, takes a deep breath, and waits.

Footsteps sound. The door creaks open.

The woman on the other side does not smile, but Onyii has learned that she has other ways of showing she is glad that Onyii has visited.

"Come inside," Adaeze says, "let us break kola together." And Onyii obeys, still unable to shake the habit she developed as a child soldier under Adaeze's eye.

Even though chairs and barstools adorn the space—kitchen and living room joined into one—Onyii and Ada sit cross-legged on the floor. Adaeze has a disc in her hands, and on it sits a kola nut encased in a hard white shell. From where she sits, Onyii can smell it, sweet and rose-like.

Ada hands the disc to Onyii, who takes it and bows.

"Who brings kola brings life," Onyii says, then looks up. "But it is you who should break the kola nut." She hands the disc back.

Adaeze hesitates, with the disc returned to her hands, like she's on the verge of refusing, before she smiles and takes the nut between her thumb and forefinger. With a small squeeze of her mechanized digits, she forces a crack through the thing, splitting it cleanly into two halves. She takes one, then hands the plate to Onyii, who takes the other. And, together, they chew the bitter caffeinated nut.

When they've finished, Ada rises to her feet. "Let me go get some palm wine."

Several old-fashioned books on the shelves lining the wall to Onyii's left lie on their sides, and though the shelves sit on the top half of the wall, the thin and thick tomes leave plenty of room.

Adaeze returns with a bottle of palm wine and fills the two clay cups she has brought with her. When she sits, Onyii can see the effort it takes her. For so long, Adaeze had lived a life of motion, and Onyii imagines her filling her days now pacing back and forth along the length of the shelves. Sitting down in an armchair only to get up a moment later. Her hair has grown out into an afro threaded with silver. Each new crevice on her face speaks of a battle or a time she faced death and managed to walk away. But now Ada is able to sit still. Maybe living in this place, far from everyone and everything, has finally slowed her down.

Onyii sips from her cup. The palm wine burns and is sweet at the same time. "Even though I never announce myself, you always seem to know I'm coming."

Ada shrugs. "You don't have to become ready if you stay ready." She brings the cup to her lips and drinks. "How are you?"

It still startles Onyii a little to hear Ada talk like this, asking after her health instead of her operational readiness. "I'm well. I have been volunteering at the receiving stations. When the refugees arrive, whether it's one or one hundred, it gives me something to do."

"Something that isn't what we used to do." Adaeze walks into difficult conversation fearlessly. She doesn't deaden her voice the way Onyii notices others do when discussing the atrocities of the war. She doesn't skip over those things. She recognizes it all. And doesn't run away. "It is good to keep busy. But you also cannot forget what we are, what we did. We will forever be haunted by it. Some of us may walk through the rest of our lives looking the very picture of health, but no one can truly know what is in another person's head." She smirks at Onyii. "Even if they have the best comms in the world."

"Is that why you stay here? Away from everyone else?"

Adaeze stretches her neck. "I stay here because my father was a goatherd, and I have his genes in me."

"No one can see you suffer out here. That must be . . . peaceful."

"The shorthorns and the bats and the two-fangs all have eyes to see me with." She tries to keep a straight face to go with her stern voice, but a smile curls her lips, and the two of them chuckle. Onyii can't remember the last time she laughed this freely. When they calm down, Adaeze pours them both more palm wine. "I have to remember to think. To live with the past. To sit with myself. For so much of the war, we busy ourselves with combat, with strategizing and fighting, as a way to stay out of our own heads. As a way to lose ourselves. We think that giving in to our basest impulses means giving in to our truest selves." She shakes her head. "But that is not who we are." She holds Onyii's gaze. "That is not who *you* are."

"And who am I?"

"You're the girl who was still wearing her school dress when she first snuck away and cut her way all through the bush to get to the rebel camp where you knew I was hiding. The one who slept on a dorm room bed with ribbons tied around your bedposts. Now that there is peace, you have time. Spend some of it with that little girl."

"I may not have all that much time."

Adaeze nods, her eyebrows creasing into a frown. "The commission."

The hostage incident at the Okpai oil fields prompted the end of hostilities. With the death of internationals, the colonial powers intervened to broker a ceasefire as prelude to a full and lasting peace treaty. But one condition the Nigerians had demanded, in the healing of the fractured nation, was a Truth and Reconciliation Commission. An accounting of the horrors that each side had visited on the other.

"Yes. If the Truth and Reconciliation Commission goes forward and the investigations uncover what I've done, then surely I will be punished. Whether dead or in prison, I will have lost my freedom."

"You were at peace with dying before. What has changed?"

Onyii looks at the cup in her hands and the ripples in her palm wine. "It was different. Dying on the battlefield in order to make Biafra a reality—that would mean my life served a purpose. I would die using my skills and my abilities to make an impossible thing happen. But this? Being judged by people who think they're better than us? Who interfered in the war when they said they wouldn't and have caused so much death and destruction but will go free and unblamed? It is . . . unjust."

Adaeze shakes her head. "It is how the oyinbo do business. They are allergic to claiming responsibility for their actions. This is their history. Perhaps they know no other way." She looks to Onyii. "Perhaps this does result in your death or your imprisonment. But what if it is the way to move Biafra forward?"

"What?"

"In the Book of Genesis, Chapter 22, the Binding of Isaac. You know this story?"

How long since Onyii even touched a Bible? She'd dismissed Christianity as a remnant of ancient colonialism, but Ada had always been a believer, even in war. And even as she continued to claim that Chukwu lived in the minerals at their feet and the sun in their sky. For so long, Onyii had been told that the Hausa and the Fulani and other tribes who united under the Nigerian banner were heretics for belonging to another faith. But, yes, Onyii remembers the story. "Yes."

"God demands a sacrifice of Abraham. His son Isaac. And Abraham agrees, bringing his son all the way up Mount Moriah. He binds his son and withdraws a dagger and is ready to kill his son in order to fulfill God's will when God sends an angel from the heavens that commands him to stop. Abraham looks up and sees a ram caught in the bushes. Now that it is known that Abraham fears God, the ram is sacrificed in Isaac's place."

"It is a familiar story, Ada."

"It is in the Qur'an too."

Onyii frowns. Why would Adaeze bring up the name of the Fulani holy book? The basis of their blasphemous faith. Is this a test?

"What do you mean?"

"In the Islamic text, there is a different son. Ishmail. And the binding comes to Abraham in a vision. Like a dream that haunts him. He tells Ishmail of his vision. And Ishmael submits willingly. When Abraham—here, called Ibrahim—is prepared to kill his son, God stops him and provides him with a ram. As a reward, Abraham will be given another son. This son will be named Isaac. And he will become a prophet."

"I don't understand."

"Some things happen in cycles. It is this way with parables."

"Which one am I supposed to be? Abraham? Isaac?" She twists her mouth around the Muslim name. "Ishmail?"

Adaeze bows her head. "I was once willing to sacrifice you for the glory of Biafra. There was a time when I would have done it without question. I let you run with me on nearly every mission. Every village raid. We killed so many people together, and I held you at my side the entire time. Watching as, bit by bit, your innocence bled out of your wounds. This is what war does. It asks terrible things of you. You were my Ishmail." A spasm passes through Adaeze's shoulders. "I let him take your arm."

"You didn't let him take both." It hurts Onyii to hear Ada talk like this, angers her. To hear her take blame for Daren maiming her, for not rescuing her in time. The anger bubbles inside her, rises. Her shoulders tense.

"Onyii, stop. Don't give in." Adaeze has a hand stretched out, but then she puts it back in her lap. "Just . . . let me feel regret for a little while longer. We need peace, Onyii. Biafra needs peace."

"And what if there is no ram in the bush for us, eh? After everything I've been through, everything I've done, what if there is no one to come out of the sky and tell me to stop and reward me for my faith?" Onyii is on her feet now. Spilled palm wine soaks the rug at her feet.

Adaeze rises more slowly. She isn't tensed for battle. Nor is she coiled to strike. She stands ready for whatever it is she expects Onyii to give her. "There is no ram for us, Onyii." She inclines her head toward her door and seems to indicate the whole expanse of Biafra outside of her home. "Be the ram for them."

CHAPTER
44

A small drizzle patters on the leaves above Ify. The elephant grass swishes around her as she moves at a crouch. Fireflies, their lights made brighter by the trace amounts of radiation in the air, flare briefly before winking out. It's almost like they float past, appearing in one place then in another a meter or two above.

Gone are the bangles and bracelets that once ringed her wrists. Now, instead, she wears thin silver wristbands, stolen from an armory at a Nigerian outpost along the border with the Middle Belt. They expand to form the laser blades she uses to cut through the brush.

In the first months, Ify missed her Accent. The longing would pass over her in waves. But then the rest of her senses learned the world. She had to engage with all of it, and she began to see and see by smelling and see by hearing. A second second sight.

Developing her natural senses had helped her skirt the outposts. It had helped her know which food was edible and which wasn't. It had helped her move fast when she needed to steal weapons and rations and her tablet.

For nine months, she had wandered and grown stronger. Now, she tells herself, she is ready.

The treeline stops abruptly at the edge of a small cliff. Below is a copse, and in it, a group of boys younger than her. She is reminded of the boys in the detention center Daren had once shown her. It seems like so long ago. She collapses her blades and kneels in the wet grass at the cliff's edge. The boys wear rags, and some of them sit on wooden crates made soft with rain, chewing meat from the jungle rats that hang from a spit above an electronic space heater. Some of the boys have holsters for their pistols. Others have their guns tucked haphazardly in their pants. The longer guns, the sniper rifles and the shotguns, lie at their feet. There doesn't seem to be any order to them all. They look like weapons taken from different armies, weapons she has seen Biafrans use, then sleeker guns she has seen on Nigerian soldiers. Metal glints off the boys. Their limbs. Teched-up arms. A prosthetic leg peeks out from the shorts of one of the boys. The skin on their Augmented parts has been applied sloppily or not at all. None of them seem to care that their machinery is out in the world for all to see. Maybe they want others to see their tech. Maybe they want people to see it all and be frightened.

The boys stir and get to their feet. In their midst stands an older man wearing a vest over his bare chest and ample belly. His arms are more muscled than the rest of him. Light flares yellow in one eye. Tech. The others turn his way, awaiting his command. He picks up a large Gatling gun from the center of their circle with ease and slings it over his shoulder, the ammo belt slapping against his chest. Ify bets that the boys see that and admire the man for his strength. Just like an old man to brag with his body. The boys crowd around him, and he gives them instructions that Ify can't hear. If she had her Accent, she would have heard the man crystal clear, but now it's just lips moving too fast for her to read.

After, one of the boys fiddles with the space heater, and it stops glowing. Then, suddenly, a settlement springs to life in the clearing. Small huts and larger adobe dwellings. A compound with walls that spread into the forest. The buildings come out of nowhere, dirt paths overlaid on the grassy floor. There are no more people where the clearing used to be, but the sound of chatter reaches Ify.

The rain starts back up again. The settlement shimmers.

A hologram.

She turns back to her left and sees, through the trees, a path. And on that path is a caravan of what look like refugees. Someone in the front lets out a cry of joy and points in the direction of the new settlement.

It's a trap. And they're heading straight for it.

Her heart doesn't fill her chest with panic. She notices it and is grateful. It's a new feeling, confronting danger and not being scared.

She hears the noise of animals around her: the soft crush of a shorthorn's hooves on fallen leaves and small branches, the cry of a bat from above. She turns slowly to see the shorthorn grazing a short distance behind her. No fear.

She sneaks a small tablet out of the pack at her waist and makes sure the light is low. It's as thin as a sheet of paper but made out of durable plastics. Facing the shorthorn, she sits in the grass cross-legged and types in a sequence of keys. There's no metal, no tech on the irradiated beast, but that is no longer a problem. It is Ify who has been upgraded.

The shorthorn's neural network appears on her screen. A few strokes and slides later and the image rotates and zooms in. This is the secret. Radio frequency.

She inputs a final sequence, then feels the soft concussive wave radiate out from her. When it hits the shorthorn, the shorthorn looks up. At first, Ify can't tell if it's startled to find a human being sitting in front of it or if it's now under her control. She types a sequence with one hand, and the shorthorn takes two steps back. Another sequence, and the shorthorn steps forward. A longer sequence, and the shorthorn dances in a circle, rearing and bucking. Ify stifles a laugh. It worked.

She doesn't have much time left. The caravan is almost on top of the fake settlement.

She lies on her stomach, so that no one looking up the small cliff will see her. Then she inputs a key sequence and waits.

The shorthorn snorts, brays, then charges down the cliff, rumbling like a one-beast stampede straight for the clearing.

Suddenly, a clamor of voices fills the air. People shouting, angrily screaming questions, boys asking what to do as the shorthorn crashes through their campsite and stomps all over their projector. The caravan comes to a halt, bunching up like the middle of a caterpillar as the call to stop passes down the line.

Someone whistles behind her. She turns just as a lightknife swings by her head. She dodges. A tuft of silver hair falls to the ground, singed. She scrambles out of the way. It's one of the boys with a machete whose blade glows and crackles with electricity. She doesn't have time to scan him. He takes one giant step toward her and swings, and she leaps out of the way and rolls in the grass. Her wrist blades activate. She gets to one knee and raises them in a cross just as the boy's machete slices down. It sizzles with electric charge. Sparks rain on her. He swings and swings, and she shifts to deflect each blow, her body swaying this way and that, feeling the whoosh and heat of the electrified machete inches away from her skin. She feels, simultaneously, hard as steel and bendable as rubber, like she can take any shape she wishes, contort herself into any position, and strike out without hesitation. Which is what she does when the boy lunges for her again. She catches him on the shoulder, then rolls and kicks him off the cliff's edge.

More whistling.

She sees shapes move in the forest and runs off into the grass.

The steps of the bandits slow around her. She hears them hissing commands at each other. *She went this way. Into the grass. Spread out.* They're not connected. Even though they're Augments, even though they have machinery for arms and legs, they can't connect over a shared comms network. Ify doesn't have time to puzzle over this as a shot rings out. The bullet grazes her shoulder. She lets out a grunt and spins from the impact, falling to the ground.

Just ahead of her are downed tree branches and the hollowed-out husks of abandoned maglev cars. She scrambles through the grass and leaps onto the roof of a car. Gunfire rips through the roof under her feet. She leaps over one of the fallen tree branches to roll onto the muddy, puddle-filled path.

Up ahead, more burnt vehicles form a barricade. This must be another place where they trap innocent refugees, she realizes.

Something rams into her with all its strength, hurling her against a fallen tree trunk. She swings her wrist blade wildly, but the boy who charged her bends back, dodging the swing. She ducks beneath his blow, and his machete sinks into the wood. She slices at his chest. The blade peels the skin back to reveal gears and a metal breastplate. Ify scrambles away and runs. Her wrist blades retract. The light around her fades. She can hear footsteps around her. People running. They don't speak, but she hears them close in. The sound of grass rustling grows nearer.

She leaps up and grabs a low-hanging tree branch. Then she hauls herself up, too fast to linger over the pain burning in her shoulder. As soon as she pulls herself up, she jumps onto the next branch, then pushes off, throwing herself through the air to grasp another branch. She leaps from branch to branch, swinging and vaulting until she can no longer hear the sounds of bandits chasing her.

When she gets back on solid ground, there are only a few patches of tallgrass around her. But she manages to crawl under a van propped up on cinder blocks. Very little of its frame remains, most of the metal harvested or recycled. But the empty, blackened van casts enough shadow to hide her from unaided eyes.

Under the burnt-out maglev van, Ify catches her breath.

Suddenly, something grabs her ankle and yanks her out from under the van.

Ify raises an arm to activate her wrist blades, but the commander smacks her wrist away so hard that sparks spray from the band. It short-circuits, dead. He takes her other arm and smashes it so hard onto the ground it cracks open her other band. His hands wrap around her throat. He slams her head into the ground. Once. Twice. She goes dizzy, the world blurring for a moment. Her hands are on his, squeezing, prying. He's too strong.

Her bag.

It's trapped beneath her. Her legs kick and flail, but he's right on her chest. She slides an arm behind her and searches until she finds what she's looking for. She snakes her hand out and slaps the small magnetized device the size of a bulubu ball cut in half onto the man's back.

He feels the new pressure and scrapes at his back, trying to reach it. It starts beeping, and the commander's eyes grow wide with fear. He leaps off her chest, twisting, turning, trying to get the thing off of him. He seizes, his whole neural network short-circuiting.

An EMP. Electromagnetic pulse. Designed to completely fry any tech it's attached to.

The commander collapses, his body spasms on the ground, then lies steaming in the grass, nothing more than junk metal.

■ ■ ■ ■ ■

Ify finds the caravan back in the clearing. The boys are gone. There are more refugees and other types of people in the caravan than she had initially thought. Many of them wear rags instead of clothes, and many of them are nursing wounds that haven't healed properly. Some of them carry sacks on their backs that hold the few possessions they have left. A few women have young children wrapped to their chests. Most people walk with nothing on their shoulders but their heads.

She skids down the small cliff and comes to a stop at the bottom. There doesn't seem to be a leader. Everyone mills around, confused.

A large trailer takes up a bunch of space in the clearing, one whole end disappearing into the woods.

Out of it steps a woman with features Ify has never seen before but with a face that broadcasts kindness like a beacon. She wipes dust from her forehead and her cheeks, and Ify notices that she has a device on almost every limb. Bands on each wrist that glow with numbers and letters. A necklace with what appears to be a wireless transmitter, an earpiece, a Geiger counter at her waist. It's as though each thing a Nigerian tablet is capable of doing has become a separate piece of tech jewelry on her body. She is probably wearing anklets to help her tell the time.

When she sees Ify, she stops, then joy and relief burst onto her face. "Child!"

Ify squints at her. She's not speaking Igbo or Hausa or even English. Then Ify remembers the letters on the woman's wristbands. Mandarin. A Beijing dialect. Automatically, the translation layers over the woman's speech.

"Oh, thank goodness you are safe."

She wraps her arms around Ify and practically lifts her off the ground, even though she looks as though holding a heavy box over her head would snap her back. When she holds Ify out, Ify sees that her arms are muscle and sinew and that the optimism that shines in her eyes has to fight through clouds of cynicism and despair. She has seen war. Maybe she has seen this war.

She looks around. "Are you traveling alone?" she asks, returning to Ify. "Are there others with you?"

"No. It is only me."

She taps her chin. "Do you know if . . . if there was a settlement here?"

"It was a trap."

The Chinese woman squints at Ify. "A trap?"

"There were bandits here. They created a hologram to trick you. And maybe steal your supplies when they were finished with you. It is okay." Ify puts her hand to the woman's shoulder. "I saved you. You no longer have to worry about them."

"What did you . . ." Her face softens. Ify can tell the woman has realized it's better not to ask. "My name is Xifeng." She puts a hand over her heart and bows slightly. "And what is your name?"

"Ify."

"Well, Ify, would you like to join us?"

"Where are you going?" Ify asks, even though she already knows the answer.

"We are on our way to Enugu. I am leading a group of Biafran refugees, and we are going to try to reunite them with their families. Now that the war is over, the healing can begin."

Ify nods. "I am going to Enugu as well." She pulls her tablet out of her sack, inputs a sequence, and a hologram of a face appears. "I am trying to find this person."

Xifeng smiles. "Good. This is good. I will do everything in my power to help you find her." Then she turns over her shoulder. "Agu!" she shouts.

Ify turns off the tablet and puts it away.

A little boy emerges from the mass of people. He has a scar

running across his face and another long one snaking from his left shoulder to his chest. In one arm, he holds a worn musicboard. Without smiling, he sticks out his hand. "Agu," he says.

"Ify," she replies, taking his hand in hers.

"Welcome."

CHAPTER
45

Onyii stands by the fence that rings the receiving center.

Outside the perimeter, armed with minimal gear, stand Biafran soldiers.

On the ground with Onyii stand those who have chosen to camp this close to the border. Still, even after the declaration of the ceasefire, a band of lawlessness wraps around Nigeria's waist in what used to be that fertile land just before the Middle Belt. Now it's a no-man's-land separating Biafra from Nigeria, filled with shorthorns, radiation, outlaws, and boys for whom the violence never ended, all of them poisoned by radiation.

Some of the people who stand with Onyii were refugees themselves not long ago. They had walked along this road or roads similar. Or they had been received in stations along the coast. Some of them had come in boats trailed by other boats, those latter boats carrying Biafran authorities or Han Chinese aid workers. And they had passed through receiving stations where they were given the first truly warm blanket they'd worn in years. Their shoes were replaced, they were given food, medics tended to their wounds. Their physical hurt was managed in places like this. It will take longer to heal the psychological damage. Onyii knows all too well that some of the people at this fence with her will wake in the middle of the night in cold sweats for the rest of their lives. She has seen grown men who have turned into something kids skip past and jeer at and call the "look-look man."

But she stops thinking about that. Now she looks at them and the hope in their eyes. The way they peer expectantly down the road as far as it will go before it vanishes into the forest. Some of them have been coming here every day for the past nine months. Watching. Waiting.

A whistle sounds from on high. Movement in the towers.

She trains her eye on the path, and the others press themselves against the fence. Some of them crane their necks to get a better look at what's coming around the corner and starting to move into view.

The caravan is arriving.

Someone approaches her from behind. It's Chinelo. She stands at Onyii's side with a satisfied grin on her face and arches her back to get the kinks out.

"You're not back at the station getting ready to hand out blankets?" Chinelo asks.

Onyii shakes her head. "I want to watch today."

Chinelo follows Onyii's gaze, squints into the distance, then chuckles. "Are you waiting for a boy? A long-lost lover?"

Onyii smacks Chinelo's arm. "Come on now."

"They've spent all this time holding a gun. And now they must learn how to hold a girl." Chinelo smirks. "Can't be all that different."

Onyii grows quiet. This morning, she had woken up with the desire to watch the reunions. She'd had a feeling another caravan would arrive. And she'd wanted to see the moment it came into view, the moment when those at the fence would begin to shout out the names of their familiars in the hopes that they would be heard. She wanted to see the refugees look up at the fence, at real live shelter, and quicken their pace. And she wanted to see everyone embrace. She will never forget the first time she saw it. The huddled mass of refugees emerging from the forest, then, with the last of their strength, making a mad dash for the gates. And how quickly and efficiently the Biafran and Chinese guards had organized them into lines so that they could, as quickly as possible, get them food packets and blankets and medical attention. She will never forget how some of those who had been working at the gate had stared, stunned, at the face of someone they hadn't seen in years, someone the war had separated from them. The cries of joy, the tears, the hugging.

She had never seen anything like it.

Chinelo wraps her arm around Onyii. She has grown more affectionate since the war ended and since she has had to spend more and more time behind a desk. And it has taken some getting used to. Those nights when Chinelo would trace the scars lining Onyii's shoulders or those mornings when they would sometimes bathe together.

One afternoon while they were unloading food crates, Onyii had asked Ngozi about Chinelo's behavior, if something was wrong with her. Maybe she was as anxious without war as Onyii was. And Ngozi had smiled and stared into space for a few seconds, thinking of something, of someone, and when she had turned to face Onyii, she had said, "Love."

Love always makes Onyii think of Ify, which inevitably makes her think of the mass grave in which she had last seen Ify's dismembered corpse, the grave the brigadier general had shown her on his tablet. So she had stopped thinking of love. For years, she had shut it out. And here it is again. Love.

"If you love someone, you kill and you die for them," Onyii had told Ngozi.

Ngozi had lowered the crate in her hands, then put her fists on her hips. "That is what love looks like in war. But sometimes, in peace, love wears different clothes." When she stares off into space again, Onyii realizes she is thinking of Kesandu and their last moments together, that kiss they shared in the Okpai oil facility.

"Love." Onyii had tasted the word on her tongue. That is what she had felt when she and Chinelo had wept in each other's arms all those months ago. It's what she felt back at the War Girls camp, when she would go on a run with Chinelo and hope they'd take the long way back to camp, just so she could spend a little more time in Chinelo's company.

And now with Chinelo pressed against her, she mouths the word again.

"Let's go for a walk," Chinelo says, as the beginnings of the caravan come into view. "We have some work to do."

And Onyii lets her lead her away from the fence, Chinelo's hand warm in hers.

CHAPTER 46

Ify uses her pack for a pillow. She bunches it up so that it cushions her neck and hides the sharp edges of her tablet and other devices, but still she is unable to sleep. Even though it's barely dusk, others sleep like the dead, piled in the back of the maglev truck, on top of each other. Many of them are likely strangers. Ify looks at them now. Makeshift mothers holding orphans, other people's children. Kids stretched out on opposite ends of the flatbed, their feet touching, unknowingly tickling each other in their sleep. A few people huddle by themselves. Some of them have the shell-shocked expression of survivors unable to process any more information.

Ify knows that look. In the months since she left Nigeria, she has seen it often. People wandering through the forest, unheeding of the fact that they were walking through a minefield. And when a shorthorn or some other animal nearby stepped on one and it exploded, they didn't even flinch. They just kept walking. Like they were half-dead.

On the road next to the slow-moving truck, two boys play a game they call *saraya* in which they take a ball small enough to fit in their palms—like the baseballs Ify has seen in pictures of the old nations of the earth, like the Philippines and the Domincan Republic—and hurl it as high into the air as they can. Some of the boys step back and forth, trying to see the ball in the sky, sometimes shading their eyes to protect from the sun. Then, they reach their arms up and open their hands to try to catch the falling sphere. Sometimes, they let it bounce on the ground, its elasticity snapping it back into the air, and one boy leaps over the other boy to catch it. Boys with Augments direct the ball with their metal arms or legs, activating its magnetic charges to sweep it in an arc along the ground before sending it up in the air again. Like this, they dance in the setting sun. And when the caravan passes through more forest and the older men and some of the Chinese soldiers hack through the bush, the boys play in the shade.

The one named Agu watches them with that battered touchboard in the crook of his arm.

From time to time, he brings it out and sits it in his lap, whether he's sitting upright or reclined, and he'll lightly tap the keys. There's no hesitation with him, no tentativeness. It's not as though he's relearning the instrument. It's as though he were born a professional and has never stopped knowing how to play like a virtuoso. His head sways to the sound of the music as it takes hold of him.

When it ends, he lets out a heavy sigh, his shoulders slumping.

The scars on his body, where they show through his shirt, have hardened and dulled. Fleetingly, Ify wonders how he got them. What kind of child soldier was he? Was he like the bandits she rescued the caravan from? Did he struggle to carry a Gatling gun with his frail body? Did a shock-machete slap against his thigh whenever he ran through the bush looking for whatever he was going to eat next? He starts to play again.

Xifeng exits her trailer a few car-lengths behind their flatbed and walks up the makeshift bridge made of pieces of metal bolted together until she gets to the platform attached to the end of the flatbed.

"Agu!" she calls out.

In the middle of his song, he stops playing, gathers up his touchboard, and walks with her into her trailer.

Ify squints at the boy. As much as she can imagine his history, he remains a mystery to her.

Evening descends and brings with it a breeze.

When Agu emerges from Xifeng's trailer, he shakes a little bit, tiny, barely noticeable tremors running through his body. Then, a new peace comes over him. The only free space in the flatbed is next to Ify, so he sits down and resumes his song, right from where he left off.

Ify is in that groggy space between sleep and wakefulness and only belatedly notices the shift in movement beside her.

The descent is what wakes her. Fast and loud like the beginnings of a storm or a battle. Her eyes open, and she raises herself on her elbows. The moon is just peeking through the canopy of leaves overhead, the sky still blue with dark. Lying still, she listens. The last note lingers.

She sees him out of the corner of her eye, and now he seems calm. He lets out a sigh, then leans against the flatbed's frame.

Ify pushes herself up onto her elbows. "Where did you learn to do that?" she asks him in a whisper.

He starts when he hears her. But instead of shuffling the musicboard where she can't see, he clutches it to his chest.

Like it's the most precious thing in the world. "My sister made me learn how to play this musicboard." He pauses and looks at the instrument he hugs to his chest. "She told me it would make me better soldier. If I am moving my fingers, I am better able to manipulate the thing I am holding. I am taking apart guns faster and faster. And putting them back together."

"Is that who you are going back to? Your sister?"

For a long time, Agu is quiet. "I stay with the caravans because I can protect the people. Sometimes, when nothing is happening, I feel fire in my head. And it is like ants are all over my skin. My clothes are becoming wet with my sweat, and I am not knowing what is happening. But when I am having gun in my hands, I am calm. I do not know why it is this way. I am thinking it is my programming. I was made for war."

"Made?"

A shadow falls across his face. Shame curls his lips in a sneer. "You're a synth."

He nods. "We are the same. Me and those boys who attacked us. I looked at them and even though their eyes are red from chewing qat and not being in their own minds, I know they want the same thing I am wanting. To lie in the wet mud and let the earth swallow me when it rains."

Synths only do what they are programmed to. Flashes of memory flit before her eyes. A woman on a bed in a health clinic in the camp where Ify was once a child. The woman playing with a mound of clay molded into a thing with stubby, waving arms and legs. The woman cradling it close to her chest. The woman detonating the bomb inside her. A synth. But, strangely, Ify is not scared of Agu. He could probably kill her easily enough, even though she would fight him. She could make him pay for it, but he would still end her life. She knows this and is still not scared of him.

"It is good, what you are telling me. I am synth. I am soldier. I am doing horrible things, but Xifeng tells me I am also boy and that, once upon a time, I am having mother and father and they are loving me." A slow smile creeps across his face. "When I am telling her what is going on inside my head, she is looking at me with water in her eyes, and I am feeling like old man because I have seen so much war, and she is only looking at pictures and holograms of war. But she is telling me I am little boy, so I am trying to be little boy. But it is tough. Being little boy."

She smiles at him but resists the urge to put a hand on his shoulder. She doesn't want to touch him, not because he is a synth but because maybe she should leave him to his moment of peace and quiet.

So she pushes herself up to her feet.

"Are you okay?" he asks her. The pistol at his waist glints in the moonlight.

"I'm fine. Thank you." She looks to the trailer from which Agu had come earlier and adjusts her satchel. "Do you know if Xifeng is sleeping?"

He giggles, and it's the strangest sound in the world to Ify's ears. But it makes her smile. "Xifeng is never sleeping. Too busy helping all of us." He picks up the rifle that was lying at his side and raises it against his shoulder. To provide watch over the sleeping refugees.

Ify spares him one last glance before heading down the walkway to Xifeng's trailer.

CHAPTER
47

The campus below, an hour's drive from Enugu and even farther from the nearest receiving station, stretches out before Onyii and Chinelo, silent and ghostly. From their perch on the hill, they can see the firing range; the domed arena where the abd practiced their hand-to-hand combat; the spare, spartan building where they had all taken their meals; and the dormitory where they had slept. Or tried to.

Below her, she sees ghosts. She sees the abd lined up behind their tables at the firing range, wispy specters, with their sisters behind them, directing their gunfire at the plastech targets in the distance. She sees them then huddled in small circles, comparing notes, sometimes with their heads bent in silence while they communed through their comms systems. She sees herself and Chinelo and Ngozi and Obioma and Kesandu and Ginika relaxing on wooden ammo crates someone has dragged into the courtyard.

"Are you crying?"

Chinelo's voice startles Onyii out of her reverie, and she hurriedly wipes the tears from her face, metal arm scraping against the metal frame around her eye. "I'm fine."

"If you ask me, I think we could do without this Truth and Reconciliation Commission nonsense. It's a shame we have to destroy this place."

Onyii remembers the day the ceasefire was declared.

Biafrans in the capital had whispered about the imminent announcement. No one but Chinelo and members of the military leadership knew when the declaration would be made, what day, what time. But new hope had filled the city. And as day turned to night, people set up monitors on their roofs and in the streets, and people filed out into the roadways, stopping all traffic, to watch the Biafran prime minister with a military commander beside him address the Nigerian president while oyinbo from the Colonies stood around them. Then the prime minister and the president shook hands, and the secretary-general of the United World Council announced in several languages that a formal ceasefire in the Nigerian Civil War had been declared.

The city had erupted. Biafrans cheering, hugging, weeping.

And Onyii and Chinelo, in their military uniforms, had stood apart from it all. Even though bodies crowded them in the street, jostling them, embracing them, even, at one point, hoisting them into the air, Onyii had felt numb, and when she had looked over to Chinelo, she saw the same numbness. They had lost their closest friends—their loved ones—in order to bring about this moment. And all the while, a single question had repeated itself in Onyii's mind: *What happens next?*

"We will be targeted by the commission," Onyii says to Chinelo now as they look down on the campus where they had trained their warriors, those boys the Biafrans will never hear about, the ones who had helped to engineer the birth of their nation. "Because of the hostage incident."

"That is how it works, right? We are the ones in the dirt, digging in the ground and planting the seeds. So when the authorities come by and ask 'Who is dirty from all this work?' there is only us, while everyone else has been watching."

"It is not like we are taking a shower, Chinelo. We will go on trial. They will hang us."

Chinelo shrugs. "Maybe they will hang some Nigerians too."

Onyii looks to the ground and whispers, "I should volunteer myself. Once we wipe this place out, the only traces that remain of our work will be us. The last pieces of evidence. I will say that I was the squad commander that led the raid on the facility. I was the one responsible for the deaths of the hostages. If they want to blame someone, let it be me."

Chinelo smacks Onyii on the back of the head. "Stupid goat! There was surveillance. You cannot say, 'I was the leader' when it is clear from the footage and their records that I was the captain of this ship." She laughs. "Do you think I will let you take credit for my work? We are not in primary school-oh!"

But I can save some of us, Onyii says to herself, remembering how she had found Agu sitting by his bed in his dorm room, his touchboard in his lap. Then the walk up the mountain. And, when she finally ordered him to leave, the human hurt in his face that he tried not to let her see.

"You will wear your eyes out with all that crying," Chinelo says, with forced playfulness.

Onyii doesn't bother wiping the tears from her face. But at least she has stopped crying.

Chinelo waits a few more moments for Onyii to collect herself. "Are you ready?"

Onyii nods.

Chinelo pulls out the detonator, gets ready to press the button, but stops. She looks at it, then hands it to Onyii. "You do it."

Onyii shakes her head. "No. It is you who should do it." She forces a smile. "I cannot take credit for your work."

Chinelo smiles without irony. "Okay."

Then she presses the button.

They both look out over the campus as explosions ripple through it, and the buildings collapse, falling inward, and the earth opens up beneath it all to swallow it whole.

Onyii reaches out with her human hand. When Chinelo touches her palm, Onyii squeezes. Their skin glows in the moonlight.

CHAPTER
48

Even though Ify steps as lightly as she can, the beams of the walkway still creak beneath her. A few of the refugees stir in their sleep as she passes, but she continues until she gets to Xifeng's trailer. It's so big it takes up nearly the entire width of the trail. The fat leaves from the trees overhead whisper in the breeze.

There are no windows to it, so she can't tell if there are any lights on.

Ify feels around for an opening. A latch, a keypad, anything. Her fingers find grooves in the metal, nuts and bolts, edges where the metal plates overlap, but nothing that suggests an opening. Frustrated, she digs in her satchel for her tablet, powers it on, and inputs a sequence. A series of nodes and edges rises before her: the trailer's security system. In a second, she hacks the thing, and the area of curved steel before her hisses open. Steam billows out, and a rush of cold air washes over her. It's a blessing in the humid night. She peeks in to see a space that looks much bigger than its outside suggests. Consoles everywhere, and headsets that hang from the ceiling. There are old tablets and papers all over the place. Drawings and ledgers cover the floor.

Her feet track in mud. She tries, as best she can, to not leave any prints on the scattered paper, to disturb nothing, to not leave a single trace that she was here. In the center of the room is a table with a surface that glows blue. When she gets closer to it, she sees that it's a map. Of Biafra. The coastline and the jungle inland, marked by a faint green. Red indicates pathways, even where trees and other foliage would disguise them from above. Some of the paths lead into open field, into clearings. And some of those clearings have a series of question marks next to them. The others bear numbers: 2, 7, 12, 89. She wonders what those numbers mean, then she gasps. Each field, each clearing, when she squints, reveals turned earth. Graves. People are buried in these places. Many people.

Beyond Biafra is a stretch of red that cuts across Nigeria like a wound. The Redlands just below the Middle Belt, the land taken by radiation. There's nothing to mark it, no recently turned earth to indicate mass graves, no markings of where battles had happened or where villages had been razed or where tent cities had erupted into being. No markings where troops from either side had been stationed. Just untouched redness.

She finds herself leaning over, focusing on the red. And looking for that site that has by now most likely been covered in sand from new dust storms. There's no reason to believe it would still be visible after all these years, but a part of her wonders if she'll be able to pinpoint that spot in the desert where her aircraft had crashed. The aircraft that had held her and Daren and Daurama. After she had been kidnapped—rescued—from Onyii and the Biafrans.

By her hand is a keypad. Though all the lettering is in Mandarin, her fingers know exactly what to do, and with the push of a few keys, the map zooms out, the land appearing as though viewed by a bird that has shot itself high into the air. Here, she is able to see all of the Sahel. That region that stretches from Senegal in the west all the way to Ethiopia in the east, the old national boundaries overlaid with the regional alliance blocs. Dotting the map in certain rural areas, Ify realizes, are space ports. Launching shuttles to the Colonies above. When she closes her eyes, she can see and feel and smell the observation tower from which she'd watched the shuttle launch with Daren. It seems like a lifetime ago.

She zooms out further until the entire African continent is in view, then out further and now the swaths of red are larger. They cover large portions of Europe. Nearly all of what was once North America. To the east, a sea of blue beats back the tide. Most of China glows a healthy aquamarine, and the glow encases Japan and Thailand and all of Southeast Asia, doubling back over India. Before now, these places were simply names to her. Now the entire world is spread before her, and divided into red and blue. It feels like she is looking at a world divided into the dead and the living: red with radiation and poisoned air and hard, unyielding ground; blue with breathable air and vegetation and drinkable water.

Something stirs in Ify, a small stalk sprouting out of a seed, and that's a sense of anger at the injustice of it. She remembers the shuttles that would ferry precious minerals into space for the Colonies that only seemed to exist to tax them. To take and take and take and never to give.

Before she can turn this new feeling over in her hands, she senses motion behind her. Ify turns slowly to find Xifeng lounging against a console pressed up along the wall. She seems completely at ease, as though she's seen girls like Ify many times before. Ify bristles against it. *You don't know me.*

"Welcome to my cave," Xifeng says with a smile. "I apologize for the mess. Here, let me bring you a seat." She heads around the corner of the table and returns, stooped over a large, bouncing ball that she rolls to Ify. "Here, sit, please."

Ify stares at the huge sphere for a long time, trying to figure out how it works.

"It's a seat," Xifeng says excitedly. "For sitting. Better for my back than stiff-backed chairs."

She's doing that annoying thing where someone thinks that if they speak more slowly, you will understand them. But then she catches herself. She turns her wrist upward toward her, and a series of buttons glow red and orange above her skin.

Ify holds out her hand. "Stop," she says. Xifeng's fingers freeze in mid-motion. "I understand what you are saying."

Ify bends down to sit on top of the ball. It takes her a moment to find her balance on the wobbly thing.

With nearly infinite slowness, Ify rests her hands on her lap. Xifeng stifles a chuckle. Barely.

When Ify feels secure enough, she lets herself bounce on the ball. Only a little, lest she toss herself off and hit her head on the table and embarrass herself more in front of this woman.

"You're from China," Ify says.

Xifeng's eyebrows shoot up. "Your Mandarin is really good. Where did you stud—"

Ify points to her temple. "I downloaded a language patch when I was young. It began my education. The rest, I learned in school."

"Ah, so you can practice on me, then."

"I speak it just fine."

Xifeng sits back. Not hurt by Ify's abruptness, but taken aback a little. After a moment, the soft smile returns to Xifeng's face. "You were looking at my map earlier."

"Why do you mark the graves?"

"The graves?"

"On your map. I figured out what the numbers are." Ify squints. "What are you doing here?" Resentment, quiet at first, starts to boil in her. So many people, the oyinbo and now the Chinese, place themselves on Biafran and Nigerian soil and try to interfere in Nigerian affairs and take and maybe give but always take, and Ify wishes they would just leave Nigeria alone.

"I am an aid worker. With the relief effort. My organization has the sanction of the Chinese government as well as the East Asian Earth Federation. We have an agreement with the United World Council as well and—"

"I did not ask you about that."

Something happens to Xifeng's face. Like she is feeling sad, then angry, then mournful, then hopeful, then sad again, all in less than two seconds. "I am a filmmaker. I work in VR. Virtual reality. Immersive experiences. I am helping with the refugee resettlement. But I am also compiling footage. I am making a record of what has happened here. And I am listening to everyone's stories. Everyone who is willing to talk to me." She lowers her gaze. "Where I'm from, not enough people care about what happens in Africa. Many of them see a black person, on a screen or in real life, and they do not believe they see a human being. And I am trying to change that. My videos create immersive experiences that I will bring back to my country. And people there can relive what you have experienced. They can see what you saw, hear what you heard, feel what you felt."

"And smell what we smelled?"

Xifeng chuckles. "Yes, that too. I want them to feel empathy. And maybe that will result in more aid." She looks off into the distance. "We have no problem sending soldiers. But sending mechs to help rebuild irrigation tunnels, ugh. Asking for that is sometimes like pulling teeth."

"You still have not told me why you mark the graves."

"There needs to be a record."

"Why?"

"To help with the healing." She pauses. "One of the things that must happen for there to be peace is an investigation. Crimes were committed, and they must be punished. It's not about revenge. Please don't think this is about revenge. It's about . . . it's about order. And balance. So I am not just making a record to help my people feel empathy and give more money for aid."

"You are gathering evidence."

Xifeng nods. Oddly enough, she has a look of guilt on her face.

"You are not worried we will try to stop you?"

Xifeng folds her arms. "I had helpers. Androids that . . . that turned into something else." She smirks and looks off into the middle distance. "But they are gone now. They went to form their own community, can you believe that? I wanted to go with them. *Someone* has to document it all. I mean, artificial intelligence growing into sentience right before your very eyes and . . ." She calms down. "I think, when they were finished with their task, they wanted only to be left alone."

Now it's Ify's turn to be surprised. Droids. Like Enyemaka?

Ify remembers the last time she saw Enyemaka, a burnt husk kneeling over Onyii, protecting her from the blast of the suicide bomber all those years ago. Had Enyemaka survived too? Ify permits herself a slow, soft smile at the thought.

"You killed the man who led those boys, didn't you? The ones who attacked us?" At Ify's surprise, Xifeng forges forward. "The ones who attacked the caravan. I tried to stop Agu, but he went off to do the same. You are both children of war. You have been made to bear things that—"

"War does not care about any of us," Ify says, surprised at the anger in her voice. "It does not matter how rich or how poor you are, how light or how dark, how old or how young, anyone can die. Anyone can be killed." Her thoughts are a jumble. She sees the detention center with the Biafran boys, the commander that had led the synths in the attack on the caravan, then she sees Onyii, and finally she sees Daren. She calms herself. "It is what it is."

"I can study your land and read about your conflict, and I can ask to hear stories, and I can plug into your braincase and relive your memories, but I can never truly know what you experienced. What Agu has experienced. I am not you. Another thing I cannot do is watch someone suffer needlessl—"

"What if that is what must be?" Ify shouts.

Xifeng jumps back against the console.

Why am I so upset? Ify is standing now. She realizes she's kicked the ball away. It careens against a standing monitor, nearly knocking it off its magnetized base, before disappearing behind the table. Her chest heaves, but she takes several deep breaths and calms down. She looks at her hands and remembers what it was like in her cell. When sometimes the only constant was the pain. While everything else swirled around her, while her world was turned entirely into confusion, the pain was always there. The hurt. Like a beacon of light toward which she could always turn in the darkness. The hurt that is now driving her to Enugu and the end of her journey. "I have lost everything. All I have left is hurt." Her bottom lip trembles at the thought of her mother. Her father. Her nose begins to run. She tries to wipe them away, but tears stream down her face.

Xifeng makes a move to hug her but then stops and thinks better of it. Sometimes, it is enough simply to be there, waiting for those suffering to pass through their private sorrow. "The young woman whose picture you showed me. Is she someone who can help you?"

Ify sniffs and nods.

"May I ask who she is?"

The lie comes easily to Ify's lips. "Yes. Her name is Onyii. She is my sister."

Xifeng raises her eyebrows, like she is just now figuring something out. "Onyii," she whispers to herself. Then, louder, "She is Biafran, and your hair, your skin . . . you're Nigerian."

Ify composes herself, shakes her braids away from her face. "I was an orphan when Onyii found me. She took me to her camp. The Biafrans treated me very well." She wipes the last of the tears away with the palms of her hands. "If I do not find her in Enugu, I will leave the city and continue searching for her."

"By yourself?"

The look Ify gives Xifeng is answer enough. Her skin itches. Her chest feels tight. She wants nothing more than to be out of this room. Where, earlier, she could let memories of her past wash over her, now they threaten to drown her. She can't find the composure she used to have, the stillness. The peace. So she heads for the door.

"Wait. Ify."

She stops at the door. But when Xifeng says nothing, Ify tells her, switching to Igbo, "Maybe we do not need the oyinbo. And maybe we do not need the Chinese. Maybe Nigeria can handle its problems on its own." The door opens into the night, and the humidity that instantly weighs down on her skin feels like an embrace. Heat she once found oppressive she is now grateful for. Familiar, hateful heat.

CHAPTER
49

Onyii has never left the country. So when Chinelo asks her to come along on a mission to space, Onyii's first reaction is to shake her head no. "I don't know space," Onyii had said. Chinelo had caught her in a bunker deep beneath Enugu, where the Igwe stolen from the Nigerians stood, polished and repaired and ready for mission orders they would now never receive. But Chinelo had given her that pleading look Onyii found it increasingly difficult to refuse. And she'd said the mission would be brief. A day's work at most. A diplomatic mission to establish relations with Colonies and other countries. To build in peacetime what had been destroyed by war. While Onyii had been sitting in the dark aching for wartime, Chinelo had been working as a government aide to various ministers, shuttling back and forth across the atmosphere, convincing the rest of the world Biafra was a full-fledged country.

"You gonna go up to space with your girl or not?" Chinelo had said at last, cocking her head to the side and mocking the oyinbo.

That had made Onyii laugh, and now she's sitting in a window seat on a ferry that has just left the bustle and activity in Port

Harcourt behind. Port Harcourt had been one of the first targets the Nigerians had bombed at the outset of the civil war. Though it would take a long time to rebuild, the place was already alive with people. People selling news bites, people selling water-filtration systems, people selling VPN devices powerful enough to disguise your IP address with one a whole country away . . .

The ferry takes them into international waters, choppy where they encroach along the shore but calmer once they get farther out. And as they ride along the coastline, they see where the walls bordering Benin and Togo have gone up to beat back the tide.

The ferry docks in the city of Cape Coast in Ghana. And, immediately, Onyii notices the organization. The major transit hub is filled with people in motion, but all of it comes together seamlessly. The main receiving station is all sleek metal and rounded edges, and a banner hangs from the ceiling that says: WELCOME TO GHANA.

Past the border-control station and the friendly but businesslike guards, Onyii sees the boards listing all the times for the ships and trains and buses leaving and arriving. Nobody seems to bump into anybody else. There is none of the patchwork Onyii has for so long associated with home. It all comes together. It all works.

Chinelo smirks at her as they make their way through security and are escorted to the high-speed rail station. Over her comms she says to Onyii, *This is what Biafra will look like when we are done with it.*

Onyii starts, only now realizing that she had let Chinelo share her mind. They smile at each other and, in short order, board a bullet train destined for Niamey in Niger, where the space station is waiting for them. It overwhelms Onyii. So much travel, so quickly. Whenever she finds a stable surface, an armrest or sometimes Chinelo's wrist, she grips it fiercely.

The landscape changes so quickly. The choppy water along bustling coastline, then calm ocean water farther out, then sleek metal halls where the cascade of thousands and thousands of footsteps echoes and a mass of too many people hug and greet and say goodbye. Then the quiet of their train car as they blast their way into the desert landscape of the Sahel, the train encasing itself in a protective shield as it enters irradiated land . . . it's enough to make Onyii dizzy.

Chinelo sits next to Onyii in their private car. Even though they're alone, Chinelo speaks softly when she leans in. "As fast as this is, once the border with Nigeria is properly opened and we can cut straight through to the station in Niamey, it will be even faster."

Onyii chuckles nervously. "Does anyone stand still in peacetime?"

Chinelo giggles and slaps Onyii's shoulder. "We are Biafrans. We never rest. Too busy being the best." She laughs and tousles Onyii's hair, then holds her face, staring into her eyes, before kissing her. When she lets go, she leans back in her chair. "Just wait until we get on that space shuttle and you see what the moon looks like up close." Her eyes soften. "There is nothing like it."

CHAPTER
50

Whistling wakes Ify.

When her eyes open, she moves about the crush of bodies in the flatbed and sees Agu on top of the big truck's cab with his rifle propped against his shoulder. Most of the other refugees are still asleep. A few of them stir at the noises. The others remain motionless, caught in their dreams.

With the whistling comes a breeze. A canopy of trees blocks Ify's vision of what lies ahead, so she climbs up onto the cab to sit next to Agu.

"The receiving station is just up ahead," Agu says. "The refugee camp is just beyond it."

"Can I see your rifle?"

After a moment's hesitation, Agu hands it to her, and, with deft fingers, she unscrews the scope, then puts it to her eye. Still, she sees nothing but green. She tries to adjust the vision, maybe catch a glimpse of something beyond the leaves. But still, nothing. The flora blocks her way. Dispirited, she hands the scope and rifle back to Agu, who reassembles it slowly, not as though he's figuring things out or learning how to do it but rather as though he enjoys it.

The jungle opens suddenly to reveal the Enugu receiving

station. It looks, from the outside, a lot like a prison, with concrete walls that rise up and towers with snipers on top. Ify can tell the barrels of the rifles are pointed in their direction. She wonders what the guards think as the caravan slowly reveals itself, coming out into the sun bit by bit.

Between sections of wall stand chain-link fences against which presses a small crowd of bodies. Anxiety makes their faces sweat, and some of them look feverishly at the caravan as more and more of it emerges from the bush. When the head of the caravan gets close enough, some of the people on the other side of the fence start ululating and frantically waving and shouting names. A child sprints out from the shadows of the jungle to the fence and is the first to be greeted by a pair of Chinese aid workers, who sweep the boy into their arms and bring him past the Biafran soldiers.

Sections of concrete wall rise, and out step more aid workers and soldiers. The caravan parts in a semicircle and forms lines along the perimeter. Some of the refugees are antsier, bouncing from foot to foot, having forgotten their earlier fatigue. A man falls to his knees at the edge of the forest and begins weeping into the soil. Ify can't tell if he's crying because he's happy or sad. A few of the children, without parents, play around and tackle each other, while the others stare in wonder at the walls that loom over them and cast a shadow that nearly reaches the edge of the forest.

The lines pass quickly through the gates.

Ify sits with Agu on top of the truck cab as it comes to a stop and more refugees spill out from around it. Pretty soon, the only people who remain are those who have grown so attached to the caravan that the thought of leaving it behind paralyzes them.

"You are not going?" Ify asks Agu, in part to put off her own decision.

Agu shakes his head. "My sister is not wishing for me to come back."

"Enugu is a big city. You could spend the whole rest of your life avoiding her." She grins. "Sneaking into alleys whenever you see her on the street walking past." She realizes she wants him to come with her. She does not know why. She barely knows him, but it feels like the most important thing in the world that he come with her.

I don't want to be alone.

He looks at her, as though he heard her thought, and for the first time, indecision makes him frown.

"Forget your sister for a second," Ify says. "What do *you* want?"

Agu looks at his gun. "I want not to become a quarter-man like the boys in the forest. Their brains are cut in half by not being a full human. Then cut in half again by war."

Then come with me.

It seems to take forever, but eventually Agu lowers his gaze, then looks to the walls of the receiving center. Already, the majority of the refugees have gone through. What lies on the other side is a mystery. Ify does not know if this will be a place where she can shower, where she can wear proper clothes with no holes in them, or if this will be a place like the detention center in Nasarawa State where boys blew themselves up and called the blood on the wall roses.

Agu turns around to look behind him.

Ify follows his gaze and sees him staring straight at Xifeng. She frowns, but something invisible and meaningful passes between Xifeng and Agu. They look at each other as though they have spent so much time together that they don't need to open their mouths to speak whole paragraphs to each other. In the end, Xifeng nods, and Agu smiles.

Slowly, just like how he fitted the scope back to his rifle, he unslings it over his shoulder and places it on the top of the cab, between him and Ify. He undoes his shoulder holster and places that next to the rifle. Then come the ammunition clips that he had taped together and held in pouches hanging from his sleeveless jacket. Finally, he unstraps the knife scabbard from his waist and sets it down, then slides another blade out of his boot, then takes a moment to stare at the assemblage of guns and knives. When he finishes, he looks like a different boy, lighter, more childlike. Like he has taken off much more than the weight of those weapons.

Agu turns one last time to Xifeng, but the Chinese woman is gone. Then he turns back around and nods to Ify. "Let's go."

They slide off the warming top of the truck cab, land with a soft thud on the ground, and walk together.

"Wait!" Ify starts, then dashes back toward the caravan. She skids to a stop right by the flatbed and vaults over and rifles through all the trash left behind, not caring how dirty her hands get. Smelly clothes, packs from military protein meal supplements, tampons and other hygiene products. Then she finds it.

She jumps back onto the ground and returns to Agu. Grinning, she hands him his touchboard. "You almost forgot," she tells him.

He takes it from her with a smile. Water pools in his eyes.

"Come now," Ify says, smiling. "Before they close the gate-oh!"

CHAPTER
51

Traveling to the Colonies in outer space, Onyii found herself in a state of near-constant marvel. The way fire had swallowed them up as they'd cut through the atmosphere, the almost overpowering quiet of outer space, the way the Colony, when it finally came into view, seemed to loom as large as the moon. But Chinelo, so sure of herself, so practiced in how to self-present, has grounded her, has given her a piece of the familiar amid all this newness. However, the rush fades quickly.

From meeting to meeting, from conference-hall speech to restaurant luncheon, Chinelo has been made to stand behind whatever man has been chosen to negotiate matters on Biafra's behalf. With each slight, Onyii bristles even more. When it was a matter of fighting and bleeding to make Biafra a reality, Chinelo stood on the front lines. Chinelo gave the orders. Chinelo held the rifle. But now that it is time for people to get rich, the men have pushed her out of the way.

It was like this when the deputy minister of education spoke with his Japanese counterpart about university exchange programs for Japanese and Biafran students. It was like this when the minister of health met with the head of a leading

Japanese pharmaceutical company to negotiate a discounted rate for vaccines and cures for the diseases that had spread throughout Biafra during the war. It was like this when the Biafran minister for mineral development had practically given away mining concessions to the Japanese in exchange for a sum of money Onyii knows will go straight to him and not to his office or the people who live on that land. Finally, during a meeting between the Biafran minister of foreign affairs and his Japanese counterpart, Chinelo had had to interject to bring up the matter of refugee resettlement. Up until then, in that cavernous meeting room with chandeliers glowing overhead and food left untouched on large glass tables, the issue had not come up once. Instead, they had spoken of baseball and their children and money. It was then that the Biafran minister had introduced Chinelo as a general governmental aide, basically an intern capable of carrying luggage and little else.

"They are giving away our country," Chinelo had growled to Onyii during a quiet moment between meetings. The two of them had found what, in this Colony station, was called the Viewer, an indoor park made entirely of glass where residents could stare at the stars outside.

Now Onyii and Chinelo amble behind Solomon Kachikwu, the Biafran finance minister, and the Japanese ambassador. Not even the splendor of the ambassador's residence can alleviate Onyii's anger. The two women follow the two men through the cobblestone lanes, past sunken koi ponds and down paths framed by sculpted hedges.

"Does it surprise you how much the inside of a Colony resembles Earth?" Hideki Kikuta wears a slim-fitting suit embroidered with what Onyii sees are kanji. The silvery lettering sways and glows in the artificial light shining down on the villa courtyard. Hideki Kikuta, Japanese ambassador to Biafra. Even though Chinese migrants and corporations have been the first to launch a presence in the new nation, Japan is the first Colonial power to establish official relations, the first voice Biafran leadership could hear from space.

Ambassador Kikuta walks a dozen paces ahead of Onyii and Chinelo with Finance Minister Kachikwu at his side.

"Well," says Minister Kachikwu in response, "it does not resemble any part of Earth that I have ever been to."

The Japanese ambassador raises an eyebrow at the Biafran man and smirks, and Onyii sees Chinelo seething.

He makes us all seem so provincial! Chinelo hisses into Onyii's comms. *Like we've never left our huts!*

Onyii understands, then she catches herself. This is the farthest away from home she has ever been. She is practically an adult, and all she has known is Biafra and, briefly, Nigeria before that.

This is why the rest of the world is always looking down on Africans. Because of stupid, greedy men like him.

Around them, androids tend to the sand in the rock gardens surrounding the official residence.

"Well," the Japanese ambassador continues, "it is only human habit to carry home with us. But that is the benefit of space. The troubles that plagued us—earthquakes, nuclear disasters, climate change—they cannot follow us here."

They return to the front entrance of the compound: a large Myōjin-style torii garden gate. It opens out onto a well-manicured walkway with water bubbling quietly around the stepping stones.

"We appreciate you making the trip to see us." The ambassador sticks out his hand, and Finance Minister Kachikwu shakes it.

"One day soon, Biafra will have its own presence here. And the journey to your front gate will not take nearly as long."

The obsequious tone from the finance minister sets Chinelo's teeth on edge. The irritation bleeds into Onyii's mind and sticks with them long after they've left the ambassador's residence.

■ ■ ■ ■ ■

The three of them arrive at the platform of a transit station. A stop for one of those four-passenger, rice-pellet-shaped train cars ferrying Colony dwellers to wherever they wish.

The platform is quiet. Even though people mill about, there is enough space for those speaking quietly to talk without being overheard.

Without warning, Minister Kachikwu whirls on Chinelo and backhands her hard across the face. "You're an embarrassment," he hisses at Chinelo. "How dare you bad-mouth me in front of the Japanese ambassador!"

In the next instant, Onyii has her metal fingers around the minister's throat. She raises him so high his feet dangle off the ground. The rest of the world vanishes around Onyii. All she sees is red. Heat fuels every vein and every piece of wiring, and she squeezes and squeezes and squeezes and . . .

Chinelo's voice, soft but urgent, breaks through. "Onyii, stop. People are watching."

It feels so good, so necessary, to hurt this man that hurt Chinelo, but Onyii hears her voice and lets go. The man crumples to the ground, then gets up and brushes off his Western-style suit.

Onyii steps between the minister and Chinelo. "She didn't say a word to either of you."

"Your comms were open!"

Onyii glances back at Chinelo, who says nothing in reply. How could she have made that mistake? Onyii had assumed they were on a closed circuit. Then Onyii sees the glint of mischief in Chinelo's eyes. She'd done it on purpose. *Still the jokester.*

That man is the joke, Chinelo says back, letting the ends of her lips twist in a smirk.

"And *you*," he says, now that it's Onyii's turn for a tongue-lashing. "Do you even realize that everyone here looks at you as if you are some sort of monster? With your machine eye and your machine hands. They look and they think to themselves that it is a wonder you do not smell bad."

Onyii knows she stands out. She had suspected why, but she knew that not everyone was hostile. What mattered was that she could defend herself and Chinelo if it came down to it. What others think of how she looks is the least of her concerns. Let this little man worry about what others think.

"Anyway," he says more calmly. "You've spent enough time making me look like I've come straight from the bush. You will go back to Earth immediately. I will have you in Enugu before the day's end. Your services are no longer needed. That goes for both of you."

Chinelo tries to put on a brave, defiant face, but Onyii sees it waver. She wants to spit a retort at this man, make him feel small, or smack him like he smacked Chinelo, but Chinelo puts her hand to Onyii's shoulder.

"Let's go, Onyii," she says, not taking her eyes off of the minister. "Our country needs us."

Chinelo's diplomatic pass secures them a private room on the shuttle home.

The first thing she does when the door closes is soundproof the room with a button on the console. Then she lets out the loudest scream Onyii has ever heard come from her throat. When she's done, her shoulders heave. Then she stands upright and breathes a heavy sigh.

"Better," she says.

The floating Colony is far enough away that it looks now like just another star in the inky blackness of space. In their room, it feels as if they have the whole shuttle to themselves.

"When is the last time you got some rest?" Onyii asks.

Chinelo, now sitting on the bed, looks up. "Excuse me?"

Onyii takes a seat beside her. "Ever since the war ended, you've been running around. Setting up meetings with this person, drawing up plans for that initiative. You are not the prime minister-oh!"

Chinelo gestures to the Colony. "You see what happens when we let the men do it?"

Maybe Chinelo won't be Biafra's first peacetime prime minister. Maybe not even its second. But Onyii has a vision of Chinelo walking with ambassadors and sitting at tables, negotiating treaties. She hears the way Chinelo speaks on these matters, so alien to Onyii. How she does so with such confidence and knowledge, like she was factory-built to lead a nation. *She is perfect for this*, Onyii thinks to herself. *She's perfect, period.*

Chinelo frowns at Onyii. "What are you smiling about?"

But Onyii has an idea. And she walks over to the console and types. When she finds what she's looking for, her grin broadens. She inputs a sequence. Suddenly, her feet lift off the floor.

Chinelo, now floating in the air, flails. "Onyii, what are you doing? Eh-eh! Stop this now!"

But Onyii can't stop smiling. She swims to Chinelo in the zero gravity and hugs her tight. Spinning, they bring their lips together.

CHAPTER 52

The journey from the receiving station to Enugu passes in a blur.

Ify barely remembers making her way through the temporary shelter after being scanned and issued a fingerprint card and rations and new clothes at the receiving station. She barely remembers passing through the body scanners. She does remember the first warm shower she took in entirely too long.

Then there was the announcement for buses to Enugu, and making her way to the transpo station, where neat rows of maglev buses sat in the parking lot with drivers at each door and a case containing packets of food and water that they handed to each person boarding.

Agu is beside her in line, and they sit next to each other on the bus, Agu by the window, asleep. Ify wonders if synths truly sleep or if they just pretend to do it to act more like humans. She resists the urge to poke him or plug his nose like the girls in the camp used to do to her when they wanted to play a prank.

She wakes him when they pass through the main gate to the city, and she watches as he stares at all the gleaming structures.

Their bus arrives at the depot, and all the refugees and other workers from the receiving station step off and murmur their thanks to the driver, who greets each one enthusiastically and wishes them a good stay in the Biafran capital.

"What do we do now?" Agu asks.

Ify's mind settles on what she has to do. With a start, she realizes that this may be the last time she ever sees him. If her mission is successful, then she will likely be dead before the day ends. He can't be a part of this.

"We say goodbye." She smiles at his surprise. "I've lived all my life alone," she lies. "It is how I know to be. Besides, I can't have you slowing me down as I learn this new city."

"Is it safe for you?"

She arches an eyebrow at him, offended that he would ask.

He smiles, then giggles, and it sounds genuine. Like he no longer has to try in order to be a little boy. "Be well, Ify."

Ify watches him vanish in a crowd of glittering jewelry and shimmering robes, swallowed by a cloud of music and chatter. "Just remember to stay away from your sister!" she shouts after him, then chuckles.

Ify tries to find a space where no one will bother her. She can't go to a café because a waiter or some other patron might see her and start to ask questions about what it was like to be a refugee in her own country and where she's originally from. Also, she doesn't have any money.

So she stands at the mouth of an alley between a restaurant and a VR gaming center. Right above her, an orb hangs in the air. A surveillance camera.

It does not matter if it sees her face. She will be gone soon anyway.

She pulls her tablet out and, in seconds, finds her way past the very complicated security systems that make up Enugu's citywide surveillance network. She uses facial recognition software to pair the holo she has of Onyii's face with residents of the city. Maybe Onyii has changed her name. Maybe she has changed more than that since the end of the war. But no matter. Ify will do this in every city she has to go to until she finds her. But when the information appears the next instant on her tablet, she realizes she won't have to. She's almost surprised at how easy it is to get Onyii's current residence—an apartment building not far away—her status as a bodyguard for diplomats, and the fact that she is an unmarried Augment. There's nothing in her profile about her being a War Girl or being the most skilled mech pilot in the Republic of New Biafra.

For a moment, doubt creeps into Ify. Maybe this is the wrong person. Even though it is her face, everything else seems so different. But she presses onward. This could be a mistake. There is only one way to find out.

The building she arrives at looks like the residential hall of a school dormitory with a courtyard and other gathering spaces for students to congregate. But there's no university nearby. Maybe this is off-campus housing.

She doesn't want to look too suspicious hacking her way into the keypad at the gate, so she waits and prepares a holo of Onyii in case anyone asks. "I am a refugee from the war, and I am looking for my sister, Onyii," she is prepared to tell anyone who asks.

A group of chattering students pass through the main gate, and Ify slips in before it closes. She rides the elevator to a random level, then wanders and takes in the place. The wood-paneled hallways, the minimalist decor, the evenly spaced light orbs lining the ceiling. This place is low-tech compared to the school halls Ify remembers in Abuja. Those halls were lined with holoscreens of the news and of announcements from the government and broadcasts of Mecca for salat. Androids that walked the halls monitoring and sometimes even greeting students who would skip past them. Vaulted ceilings high overhead and libraries so tall they could poke the moon. She can't help but think that the Biafrans have always been backward, even if war has reduced them.

She takes the elevator to another floor and steps off, just barely stifling a gasp when she spots Chinelo walking in her direction. Ify's head swivels back and forth, looking for a way out before Chinelo notices her. Memories scramble through her mind, of the camp and the attack, of Chinelo and Onyii, always together. Ify darts off in the other direction, trying to keep her footsteps as quiet as possible.

She waits with her back pressed against a wall around the corner from the elevators. She sneaks her hand into her satchel and grips the pistol she has snuck in with her. Before going into the receiving center, she had asked Agu if he could disassemble it one last time, and he had not asked why. He had only done it. She knew that if she had asked him to put it back together after they reached Enugu, he would have grown suspicious, so she had spent her moments alone in the receiving center painstakingly figuring out how to reassemble the pistol. Her thumbs are still torn and red from the effort.

A ping sounds from the elevator, and then footsteps, then doors closing. Then nothing.

Ify waits a whole minute before peeking her head out from around the corner. Nothing. No movement. The air is still. She forces herself to move and peels off of the wall, then walks at a crouch, not caring that she would look ludicrous to anyone watching her now. She's so close.

She walks the way Chinelo had come, retracing her steps until she gets to a door that she knows to be the one. She doesn't know how she knows. She has no Accent to see past the metal. Her tablet is off. She has only her naked eyes and the body she was born with. And the certainty that grips her heart. This is it. Blood pounds in her ears.

She pulls her gun out, tries to still her restless hand, then takes a heavy breath. With her free hand, she knocks.

The soft sounds on the other side of the door stop, and Ify realizes someone must have been talking inside the room. Her heart hammers in her chest. She forces herself to knock again. This time, more insistent. She can't hesitate. She can't lose her nerve. She has been moving toward this very moment for what seems like an eternity. It guided her to freedom when she was a captive in her prison cell. It led her through the tangle of forest to the caravan months later. It has driven her in the aftermath of war now that she has lost everything and everyone she has ever loved. Propelled her. Become her engine. Imagining this very moment.

Footsteps.

She plants her feet, moves her bag so it's out of her way, and waits.

CHAPTER
53

In her room back in Enugu, the memory of outer space is still fresh in Onyii's head.

After she and Chinelo separated at the transpo station, Onyii came back to the apartment Chinelo has set up for her.

Experiencing the city as a civilian still takes some getting used to. In the face of the capital's expansion, flight paths for the maglev cars haven't yet been figured out. And everywhere, half-built stuctures—towers, university extensions, shops—are draped in scaffolding.

During the war, the city was sparsely populated, mostly a military town. Its outskirts were the perfect place to hide the training camp for the Abd Program. The city was a place soldiers would sometimes come to when they were on furlough or if they had been relieved from duty by a really bad wound. Not the type of place where someone could get into trouble. Nor was it the type of place to make you forget there was a war going on, but that's what it feels like now.

It looks like a place in a hurry to forget.

But in her room, with sound sheets muffling the noise from outside while she's able to keep her window open, she finds peace. Something like what she felt with Adaeze on that hill on the border with the Redlands.

If all goes well, it won't be like this for much longer. This military dorm will be turned into some other type of building, and, with talk of the Truth and Reconciliation Commission dying down, Onyii will transition fully into diplomatic work. Money will carry this place into the future. Stores will pop up, people will walk down these streets dressed in the most shimmering fabrics and studded with the brightest stones. And music. Everywhere, music. Thumping through the sound systems of maglev cars, blasting from the speakers set up on back balconies and front porches, crackling out of the speakers of mobile devices.

She's not ready for it yet, all that life buzzing and humming and shouting around her. But the thought does put a smile on her face. Just like you can tell the level of an Igboman's prosperity from the size of his belly, so you can tell a nation's prosperity from the amount of noise its capital makes.

This is what she did it all for. This noisy, crowded, beautiful city, bursting with life.

She walks over to her desk, slides open a drawer, and powers on the tablet she keeps inside. Returning to her bed, she swipes until she gets to the folder she's looking for. She opens it and plays the first video. In it, Agu is on one knee, drawing with his finger in the dirt of the courtyard. He looks completely absorbed in his task, not even noticing the camera aimed at him. The camera holder inches closer and closer, until he senses the person, then snaps upright and stands at attention. Onyii doesn't snicker in the video, but she snickers now, on her bed, watching it.

"What are you drawing?" the camera holder asks. "Battle formations?"

"No, sister," says Agu, foot sneaking toward the drawings to dash them out.

The camera swings down, and the camera holder says, "Oya, let's go. Time for your diving training. You like diving training, right?"

"It is a necessary part of my training."

Then the camera cuts out. When it had swung downward, Onyii was able to catch a glimpse of what remained of the drawing: it was her face. In profile, etched into the sand, an almost exact replication.

Just as she's about to open another file, her finger freezes. Was that a knock at the door?

She waits, then hears it again. This time louder.

She slips the tablet under her pillow, then walks to the door and presses her thumb against the keypad.

The door slides open, and Onyii's heart seizes. The world goes fuzzy. Blood pounds in her head. Her mouth dries. She can't swallow. Can't breathe. It can't be.

"Ify?" Her body trembles. "Ify, is that you?"

CHAPTER
54

The sight of Onyii, close enough to touch, snatches the air out of Ify's lungs. For a nanosecond, she stands there, frozen at the sight of the tech over Onyii's right eye and the way it connects with her Augmented arm, at the new wrinkles at the corners of her eyes, at the scars on the fleshy part of her cheeks, at the curliness of her hair, at the entirety of her beautiful, weathered face.

"You killed my family," Ify hisses. Her arm swings up, gun in hand. Everything moves at once. Onyii opens her arms and takes a step forward. Ify puts her finger to the trigger, pulls. A bang, and something hard smashes into Ify, knocking her all the way down the hall until she lands just under a window. The apartment door slams shut, leaving Onyii on the other side. Her gun is gone.

Ify pushes herself to her hands and knees. When she looks up, she sees Agu at the other end of the hall. He spares her one expressionless look—Ify can't tell if it's a glare or confused frown—before he dashes toward her.

She scrabbles away, forgetting the gun, but then a deep rumble shudders through the building. It feels like an earthquake.

Everyone stops.

Then again. Faint thunder getting closer, like a stampede. Suddenly, the building pitches to its side.

The window above Ify shatters. The building shudders again. Wood bursts into splinters above her. Concrete breaks apart. The floors are collapsing. The door to Onyii's room crumples, then goes flying across the hall. The shifting building tosses Agu against a side wall. His gaze doesn't leave Ify. It stays locked on her like a self-guided missile.

He pushes himself off the wall and uses the shifting momentum from the collapsing building to spin himself into Onyii's room.

The stone behind Ify cracks. Then the wall bursts in. She shields herself from the flying debris, then clings to the ground as the building rocks. The new opening in the wall opens out onto the chaos of Enugu. Suddenly, the ground is getting closer. The angle of the floor gets steeper, and Ify tries to scramble up to the corner, where she can get a grip on the wall, but the building is falling too fast, and suddenly, she is flailing, trying to grab at bits or pieces of shattered wood or stone, then she's flung into the air.

CHAPTER

55

Onyii has been shot before. She's had bullets graze her, pass through her, lodge themselves in muscle tissue, miss vital organs just barely. She's even had them ping off the metal of her arm. But never has a gunshot burned with such fire as the one in her shoulder does now. It hurts so much she can't even get up off the floor to see the tussling outside her door. It sounds like two bodies wrestling. She tries to move, but the wound has her paralyzed.

It has to have been a ghost. There's no way that was Ify standing outside her door. With a gun in her hand. There's no way that was Ify aiming her gun squarely at Onyii, then vanishing at the last minute as it went off, knocked off-balance by something too fast for either of them to see. It couldn't have been. Ify is dead.

A pool of blood spreads beneath Onyii's shoulder. She can feel the warmth blossoming. Radiating outward with the hurt. The bullet has ripped through her human shoulder. Her flesh-and-blood shoulder. Her weak shoulder.

She tries to get up on one of her elbows, but the pain is too great. That couldn't have been Ify. It couldn't have been.

I saw you in a mass grave. I saw your dismembered body.

But a tremor of doubt runs through her. Had she truly seen Ify's body? Most of the faces had been disfigured beyond recognition. The victims had been turned from people with full lives and hopes and fears into nothing but mangled bodies. Numbers. Flattened out into a single horrific sight. Had Ify really been there? Lying on top of the pile or even buried beneath the mountain of corpses? Had Onyii truly seen that?

All these years, and Onyii had not dared hope. Had not permitted herself even a moment of wondering. The thought of Ify had always come with thoughts of bloody revenge. The thought of Ify was what had driven her in every battle, what allowed her to forget herself in combat and let instinct take over. It had turned her into the feared Demon of Biafra, so fierce and unrelenting and skilled a mech pilot that word of her had crossed enemy lines. Known through both Biafra and Nigeria as the most skilled warrior on either side. And it had been because of Ify's death.

The ground shakes again beneath her, this time throwing her to the other side of the room. The jolting sends new shock waves of pain through Onyii's shoulder.

Another short rumble, then, faintly, in the distance, a small whisper of thunder getting closer and closer, like waves rushing toward the shore, until she recognizes the sound. Explosions. Even after all this time in peace, she knows that sound.

It's an attack.

Struggling, she manages to get up on one elbow. She grits her teeth against the pain in her shoulder, and when she feels the wound, she sees her sleeve is soaked. Her left arm has gone numb. But just as she's about to stand, the building pitches to the side, slamming her over her bed and against the wall. She grunts in pain, then tries to get her legs steady beneath her. The building sways, and she looks around for something, anything, to grab on to. She takes a step toward the door, then another, but the building pitches again in a different direction, and she flies off her feet toward the window. She flips and scrabbles at the floor for any purchase, but her fingers just slide against smooth wood until she smashes backward through the window with the full force of her body.

Wind buffets her, and she prepares to curl into a ball to help minimize the damage to her organs when she hits whatever she's going to hit, but something latches on to her leg, stopping her fall. It holds her still, and she swings, banging into the edge of the building, but hanging now upside down.

She looks up. It's Agu.

This time, Onyii takes no time wondering if this is a ghost or a vision. The truth is that she's hanging from the edge of a building on the verge of collapse. And something is keeping her from falling to her death. Whether it's an edge of broken metal that her pant leg has caught on or the hand of a little boy she had fought in war with, right now it doesn't matter.

She bends at the waist to reach up and grab his other hand, her stomach on fire with the effort. He's leaned over the window's ledge, broken glass all around him. Just as he's about to pull her up, the building shudders again. There's not enough time.

"Sister," Agu says in a low, insistent voice, and Onyii knows from that tone exactly what he means. *Let me protect you.*

So she lets him swing himself around and wrap his synthetic body around hers, shielding her head and vital organs before letting them both fall through the open window.

CHAPTER
56

When Ify wakes up, it looks and feels and smells and sounds like the world is ending.

Screaming and shouting and pleading. Brimstone and smoke. The taste of copper in her mouth.

Everywhere, collapsed buildings. Food stalls, shopping malls, school halls. Fires rage. Bots fight to extinguish the blazes. People run, and traffic bots try to steer them. The katakata has disrupted the flight paths so that maglev cars and buses crash into each other, their burning shells littering the streets of Enugu.

Gritting her teeth, Ify pushes herself to her feet, and that's when she notices her right arm hanging limp at her side.

A short distance down the way, flames lick the glass inside a fabrics store. The windows burst open. Ify skips into the front display and tears at the dress on a mannequin until she is able to rip off a long enough piece of cloth. Using her teeth, she ties a sling for her broken arm, then heads to the bus depot.

It's strangely empty, but on the way, Ify sees the telltale marks of destruction. In open stretches of street, craters sit like perfectly formed half-circles in the concrete and metal. Towers stand with nearly entire spheres cut out of them. Who planted those bombs?

While a few of the buses remain standing, the depot itself is little more than shattered flexiglas and twisted metal.

She sees, in the parking space beyond, a row of mismatched hoverbikes. No one else is around. Once she's on one of them, she looks for somewhere a thumbprint is supposed to go but finds nothing. The fingers of her good hand go to her bag for her tablet, and that's when she realizes her bag is gone. She has no idea when she lost it or her tablet, her key to the world.

Panic grips her heart. She looks around. Her gaze settles on a dead Biafran dressed in a multicolored agbada. His upper torso sticks out from under a pile of rubble. She rushes to him and yanks and yanks until she's able to get him partially free, then, taking a guess, she brings the bike over and lifts his bloodied hand until his thumb reaches the catch for it.

A tense moment of silence follows, then the bike hums to life. She hops on. It rises off the ground. Its wheel spokes unfurl to create magnetized bases, then she's off.

She wonders what happened to Agu. A chill runs through her. He was a synth. How many more synths had there been in that caravan? How many of them had been carrying in their stomachs or in their chests or in their braincases the bombs that had ripped through Enugu? That had left Onyii crushed beneath a mountain of steel and rubble.

CHAPTER
57

Onyii closes her eyes and prepares for impact.

They hit tree branches first. She hears snapping and hopes that it is a tree branch instead of Agu's ribs. He lets out the tiniest grunt when they land on top of a maglev car. The thin exterior crumples beneath their weight.

A moment passes, then Agu lets go.

She unfolds her limbs and rolls off of Agu and the top of the car to land on the ground. The pain in her shoulder has subsided, but she still struggles to move her left arm.

She waits for Agu to get off the car, but he doesn't move.

"Agu?" She creeps closer. "Agu, get up." She nudges his shoulder, then grabs his arm, shaking him. "Agu, oya, get up!" Her breath comes in short gasps. She climbs back on top of the car and feels along his neck for a pulse. "Agu?" She listens for breath, squeezes his wrist. "Agu! Agu, wake up!" She can't stop shaking him. She knows from the coldness in his body, the way his limbs hang limp, the way no machinery hums in his frame, that he's gone, but she can't stop shaking him. Not now, not after everything. "Agu, please." *No no no no no.* Then the tears come, and all she can bring herself to do is press her forehead against his motionless chest and sob.

Agu.

Screams. Sharp and piercing.

She gets up from where she kneels and slides off the car. She wants, needs, to do something for him. Prepare him for burial, fix his clothes, something. But the wailing in the city grows louder, more urgent. She can't just leave him like this.

Fire bursts through the windows of the collapsed apartment building above them.

She glances at him one last time, his eyes frozen open, his lips turned up into the faintest smile. She was the last thing he ever saw. He died happy.

He died happy. That's what Onyii tells herself as she rushes into the chaos.

Buildings groan on poor supports all around her. Church spires tumble to the ground. Markets cave in on themselves. Onyii strains her ears to hear a familiar noise. She searches and searches and searches but doesn't hear it. No gunfire. If this were a proper attack, they'd set off the explosives, then follow through with gunfire. Onyii looks up. Though smoke clouds much of her vision, the blue sky bears no chemtrails. Of all the sounds to assault Onyii's ears, she does not hear the screech and boom of aerial mechs ripping through the sound barrier. Nor does she hear the ominous growl of that special mech's beam cannon charging for a shot that would turn half of Enugu into dust.

Nearby, a building's struts snap, and its columns hit the ground, raising monstrous clouds of dust thick with shards of concrete. Onyii does not give herself time to hate, to feel anger toward the Nigerians or let herself give in to the thirst for vengeance. That will come later. For now, she runs toward the building, a section of an apartment complex, and waves over others, some of them too stunned to know where they are. Many of the pedestrians on the street, covered in dust, some of them bleeding from wounds they do not even realize they have, stare blankly at Onyii.

Before them lies a metric ton of broken stone and brick. Onyii calls and points to specific people and directs them to various spots along the edge of the rubble. "Start digging!" To a man who looks dressed in the clothes of an engineer, she turns and says, "Go to the barracks and bring out the Diggers. Radio, if you can, to let your colleagues know. And pray to Chukwu that the doors open."

Onyii leads the others in attacking the rubble at the edges. Lifting stones and tossing them out of the way. Many of the Augments here don't have increased strength built into their machinery, so they're as weak as red-bloods, but they dig with the intensity of people in crisis. Pretty soon, the skin has been worn away from fingertips, and everyone is awash in dust and plaster.

The Nigerians have broken the ceasefire. Stunned by the devastation, by its suddenness, this is all she can think.

A dozen paces away, Ngozi runs with a group of androids carrying a body on a stretcher. Onyii's heart sinks.

"Chinelo!" she screams as she dashes after them.

The group doesn't break stride as they rush Chinelo's body to the hospital. Onyii runs faster than she ever thought possible to catch up to them. She runs alongside them and tries to get a glimpse, but the flexiglas shield over the stretcher is covered in dirt. Dried blood smudges the surface in splotches.

Ngozi says, "We found her under the Central Flats." She's out of breath, but she continues to push her body. "She was still in the building when it collapsed. She was in one of the upper floors that fell last. It took us over an hour to get her out."

"Is she breathing?" She can't stop the panic in her voice. "Is she alive? Ngozi, tell me. Was she breathing?"

Ngozi just shakes her head at Onyii's questions.

Even as they rush through the jammed-open ground-floor doors of the hospital, outside of which wait many wounded, Ngozi says nothing.

The first-floor corridor is so crowded they can't get through.

"Let us through!" Onyii shouts. "We have a commander in the Biafran Army! Let us through now!" She does not care that there are others just as grievously wounded as Chinelo, maybe even some on the verge of death. Onyii can't remember the last time she wanted something so badly as she wants to get Chinelo into a healing pool.

At a set of double doors, a doctor in a bloodstained smock holds his hands out. "You can't go in there. We're beyond capacity as it is."

Onyii bares her teeth in a snarl and snatches Ngozi's pistol from her waist, then aims it at the doctor's head. "You will let us pass."

"There is a *child* in there!" the doctor pleads. "A child."

Onyii's hand wavers. Her shoulders heave.

"A child," the doctor whispers, one last time. When Onyii doesn't move, he gestures to the mass of people behind her, crowding every inch of the ground floor. "All these people are in dire need of medical attention. The blasts decimated our wireless systems. We're operating on generators now. We're strained past our limit. There's no telling how long they'll hold out."

Onyii wavers. The gun shakes in her hand. She grits her teeth and hisses, "This woman has valuable intelligence about who committed this terrorist attack. If she dies, it dies with her. This is a matter of national security." Her arm stiffens. She cocks the hammer back. It is a lie, but the lie is all Onyii has. "As an officer in the Biafran Army, I order you to step aside."

After a moment, the doctor sighs and gets out of the way.

The group rushes through the swinging double doors to find two doctors holding a limp child in a bodysuit, positioning her over the healing tank. Onyii points her gun at them.

"Away from the tank!"

The doctors' eyes grow wide. "What is going . . ."

Onyii breaks away from the group and presses her gun to the protesting doctor's forehead. "Step aside."

After a moment, the doctor does as ordered, and Onyii and Ngozi strip off Chinelo's bloody clothes, hurry her into the tank, fit the breathing mask to her face, then slam the tank door shut. Onyii turns the lock.

When the machine hums to signal it's working, tension seeps out of Onyii's shoulders. She wants to collapse but knows that she can't. Not yet. She lowers her gun and wants to say thank you to the doctor she threatened but knows that the doctor is just as likely to spit in her face as she is to accept her gratitude without a word.

If she stops moving, the thoughts racing through her mind will catch up with her, and she'll have to deal with Agu's death, how he died protecting her after she had tried and failed to protect him. She'll have to deal with Ify's betrayal. She must have been behind the bombing. Did they not trust the attack alone to kill the Demon of Biafra? Did they think they really needed to send someone once so dear to her heart to make sure the job was done? Did they need a visual of her body to confirm the kill? To know that they had cut the head off the snake? She turns to leave, but Ngozi grabs her wrist.

"Where are you going?" The look in Ngozi's eyes turns the question into: *Please don't leave.*

But Onyii shakes her wrist loose. "This was a violation of the ceasefire. I'm simply going to give them a chance to explain themselves."

"Alone?"

"I'm the one they want." By the door, syringes sit in a cabinet drawer on top of dozens of steroid packets. With her metal fingers, Onyii takes a syringe, punctures one of the packets, draws the fluid into the syringe, then plunges it into her damaged shoulder. Instantly, strength returns to her. She flexes her fingers, curls her arm, and smiles grimly. Then she gathers up the remaining packets and stomps out. It won't last forever, and the crash, when the boost wears off, may cripple her, but the packets will last long enough for her to do what she needs to do.

She leaves the hospital in a hurry. The crowds of injured people in the halls and outside become a blur. No more fires rage outside. Instead, it is oddly silent. An eerie quiet, punctuated by the occasional collapse of rubble.

But she walks with purpose, ignoring the cries for help and the sobbing of those who have just lost loved ones. In her mind, she is telling these people, *Do not worry, I will take revenge for you. I will punish them for what they've done.*

And when she arrives at the bunker on the outskirts of the

city, she is glad to find that the elevator down to the basement has escaped damage.

Her footsteps do not slow in the darkness. Motion-sensor lights pop on to light her way until she gets to the grand room, where what she is looking for is stored. She stops, and for several moments she looks up at her Igwe. The aquatic capabilities have been stripped away for increased mobility. One of the plates has been refashioned as a shield with a sword clapsed inside it for easy release. The shoulder cannons are attached to the ammo packet on its back. A retractable spear is bound tight at its waist. Though the metal plating of the arm seems unbroken, Onyii can see the joints that, upon command, would open up to reveal the Gatling guns at her elbows.

Amadioha. The name she has chosen for her Igwe. The ancient god of thunder and lightning, whose governing celestial body is the sun and who represents the will of Chukwu. Amadioha. Of the people. Before there was a Biafra, before there was a Nigeria, there was Chukwu, Supreme Being. Daren had mocked them by calling his mech an Alusi, naming it after the spirits of Igbo religion. Well, Amadioha was the Alusi of justice.

She presses the lift button by the wall, and a platform descends. She walks onto it, and it rises to bring her to a bridge right in front of where Amadioha's cockpit will open. She takes a moment to touch its chestplate. Her body tingles, as a prelude not to the pain that will soon engulf her if she does not take another steroid packet but to the fact that soon she will be where she is most comfortable, where she was born to be.

Whatever was done to Ify during her captivity among the Nigerians, this is what it turned her into. A terrorist who brought death to an entire city.

They had tried to kill the Demon of Biafra, first through peacetime, then through direct attack. Familiar feelings grow in Onyii's chest, and she lets the warmth spread through her entire body, filling her face with heat.

She gets to fight once again.

■ ■ ■ ■ ■

When Onyii arrives at the fortified Nigerian border, their army is waiting for her.

Smaller ibu land mechs and, behind them, larger models. They see the dust trail her Igwe kicks up in its wake, and they aim their laser cannons at her. She comes to a stop in full sight of them. They form a line that stretches for miles in both directions. She licks her lips. Her steroid packets sit in a container at her side, ready for her. Her fingers don't twitch on her gearshifts or her directional pad. Nor does her hand shake when she grips her joystick. She is as calm as she has ever been. This is where she belongs.

Amadioha rises to its full height.

She turns on her comms and programs her sound system to broadcast her voice loud and clear over the sparse plain, with the expanse of redland just behind her. Now that she has passed into territory protected from radiation, the rust on her Igwe heals. Its red and green and black paint glows in the unforgiving sun.

"The Biafran capital has been attacked," she proclaims, "by an insidious Nigerian element. Dozens have already been killed and hundreds injured. We have not yet finished counting the bodies. It is a terrorist attack in violation of the ceasefire and in violation of the human rights accords your nation, in its hypocrisy, claims so proudly to support. The attack is a wickedness that one can only attribute to your kind. And I hereby demand that the enemy agent who plotted and executed the attack be brought before me, so that she may face justice in a Biafran court of law." She has no idea if Ify is here or whether she lies crushed beneath a building the Nigerians blew up. Ify could be riding through the Sahel or she could be dead. But Onyii does not care. This demand is a mere formality. "If you will not forfeit the enemy agent, then we shall be forced to take her ourselves. So speaks Onyii, the Demon of Biafra."

She can sense the tremors that ripple through the line of pilots. Maybe they had thought the Demon of Biafra had vanished once peacetime had arrived, whisked away into obscurity now that she was no longer needed. But here she is. It pleases her to see them cower before her.

"Her?" The voice beams into Onyii's comms network, and a face appears on her screen. It wears a mask, hiding the features behind it, but that voice . . . she will always recognize that voice. The pilot who had decimated their forces during the attack on the oil facility. The pilot who had taken her right arm. "How do you know the agent was a 'her'?"

The line of mechs parts at its center, and through the opening walks a mech that she never thought she'd see again. Why should she be surprised? Of course they were fated for this very moment.

"Daren." She says his name below her breath, tastes it on her tongue.

"Out of my way, pilot," she says.

He's holding his massive energy cannon in his hands. It's aimed directly at her. "You speak of a little girl, no? Who called herself Ify?"

He admits it.

"Hand her over."

"Ify is no longer under our command. When she revealed herself to be a traitor to the republic, she was exiled. Whatever she has done since, she did on her own."

"Typical liar." Amadioha grabs the hilt of its sword and slides it out from inside its shield.

"We too believe she has committed a heinous act. As I speak, we have forces now tracking her down. She will be brought to justice." His mask does not hide the lower half of his face. He's smiling.

So she is alive. Very well. "She does not belong to you. Out of my way, or you shall be accused of harboring a terrorist, and I shall have no choice but to cut you down."

"There is no need for all of that. I know that I'm the one you're after. After all, I taught Ify everything she knows. Let us battle alone. Whoever wins shall have the pleasure of capturing the traitor. I will enjoy taking your head." The transmission ends.

I will cut you down. Then I will find Ify and have her answer for her crimes. All Onyii has left is herself. Chinelo lies in a coma. Agu lies dead and unburied in a city on fire. Everyone she has ever loved is dead or dying. She remembers that shuttle flight back to Earth from the Colonies. Her hand trembles on her joystick.

She tears open another steroid packet and pours it into the sieve that connects, by way of wires, to her metal arm. Her mech is plugged into the back of her neck. She is as connected as she can be.

Amadioha gets into its fighting stance.

Daren's Igwe powers up its cannon. The air between them shimmers with energy.

Then he fires.

CHAPTER 58

It's night by the time Ify emerges from the forest and sees it all laid out before her. What had once been her home and the home for so many others is now a rusted ruin. The War Girls camp.

Elephant grass grows over paths that had once been hardened into dirt roads by the passage of so many feet. She remembers the girls on their way to school or on their way to the health clinic or on their way to whatever open spaces allowed them to congregate and joke and make fun of each other and play. She pushes her bike until it can go no farther, then stops at a rusted tank that had once been their filtered-water supply. Some of the pipes that had run underground to pull moisture out of the soil or to provide a conduit for what came down in the monsoons now poke through the ground in parts, the wiring exposed where some scavengers have carved away the metal sheeting for barter.

Her bike catches on a piece of exposed piping and won't move. She jerks it once, twice to try to get it free, but it's gone. She kicks it, then bites back a yelp. Pain shoots through her toes. She stumbles a few paces, one-footed, before settling into a limp.

There's nothing left of the greenhouse, just a few vanishing indents in the ground where they had made space for groundwater and the shattered glass that crunches beneath her boots. A memory flashes before her eyes. Onyii picking mangoes from the trees, while, many rows down, Chinelo fingers the petals in a bed of roses. Chinelo glances at Onyii when she thinks Onyii's not looking. In the memory, Ify watches all of this from an upturned crate, her school tablet on her lap as she swipes through the day's lessons and tries to work through the polynomials she had learned that morning.

She shakes the memory away, then limps toward the center of the camp, where the Terminal once stood. It's now a single hunk of metal, a broken thing with sharpened edges that poke into the air. The metal stairway hangs off its side. It used to loom over her when she was little. Now she can nearly see over the edge of the standing platform.

In her mind, explosions sound and the chaos of war surrounds her. She closes her eyes and lets the scene swirl around her. Dodging figures in black, sliding through grass and dirt and leaping over fallen half-mech panthers and boars. Defeated mechs crashing down from the skies and crushing buildings beneath them, thundering when they land on the ground. A crabtank stomping through the camp, its turret guns swiveling and shooting at anything in its path.

When the memory threatens to overwhelm her, she opens her eyes.

This is where she stands. The ruined remains of the place where she had grown up.

She gets to a small field where a platform had once stood with walls shielding one end. There had been piping, but their bathroom was still a rickety structure, and, when they were children, the distance between the stalls and the dormitory seemed like forever in the dark. Now Ify walks that distance in a few dozen paces. She stands where the dormitory had once stood. Only a few broken wooden beams and supports remain strewn over the ground like fallen tree branches.

One night, they had all gathered together on one of the few occasions when Ify was allowed to spend time with them. And someone had pirated a vampire movie, and they'd all sat or lain down as best they could to get a view of the small tablet screen, their faces bathed in its glow. And Ify had watched the horror on their faces, had heard the stifled screams and the giggles, had felt how the girls shook with fear afterward and how, at one point after the movie, one of the girls whispered to another that she needed to pee. And the older girl had brushed the littler one aside. Another had told the girl to just go by herself, that it wasn't that far. Then Ify heard another girl shiver beside her, trying to hold it in. And she still doesn't know where the idea came from, but she remembers standing up suddenly and saying, "Toilet parade!" And she gathered the girls together and told them that they'd make a parade, like those celebrations they watched on the holos sometimes, so that they could all go together and no one had to be alone. Some of the girls looked at Ify with admiration, the same ones who had stayed quiet while the older girls had tormented Ify for her hair or her skin or the way she sometimes sounded when she spoke.

Ify's fists clench at her sides. Angrily, she wipes tears from her eyes.

A dozen steps later, she stops. The grass is so tall it nearly hides the pieces of metal bent into crosses and arrayed in neat rows before her. Weeds grow in patches over the land. Ify walks forward until her foot hits the first mound.

Graves.

Who did this?

There are so many of them. Maybe some passing aid worker, someone like Xifeng, had come through and buried the dead. They could not have found this place after the raid more than four years ago. War was still happening. Maybe it was a soldier. It does not matter which side. Ify does not linger. She continues on.

She walks and walks until she finds the cliffside where she used to spend so much time with Enyemaka. The android, when Onyii and Chinelo had first built it, didn't speak at all, just did as commanded. Then they programmed it to speak, but it would only respond with *yes* and *no*. If Ify wanted to do something she wasn't supposed to, Enyemaka would block her path, too hard to hit or move. Then the more nanobots Onyii injected into it, the more its voice started to change. And it would respond to Ify, and then it began to joke, and then it started to sound like Onyii. Like a kinder, less wounded version of Onyii. Onyii if she had known anything other than war. Enyemaka had slowly turned from *it* to *she*.

And she had spent her very last moments crouched over Onyii like a shield, after she had tossed Ify free of the blast from a synth suicide bomber.

Ify sits on the grass. As soon as she does, a breeze wafts through the camp. After the blood and dust that had covered her in Enugu, after the ever-present chill of her prison cell and the torture from her interrogator, this is the kindest thing that has touched her skin.

She lets her eyes drift closed. The breeze grows fiercer. On the winds, Ify hears a noise: jet propulsion engines. She listens for what will inevitably follow.

CHAPTER 59

The laser speeds toward Onyii.

Just as the laser reaches her, she leaps into the air, adjusts course, then rides just above the laser beam, sword pointed at her target. She strikes, but only hits his arm. He skids away, kicking up a cloud of dust. His laser cannon, pierced through by Onyii's sword, lies at her feet. Onyii pries her sword loose, then faces Daren, who she can tell is gazing at her in wonder, trying to figure out how she can move so fast.

She dashes toward him. He raises his shield just in time to catch her. She pushes him back, each swing denting his shield. The sound booms over the plain.

He spins himself in a half-circle, taking the hammer attached to his back, and swings with full torque. Onyii absorbs the blow with her shield, but it sends her clear over the plain. She flips herself and lands on her feet, skidding back. Her sword tearing through the ground until she comes to a stop.

She flies forward. Daren rushes to meet her. Their weapons clash, sword against hammer. They hold, then break away, then clash again. Spinning. Onyii braces herself with her other hand as Daren spins them around. He angles up. Onyii sees it too late. Daren spins her into the ground. Dirt erupts around her. Her cockpit shudders. Daren raises his hammer and plunges it down. Onyii powers her thrusters to lift her up, then backward, just out of the way of his strike.

When she's standing again, her sword is gone. She looks around for it, then sees it a mile off in the direction of the Nigerian mechs. She speeds off toward it, away from Daren. But just as she reaches it, a spearhead attached to a winding cord strikes it out of reach, pinging it behind enemy lines. The cord writhes and wraps around her wrist. It's attached to Daren.

The cable retracts, pulling her along. She engages her thrusters, trying to pull back. She grips the cable with her free hand, and they're stuck. But she's slowly losing, inching closer and closer. Until Daren speeds toward her, the cable slackening, falling off. Onyii skids to the side just as Daren swings his hammer, smashing through several Green-and-Whites, tearing them in half as though they were paper. The pilots' cries fill the air. Onyii raises her shield to catch another hammer blow, then another, then another. He swings again. She times her spin so that she can grab his arm. Just as she goes to tear through it with her hand, he vaults into the air, using his hammer as a pole, and kicks her away. She stabilizes in the air. He pulls his spiked hammer from the ground and charges again.

What?

She looks behind her. The full weight of Daren's hammer crashes into her back. Her entire world goes white with pain. She hears her ammo pack crunching behind her as a series of explosions spin her forward and propel her to the ground, then bounce her off into the air. Each one damages her further. She spins without control. Her monitors fritz with static before going dark.

When she finally rolls to a stop, she coughs blood onto her console. Another hammer blow sends her spinning into the air. She hears his jets flare again before yet another hammer blow sends her crashing into the ground. She's defenseless.

His hand jams onto her mech's head and squeezes. Glass breaks, gears snap.

She lies limp in her seat.

"You Biafrans," Daren hisses through Onyii's comms. She can't see his face, only hear the venom in his voice. "So easily duped. So easily manipulated. So stupid." He slowly crushes her head. "Even your precious little Ify. She had no idea we were tracking her." He chuckles. "No need to worry about me betraying my plan to the others. Only you can hear me. During her captivity, we injected her with a tracking device, knowing that she would lead us to you. You see, all that time she was with us, we were grooming her for her true purpose: bringing down your foolish little nation. Then, when we were done, we could wipe our hands of her. And she led us straight to you. All our bombers rode the caravans with her. So know that nowhere are you safe. You can never escape us. We will crush you." He pushes harder. Stone grinds against stone as a crater forms around Amadioha's head. "Attack the Biafrans, draw out their warrior, then cut the head off the snake, and you played into our trap perfectly." He flips his hammer in his free hand and raises it. Its spiked head blots out the sun.

"More," Onyii growls, hungry.

Daren pauses.

It stirs inside Onyii. That energy, that fury. It bangs itself against the cage around her heart, but now she opens the gate. She has nothing holding her back. There is only this. This fight. This act. This moment. "More."

Energy and information gush through the cables attaching Onyii's neural network to Amadioha. Blood spills from her nose.

"More."

Cracked, external plates break off from Amadioha, revealing more of its metal rib cage and the inner machinery of its arms. One arm folds at the elbow. The Gatling gun fires, knocking Daren off-balance. Onyii spins to her feet and charges after Daren, who has sped backward. His speartail ejects from the back of his Igwe. As she chases him, the spearhead darts at her, trying to pierce her mech's frame. She dodges to the left. Dodges to the right. It moves faster and faster, but she beats it every time. It darts for her head, and she grabs the cable just behind it and flies even faster.

Daren twists at the waist, ready to spin and swing, but Onyii dodges, and Daren twirls himself into the trap, wrapped up in his own cable, arms pinned to his sides. Onyii grips the cable with both hands, twisting it around her forearm. She pulls tighter. Bolts of lightning shoot up and down the arms of Daren's Igwe. Tighter. He drops his hammer to the ground. Tighter. The metal arm plating cracks. Tighter.

The Igwe's engines burst, and the metal that had folded like wings on its back flare open, snapping the cable. Daren turns around and fires missiles at her. Onyii flies backward, but the missiles are too fast. She fires from her Gatling guns. The explosion engulfs her. Her cockpit screens show her nothing but flames. A panel of glass cracks. But when the smoke clears, she is still standing.

Blood leaks from her nose down to her chin.

She licks her lips. "More."

Onyii charges forward. Daren grabs the hammer and swings upward. Amadioha digs its fingers into the ground and spins around, then grabs the insides of Daren's wings and pulls, ripping them off the Igwe's back. She kicks Daren forward. Daren swings again. But too slow. Onyii catches the blow with one wing and, using the other, pierces Daren's arm at the elbow. It sparks with electricity until Onyii drops the shield in her free hand and grabs the arm holding the hammer and yanks it free.

"More," she whispers.

Daren grabs for her with the other hand, but she grabs that and slams Daren to the ground, driving the wing she's holding straight through his bicep.

Daren's Igwe squirms and writhes beneath Onyii. She kicks him over so that he's staring up at her, armless. Her chest shudders with each breath she takes.

It's done.

"You will never find her, and you will never have peace," Daren manages to sneer through bloodstained teeth. "Even after I am gone, we shall war until we destroy you."

Onyii looks down on him. "I have no need for peace." She raises the shield with both hands and drives it straight through the Igwe's breastplate.

After a moment, the light in Daren's Igwe dies.

Calm settles over the plain. Craters pockmark the ground.

Smoke billows from them. Onyii bows her head. Her nose has stopped bleeding. When she opens her eyes, her vision blurs. Static fritzes the world around her. Her Augmented eye. It's busted.

She hears a steady beeping coming from below. Daren's Igwe. A red light glows on and off, on and off. His comms channel is still open, and she sees on his screen a map. The dot on the map moves slightly, then stops.

Onyii registers no surprise, no shock, no reaction. She knows what this means. With one hand, she grips the head of Daren's Igwe. Metal grinds against metal, cables snap, then the head comes loose. She holds it in her hand. It will lead her to where she needs to go.

Without sparing another look at the destroyed mech beneath her or the army arrayed behind her, she bursts into the sky, heading south.

■ ■ ■ ■ ■

By the time Onyii lands in the forest clearing, it's night, and Amadioha's left arm has come loose. Upon contact with the soil, the jolt shakes it further, and it hangs by a few cables before those snap and the arm falls to the ground with a heavy thud.

The cockpit opens up. A breeze kisses Onyii's cheeks. She closes her eyes against it, then shakes herself awake. The trees of the forest blur together. With her human arm, she fishes around for more steroid packets. Her fingers alight on one. She's barely able to bring it to her mouth, but she manages to get the thing in her teeth. With a jerk of her head, she rips it open and swallows the juices. They stream down her chin, but the foul-tasting elixir burns her throat and sends fire back into her veins. Her vision clears.

She inputs a sequence on her console, and Amadioha folds in on itself, lowering her to the ground. She disconnects, wires snapping back into place in her headrest, and climbs out of the cockpit. When she sets foot on the grassland, she topples over but catches herself just in time.

She coughs, then spits blood into the elephant grass.

Unconnected, her metal arm hangs useless at her side. But she is able to hold her pistol in her human hand, and that's all that matters.

Slowly, with halting but determined steps, she makes her way out of forest and into the camp. It lies more disfigured and broken than she remembers. But nearly half a decade has passed, and the jungle hasn't yet overtaken the place. Vines wrap around the remains of buildings that were once schools and medical clinics, recreation spaces and the armory, the mess hall and the library. And elephant grass tickles the husk that had once been their Terminal. Only a nub of their Obelisk is left.

She walks through it all, but no memories come to her. She half expects them, but there is only silence. No crackling from dying fires. No sparks flying from damaged machinery. No squish of her boots in pools of ash and mud. Even the wind that bends the grass makes no noise. She sees footprints in the sand, but she knows they don't belong to anyone she would recognize. Those people are either dead or gone. Swallowed up by the war that has just spat her out. She walks and walks and walks.

She knows where the homing beacon is leading her. Can picture the spot perfectly.

And when she arrives, she sees her sitting on the edge of the cliff overlooking the beach.

She flicks the safety off her pistol. The girl at the cliff's edge doesn't move.

Doesn't make a sound, even as Onyii presses the barrel of the gun to the back of Ify's head.

CHAPTER
60

"Get up."

It takes Ify a moment to register the voice. She had been so ready for this moment. Yet it still surprises her. She comes to her feet. Her hands shake at her sides, but she clenches them into fists. She can't waver now. Not when everything that has happened has finally caught up to her. The murder of her family, her life with the Biafran War Girls, her kidnapping, her time with the Nigerians overseeing the detention of children dubbed "enemy combatants," her time in prison when she had lived as an accused traitor, her attempted assassination of the person who had slaughtered her family. All of it has been leading to this moment. This moment when she is adrift, belonging to no one and nowhere. On her own. Neither Biafran nor Nigerian. Just Ify.

"Turn around."

Ify does as ordered.

What she sees is a shell of a person. Blood has dried in streams over Onyii's face. Her plaited hair is a frayed and reddened mess around her cheeks and down past her shoulders. Her shirt is torn in places. Her right arm hangs limp against her side. She is slightly crouched, one leg bent awkwardly beneath her. Her gun arm shakes. The pistol wavers but never loses sight of Ify.

For several seconds, they stand in silence, facing each other.

"Did you know?" Onyii hisses through her teeth. Her right eye flickers on and off.

"Know what?"

"That they were tracking you?"

So that's how it happened. Ify had led the shaheed straight to Enugu. Straight through the security checkpoint. She feels a twinge of regret but smothers it. She had not meant for all of that death. But it can't be helped now. She can't go back in time. What's done is done. "No," she says to Onyii. "I didn't know." She glares at Onyii. "But it doesn't matter."

Onyii looks taken aback for a second before reasserting herself.

"Revenge is revenge."

"Revenge? For what?"

"So you do not even remember." Ify trembles with fury. When Onyii is still silent, Ify makes to take a step forward, but stops herself. She takes several deep breaths, calms herself down. "I suppose you were *just following orders*." She spits that last part out like venom.

Onyii's gun hand wavers.

"You did it. You came to a village in Abia State. You murdered my family. Then you kidnapped me. That's where I came from, isn't it?"

Onyii's arm trembles. For nearly a minute, she holds the gun to Ify's forehead. But she doesn't pull the trigger. Then her hand falls to her side. The gun dangles from her fingers before landing softly in the grass.

Tears well in Ify's eyes. "Why couldn't you just kill me?" Her bottom lip trembles. "Why couldn't you let me be with my parents?"

"Ify, I—"

"My family!" Ify shrieks. "You took my family from me! And you lied to me. My whole life, a lie!" She lashes out at Onyii, cracks her across the face with her fist.

Onyii doesn't move, merely takes the blow. She doesn't even stagger backward.

Ify looks and sees that she didn't even bruise the young woman she had once called her sister. But then she sees the way her metal arm hangs at her side and the way her legs bend beneath her and the way blood has crusted on her body, and she knows that no blow from her could match the damage she has endured at the hands of others.

Onyii continues to look away, no expression on her face. There's a terrifying dullness in her eyes, as though she's not really there.

Ify picks the gun up off the ground and holds it out to Onyii. "So do it. Send me to them. I have nowhere else to go." When Onyii doesn't move, Ify grabs Onyii's human hand and thrusts the gun into it, then raises Onyii's hand to her forehead, cold gun barrel pressed against her skin. "Do it. Do this one last thing. All you can do is kill." Ify spits the words out. "Kill me, then. This dirty Nigerian. Send me to heaven. Or to hell, wherever Biafrans think I'm supposed to go." She jams the gun harder against her forehead. "Do it," she hisses. "Do it!" Nothing from Onyii. "DO IT!"

But Onyii's hand falls away. She turns and begins walking. "No more," she whispers.

"Wait. What are you doing? Come back here! Onyii! ONYII! Come back here and do it!"

Onyii keeps walking until she vanishes from sight.

Ify chases after her and follows her into the forest, tripping over exposed roots and getting cut by thorned vines. She stops when she sees Onyii at the edge of a clearing, staring up at her beaten and battered Igwe. In its condensed form, it looks more like plates of metal stitched together than anything resembling a mech.

Ify creeps closer.

She gets to within a dozen paces of Onyii when Onyii says, "I'm done." Onyii turns to face Ify. "I'm done killing." She uses her human hand to cradle her metal arm. "If you want someone to put a bullet in you, find someone else." Then she walks away.

Before she's out of sight, wind buffets them. Tree branches sway. Grass parts. The sound of propellers cuts through the silence.

Spotlights shine down on the two of them, sweeping in small arcs.

"Ifeoma Diallo, surrender your weapons now!" comes the booming voice from a loudspeaker in one of the aircraft above.

Ify squints. The insignia of the Biafran flag is painted on its wings.

"You are under arrest!"

Soldiers clad in black emerge from the forest with their rifles pointed at her. They come from all sides. Onyii stares dead-eyed at Ify the entire time.

Ify growls, feels herself glowing with anger. But she wonders what she's angry at. That Onyii couldn't bring herself to admit to her crime? That she could not kill Onyii and truly avenge her family's murder? Or that she was denied her glorious death?

What does it matter? The rage is real, and Onyii is the nearest target. "I will never forgive you," she hisses, as Biafran soldiers kick her legs out from beneath her and force her to her knees. The first blow from someone's shockstick is enough to knock her unconscious.

CHAPTER
61

How quickly Enugu falls back into wartime formation, Onyii thinks.

The city is still bathed in scaffolding. Streets littered with rubble, buildings still hollow and deformed. But now it is suddenly filled with military uniforms. Soldiers hurry past her with their rifles and their ration packs. Old officers who had seemed so acclimated to being civilians now revert back into their wartime selves with an ease that startles Onyii. Everyone has become hard again.

Diggers are being retrofitted on the outskirts of the city for tunneling operations. Mechs, heavy with shoulder cannons and Gatling gun arms, appear aboveground for the first time in almost a year.

People still mourn their fresh loss, but they weep for their dead lover or their dying children in the shadows. *We will have plenty of time to cry when this is over. Or when we are dead.* That is what Onyii wants to say as she makes her way to the hospital, but she can't say those words out loud.

Because her steps lead her straight through the still-charred front doors, down the hallways where the blood in places still has not been cleaned, to the recovery ward where healing baths lie in rows, filling the room. They look like coffins.

The machines beep regularly and in unison. There's no one here. Even though there is no darkness for Onyii to hide in, no shadows to mask her sorrow, she can mourn here with no one watching.

There are no chairs, so Onyii stands. She puts a hand to the flexiglas surface through which she can see the mask fitted to Chinelo's face.

"We're back at war," Onyii says at last, because it is the only thing she can think to say. "I thought I would want this. You saw how awkward peacetime made me. How unused to it I was. I . . ." She takes her hand off the flexiglas to look at her metal fingers. "War is what I was built for. But I don't want this. None of me wants this." As she speaks, she digs inside herself to find that familiar hate, that power that had driven her in combat. She wants that rage, needs it. But she searches and searches and searches and finds only heartache.

The console attached to the head of the healing bath shows Chinelo's vital signs. As close to normal as one can hope for. But when Onyii looks at the brain activity, everything is a hopeless gray. There is no part of her brain that glows. She is not even dreaming. Just trapped. In a pitch-black slumber from which she will never wake.

"Maybe it will always be like this." Onyii's voice is leaden when she speaks. Like it's made of the same metal alloys as her arm. "Maybe neither of us will live to see what Biafra might become. This war. It . . . it swallows up everything." And she knows that if Chinelo can hear her, Chinelo will know what she means. She means Agu and Chiamere. She means the sisters in their program who have died: Kesandu, Obioma, Ginika. And all of their abd. She means the camp where they'd made a life for themselves as girls. She means Ify.

There are no tears when she thinks of Ify. There is no rage. Nothing.

"She's alive." An emotionless chuckle leaves Onyii's lips. "After all these years, she survived. I don't know how she did it, but she did it. She survived. She survived, and I . . . I abandoned her." Then the tears come. Her chest closes over whatever words she had left. Her shoulders shake. Her legs tremble. "I abandoned her. I . . . I thought she was dead."

The emotions rush in a wave through Onyii. Her legs buckle. She grips the flexiglas surface and just barely keeps from collapsing. Suddenly, her sobs turn to laughter. Bitter, acidic laughter.

"I abandoned her, and now she is here to kill me." Like an operating system rebooting, Onyii regains control of herself. She sniffs away a sob and wipes away her tears. "When I found her and brought her back to our base all those years ago, you never asked where she came from. You never asked why I had brought back this little girl who offered us no tactical advantage. She was too young to be a friend. She didn't speak our language. She might have even been a spy. We had no time to teach her how to fire a gun. Not in those early years. I brought her to us, and you just accepted it."

No change in the rhythm of the beeping. Onyii knows it is foolish to hope that Chinelo might hear her, might respond, but she still hopes.

"She will go on trial tomorrow. They'll execute her immediately after." She grits her teeth, clenches her metal hand in a fist. "I wish you'd asked me why I did it. All those years ago, bringing a stranger into our family. I wish you'd asked me. But you didn't. Maybe you knew. You were smarter than the rest of us, so you probably did know. You knew that if you'd asked me, I would have told you, 'I don't know,' and that would have been the truth." Onyii stares into space for a long time, looking at nothing, seeing everything. "I couldn't do it. I couldn't kill her. And now our nation might die because of it." She turns her gaze to the serene expression on Chinelo's face. "I'm sorry," Onyii says.

■ ■ ■ ■ ■

Onyii's footsteps echo down the prison corridor.

She stops when she gets to the last cell in the corridor.

Ify sits cross-legged on the floor, her head bowed, her forearms bound by metal restraints that she lays in her lap. She doesn't look up when Onyii stops in front of her. Her bed is untouched. The white of her prison jumpsuit is the same color as the walls around her. All that marks it is the dried blood along her collar and running down her front. She makes no noise.

"Tomorrow, you will go on trial," Onyii says. "You will answer for your crimes. And you will be executed." She clenches her fists. "You will die by lethal injection."

Ify doesn't move.

"Consider it one last kindness."

At that, Ify looks up and sneers. Her sneer turns to a grin. But she says nothing.

When did you become this? Onyii wants to ask her. Was it during her captivity? Was it before then? Did this person exist when Onyii had brought her to live with the War Girls? Was she always there?

"One last kindness?" Ify growls in a voice Onyii does not recognize. "I am a Nigerian. A Yoruba. You gave me an Igbo name, but it was a lie. You gave me a life as an innocent girl, but it was a lie. You gave me hope for a future where I am some stupid little girl studying nonsense in America. But that too was a lie." She looks up and stares Onyii in the face. Her left eye is swollen shut. "Even now, you lie. You have chosen lethal injection not out of kindness but because you are a coward."

Silence thickens the air between them, makes it more impenetrable than any concrete wall. Onyii waits for a denial, waits for Ify to tell her that she didn't know she was being tracked, that she had no idea the bombing was going to take place, that she'd wanted only to shoot Onyii. Onyii waits.

But there is only silence. Ify won't deny the massacre. Perhaps she even wanted it.

Ify won't die tomorrow, Onyii says to herself, as she turns to walk away. *Ify died a long time ago.*

CHAPTER 62

Ify's body quakes when she watches Onyii turn her back.

"Is this how it ends, then?" Ify wants the same hardness in her voice that Onyii has. But she can't get there. When she speaks, she hears the note of pleading in it. And she hates herself for it.

Onyii stops. "This is war. This is what happens. This is how it happens. No more, no less." But she doesn't move. She doesn't leave, and that fact sends a shudder of hope through Ify's body. She can't let go. Not yet. "I . . ."

"Tell me it was you." The metal restraints are so heavy around Ify's forearms and hands. "Tell me it was you who killed my family. I need to know." She feels herself fumbling for that hatred she felt just hours ago.

For a long time, Onyii is silent. "It was July. The sixth of July. I remember because it was someone's birthday. Someone in our group." Onyii shakes her head. "I can't remember her name. But we had celebrated earlier that day. We did night missions, so we had the mornings and the afternoons to ourselves. And we could be regular girls again. We hadn't completely lost that. On the sixth of July, we celebrated a birthday. Then, that night, we crossed the border into Abia State, and we found an unguarded village. The girl whose birthday we celebrated didn't want to attack it. She only wanted to fight soldiers. She didn't want to kill innocents. But our commander kept telling us that, in war, there are no innocents. So, when we knew that everyone was asleep, we raided.

"There was no armory. There were no weapons. There was just . . . food. Food and farming animals and calabash bowls. Nothing of military importance. But we took hostages. We didn't know what else to do. This wasn't a military outpost. This place wasn't of any use to us. But it was our commander's idea to make a broadcast. To give a speech that would be shown to the Nigerians. Justifying what we were about to do.

"He made me and the other girl stand with the hostages. The rest of our squadron were young men, boys, and some older men. Some of them were reluctant. Some of them were hungry for blood. Maybe they had been wronged in the past. Denied a job or a wife. Maybe a Nigerian had treated them rudely. Maybe they just had a grudge. That was the thing about war, especially in those early days. It was a convenient way to settle a grudge. At the end of the day, you could say the person you killed was your enemy. You could say they were trying to kill you. Even when they weren't."

She stops, like she's run into a wall she can't go around or climb over. Then she lets out a sigh. "While some of the others were setting up the recording, a woman with silver braids running down her back and a dress patterned with blue and red and gold flowers tried to attack the girl whose birthday it was. So I shot her."

Tears stream down Ify's face as she listens. "You killed my mother," she whispers.

"I was a child!" Onyii roars. "I was just a child." Now tears pool in Onyii's eyes. "I was a little girl with a gun in my hands. I did what I was told. I had no one! No family—"

"So you took mine."

"I . . ." Her voice lowers. "I was a child." She sniffs and wipes her face. "That gave the others the courage. When they saw what I had done, they knew they could do it too. So our commander gave his speech, then lined up the remaining hostages from the village. And we shot them dead."

A single question haunts Ify. "Why didn't you kill me?"

Onyii's eyes are soft again, and Ify reels from a memory of looking into them as she's lying on her cot, waking up in a camp surrounded by girls her age, on any regular morning before she is to begin her lessons. That look. So many times, Onyii had given her that look, and so often Ify had wondered what was behind it. It seemed to hold so much more than love or gratitude or kindness. It seemed to hold . . . regret.

"Why didn't you kill me?" she asks again.

Onyii's bottom lip trembles. She shrugs. "I thought . . . We had just celebrated a birthday, and it was the first time I'd seen the girls smile in a long time, and . . . and I wanted to do that again. I thought maybe it could be your birthday too. And no one should have to die on their birthday." Onyii wraps her arms around herself. "I'm sorry," she mouths.

Then she turns on her heel and hurries away.

Later, when the guards arrive to take Ify to the courthouse for her trial, they will think her silence is defiance. Some of them will think that maybe she has taken a drug to fortify herself. Maybe they will think she's praying. None of them will know the truth. None of them will know what Onyii has just given her.

Peace.

■ ■ ■ ■ ■

Plaster covers the floor of the courtroom. Guards escort Ify to a booth in full view of the people assembled to watch the hearing. On the way from her prison cell, she'd seen the destruction wrought by the suicide bombers. Even though construction was under way, rubble still filled the roads, stone and concrete and metal piled on top of each other like small mountains.

The large room fills with murmurs when they first bring Ify in. The hum continues as she's sat down and the guards fit manacles to her ankles. She still wears the same white jumpsuit they'd given her when she was first brought to prison, marred by dirt and dried blood.

Ify searches the crowd for Onyii's face, even as the judge reads her charges. One count of terrorism; 259 counts of premeditated murder; five hundred counts of maiming; one count of the possession, acquisition, and use of explosives to commit an act of terrorism.

The judge, who wears a military uniform, stops reading, then looks up from his screen. "Were this a peacetime incident, the penalty for these crimes would be life imprisonment. But the ceasefire does not qualify as peacetime. We are, unfortunately, still at war. Thus, the accused is not a civilian. She is an enemy combatant. As such, her punishment shall be death by lethal injection."

She has known this was coming. It still snatches her breath away to hear it. She is going to die.

Her steely expression slips. Her eyes dart through the crowd, hoping for a chance to see Onyii's face one last time. To take it into her memory. To have something to look at when she closes her eyes for the last time. But the room is too crowded. Onyii is nowhere to be found.

She searches for Onyii in the crowds that flank her as guards take her from her booth, through the gathered mass of people outside the courthouse, to a van. And as they bring her out and lead her down into the basement of a nondescript building, Ify still searches. She glances from face to face as new guards wearing masks take hold of her and lead her into a room with a metal platform in the middle, shaped like a cross. Next to it is a small machine, as tall as Ify's chest, on spindly metal legs. A man in a robe as white as the walls of this room stands by it.

The masked guards strap Ify to the board, then the board groans as it rotates vertically. The man operating the machine taps Ify's left arm, raising the veins, then inserts a needle and tapes over the injection spot with mauve-colored adhesive tape.

With the board raised, Ify finds herself staring into a wide pane of glass. In it, she sees her reflection. Her wild afro, the red and black that stain her shirt in patches, the flecks of gold in her purple irises. Eyes that she has learned are beautiful.

Maybe this mirrored glass is meant to give criminals one last moment of reflection. This is what Ify thinks when the man operating the intravenous injection machine pushes the button that sends it into action. Perhaps the mirror is there to remind the criminals of who they are, what their act has turned them into. Perhaps the criminals are expected to see a monster.

Maybe they're expected to see the child they once were.

Why, then, is Ify's last sight before darkness closes in of Onyii with that look in her eyes? That look she would give Ify every morning when Ify woke up. Another vision, then? One not conjured up by her Accent but made purely out of her fears and hopes and dreams.

The image of Onyii blurs as tears fill Ify's eyes.

That look. As though Ify is the only thing in the world that truly exists. But it is different now.

There is no more regret.

■ ■ ■ ■ ■

When Ify comes to, her face is pressed against carpet.

The world is a mass of colors. Moving, battling each other. Piercing through the fog is a voice. Voices.

Her body feels as though she's been crushed beneath the foot of an ibu mech. But she manages to roll over so that she can stare upward.

The colors stop their dance. Slowly, they grow shapes and edges until a face forms.

A stranger's face. Older. With gray in her braids and wrinkles along her forehead and cheeks. She wears a smirk.

"She's awake," the woman says in a deep voice that Ify has never heard before. The woman breathes a chuckle. "Is this revenge for how poorly I've treated you all these years?" the woman jokes to someone Ify can't see.

Ify hears a murmur. This voice is familiar, but she can't turn her head.

"So, you brought the most wanted person in both Nigeria and

Biafra to my home. Always causing me problems, aren't you, Onyii?"

Ify's eyes shoot open. With strength she did not know she had, she pushes herself up onto one elbow. She has to see. She has to. And when she finally comes up onto her knees, she sees it. That face. That look.

Onyii.

CHAPTER

63

When Onyii can tell that Ify is strong enough to eat, she brings her a plate of gari and a bowl of steaming egusi soup from the kitchen. Then she sits and watches Ify stare blank-faced at the food for a moment before digging in. Adaeze raises an eyebrow at Onyii.

"It's a wonder she didn't clear out the pantry when she stayed in your camp." Then she looks at Ify, and there's a glint of wonder in her eyes. "Did she always eat like this?"

"A side effect of the chemicals."

Ify pauses mid-bite, her right hand slick from the soup, covered in bits of gari. "Chemicals?"

Onyii sees the questions swimming in her eyes. "I switched out the chemicals they injected you with," she says to Ify. "That was where I went after we last spoke. In the end, I didn't know if they would check and ruin my plans by switching them back. That's why I had to stay and watch. It was the longest hour of my life."

Ify swallows the gari in her mouth. "I'm not dead?"

Adaeze sucks her teeth. "Eh-eh! You think dead people are this hungry?"

Which gets Onyii chuckling.

Onyii gestures in Ada's direction. "Ify, this is Adaeze. She . . . she trained me. When I was a child." Ify's face darkens, and Onyii knows that Ify is remembering that when Onyii was a child, she had murdered her parents. "She took care of me."

Adaeze shrugs, as though the whole thing were nothing to her. "And now I am taking care of a fugitive."

"I had nowhere else to bring her," Onyii snaps.

Adaeze raises her hands in self-defense. "This is just typical Igbo hospitality." Ada grins, and for a second it feels like they're young and full of energy again instead of older and chewed up by war. "So. What will you do now? Onyii, I know it is out of character for you to have a plan."

It's true. There is no plan. Onyii hadn't thought beyond saving Ify from execution. She had switched the chemicals, hoping they would only render Ify unconscious and not kill her. Then she had watched them cart Ify's body away. Later, Onyii had snuck into the mortuary to find her and had wrapped her in a separate body bag stuffed with insulation to warm her body back up. Then she'd stolen a hoverbike and come here. Far enough away from Enugu to give her time to breathe.

"Or were you just going to let this little one eat me out of house and home?"

"Get to Ghana. Apply for asylum, maybe? Go anywhere that's not here."

"You didn't hear? With the ceasefire broken and war now happening, Ghana has closed their overland border. No more refugees."

"We could go east, then. Sneak into Cameroon. And figure out a way from there."

Adaeze shakes her head. "Jumping from one war into another. Besides, Cameroonians have no love for Nigerians these days."

"Space," Ify says.

All heads turn her way. Onyii has been so focused on figuring out how to get Ify to safety that she'd forgotten Ify was sitting right there.

"We need to get to a space station."

Onyii's eyes light up. The route! "That's it. We don't have to go to Cameroon. As soon as we get into international waters, we're safe. We get to the nearest available coastline to the west, then book passage to the station in Niamey." The memory of Chinelo and their trip to the Colonies bites at Onyii's heart, but she stuffs it down.

"Niger?" Adaeze shouts. "That's fifteen hundred kilometers from Port Harcourt. By land! And you want to go around?"

"Ada, what choice do we have?"

Ada holds up a finger to silence her. The room goes quiet. Then they hear it. Jet propulsion engines. Mechs. "Get down!" Ada dives for them just as bullets blast through the window and ricochet off the far wall.

"How did they find us?" Onyii asks, her body pressed over Ify's. Egusi soup stains the carpet. Another volley of bullets. The engines are closer. If Ify's marked for death, then they will have no problems blowing this whole place into splinters. "We have to get out of here."

Ada rushes into another room, then comes back out and tosses a shotgun to Onyii. Onyii grabs it and spins, just as the first soldier appears at the window. A single boom sends him flying back. Ada posts up by another window, an assault rifle at her shoulder, and fires in short bursts. Between rounds,

Ada shouts, "There's a bag in the other room. Money, guns, bodysuits. And fuel cells for your bike. Take it."

Those must have been for Ada. Maybe she'd always known a day like this was coming. Maybe she'd planned on leaving alone. Maybe she thought she was the only one she would need to save.

She fires another round, then takes a concussion grenade from the belt at her waist. Bootsteps sound up the path along the cliff. Ada tosses the grenade through the window. She shouts, "Go!" But the rest is swallowed up by the roar of the explosion.

The force hurls Onyii and Ify back.

"Little one, there's a gun in the kitchen. Get it."

At Ada's command, Ify vanishes.

Onyii rushes into the other room and sees the duffel bag ready. This was Adaeze's escape. And now it's Onyii's. And Ify's.

Onyii snatches it up and, when she finds Ify crouching in the middle of the room with a pistol in her hand and a jacket whose pockets bulge with ammo, she grabs Ify's hand and hurries for the back exit. She turns to say goodbye to Ada, but Ada has moved to another location. An explosion takes a chunk out of the front wall.

She will survive. That's what Onyii tells herself as she runs, then skids, down the backside of the cliff face into the shadows, where she'd hidden her bike. When they land at the bottom, Onyii pulls out the bodysuit and thrusts it at Ify.

Ify quickly undresses, then slips into the suit and presses a button that fits the whole thing tightly on her skin. A paper-thin visor slips over her face.

Another boom.

When Onyii looks up, Adaeze's whole cottage is in flames.

A soldier rounds the corner of the hill. Onyii sees him just in time to blast him. "Grab the bag and start the bike."

Ify runs and does as ordered, while Onyii picks off more and more soldiers. They swarm the hillside. Onyii fires, turns, fires, turns, fires. Until she hears the familiar revving of the bike.

She fires one last time, then darts for the bike. Bullets tear apart the grass at her feet. She leaps on, Ify in front, grabs the handlebars, and they're gone.

As they escape, Onyii cranes her neck to look behind them. Three mechs crest the hill, leap off, and crash onto the ground, cannons trained on their vanishing silhouette.

CHAPTER
64

Ify has the duffel bag in her lap as the bike guns forward over the plain.

Bullets rip into the ground in their wake. A moment of silence, then a soft *fwoomp*. Onyii swerves the bike to the right just as a column of red sand shoots into the air. A sound like thunder booms overhead. The force of the blast nearly knocks them sideways, but Onyii, without a word, gets them straight again. Onyii pushes the bike to go even faster and get out of range of the heavy artillery.

Ify ducks under Onyii's arm and peeks behind her to see small shapes growing larger along the horizon behind them. More soldiers. They're on their own bikes: armored hovercrafts that cut through the air and raise walls of sand as they speed through the desert. Ify and Onyii are no match.

"Drive!" Onyii shouts, then slips the shotgun out of the holster by her thigh and reloads it. Another boom sends sand spraying at them. The soldiers have shotguns of their own.

Their bike leaps off a ledge. The landing jolts Ify and she nearly flies off, but with her free arm—her human arm—Onyii grips her tight.

One of the soldiers appears right next to them. Onyii twists and blows him off of his bike. Blood explodes from his chest as he backstrokes through the air and onto the ground.

Their bike dodges shrubbery that breaks apart with each gunblast from the soldiers right behind them.

Something large drowns them in shadow. Ify looks up to find an aerial mech right above them. It makes a sound like a thousand snakes hissing at once. Then missiles rain down on them. Ify swerves back and forth, screaming. Onyii's legs lock on to her seat, but she sways so much she nearly drops her gun. The soldiers on bikes have fallen back, but as soon as the missile volley ends, they appear through the smoke and draw closer.

Ahead of them, the land is a deeper red. Instinctively, Ify slows down. The Redlands.

"Ify!" Onyii shouts. "Keep going!"

"You're not wearing a bodysuit!" Without one, the air might kill Onyii. The radiation in the Redlands is so thick it has even supposedly made monsters out of ordinary animals, twisted and contorted them into unimaginable beasts. It mutates the flesh. It burns the mind. She might go mad in an instant. But if Onyii hears Ify over the boom of her shotgun, she doesn't respond.

Their bike skirts the side of a ridge. A soldier on his bike leaps into the air above them. Onyii angles her shotgun up and fires. The explosion swallows the soldier whole.

"Keep going!" Onyii shouts again, so Ify obeys. "It's the only way to shake the mechs!"

And Ify realizes that Onyii's right. The radiation would rust the mechs and disable their comms. Even if they are foolish enough to follow, they won't get far.

The three aerial mechs chasing them all open their shoulder cannons. Then that hissing sound again. Ify crouches over the handlebars. Just a little bit farther. The missiles move faster than they can, but suddenly, they arc downward and detonate just behind them, explosions blowing the soldiers behind them in all directions and sending Ify and Onyii flying into the air. The homing beacons must have short-circuited.

Pieces of bike and soldier, all in flames from the explosions, bounce and fly around them, the enflamed frame of a bike arcing just over them before rolling to a stop a hundred meters ahead.

That's when Ify looks up and sees the wild expanse of red before her. The Redlands. No one comes out of this place the same way they went in. If they come out at all. Its borders are invisible, but you always know when you've crossed them. No matter how much protection you wear, there is always a tightness in the chest, a prickling on the skin so sharp and intense it brings tears to the eyes. And the sudden drying out of skin. Ify can feel her bodysuit working with extra energy to moisturize her skin.

Nearby, an outcropping looms. In the shadows, they won't find any protection from the poisonous air, but maybe it can afford Onyii enough time to slip into her own bodysuit. Already, rust has swallowed half her metal arm. The only sign she shows of the pain she's in is a tightening of her features, like her face is struggling to hold itself together.

Ify steers them toward the shadow cast by the outcropping and powers down the bike, though she doesn't turn it off completely.

Onyii falls off.

With fumbling fingers, Ify goes through the duffel bag, careful not to expose too many of its contents to the elements, then, as fast as she can, she slips Onyii out of her clothes and into the bodysuit. As it tightens around her frame, Onyii lets out a sigh, and her face loosens again. The suit bulges awkwardly around Onyii's Augments, and her visor has trouble shutting completely, but when Ify looks at her, for some reason, she can't help but laugh. Onyii joins her, lying on the ground, clutching her stomach, then calming down as Ify pulls her to her feet.

Ify's about to ask Onyii where to next when she senses movement to her left. She squints. Far along the shoreline, a shape moves. She stands to her full height to get a better look at it. Then the silhouette turns into two, then three, then four.

A bullet whizzes by her face. Her mask cracks at her cheek. She falls to the ground. When she looks up, she sees them. With white-and-red bandannas over their faces and bikes beneath them, hurtling straight for her. Bandits.

Ducking, Onyii hauls Ify onto the bike, then gets on.

Bullets stitch the ground at her feet.

Onyii inputs her sequence in the bike's console, but it fritzes, sending sparks into the air before going dark. More gunfire pings toward them.

The radiation.

Ify slides off the bike. Her fingers search for a side panel, any sort of groove in the metal. When they catch, she yanks the plate open to reveal blackened fuel cells. That's what it was. The radiation drained their battery. Ify rips the spent fuel cells out of their slots and hurls them behind her before jamming in the new ones. They don't glow as much as they should. But it's enough to get the bike roaring again. A green confirmation light blinks at them from between the handlebars.

Cannon fire explodes near them, tearing a chunk out of the outcropping. Ify holds on tight to the handlebars and guns it into the uncovered plain. She lets instinct govern her. Nothing matters but getting away from them. A heavy weight presses onto her back. Onyii, unconscious. That's why she hadn't been shooting back. She hasn't yet healed completely.

Ify manages to glance behind her. There are eight of them in total, swerving through the hills and leaping into the air, belting out war cries. The sound chills her. *They're going to kill us.*

Everywhere, red. The dirt, the rocks, the sky. Ify, with Onyii on her back, darts through the sand. Massive clouds of red dust rise in her wake. A shot pings off the back of her bike. The left side dips, and she swerves left to right, right to left, not daring to slow down. She careens up a hill but can't stabilize. They fly through the air. With one hand, she grips the handlebars. With the other, she wraps Onyii's metal arm around her waist. She can't let go. She can't fall off. She can't lose Onyii. She can only pray that when she lands, it won't be on her back. The bike rights itself and lands so hard that it jolts her teeth together. Onyii flies off the side of the bike, but Ify reaches out just in time to grab her wrist.

"Come on, Onyii," Ify whispers. "Come on! Wake up!" The extra weight slows Ify down. Their bike speeds forward. The ground tears Onyii's bodysuit.

A new sound reaches her. The thundering of hooves.

Shorthorns.

The bandits hear it too.

Behind the herd of shorthorns, a sandstorm looms.

An idea comes to Ify. She stops the bike, then pops open the bike's front console and pulls a cord out. Her fingers tear at the back of Onyii's bodysuit, just at the base of her neck, and Ify plugs the other end of the cord in, praying it fits.

Click.

Then she jams her foot on the pedal, sending electrical currents straight into Onyii and jump-starting her sister.

Onyii jolts awake. She takes a nanosecond to note her surroundings. Then she snatches an assault rifle out of the duffel bag, gets on one knee, and fires. Short bursts that hurl the bandits off their bikes.

She climbs onto the back of the hoverbike, disconnects, and they're off again.

Ify presses her foot harder on the pedal, tries to will her bike to go faster. Behind the bandits, shorthorns three times as tall as her, made into giants by the radiation, emerge from clouds of red dust. A whole herd of them.

One of them ducks its head, then catches a biker from behind, flinging him into the air. Dust clouds swallow him and his cries.

Another shorthorn catches up to two bikers and swings its head from side to side, the bikers skidding, then crashing, the explosions so loud that the sound rumbles across the plain. Fuel tanks. They're not just using minerals to power their bikes. They're using old tech. Oil.

She hears a *fwoomp* behind her. Something small shoots into the air behind her, flying in a parabola straight for her. It gets larger as it closes in, then opens up. A dozen small missiles crash into the ground around them. Onyii hugs her tight, pushing her against the bike's frame, protecting Ify's body with her own. Ify screams as she swings her bike back and forth to avoid the detonations. Explosions boom all around her, covering them in fire and thunder. She closes her eyes against it all and races ahead, astounded when she gets through it that she's still alive. Smoke chokes her lungs. Even through her visor, her eyes burn.

Ahead of them, the land is gray with fog. Moisture? In the Redlands? Ify bats aside her questions and urges the bike faster.

Mutated jackals appear behind them, some of them keeping pace while others nip at her heels. Their ridged, black backs glisten like the stones that suddenly cover the desert floor. If this can still be called desert.

The rusted carcasses of mechs and airships long reddened and decayed with radiation poisoning rise like fingers out of the ground, bent and twisted and broken and brittle.

All of a sudden, it's quiet. They're in the fog.

More bandits burst through the mist, their bandannas turning them into ghosts beneath the newly darkened sky. Fog swirls around some of them, forming small cyclones that drive sinkholes into the earth. The ground collapses beneath one bandit. It ripples beneath them all in waves, loose rock shuttling toward them, bruising shoulders and toppling more riders.

Other jackals materialize out of the mist, barking and baying.

Onyii spins in her seat and shoots one jackal through the forehead, while one of the bandits, so close Ify can see his black eyes, shoots another that had leapt up to try to take him from his bike. Oil-colored blood spurts from the thing as it loses its life in midair and crashes to the ground.

Sand whips about them in walls, and the men wrap their scarves tighter around their faces to keep the dust out of their mouths.

Sand.

That means they must be close to the end of this place.

There's light up ahead. They race toward it. Brown sand turns to ash that swirls and corkscrews around them and up into the sky.

A massive screech tears through the air, a sound worse than when her captors had manipulated her Accent. A screech and a roar at the same time. It nearly pierces her eardrums as it falls on her whole body like a wave, scattering the mist in all directions. It stops just as suddenly as it started. Ify looks up to find dark clouds swirling. Farther down, she sees the same. Then a funnel cloud dips out of the sky and touches down, and wind whips so hard around Ify that she nearly flies off her bike. One by one, more and more spiraling clouds touch down. Then, to her left, a wall of smoke like a sandstorm but made entirely out of mist. In it, shapes move, then suddenly a winged aerial mech so large it could blot out any sun emerges. It is all metal, like any other mech. But its eyes glow an otherworldly green. Is there a pilot in there? Has the machine grown its own mind? Has the radiation mutated the metal into a whole other monster?

The first of the aerial mechs swoops down, then bounces back into the air, another following in its place.

There's no gun in their arsenal big enough to take that thing on. So Ify wills her bike as fast as possible toward the light.

The bandits are close enough that she can hear them now, shouting orders at each other, then another screech, and in the wake of it, they all grow silent. One of the mechs is practically on top of all of them. With each pulse of its jets, it clears away the mist around it. The tornadoes get closer, tearing through the stone on the ground.

Ify banks wide to the right, just as the giant mech dips behind her.

Suddenly, the sun is shining and the land is red again.

Ify looks behind her to see the aerial mech bursting from the clouds with wind funnels lining its body and connecting to the red earth: swirling, dark fingers pulling at the sand. And around those funnels spin the vehicles and bodies of all the men who had been chasing them. Their weapons detonate to make a spiral of explosions, pirouetting until they hit the mech's wings and body and face. It lets out a wail that loses its strength out in the red expanse. Then the mech turns to head back into the darkness.

Ify has never heard a mech scream before. The sound haunts her all the way to the border, from which they can both see forest, glistening and green before them. "We did it," Ify says to Onyii. "We made it through the Redlands."

Onyii coughs into the crook of her arm. A dark splotch stains the inside of her helmet. As she looks back the way they've come, her breath sounds like it's rattling in her chest. "We did, didn't we."

She turns back to Ify and smiles from behind her visor. Then she pats her on the shoulder, and they're off.

CHAPTER
65

The bike becomes too cumbersome to maneuver through the forest, so Onyii brings it over to a small patch of shoreline by a river. Then she gathers branches and leaves to toss over the thing. They decide to keep the fuel cells with them. In case they may need another bike. The two of them change out of their bodysuits and pull their dirt-covered clothes out to wash in the river nearby.

As they scrub, Onyii glances up at Ify and shakes her head in wonder at the person she's staring at, the woman who maneuvered them through the Redlands, who outran bandits and sandstorms, who didn't freeze in the face of monsters that had chilled the marrow in Onyii's bones. She worries, though. She worries that the toughness has buried whatever it is that Onyii saw in Ify when she was figuring out equations on her tablet or when she was working her way through her stellar configurations. Whatever it is that ran through Ify when Onyii found her sneaking in video recordings of workers outside the Colony Stations, joking at the camera about the work they'd done to make this beautiful thing spin with such majestic slowness in space.

Ify looks up and then hides her face. "What?" she asks shyly. "Nothing," Onyii says.

They bathe, then change back into their clothes.

Onyii has the duffel bag slung over one shoulder, rifle slung over the other, and the shotgun in her hands. She moves them forward, while Ify takes stock of the rear in wide sweeps with her pistol. Every so often, the world buzzes, then sparks, and static fills Onyii's vision. Her busted eye. She looks around with her good eye. They're near shoreline. If they're far enough along this coastline, then they should be near Lagos.

The beginnings of a plan swirl in her head. Make it to Lagos and hope it has reverted to its earlier form: a lawless, free-for-all kind of city filled with bounty hunters and bandits and smugglers. There, it should be easy enough to get someone to take them wherever they need to go.

They make their way as quietly as possible through the brush until Onyii stops. The setting sun has splashed purple and gold over the horizon and turned the underbellies of the clouds into red tongue-shaped things. And one of these rays, aimed into the forest, alights on the heaving form of an Agba bear. So near to them, it had looked like a boulder. But Onyii watches its hulking form, curled in on itself like a hedgehog, expand and contract with each sleepy breath it takes.

Throughout the forest, the sun's rays illuminate other creatures. Goats whose coats turn iridescent and shimmer, their horns spiraling out for the whole length of their backs. Baby wulfu that tackle each other and roll around in the grass, each of them as big as Onyii. Lizards that slither up and down the trees around them. Everything is gilded. Onyii can't help but lower her shotgun and stare at the sight. Even though static interrupts the vision from time to time, she can't stop staring. They've all been touched by the Redlands.

Ify appears at her side and holds her free hand. They look at each other, then back at the forest. The animals slowly peel away. Onyii takes that as their cue to keep moving. Darkness is falling. While that might make it easier for them to hide from Biafran soldiers, it might make them easier targets for bandits. Onyii knows how some have been taught to move through darkness. She's been taught that herself.

But when they take extra care to move as silently as possible, it's not simply out of caution or a wish to keep from being seen. Onyii is thinking of that scene in the forest and knows that Ify is too. This is how they pay their respects to this place.

The sounds of Lagos reach them soon enough. A buzzing sound shot through with shouting and occasional gunfire and the general katakata of a place bursting at the seams with too many people. All of that makes its way through the air over the lagoon as though to say to them, *Welcome to Lagos. Enter at your own peril.*

Twice on their way through the crush of bodies and kabu-kabu to the Third Mainland Bridge, Onyii almost loses Ify and is seconds away from shooting into the air to disperse the crowd. People walk around with their weapons in plain sight, although none of them are as heavily armed as Onyii. Ify has her pistol tucked into her belt at the small of her back, her shirt hanging over it.

Keke Marwa tricycles and kabu-kabu clog the bridge. Residents and commuters and smugglers wind their way through the traffic on foot like sand moving through a jar filled with rocks. Past the docks is a string of islands, and on those islands, mansions, office buildings.

Past the main thoroughfare that the bridge bisects, young men stand at the docks with obsolete tech hanging like jewelry around their necks. Chinelo would have loved it here. One of them wears a belt on his head, curled hair, dyed blond, poking out in knots. He grins, revealing teeth that glimmer. His hands are filled with bands of money in at least four different currencies.

"Credit?" he sings to the bustle of people moving around him. "Credit? You got credit, come see me, I chop your dollar. Abeg, make big money bigger. You do not know, eh. Whatever you want, ask me, it's yours. I have containers from Korea or Dubai."

Ify smirks at the boy's boasts. Tattoos cover his shirtless torso.

Onyii marches forward. "We need a boat."

The boy takes in the two of them and how their clothes haven't completely dried yet. He also doesn't fail to notice the shotgun in Onyii's hands. "Chai! Bank robbers, nah! Eh, if you are going to raid the presidential palace, ah, you will need more than just the two of you, especially with this one"—he flicks his wrist at Ify—"too skinny."

Onyii steps up to him, blocking his view of Ify. "A boat."

He frowns, and Onyii wonders for a second if he's Augmented and scanning her face to see if there's a bounty out on her. If it comes to it, Onyii can aim and fire her shotgun faster than most people on this platform. But then there's Ify to worry about.

"You have coin? Dollah? If you want to sail the seven currenSEAS, I will need to see some currenCY."

"You don't even know where we wanna go yet." This from

Ify, who has stepped closer so they can all speak without being heard by prying ears. "Tell us your rates first."

The boy looks at her with shock, like he can't believe what she's just done. Then he turns back to Onyii. "Is desperation tax. Does not matter where you are going. You have a shotgun, she has a pistol practically hanging out of her buttocks. And I know for a fact that there are more guns making clack-clack in that bag of yours. You no say, 'I want boat to Abidjan' or 'I want boat to São Tomé.' You just say, 'I want boat,' which means you do not care where you go to, only where you are coming from. Which means that you are desperate. And if you are desperate, then you are trouble. And for trouble, you must pay extra."

Onyii grits her teeth.

Behind the boy, the dock platform branches off, and by each separate platform running along the shoreline floats a submersible guarded by strongmen.

With ease, Onyii could toss this twig of a man over into the churning waters below. But, since the desert, they've managed to avoid bloodshed. And Onyii finds she actually prefers it this way.

Ify brings her face closer. Sweat beads her forehead, slides down her face.

Behind the boy, more and more submersibles descend into the water. After the next two, there won't be any more until the next fleet arrives. Who knows when that will be?

"Okay," Onyii hisses, "how much to Accra?"

"Ghana?" He flings his head back in astonishment. "Chai! Such a long trip. Or, at least, it used to be a long trip. I can get you there in no time round. You know how they used to say, 'No time flat'? I say, 'No time round.' Why? Because I'm different."

He's stalling.

Ify puts a hand to Onyii's shoulder. She feels it too.

Onyii tries to get her braids to fall over her face while her gaze runs over every set of eyes, trying to gauge their intentions.

Ify squeezes.

Onyii spins around just as four Augments storm the bridge. Bounty hunters! One of them sticks his massive metal arm out. His hand comes apart at the wrist to reveal a grenade launcher.

The boy smuggler wildly waves his hands, then dives out of the way when the projectile arcs straight for them. Onyii tears a chunk of concrete out of the bridge and hurls it at the grenade. The explosion hurls everyone down and throws taxicabs into the lagoon. Ify lies on her side, her pistol just out of reach, her eyes blinking lazily. There's one submersible left.

Through the screaming, bullets strike the metal taxis and the concrete. Gunmen shoot wildly through the smoke.

Ify staggers to her feet.

Onyii grabs her, and they hobble forward through the smoke and gunfire. The last submersible is sinking. They dash straight for the end of the platform. The guard there turns and raises his rifle. But just as he's about to shoot, three pistol shots ram into his chest. He topples over the edge of the railing. Ify's gun hand drops. The pistol dangles from her fingers.

"We gotta jump," Onyii pleads. "Stay with me."

Ify nods her head.

The dark water bubbles as it swallows more and more of the submersible. More gunfire behind them.

Onyii hauls Ify forward, breaking into a sprint. Just as she leaps, a bullet clips her calf, and she flails. She can't let go of Ify. No matter how sharp the pain in her leg, no matter how much she knows crashing into the top of the submersible's hull will hurt, she can't let go.

She lands on her stomach. Several ribs snap. But she holds on to Ify with every last bit of strength she can find. Swallowed by pain, she pulls Ify up to her chest and gets to one knee. With her human hand, she holds Ify still. With her other hand, she bangs on the door. "Let us in!" she screams. She bangs again. And again and again and again, pounding a dent into the hull while the water rises and bullets whizz past them. "Let us in!"

They're sinking.

Onyii fits her fingers under a groove in the round entrance seal and pulls. A gear pops loose in her arm, but she keeps pulling and pulling. Wires snap. Their loose ends spark. Tears well in her eyes. Ify lies limp in her arm. She has to open it. Water pools around her knee, then rises above her ankle. She tries to hold Ify up as the water rises. Pain doubles her over.

"Let us in! Please!"

The water is up to her waist and getting higher. Now her chest. She struggles to keep Ify's head above the waves that crash into her body. Ify slips out of her grasp and sinks. Her head vanishes below. Onyii's losing strength. She pulls and pulls, but the seal won't give. Then she's completely submerged. Underwater, her head turns. That's when she spots Ify's body, drifting lower and lower into the blackness.

Onyii dives and kicks toward her. Shadows form at the edges of her world and close in. She kicks and kicks.

No. Not after everything they've survived. Not when they're so close to freedom. Onyii can't stop. Not yet.

But she feels fire in her lungs and fire in her legs and fire in her arms and fire in her head, and a light glows softly somewhere nearby, and Onyii has heard of this light, the thing you see just before you die, and Onyii wants to swim away, wants to find Ify and get away from the light, but it's getting closer and closer and closer. Until it takes her completely.

Current sweeps her, grips her leg, and pulls her away while Ify drifts farther and farther out of reach until she's gone, sucked suddenly into a space too dark for Onyii to see.

■ ■ ■ ■ ■

When she comes to, she vomits water. It splashes onto a metal floor. She's alive. Wait. She's *alive*. But as soon as she tries to push herself up, she falls, and her head hits the metal grating.

"Ify," she mouths, no strength to even say her name out loud. "Ify . . ."

Footsteps pound on the metal. Hurrying. She hears voices. Speaking pidgin.

She remembers Lagos.

The boy.

The submersible.

Nothing but water around them. But where is she?

She hears an unfamiliar voice. A woman. Her pidgin is halting. Worse than a child's. But her voice slackens the muscles in Onyii's body.

Onyii tries again, and this time, she's able to sit up. Thankfully, there's a nearby wall for her to rest her back against.

The woman kneels before Onyii, wraps her in a blanket, and opens a small bag that has needles and vials of chemicals in it. Beside her, what looks like a fuel cell. She has her head bowed while she works, so that in the tornado of colors, it looks like her face is all black. But then the woman does something that sends steroidal energy into Onyii and wakes her up. She can see.

But right behind it is the pain. Pain so great, she feels like it will crush her. A moment later, it subsides. Her chest heaves from the effort of not crying out.

"Who . . ."

"Shhh," the woman says, then packs up her tools. She looks off to the side.

Onyii follows her gaze. Her heart skips. Her first instinct is to leap up, but her body refuses to obey her. So she must sit still, paralyzed, as Ify rushes to her and wraps her arms around Onyii's neck, sobbing into Onyii's already sodden shirt.

Onyii tries to move her mouth. Not to ask any of the questions darting back and forth in her head, but to quiet Ify, to calm her.

Ify breaks away, tears streaking her face, and sobs a laugh. "Onyii," she says, "this is Xifeng. She's an aid worker. She escorted the caravans. And she works with . . . with children who've lived through the war. And, Xifeng, this is Onyii. My sister. Who I told you I was searching for." Hope springs in Ify's eyes. "Xifeng is going to take us to space."

CHAPTER
66

Xifeng bandages Onyii's wounded leg while she speaks. "There are a few shuttles operating out of Gabon. Libreville, mostly. But Franceville too. They can take people up into outer space, where they'll be able to begin the asylum process in the Colonies. Libreville's right along the coastline down into Central Africa."

Ify has finally calmed herself enough to notice the other men, some of them bare-chested, others wearing vests with ammunition clips in them, stalking through the submersible. Some of them mutter to themselves while others joke loudly. Some of them reek of alcohol. But they all walk around with that certainty of step that shows they've spent much of their life on submersibles like this. They look like they know what they're doing. Still, after their encounter with the boy smuggler in Lagos, Ify trusts no one. No one except Xifeng. And Onyii.

"Will I need identification?" Onyii asks. Then, at the question in Xifeng's eyes, she says, "Ify and I are the two most wanted people in Nigeria. And we will be a problem for any country that has us. They can't know where we are. And they cannot see our faces."

Ify jumps in. "There were bounty hunters in Lagos. They

found out who we were. We've been on the run since . . ." Her heart drops.

"Your tracker," Onyii says. And when Ify looks up, she can feel the color leak from her face. "The Nigerians put a tracker in you before they let you go." Onyii coughs violently, then lets out a sigh and leans her head back. "That's how I was able to find you in the camp. The Biafrans can track the signal too. That's how they found us at Adaeze's."

Ify's eyes widen in recognition. "We have to . . . we have to remove it."

Xifeng puts her arms out, as though to stop the two. "But wait. The Biafrans and the Nigerians won't cross international borders to catch you! That might start a war with other countries. Their mobile suits wouldn't dare fly into foreign airspace."

Onyii looks grimly to Xifeng. "That doesn't mean they won't tell other governments who we are. And those governments will chase us, capture us, then extradite us. They will send us back."

Ify looks at her lap. "Nowhere on the continent is safe for us." Determination hardens her features. "But first, we have to get rid of the tracker." She starts to rip apart her shirt to expose her chest. "We have to take it out." She grits her teeth. "Or else they'll know exactly where we are."

Xifeng sputters. "But I don't have the right tools."

Onyii pushes herself forward. "Just show me where it is. I'll take it out."

Xifeng's eyes shoot open in shock. She looks from Onyii to Ify and back again. Onyii can tell she is seeing the silent communication happening between them, the worlds of information, the dialogue exchanged in their gazes, them coming to a grim agreement. She sighs. "Okay. But let's prepare a room."

They find a bedroom in another part of the submersible, and Xifeng lays plastic sheeting on the ground while Onyii ties her braids back. Xifeng has more chemicals with her and sterilizes all her knives and blades, as well as Onyii's hands. Then, Xifeng takes a signal reader, the same size and shape as a brick, and runs it over Ify's body until, arriving at her chest, the beeping turns into one long whine.

Ify's breath quickens. Just beneath her left breast. That's where the tracker is.

Xifeng turns the thing off. "At least it's not on her heart. That would have made it impossible to remove without damaging the organ."

Small mercy, Ify thinks to herself as she lies on her back. She angles her head toward Xifeng. "Do you have anything? For the pain?"

"Your body and brain have not fully recovered from almost drowning. Anything I give you might stop your heart completely. I . . . I'm sorry."

Ify holds Xifeng's gaze for a long time before turning to Onyii. Their eyes lock. When Ify's breath quickens, she breathes through her nose. Onyii gestures to her belt. Xifeng, understanding, unclips it from Onyii's waist, then folds it and slips it between Ify's teeth.

She sterilizes Onyii's hands one last time, then hands her the first of the knives.

The first cut, an incision along Ify's rib and just below her breast, is bearable, but the knife digs deeper and touches something in Ify that sends bolts of lightning into her brain.

The belt muffles her scream, but her cry is loud enough to make the knife hesitate. Onyii pauses. Then the knife moves horizontally. Cool liquid slides down Ify's side, and she knows, even though pain blocks out almost all rational thought, that this is her blood.

Then something presses into her wound, pulling the flesh apart. Ify nearly bites through the belt. Her eyes flare wide. She sees nothing. Hurt turns the entire world white. Her back arches against the floor. She screams and screams around the belt in her teeth.

Onyii's hand slides out of the wound, and Ify slumps. Her screams turn to moans. Tears waterfall down the side of her face. She looks away as other hands busy themselves sterilizing her wound and sealing it with MeTro sealant.

As these hands wrap her in bandages, Ify's breath slows, and the world dissolves into a haze.

It's this haze that blankets her as something coarse is wrapped around her to keep her warm. The haze raises her above water, through the top of the submersible, and into the open sun. Voices swim around her as the haze carries her into the back of a truck and rolls another blanket over her.

Time collapses.

Onyii's face is suddenly before hers. Her sister is on one knee, grabbing the strap hanging from the ceiling of the truck's carriage. "We're almost there," Onyii whispers.

Ify can barely make the words out, but that's what it sounds like. *We're almost there.* She blinks herself awake, but confusion knits her brow. "Why are you wearing a military uniform?" But it comes out as an incoherent murmur. She knows this, because Onyii smiles at her words.

"Just rest, little one. I love you." Then she blows softly on Ify's forehead, like she used to do when the sun grew too hot or the weather in the camp became suffocating. A small piece of relief from her suffering.

I love you too, Ify tries to say, but it comes out as one long, jumbled sound. Then she falls asleep.

CHAPTER
67

It was easy enough to knock out the Gabonese border guard on the periphery of the border station and steal his uniform while Xifeng rolled her truck through. Simply flashing her Xinhua Aid Agency ID and telling the remaining guards that she was coming from war-torn Cameroon got her through. Then, when they were far enough ahead, Onyii had leapt into the back of the truck. She had cut off her braids and shaved her head before leaving the submersible to make their plan run more smoothly. It would expose her face, but the more like a man she seemed, the less likely people were to give her a second look. Xifeng had sprayed skin shielding over the metal on her face, and when Onyii saw her face in a mirror, she gasped. Her fingers had gone to her eye. It glowed yellow, but there was nothing else to indicate on her face or her arm that she was an Augment.

"Cosmetics," Xifeng had told her, in response to her shock. "Aerosol skin cream from China. Some use it for burn wounds. Others use it instead of standing beneath the sun to tan."

"They want to get darker?"

And that's when Xifeng had suddenly looked at Onyii, then blushed and grown shy. "We find you attractive," Xifeng had said, as though she were responding to an order from a commanding officer.

The trip to Libreville is brief. Before them lies a long and wide seafront boulevard populated with parks bearing a multitude of marble sculptures. The open-air Mont-Bouët market spreads out away from the coastline. In the distance looms the presidential palace. The whole place seems so wealthy. So carefree.

It's too risky to chance a ride on the Trans-Gabon Railway to Franceville in the country's interior, so Xifeng and Onyii take the roadway running along the rails.

Night nears by the time they see glistening Franceville in the distance. And past the river, peeking over the horizon, is the space station. It's a small hub, but with so many wars in neighboring countries, it has begun to expand. Money finds its way to stable countries, countries that can take advantage of the chaos around them.

At the bridge crossing, two guards amble to the back of the truck and make a show of inspecting. When they see Onyii, legs hanging over the end of the flatbed, trying to look as calm as possible and not open her mouth, they start chatting. One of them asks the other a question, then arches an eyebrow at Onyii, waiting for an answer.

If she says a single word and they hear her accent, they will be able to tell she's not Gabonese. Then it's all over.

She snorts a laugh and looks away, like she can't be bothered to answer. That gets one of the soldiers belly-laughing. While the other fumes, the first one waves them along. As they pull away, Onyii tries not to let them see the mountainous sigh that shakes her shoulders.

They pull over into a vehicle lot. Not far from them is a large warehouse structure. Closer to the station, aerial mechs stand guard around the shuttle. Passengers have formed a line by the escalator leading up to the shuttle's entrance.

Xifeng turns the truck off, then joins Onyii at its back. Together, they tie back the curtain, pull away the plastic sheeting, and lift the bundle holding Ify into a cylindrical container just barely large enough to fit her. Inside the opening is an oxygen pump connected to a tank. From it dangles a mask. Onyii fits the mask to Ify's face, inputs a command into the machine to begin pumping, then takes one moment to memorize her face, so soft and serene in slumber, before closing the lid.

As wrapped up as Ify is, she should avoid detection from any scanners. And her tracker lies at the bottom of Lagos Lagoon, so neither the Biafrans nor the Nigerians will be able to find her.

Onyii and Xifeng hoist the heavy cylinder onto their shoulders and bring it to the shuttle. A woman in a pilot's uniform idly swipes at her tablet.

"Storage?" Xifeng asks.

"Are you scheduled to be on this flight?" the woman asks in French. "Is your name on the manifest?"

"No, I'm not on this flight, but—"

"Then I cannot take your package."

"But there are aid materials in here. Desperately needed where this shuttle's going. Please, it's time-sensitive." Indeed, Ify only has a finite amount of oxygen before the compartment is timed to pop open and release her. "I'm with the Xinhua Aid Agency." She awkwardly tries to fish through her pockets with one hand. "My name is Dr. Liu Xifeng. I—"

"This is heavy!" Onyii barks in her best imitation of Gabonese French. "Take her package now! What are you wasting our time for? You have space, don't you?" Complain loudly enough while wearing a military uniform and people will generally do what you ask. Onyii has seen it enough times to know it works.

At that, the woman lowers her tablet, sucks her teeth, then points in the direction of a carousel that sends suitcases and oddly shaped containers into the shuttle's baggage compartment. When they finally lay the cylinder down, the carousel beeps loudly from the weight and stops. Onyii glares at it, and it starts moving again.

The two of them watch until the whole cylinder is swallowed by the shuttle and the storage compartment closes shut.

It's done.

An alarm blares as all the compartments shut, and the shuttle becomes a single, sleek craft that will spirit every soul onboard into the stars.

Onyii starts when she feels tugging at her sleeve. Xifeng. Around them, launch station personnel busy themselves, clearing the launch area, and Onyii and Xifeng hurry back to their truck. A coughing fit takes Onyii. She struggles to keep up. Even as the ground beneath them begins to shudder and the metal supports running along the shuttle's vertical frame fall away, Onyii keeps looking back over her shoulder. As the jet propulsion process begins and smoke billows like a skirt under the shuttle and Onyii's coughing threatens to double her over, she keeps looking back. The main walkway detaches and moves away on its own. All the while, station personnel mechanically direct the traffic. Like this is something they see every day.

But Onyii can't stop staring.

"Why aren't you going with her?" Xifeng asks softly when they get back to their truck.

For a long time, Onyii is silent, her face inclined skyward, watching the shuttle grow smaller and smaller and smaller until it escapes the earth's atmosphere and every war being fought beneath it. "In less than two weeks, I will be dead." Onyii squints into the stars. "We rode through the Redlands before we made it to Lagos. For much of the journey, Ify had on a bodysuit to protect her from the radiation. I did not." Onyii can feel Xifeng's eyes on her back, but she doesn't turn. Her gaze remains fixed on the stars. "The shower we took in your submersible only helped to ease the pain. But the cancer is already taking over my kidneys. Another cancer has metastasized on my throat. Soon I will be unable to speak. Then it will take my lungs. I couldn't let Ify watch me die like that." She looks down at her hands, wet with the blood she coughed into them. Rust swallows the metal. Static breaks her vision. "I want her last sight of me to be of me whole. That's how I want to be remembered."

Xifeng says nothing, merely takes a step to Onyii's side and stands close, closer than anyone worried about radiation poisoning would stand. She doesn't touch Onyii, only smiles and raises her chin just as Onyii does, to watch the stars against the darkening sky.

Bursts of static chop up Onyii's view of the constellations. Just as she pieces one together, static obliterates it. A shorthorn. Static. A crown. Static.

"Keep her safe," Onyii says to the sky.

A girl. Hand raised to wave goodbye to her sister.

Then static.

AUTHOR'S NOTE

The Biafran War, also known as the Nigerian Civil War, began on May 30, 1967, when Colonel Odumegwu Ojukwu, then a regional governor in Nigeria, declared the Eastern Region of Nigeria to be the Republic of Biafra. In July of that same year, Lieutenant-Colonel Yakubu Gowon, Supreme Commander of the Nigerian Armed Forces, declared war on the fledgling republic.

Nigeria had gained its independence from the United Kingdom in 1960, inheriting a colonial administration that held little regard for the nation's cultural and ethnic diversity and privileged some groups over others, leaving large swaths of the country disenfranchised. Thus, the Igbo people, who lived largely in the Eastern Region, saw almost none of the riches generated by the oil that foreign companies took from their shores. When Biafra seceded, it was believed that the Igbo people would be properly compensated for the resources that lived, all this time, beneath their houses.

What followed was three years of war, starvation, and disease. By the end of the conflict, two million civilians had died of famine during a blockade established by the Nigerian government. Between two million and four and a half million people had been displaced.

While it could be said that the conflict was over oil, the spark had landed on a mountain of tinder made up of years and years of resentment fueled by lack of representation in government and in the military. Prior to the declaration of secession, pogroms put into place in Northern Nigeria saw up to 100,000 Igbo people, almost half of them children, murdered. In that time, nearly two million Igbo refugees fled to the Eastern Region. Massacres and coups and counter-coups, all of these preceded that fateful May 1967 declaration of secession.

My family is Igbo, and my mother was preparing for grade school when the war broke out.

As a child, I only heard of the war in conversational asides when uncles and aunties would come to visit or when Mom was on the phone with relatives from Nigeria. I'd always tuned them out when conversation turned to Nigerian politics; they all always expressed that same content exasperation that seems to come with being immigrants who still maintain ties, however tenuous, to the land they came from.

As I grew older, the stories became more and more detailed, and my mother began to appear in them.

To write this novel directly referencing perhaps the most painful episode in Nigerian history, I drew most heavily from my mother's recollections. She was my central resource in learning what it was like to live as a child through the political conflicts I had read about as a political science major in college.

War Girls is also a commentary on the wars that ravaged the African continent in the 1990s and 2000s; wars in which children were drafted as soldiers, drugged and assaulted and manipulated and given guns as tall as them; wars in which millions upon millions of people were forced to leave their homes; wars in which mass propaganda greased the wheels for the systematic slaughter of innocents simply because they belonged to a tribe that was not yours.

For my research into the Biafran War and these additional conflicts, Chinua Achebe's memoir, *There Was a Country*, was invaluable. Chimamanda Ngozi Adichie's chronicle of the war, *Half of a Yellow Sun*, revealed not only the ways in which war can touch the lives of individuals but also the frightening lack of literature that exists about this period in Nigerian history. The Nigerian Civil War is not taught in schools, nor is it generally written about aside from nonfiction histories from military commanders or politicians, each with the aim of exonerating themselves and putting forward their own political agenda. *War Girls* aims to be a corrective to this dynamic.

A Moonless, Starless Sky by Alexis Okeowo painted portrait after portrait of Africans in Mauritania, Somalia, Nigeria, and elsewhere fighting extremism in their own way, whether through civil rights campaigns or aspirations to play professional basketball. *How Dare the Sun Rise: Memoirs of a War Child* by Sandra Uwiringiyimana and *A Long Way Gone: Memoirs of a Boy Soldier* by Ishmael Beah were both heartrending chronicles of surviving war and massacre and trying to find life after.

The earliest seed for this book was planted, almost without my knowing, a decade and a half ago when I came across the novel *Beasts of No Nation* by my fellow countryman Uzodinma Iweala. I was forever changed by that book.

The Biafran cause did find its champions outside of Africa's borders. Novelist Frederick Forsyth, most famous as the author of the acclaimed thriller *The Day of the Jackal*, was a staunch advocate. His book *The Biafra Story: The Making of an African Legend* has been held up as a hallmark of war reporting, not only for its detail but also for the outrage he felt at the violence perpetrated against the Igbo people during this brutal conflict.

And he takes to task the uncaring and dishonest attitudes of the British and American governments that actively aided in that violence. The outrage is palpable in Kurt Vonnegut's "Biafra: A People Betrayed" as well.

There has been writing about Biafra, but not nearly enough. And not nearly enough of it by those who can still feel the imprint of the conflict on their lives. Even now, as calls for secession grow anew, an entire generation has been raised in ignorance of the conflict. It is my hope that *War Girls*, in directly referencing this past, can act as some sort of salve to the national wound and keep it from growing into something worse and, worse yet, inoperable. It is my hope also that *War Girls* will become only one of many such books. And that it will exhibit that emblematic Nigerian quality of taking pain and despair and dysfunction and transmuting it into something heartier, more fulfilling, more nourishing. Of sifting poison out of the water drawn from the well.

ACKNOWLEDGMENTS

When I pitched my agent, Noah Ballard, about a book I wanted to write, and I told him I was thinking Gundam in Nigeria, he did not hesitate for one second before saying, "Yes, go write it." And for that, he has my immense gratitude.

Ben Schrank and Casey McIntyre helped rally the House behind this book and were among its first cheerleaders.

And I must thank my editor, Jess Harriton, for believing in this book, pushing and pulling where necessary, steering me away from my own excesses and urging me forward when despair threatened to derail my efforts.

The significance of this cover is not lost on me. Many have remarked to me what it has meant to them to see a dark-skinned black girl staring daggers at you from the front cover of a young adult novel, a protagonist, a hero, a badass. Though there is much work to be done in the publishing industry with regards to better, more inclusive representation on both the inside and the outside of a book, I look at this cover and I see a victory. The people responsible are Tony Sahara and Kristin Boyle, our in-house designers, and, most importantly, the esteemed illustrator, Nekro, talented beyond measure. They have spoiled me with their work.

I will be forever indebted to my copyeditors, who wrangled this book into readable shape.

And I send a sincerest thank-you to my family, because every minute spent with you is a minute stolen from heaven.